Berg's *Wozzeck*

STUDIES IN MUSICAL GENESIS, STRUCTURE, AND INTERPRETATION

Terry Riley's, In C Robert Carl

Beethoven's Diabelli Variations, William Kinderman

Beethoven's "Appassionata" Sonata, Martha Frohlich

Richard Strauss's Elektra, Bryan Gilliam

Wagner's Das Rheingold, Warren Darcy

Beethoven's Piano Sonata in E, Op. 109, Nicholas Marston

Mahler's Fourth Symphony, James L. Zychowicz

Vaughan Williams' Ninth Symphony, Alain Frogley

Debussy's Ibéria, Matthew Brown

Berg's *Wozzeck*

PATRICIA HALL

2011

OXFORD
UNIVERSITY PRESS

Oxford University Press, Inc., publishes works that further
Oxford University's objective of excellence
in research, scholarship, and education.

Oxford   New York
Auckland   Cape Town   Dar es Salaam   Hong Kong   Karachi
Kuala Lumpur   Madrid   Melbourne   Mexico City   Nairobi
New Delhi   Shanghai   Taipei   Toronto

With offices in
Argentina   Austria   Brazil   Chile   Czech Republic   France   Greece
Guatemala   Hungary   Italy   Japan   Poland   Portugal   Singapore
South Korea   Switzerland   Thailand   Turkey   Ukraine   Vietnam

Published by Oxford University Press, Inc.
198 Madison Avenue, New York, New York 10016

www.oup.com

Oxford is a registered trademark of Oxford University Press.

Library of Congress Cataloging-in-Publication Data
Hall, Patricia (Patricia Ann)
   Berg's Wozzeck / Patricia Hall.
       p.   cm. — (Studies in musical genesis, structure, and interpretation)
   Includes bibliographical references and index.
   ISBN 978-0-19-534261-1
   1. Berg, Alban, 1885-1935. Wozzeck.   I. Title.
   ML410.B47H34 2011
   782.1—dc22   2010018837

Companion illustrations () are available online at www.oup.com/us/bergswozzeck
Access with username Music2 and password Book4416.
For more information on Oxford Web Music, visit www.oxfordwebmusic.com

1 3 5 7 9 8 6 4 2
Printed in the United States of America
on acid-free paper

To my son

SERIES EDITOR'S FOREWORD

The Oxford series *Studies in Musical Genesis and Structure* began under Lewis Lockwood's editorship in 1985, with Philip Gossett's volume on Donizetti's *Anna Bolena*. Each volume since then has sought to elucidate the detail of musical creation in a single work by a major composer. Around the turn of the millennium the series expanded its purpose to include associated issues of interpretation, with a view to placing these individual masterworks within a continuum from sketch to score, and on to première. Sometimes the path has led even beyond, to issues of legal interpretation and the work's rich life even after the death of its composer.

From a base in the central canon of classical and romantic repertory, the series has gradually caught up with selected works from the twentieth century. Recent volumes have featured works by Debussy, Vaughan Williams, Bartók and, in 2009, Terry Riley, whose *In C*, a work from the 1960s, lacks a definitive form at all. In the coming years *Studies in Musical Genesis, Structure, and Interpretation* will start to confront another frontier, with volumes on works that have been digitally incubated and born, and genres in which the work is sometimes its own performance. Although a long way from the traditional, romantic-period sketch studies with which the series began, these emerging essays on musical genesis from the computer age lead to the same endpoint: better understanding of the ways in which great art comes about.

Right from its inception twenty-five years ago the series has demonstrated that opera is a particularly fertile ground for genetic investigation. The inter-relationship of music, words, and staging, as well as the different creative approaches of composer and librettist, leads to complexities and speculations that sometimes even defy the two-dimensionality of the traditional book. Hence, in this current study the series augments the book with accompanying digital materials, so that readers can pursue their own, independent sleuthing of significant slabs of primary-source documents and explore the fuller detail of catalogues that would otherwise be reserved for specialist library visitors only.

Patricia Hall comes to this study of the autograph sources of Alban Berg's *Wozzeck* with an impeccable pedigree both in Berg studies (her 1996 study of the sources of Berg's *Lulu*, for University of California Press) and sketch study (her edited handbook of 2004, with Friedemann Sallis, for Cambridge University Press). Even the most casual student of music history knows of Berg's *Wozzeck* for two reasons: it is a rare example of total artistic synergy across the divide of centuries, between Berg's music of the early twentieth century and Georg Büchner's fragmentary text of the early nineteenth century; it is an equally rare example of the total sublimation of musical forms to dramatic priorities. Patricia Hall's study gives fresh evidence for the reassertion of both these truisms. In the first four chapters she systematically leads us through the decade from first conceptions of 1914 to the much-reported première in Berlin late in 1925. There are frequent revisions of the work's previously accepted creative chronology as well as an extended tutorial in unraveling the detail of Berg's working method. Hall's last three chapters, with their respective emphases upon the connection with Büchner's text, transition, and pitch structures well elucidate the opera's formal construction, from largest to smallest levels. Here we find real evidence for that compellingly pneumatic character of the opera, in which, to quote Hall, Berg so frequently balances "the emotional malaise of atonality with the expressiveness of tonality."

Malcolm Gillies
London Metropolitan University

ACKNOWLEDGMENTS

As with my previous book on the sketches for *Lulu*, it has taken me nearly as long to grasp the complexities of these sketches as it took Berg to complete his opera. I sympathized with Berg's abbreviated summer periods of composition, since I usually spent only ten weeks each summer working with Berg's sketches in Vienna. I used these forays to Berg's home ground to immerse myself in Viennese concert life and exhibitions, to frequent the same coffeehouses, museums, and concert halls as Berg, and to visit Berg's summerhouse, where he composed his masterwork.

I doubt if Berg's neighborhood in Hietzing has changed much since he lived there. Certainly his apartment is literally frozen in time. I thank the Alban Berg Stiftung, Dr. Regina Busch, and Klaus Lippe for allowing me to periodically visit this altar of history and to examine Berg's copies of Büchner's *Woyzeck*, as well as his Tagebücher for the critical war years. Klaus Lippe and Mark DeVoto generously agreed to read the entire text, and I am especially grateful for their many suggestions.

I developed a strange fixation with the history of World War I during the writing of this book, which I began to see as not only a major influence on Berg's opera, but as a defining event in twentieth-century art, music, and literature. I read voluminously from German, English, and French sources, even visiting locations on the Western Front. (I should thank my mother here, who gamely accompanied me to various World War I museums and battlefields.) It seemed curious to me that a fragment written in the 1830s was so uncannily relevant almost a century later. I suppose one could make the same analogy about war and collective amnesia from one generation to the next. The Vietnam War, embedded in the memory of my generation, is an abstract event to my students, related to them secondhand by their fathers and uncles.

After twenty-five years as a Berg scholar, I have come to appreciate the fortunate consistencies that can occur from one book to the next. My research was again generously funded through General Research Grants from UCSB. The Fulbright Commission, who funded my research as a graduate student on the *Lulu* sketches, and the resulting book with UC Press, awarded me a Faculty Research Grant to Vienna. (I became what the Fulbright Commission referred to as a "repeat offender.") This, my only extended period of study in Vienna, allowed me to study the sketches for two very difficult preceding works, the *Altenberg Lieder* and the Three Pieces for Orchestra. Edmond Johnson produced the beautiful and tremendously difficult examples and transcriptions. Andre Mount took on and brilliantly completed the onerous task of arranging and editing the color images of sketches, and formatting the entire manuscript for Oxford University Press. Laura Emmery graciously measured a number of complicated fragments at the Musiksammlung of the Austrian National Library. Anita Ip made the first translations of a number of the reviews of the 1925 Berlin premiere. Maura Jess expertly edited and scanned some of the most problematic sketch images. Lee Rothfarb, a fellow graduate student at Yale and now my colleague at UCSB, generously reviewed many translations.

The Austrian National Library has become my home away from home. I thank them for patiently allowing me to work with the original sources summer after summer, and for allowing me to photograph Berg's sketches. In particular, I would like to thank Josef Gmeiner and Dorothea Hunger for helping me decipher Berg's handwriting. In this regard, a new friend Professor Herwig Knaus, never failed to interrupt his work to confront my latest deciphering nightmare. I am also deeply grateful to the Beinecke Rare Book Library at Yale, the Music Division of the Library of Congress, and the Houghton Manuscript Library at Harvard of allowing me to photograph there as well. The remaining archives, the Bayerische Staatsbibliothek, Munich, and the Staatsbibliothek Preussischer Kulturbesitz, Berlin kindly supplied scans of their respective sketches.

Martha Hyde, my dissertation advisor at Yale, read Chapter 2 and made many helpful suggestions during the early stages of writing. I am very grateful for both her optimism and realism in difficult times. Just as Berg described himself as "always a student of Schoenberg," I consider myself "always a student of Martha Hyde."

Malcolm Gillies, whose studies of Bartók's sketches I greatly admire, was the ideal series editor, acting as a conduit to Oxford University Press, offering enthusiasm and suggestions with which I always agreed. Suzanne Ryan, Music Editor at Oxford, significantly shaped this book with her suggestions for additional material. Three anonymous and expert readers made myriad constructive suggestions about the content, as well.

My son, now an actor, collector, and translator in Tokyo, is also well acquainted with the world of academia, having grown up at Yale as well in the Music Departments of various universities. I thank him for reading several chapters, and noting every phrase that made sense to me, but no one else. It is to him this book is dedicated.

For permission to print the many sketches appearing in this book, I thank the Österrichische Nationalbibliothek and the Alban Berg Stiftung. Part of Chapter 7 was originally published in *The Cambridge Companion to Berg*, ed. Anthony Pople (Cambridge: Cambridge University Press, 1997), pp. 184–187, and is reproduced here by permission of Cambridge University Press. Chapter 2, originally published in *The Musical Times* (Autumn, 2005): 5–24, is reproduced by permission of *The Musical Times*, Ltd., and Chapter 5, which originally appeared in *Theory and Practice*, 33 (2008): 249–271, is reproduced by permission of *Theory and Practice*.

CONTENTS

Berg's *Wozzeck*

Introduction

> At first, I didn't have the slightest hope that I would succeed in deciphering it. Before me lay four sheets of dark grey, brittle paper, written on in all directions with long lines of very fine, very pale, yellowish strokes. There was not a single legible syllable. In addition, several small sheets of white paper, covered with similar strokes. Since the marks were larger here and the background lighter, here and there a word could be deciphered, but nowhere as much as a whole sentence.[1]
>
> —Karl Emil Franzos

It is difficult to imagine a more daunting set of conditions for deciphering Büchner's *Woyzeck,* one of the "most performed dramas of the 19th century."[2] Through the tenacious efforts of scholars, the text of the play has nonetheless appeared in progressively more accurate renderings, from Franzos's pioneering effort in 1879 (described above), to the electronic facsimiles of the present.[3]

Berg's sketches for his opera *Wozzeck,* in many ways a cumulative creative record equivalent to Büchner's handwritten fragment, present similar challenges for study, for while Berg, unlike Büchner, actually finished the work, his sketches that should bear witness to this effort are woefully incomplete.

Granted, by definition, sketches are fragmentary. In his chapter, "Coming to Terms with the Composer's Sketches," Friedemann Sallis reminds us: "Sketches are private documents, not normally intended for public scrutiny, and their function is primarily mnemonic. Composers write down that which cannot be committed to memory."[4] Further, we cannot realistically assume that a composer—even one as meticulous about his private documents as Berg—kept every one of his sketches. Still, there are large sections of the opera for which no sketches whatsoever exist. David Fanning's remarkably detailed catalogue of the sketches lists drafts of only 32 measures for Act I, scene 2, a physical impossibility, even taking into account that Berg composed at his piano and the pencil-written *Particell* served as a stage of compositional process.[5] Similarly, there are only twenty measures of sketches and drafts for Act I, scene 4. In all, there are approximately 250 pages of what might be termed sketches and drafts, housed in four archives. (This excludes Berg's editions of the Büchner text, housed at Harvard, the Austrian National Library, and Berg's apartment in Vienna.) This collection of sketches and drafts, most of which resides in the Music Division of the Austrian National Library, includes three sketchbooks, assorted loose leaves and fragments of leaves arranged in folders, and a few sketches appearing in notebooks of non-musical material. Certainly, the discovery of 23 leaves of an early *Particell* and sketches for Act II, scene 2 (the first scene Berg composed), is gratifying, but there is no telling how long we will have to wait before others emerge.[6] Having personally witnessed a tiny snip of a *Wozzeck* sketch presented as a gift to a guest at a dinner party in 1985, I think it could very well be forever.

The study of Berg's sketches, like Büchner's is also complicated by Berg's notoriously difficult handwriting. It is not "microscopically small," but it is equally illegible.[7] (There are probably only a dozen scholars who can read it, with some effort.) And Berg too relied on frequent abbreviations; he routinely abbreviates instruments (Gr. Tr. for Grosse Trommel), characters in the opera (W for Wozzeck, Hpt. for Hauptmann), and commonly used words (v for von, u for und, kl for klein, etc).

The physical condition of the Büchner and Berg sketches is also problematic. It is horrifying to learn that the chemical treatment Franzos applied to Büchner's manuscript left it even more faded than before, causing punctuation marks to become "an open field of editorial decisions."[8] But we are equally guilty with Berg's manuscripts in the twentieth century: the *Partitur* to *Wozzeck*, sold by Berg for 6000AS to the Library of Congress in 1934, was treated (probably in the 1940s) to a preservative varnish that ironically caused the colored ink in the manuscript to run.[9] Even the condition of the paper between the two collections demonstrates parallels: in 1921, during a period of Austrian postwar inflation, Berg's favorite manuscript paper was of such poor quality that, like Büchner's, it became brittle and discolored over time.

It is hardly surprising then that there have been no book-length studies of this relatively small collection of sketches, even if they are (like Büchner's) for one of the most performed works in the repertoire. We are helped very little by Rosemary Hilmar's catalogue of the sketches, which, like the rest of her book, is so ridden with errors that it warrants a disclaimer.[10] In his book on *Wozzeck*, Peter Petersen, like David Fanning, corrects some of the worst errors in chronology committed by the Hilmars.[11] Petersen also summons the sketches as convincing evidence that Berg made changes in his text based on the Witkowski edition of the play that appeared in 1920, six years after Berg began his opera, and for a detailed analysis of the opera's characters and associated music. Which raises the question, are the sketches better used, as Petersen employs them, as supplementary evidence in a larger study of the work? Even Fanning openly concedes at the end of his catalogue: "a close examination [of the sketches] will probably not yield more than a modest addition to our understanding of the work."[12]

This book, a study of the source materials for *Wozzeck*, addresses these challenges by examining the opera as a continuum—relying stylistically on works that immediately preceded it, evolving in the course of composition, and contributing in turn to works that followed it. Thus, it is not a self-contained uniform entity, but an evolving work influenced most profoundly by his teacher, Arnold Schoenberg, and Berg's involuntary participation in a world catastrophe: the Great War, and the ensuing financial debilitation of Austria. The physical documents associated with *Wozzeck* are hardly self-contained either. To give a truer picture of the slow and at times interrupted creation of this masterwork, one must consult Berg's correspondence, diaries, calendars, notebooks, his personal library, preceding and following works—and sometimes even works from which the themes for *Wozzeck* were borrowed. Further, sources that are not technically sketches or drafts, like Berg's autograph *Particell*, or his annotations in his Büchner text, can sometimes reveal more evidence than a sketch per se.

One could view this entire collection of documents as an enigma to be deciphered and solved, whether by transcribing a document, establishing the chronology and order in which Berg composed the fifteen scenes, or decoding the significance of a series of numbers appearing in a sketch. And like the various editions of Büchner's play, my work has benefited from earlier scholars' studies of the sketches, beginning with Ernst and Rosemary Hilmar, and continuing with the work of Peter Petersen and David Fanning, as well as from the analyses of Jarman and Perle. I have had the advantage of working over an extended period of time with the actual documents, rather than a microfilm. This has allowed me to examine physical properties such as paper types and writing implements that add significant evidence to the total picture. Further, I have attempted to decipher the sketches I discuss as completely as possible, to the point of enlisting color computer scans, manipulated by various parameters. Even seemingly meaningless annotations in the margin can suggest significant facts about chronology and the stylistic evolution of the work over the eight years in which it was composed. Contrarily, evidence that at first seems a given, for instance, physical proximity to the sketches for other works, often leads to blind alleys and gross missteps.

Manuscript study is a humbling experience. Even if we manage to decipher the sketches (we often don't), how can we presume to look through what Richard Kramer so poetically calls "the window of the artist's soul"—a person we have, in most cases, never even met?[13] At most, the sketches give a glimpse of a creative act.

We begin our study with sketches showing Berg's first attempts at orchestration in the *Altenberg Lieder*, Opus 4, and attaining large-scale form in the *Marsch* from the Three Pieces for Orchestra, Opus 6. Chapter 2 is a study of the inception of the opera, dating to shortly after Berg first saw Büchner's play performed in 1914, and drawn out through 1918 by the First World War. The second phase in composition, discussed in Chapter 3, traces Berg's steady progress to complete the opera in post-World War I Austria, extricate himself from the many duties his teacher, Schoenberg, required of him, and become a famous composer in his own right. This phase in Berg's development comes to fruition during the critical years 1923 to 1925, covered in Chapter 4, when Berg's opera premiered in Berlin. Chapter 5 demonstrates through annotations in Berg's Büchner text how he used text to derive form in two scenes: Act II, scene 2 and Act II, scene 4. Chapter 6 examines Berg's sketches for large-scale form that surprisingly evolved over the course of the opera. Chapter 7 discusses the many analyses that Berg completed in the sketches for *Wozzeck*, and how these analyses reveal a distinct evolution in his style over the eight-year span in which he composed the opera. And, finally, in my conclusion I consider the significance of *Wozzeck* in terms of Berg's overall compositional output.

CHAPTER One

The Path to *Wozzeck*

I've finally composed something again, a short orchestral song on a picture postcard text by Altenberg, to which I will add several more as soon as the concerts here are over. I will give the completed one to Webern, whom I see often, to take along for you. For after this long period of stagnation I am completely incapable of judging my work and really can't say whether it's any good or the greatest rubbish. And so I ask you, dear Herr Schönberg, as soon as you have time, to look at what I've composed and tell me, or let me know through Webern, what you think of it, that is to say, whether it is good or bad, and <u>what</u> it is that's bad. I must get on the right track again so that <u>at the very least</u> I'll be able to apply what I already knew, namely the infinite number of things I learned from <u>you</u>, Herr Schoenberg. Moreover, considering my limited talent for <u>orchestral writing</u>, this will no doubt turn out badly, at least at first. Perhaps I could learn something more in <u>this</u> regard, too, particularly if you'll be so very kind as to make corrections, i.e., criticize some of it—all of it would no doubt be asking too much.[1]

—Berg to Schoenberg, March 10, 1912

It is difficult to recognize the composer of *Wozzeck* in this letter, both in its apologetic tone and self-disparaging content. Even after Berg received reassurance from Schoenberg, Berg's insecurity about orchestration is unassuaged: He responds, "[…] how happy your judgment that the songs are not altogether bad has made me. Especially in respect to the orchestration, where I feared, in view of my unfortunate beginnings, that in every bar—though it urged itself upon me with the intensity of something *heard*—I might have committed some imbecility."[2]

Yet a little more than two years later, Berg had completed an approximately thirty-minute work for large orchestra (Opus 6) that embraced not only atonality, but nontraditional form. In his "Lecture on *Wozzeck*" (1929) Berg is confident enough to comment, "Until [*Wozzeck*], works of bold dimensions—such as four-movement symphonies, oratorios and large-scale operas—were missing in the sphere of atonal composition."[3]

How then, did two critical works, the *Altenberg Lieder* and the Three Pieces for Orchestra, prepare Berg to write an opera containing fifteen scenes and lasting approximately two hours? In this chapter we examine sketches for two particularly illuminating movements, "Sahst du nach dem Gewitterregen" from the Five Orchestra Songs on Postcard Texts by Peter Altenberg (Opus 4) and the *Marsch* from the Three Pieces for Orchestra (Opus 6). As we shall discover, the sketches for these movements reveal the compositional strategies by which Berg consciously overcame the complexities of orchestration and large-scale form.

One could argue that the *Altenberg Lieder*, with its five movements and leitmotivic repetitions of text, constitutes a miniature monodrama. After a relatively lengthy "overture" the songs present a journey of the (female) soul, punctuated by climactic ecstasies. From the hopeful "Soul, you are more beautiful, profounder, after snowstorms," to the suggestion of abandonment in the third movement ("Over the brink of beyond musingly wandered your gaze; never a care for house and hold!"), to the certain despondency of the fourth song ("Nothing is come, nothing will, to still my soul's longing.—So long I have waited, have waited so long, ah, so long!") to the sorrow and resignation of the last movement ("Here I give cry to my unfathomable, measureless sorrow that would consume my very soul [...])," the cycle traces a romantic downward trajectory.

Each movement, or "scene" is further structured by the individual lines of the postcard texts. For instance, in the second song, "Sahst du nach dem Gewitterregen," the three lines of text constitute an exposition, development and recapitulation in the short expanse of eleven measures:

Did you see the forest after the thunderstorm?!?!
Everything shines, blinks and is more beautiful than before,
See, woman, you need a thunderstorm, too!

The first line, sung with minimal orchestral accompaniment, is framed by a semitone/major third motive in prime and transposed inversion: (B-flat-B-G), (D-C-sharp-E-sharp) (Example 1.1). This last statement of the motive links with the F of the orchestral accompaniment (measure 2) to form a chain of two thirds connected by semitones, which foreshadow a long melodic chain of the same form of the motive in the orchestra, beginning on B. The chromatic triplet figure in the first line of text leads to the ascending F-E-flat dyad "Ge-wit," which, like the G-B dyad that precedes it, becomes fixed in register for the remainder of the song.

The second line of text develops these motives, particularly in the vocal line, where the final note (F) of the first vocal line forms the axis of two symmetrical melodic strands: F-sharp-G-A-flat and E-E-flat-D. This leads to a melisma, (measure 5) that reiterates the first three notes of the vocal line, before resolving in a chromatic ascent (again in triplets) and a descending minor seventh to form an ordered inversion of the opening "nach dem Gewitt," replicating the pitches F, F-sharp and G. The accompaniment, meanwhile, articulates three series of a semitone plus a third, the first beginning on B-G-sharp, the second on A-C-sharp, and the third on the familiar G-B dyad.

Finally, the third line is set to a two-part canon, using the same G-B series as in measure 5, now in retrograde inversion, as well as the perfect fourth series from "Gewitterregen" set identically with E-flat-B-flat-A-E. The vocal part of the third line again elides with the last note of the previous line, now by duplicating the "A" of

Example 1.1: Score of "Sahst du"

"zuvor," however two octaves higher. The final F octave (measure 11) appears in the same register in measures 2, 6–7 and 11, punctuating the end of each line of text.

Berg's initial sketches for the second movement (Figure 1.1a, transcribed in Figure 1.1b) bear important similarities to sketches for his later operas. For instance, Berg attaches small motivic figures to fragments of text (Schöner,

(a)

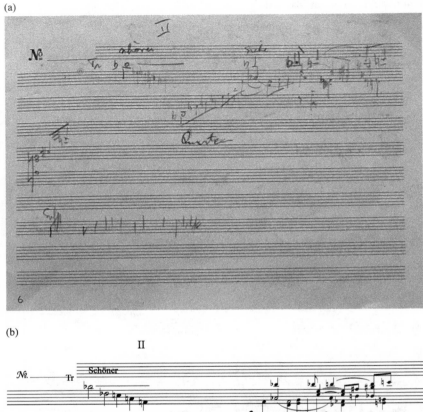

(b)

Figure 1.1: F 21 Berg 65 fol. 6ᵛ

siehe, sahst), suggesting that these words acted as the creative impulse for their accompanying music. ("Schöner" and "siehe" appear in other movements, as well.) We also observe Berg's minute attention to vocal delivery—the orchestration of the voice, so to speak. Adorno, one of Berg's most insightful analysts, enthusiastically describes the "coloratura-like melisma" (measure 5 of the song and staff two of Figure 1.1a; elaborated in more detail in staff 7 of Figure 1.2a and its transcription in Figure 1.2b), noting, "There was nothing like it again until Boulez's *Marteau sans maître*."[4] In this second, more detailed sketch, Berg eliminates the orchestra at the critical opening of the recapitulation ("Siehe Fraue"), exposing the voice on its highest pitch, A6 (with a dynamic of *ppp*, no less). This recalls Berg's carefully described

(a)

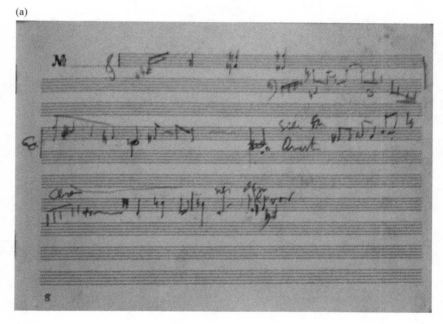

(b)

Figure 1.2: F 21 Berg 65 fol. 8ʳ

technique in a concept sketch of the previous song, appearing in the same sketchbook (Figure 1.3a and its transcription Figure 1.3b), in which he specifies that his
"Hauch Akkord" (breath chord) which he gives the motivic designation Z, "often
appears in fortissimo locations, unheard, or continuing to sound." In his diagram

(a)

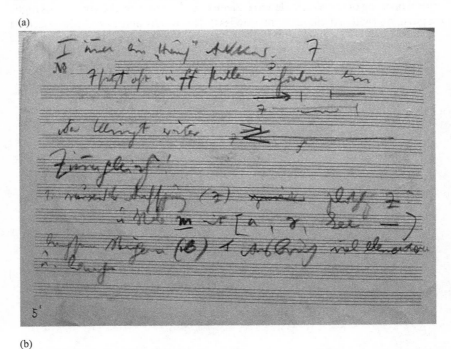

(b)

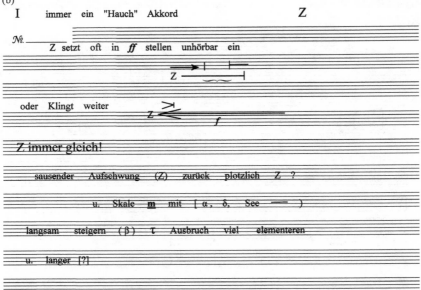

Figure 1.3: F 21 Berg 65 fol. 5ᵛ

(staff 2) this sonority is suddenly exposed by the silence of the other parts, or gradually exposed by the tapering off of the orchestral parts (staff 4). In one of his many analogies between painting and Berg's compositional process, Adorno comments:

> Colors are not just painted as if pre-existent, they are developed; the process by which they are created becomes their justification [. . .] the chord enters inaudibly in the third section amid a tutti fortissimo and is only thrown into relief through subtraction, through the extinguishing of all other articulated events. That way it establishes itself as something that has been there all along.[5]

A final similarity between the Altenberg sketches and Berg's operatic sketches is the rhythmic shorthand that Berg used to set text before he filled in pitches (Figure 1.1a, staff 8). This has the effect of establishing the rhythmic parameter before Berg moves on to the exact pitches, a technique he will also apply to orchestration. Here the sketch (and the entire leaf) is so experimental and tentative that the contour of staff 8 bears little resemblance to the final score.

In this miniature monodrama, Berg assiduously attends to the smallest musical component, the interval. Hence Berg's annotations in both Figure 1.1a, staff 4, and Figure 1.2a, staff 4, "Quarten" (fourths), referring perhaps to the series of ascending fourths in the 'cello that lead to the fermata of the first half (measure 6). In general, these initial sketches have characteristics of a concept sketch rather than a draft: We are confronted with ideas for individual events in the piece, for instance, the melisma (measure 5) or the symmetrical formation shown on the top staff of Figure 1.2a.

It is not until the final draft that Berg even approaches orchestration (at least in this movement) (Figures 1.4 and 1.5). It is as if Berg must master the complexities

Figure 1.4: F 21 Berg 65 fol. 8ᵛ

Figure 1.5: F 21 Berg 65 fol. 9ʳ

of pitch before even considering orchestral color. As chaotic as this draft initially appears, it features a logical, almost analytical layout of the movement, in two halves; the first leaf ends with the sustained chord, measure 7, the second leaf begins with the recapitulation (measure 8) and sketches through the end of the song, measure 11. If we adopt Adorno's painting analogy, then Berg lays out his palette of instruments at the top of the draft: *Cl[arinette]*, *Br[atsche] getheilt 2 Fl[oten]*, etc., and begins to apply his hues by delicately dabbing within the body of the draft. In general, Berg seems to be aiming at multiplicity of color—for instance, our referential F at the end of each vocal line is orchestrated differently for each of its three appearances. Further, Berg uses color to segment uniform sequential passages into smaller statements: the long, descending third sequence of measures 8–11 is divided into three segments colored by the oboe, trumpet, and finally trombone. Berg orchestrates the point of densest texture and broadest register span, the sustained chord of measure 7, with nearly every instrument available to him, before allowing the voice to enter unaccompanied in the next measure. It is apparently such a critical moment that Berg devotes an entire sketch to it, where he maps out the orchestration of this section in more detail. One could contrast the variety of orchestral color appearing in this song with Berg's very limited and utilitarian set of motives; the third semitone motive appears a total of 21 times in eleven measures. Yet we are no more bothered by these repetitions than by the endless triads in tonal music. Nor does this movement reflect the analytical complexities of some of the other movements, which exhibit compositional techniques that foreshadow those in *Wozzeck*. In the sketch, for instance

(Figure 1.6), from the opening movement of the *Altenberg Lieder*, Berg is wrestling simultaneously with five transforming ostinati, while meticulously ticking off their pitch content as it relates to two statements of the total chromatic. Berg's chromatic list reminds us that this movement also features the first appearance of a twelve-tone theme—nine years before Schoenberg—again anticipating Berg's musical language in *Wozzeck*.

As brief and fragmented as they are, we are fortunate that Berg's sketches for "Sahst du nach dem Gewitterregen" are so detailed and, moreover, that they appear together in a sketchbook, allowing us to see each successive stage of his creative process. This separating out of parameters, from motivic ideas generated by the text, to rhythmic sketches representing themes, to total placement of the pitch content in a *Particell*-like sketch, continues in Berg's act of orchestration, as well. After listing his colors, Berg finally begins to add orchestration as a final step—whether he had conceived these colors earlier in his creative process or not. If anything, this strategy of isolating parameters will become more pronounced in the *Wozzeck* sketches, in which he lists and annotates its complex orchestration only in the *Particell*.

Given the apoplectic reaction of the audience to this movement at its premiere in the "Skandalkonzert"[6] of March 31, 1913, as well as Schoenberg's utter rejection of Berg's foray into this abbreviated style,[7] it is surprising that Berg didn't destroy the work, sketches and all. Even so, we have Mark DeVoto to thank that this work became concert repertoire, or for that matter, even

Figure 1.6: F 21 Berg 65 fol. 3ʳ

known. The title of his article, published in 1966, reflects this: "Some Notes on the Unknown *Altenberg Lieder*."[8]

The *Marsch* of Opus 6: A Carefully Crafted Chaos

The Pieces for Orchestra (Opus 6) is the first work by Berg to anticipate the sound world of *Wozzeck*. And indeed, the *Marsch* was begun in 1914, the same year Berg decided to compose his opera. As we shall discover in our study of the chronology of the opera, however, Berg did not compose these passages from *Wozzeck* in 1914; rather, he gravitated back to this style when he returned to his opera after the war.

Berg called his score of the *Marsch* the most complicated ever written, and analysts have endlessly attempted to decode its form. Here are descriptions by several leading Berg scholars:

Fragmentary rhythmic and melodic figures typical of an orthodox military march repeatedly coalesce into polyphonic episodes of incredible density that surge to frenzied climaxes, then fall apart.[9]

—George Perle

[...] the three-sectioned sonata design, distinguished in the background plan of the piece, is exploded by constant motivic development and the unrelenting presentation of apparently new material; sonata form is here destroyed from within by its own developmental tendencies.[10]

—Douglas Jarman

A Bogenform [. . .] the Marsch really reflects none of the classical forms so central to other works by Berg, but rather only a series of episodic sections set off from each other by changes in texture or tempo, or by the prominence of one or another theme—in other words, what one might expect, formally speaking, in a military march by any of a hundred composers of band music.[11]

—Mark DeVoto

And, finally,

I make no bones about saying that I find it the most difficult and perplexing of Berg's instrumental compositions; any comments I have on it must therefore be taken as provisional. But there are hints of an understanding of it in Berg's own markings. Among the plethora of indications [. . .] [h]e was content to build a piece around the interaction of tempos without exploring any further ramifications.[12]

—Derrick Puffett

A second generation of scholars (Melchior von Borries and Don McLean), have employed Berg's sketches in this Mount Everest of analysis.[13] This is, ironically, often a more difficult task than hypothesizing a form based on analysis of the finished score; it involves deciphering Berg's very difficult handwriting, interpreting the meanings of complex thematic lists, as well as finding the location of these themes—which often, because of compositional changes, can appear ten measures or more later than annotated in Berg's sketches. In my own investigation of the sketches, I am primarily interested in exposing sketching techniques that allowed Berg to make the giant leap from the miniatures of his previous style to large-scale form. These include actually assigning letters to each of his many themes, completing his de facto analysis. But I shall also interpret what new insights Berg's sketches suggest about the form of the movement: that rather than a traditional form, it consists of a series of thematic groups.

Figure 1.7a, and its transcription Figure 1.7b, for instance, one of Berg's earliest sketches for the *Marsch*, features a virtual flow chart of thematic groups recalling the system of thematic notation Berg used in the same year for his *Gurrelieder Führer* (Figure 1.8).[14] In both examples, each motivic entrance is assigned a letter and subscript to denote its location in the thematic group. In contrast to the delicacy of some of the sketches for the *Altenberg Lieder*, this sketch for the *Marsch* fairly careers across the page. Since Berg identified the locations of these thematic groups in compositional drafts, it is often possible to identify the content of these themes, including the A6 noted at the bottom of the sketch and the C2, which, he notes, will eventually metamorphose into the extended C4.

For example, even though Berg's draft of the initial A section (Figure 1.9) is horribly smeared, one can discern numbers indicating the entrance of themes. A1 through A6 are systematically introduced in the opening and stated in retrograde order at the end of the A section, forming a palindrome. (These denotations, as Don McLean has noted, exactly correspond to Mark DeVoto's list of themes for the A section.)[15] Berg had already used this technique of formal retrogradation in the first song of Opus 2, and "Sahst du Nach dem Gewitterregen" relies on a similar formal technique, the retrogradation of the opening succession at the end of the movement.

Several things seem significant in this sketch. First, Berg is working with a much larger group of thematic ideas than in the *Altenberg Lieder* (he has already generated six ideas in the opening nine measures). Second, he uses the same technique to delineate sections that he used in slightly earlier opuses to create entire movements. And third, each thematic idea is characterized by a unique orchestral color and range (Example 1.2).

Berg uses orchestral color to delineate entire sections as well. For instance, he describes the transition to the first section as percussive (Figures 1.10a and 1.10b): "Übergang zum ersten Theil ist schlagwerkartig." These specific indications of orchestration appear in early concept sketches, in contrast to the "paint by number" technique Berg used in his final draft of the second song of the *Altenberg Lieder*.

Berg's sketches for the B section (which he identifies in his drafts as beginning in measure 22) show specifically how Berg produced extended forms by successive additions of material. In Berg's initial sketches for the B section we see a phrase construction consisting of a neighbor-note-like motive (G-A-flat-G) that is repeated, and completed in its third statement. It is no longer in length than one of the phrases in the *Altenberg Lieder* (staves 1–2 of Figure 1.6a). Berg makes the annotation at the top of the sketch, "*auspinnen*" (develop). In Berg's later drafts, he inserts thematic

(a)

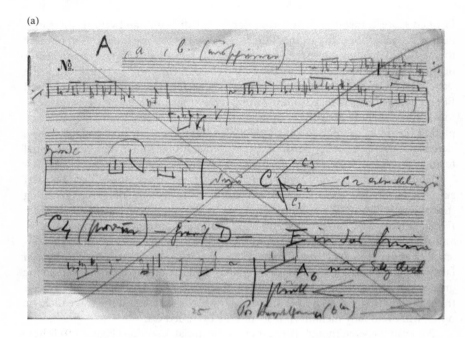

(b)

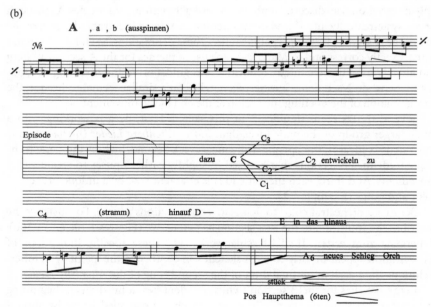

Figure 1.7: F 21 Berg 13/II p. 25

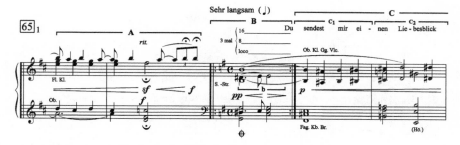

Figure 1.8: Gurrelieder Führer (first line)

Figure 1.9: F 21 Berg 13/II p. 14

Example 1.2: Motives for the A section

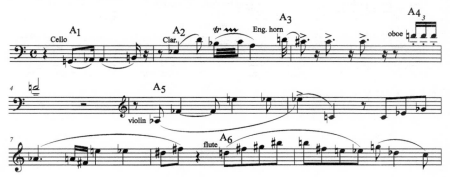

(a)

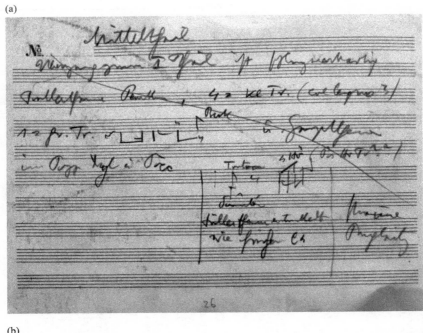

(b)

Mitteltheil

№.

Übergang zum I Theil ist schlagwerkartig

Trillertheme Pauken , 4 = Kl. Tr. (col legno ?)

Beck

1 = gr. Tr.

u. Hauptheme

im Pizz Xyl u. Picc

Tamtam 4 Hr (Pos Hr Tr ? ?)

daunter

triller theme entwickelt

wie früher C4

stramme

Begleitung

Figure 1.10: F 21 Berg 13/II p. 26

material between the two halves that foreshadows themes from the C and D sections, extending it by ten measures. The opening of the B section (measure 22) rather than announcing itself, precisely meshes with the closing phrase of section A, both thematically and instrumentally (Example 1.3). This elision is the same technique Berg uses in the developed restatement of section D (measure 91). His tempi, as one would expect from Berg's other works, do act as a structural element, to emphasize the parallel changes suggested by the themes and general pitch content. For instance, Berg's entire B section features a progressive de-acceleration that transitions to his next major section, C, beginning in measure 39. Given that Berg mentions a D7 in one of his sketches, we begin to suspect that Berg must have completed a "Führer" for his own composition. But lacking such a chart, we can construct the following plan showing the arrival of themes up to the restatement of D:

A (m.1) – B (m.22) – C (Episode)(m.39) – D (m. 71) – E (m. 80) – D' (m. 91)

Example 1.3: Transition to B section

Although Berg was clearly capable of writing neatly organized forms, for the *Marsch* he chose a "*modernes Form*," that is, one that is developmental and through-composed in character. If there is a recapitulation, it is the "Höhepunkt" of measure 125, in which he again elides into the A5 theme of measure 5 (Example 1.4). But here as elsewhere, the texture is so dense and the arrival of A5 so smooth, that it is not a recapitulation in the traditional meaning of the word. And Berg's sketches do suggest an overall form that subsumes his thematic groups. The sketch cited at the beginning of this study, for instance (Figure 1.9), mentions a percussive transition to "the first part," which, based on the evidence in the sketch, appears to be the above-mentioned recapitulation.

Example 1.4: Recapitulation

In general, Berg's thematic groups (A B C D E) alternate between an expositional and a developmental character. The C group (beginning in measure 39) is much calmer, more clearly organized, and the arrival of each subsequent C theme more recognizable. Again, this is also a result of the unique sound color of each entrance. For example, C3 is played by a muted solo viola, while C4 (*grazioso*) features a solo oboe (Example 1.5). This is not a neat parceling of thematic ideas, as in sonata form, but one in which themes are spewed about in a Kandinsky-like design, often arriving (but not developing) before their location proper.[16] Put another way, themes often play supporting roles before being featured as soloist. Further, these themes often appear in a density that, despite Berg's careful annotations of "Hauptstimme," makes it nearly impossible to extract them from the surrounding musical texture. It is no wonder that the *Marsch* has produced so many interpretations; ambiguity is an inherent aspect of the work.

Example 1.5: C3 and C4 themes

The sketches for the *Altenberg Lieder* and the *Marsch* reveal the twenty-seven-year-old Berg's rapid development as he quickly acquires techniques of orchestration and large-scale form and employs them in subsequent movements. In the *Altenberg Lieder*, Berg tended to isolate parameters in his sketches, moving from motivic analysis, to rhythmic sketches, to drafts, to orchestration. In the Three Pieces for Orchestra, Berg assigned thematic tags in the early stages of composition, which allowed him to move quickly to continuity drafts representing most of the work. Berg would draw on these sketching techniques, as well as his compositional innovations for both works, in his sketches for *Wozzeck*.

CHAPTER Two

The Inception of *Wozzeck*: 1914–1918

I saw *Wozzeck* performed before the war, and it made such a huge impression, that I immediately decided (after a second hearing) to set it to music.[1]
—Alban Berg to Anton Webern, August 19, 1918

Despite Berg's determination to compose an opera on Büchner's play, it is doubtful if he made much progress until the end of the war. Several authors have argued that a sketchbook including nearly all the extant sketches for Act I, scene 2, and Act II, scene 2, dates from 1914, that is, before the beginning of World War I and Berg's induction into the military.[2] This chronology is also supported by a remark by Berg's student Gottfried Kassowitz that Berg began to sketch two scenes immediately after seeing the play.[3]

Yet, in Berg's lecture "Pro Domo," dated May 23, 1927, he claims, "It is difficult for me to fulfill the request today to say something about my opera, because it has been ten years since I began to compose it," thus identifying the inception of the opera as spring 1917.[4] Berg makes an even more conservative assessment in a letter to Webern in the summer of 1921.[5] Citing the three interruptions he has thus far endured between summers of compositional activity, Berg places the beginning of composition at 1918.

As important as this delay is to the development of the work was the effect of the war on Berg's creative evolution. When Berg began—even in the most tentative form—to compose the opera in 1914, he was stylistically in the world of the *Marsch* of the Three Pieces for Orchestra, Opus 6, which he had completed that summer. Certainly Berg's military experiences allowed him to identify with the oppressed soldier of Büchner's play, generating a number of musical and programmatic ideas for several scenes of the opera.[6] At the same time, however, I will argue that Berg's creative powers were so hampered by military service and inactivity that he remains mired in the style of the *Marsch* in 1918, to the point of mimicking passages from it in Act I, scene 2.[7]

In this chapter, then, I decipher several sketches from a frequently cited sketchbook for *Wozzeck*. But I also turn to a less likely and largely ignored source of evidence, the notebooks Berg compiled as a soldier in World War I. As we shall discover, in addition to finally clarifying the chronology of Berg's tentative beginnings on the opera, these notebooks, with their many diagrams and biographical annotations, depict Berg's struggle far more poignantly than narrative alone. It is an astonishing drama in itself that an essentially unknown composer of thirty, facing the Great War, post-war inflation, and a complete breakdown of his health, composed an atonal opera which—despite the misgivings of his famous teacher—became one of the masterpieces of the twentieth century.

∾

There is a little bit of me in his character, since I have been spending these war years just as dependent on people I hate, have been in chains, sick, captive, resigned, in fact, humiliated.[8]

—Alban Berg to Helene Berg, August 7, 1918

Like many men his age, Berg enlisted for military service well after the outbreak of war. His calendar for 1915 bears the word "*Einrückung*" (report for duty) for the date August 15.[9] His personal notebooks from this period confront us with detailed diagrams of such inartistic subjects as the "Spanish rider," the "wolf pit," dugouts, fire steps, and other subtleties of trench warfare (Figures 2.1–2.2). These brutal images, copied from manuals Berg received in reserve officer training (Figure 2.3), would be alarming, interpreted perhaps as a psychological defense

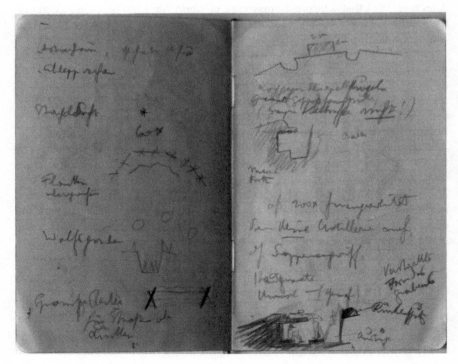

Figure 2.1: ÖNB Musiksammlung F 21 Berg 479/19 fols. 3ᵛ–4ʳ (catalog #: 298 & 299)

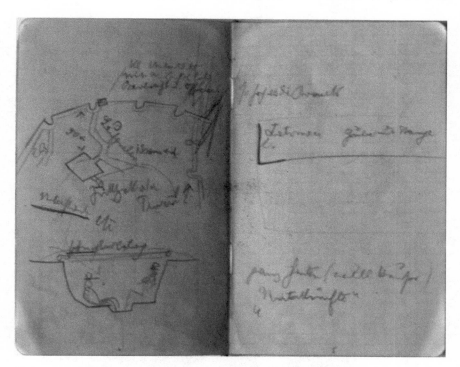

Figure 2.2: ÖNB Musiksammlung F 21 Berg 479/19 fols. 4ᵛ–5ʳ (catalog #: 300)

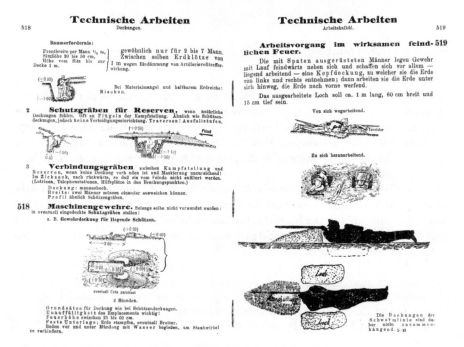

Figure 2.3: Austrian Unterofficier Training Manual for 1915

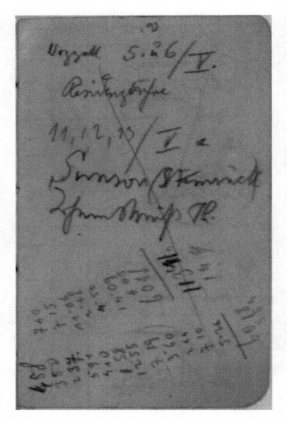

Figure 2.4: ÖNB Musiksammlung F 21 Berg 479/48 fol. 56ᵛ

against the foreignness of military life, if Berg in private life were not the con-
summate list maker. In fact, his notebooks are filled with grocery lists, expense
lists, correspondence lists, lent book lists—and even performance lists! It is one
of these informal performance lists that reveal the inauspicious beginnings of
Wozzeck: the two performances of the play that Berg happened to attend in May
1914 (Figure 2.4).

Berg's horror of military life is well documented; in frequent letters to his wife,
as well as to his student Gottfried Kassowitz, he described his disgust with group
living, his insomnia in the barracks, the "abominable" food, his "senseless" duties,
and the "revolting" latrines.[10] Typical in tone is the following letter to his wife written
a day after he had enlisted:

> Two hours pass, chatting, before I get my uniform. Who goes there? Linke—what a
> coincidence! I pay a tip of two Kronen and get a uniform. You can't imagine it—the
> smell! Still, thanks to the two Kronen it's at least fairly clean, though trousers are
> too short. But the great thick cap, and the haversack—someone must have bled all
> over that![11]

Lest Berg be dismissed as the hypersensitive artist, we also have the following letter to his wife from the same period, outlining the typical exercise routines of Austrian infantry:

> We had such a strenuous exercise today, my Pferscherl, that this will have to be a shortish letter. From seven in the morning till one in the afternoon we were marching, running, charging across hill and dale, through the swamps and the marshes, down on the ground, up again, and so on. I've got a crust of mud all over me. Afternoon out again, but at least without pack or rifle.[12]

There is a touching letter of July 13, 1915 to Webern, who had enlisted in the military even earlier than Berg. Berg pleads in a nearly maternal tone:

> Forgive me if I make you aware of something that, to me, seems very important. Do your superiors know how things stand with your vision? Is it clear to you to what extent you can trust your eyes and to what extent you can rely on them? [. . .] Shouldn't you make your superiors aware of this again, *before* you go to the front?[13]

Berg's own health dilemma, debilitating asthma attacks, caused a breakdown in his health that plagued him for the rest of his life. After hospitalization in November 1915 he was transferred to watch duty and finally, in February 1916, clerical duty for the remainder of the war.[14]

The first clearly dated sketches for *Wozzeck* come from the time of this emotional hiatus of 1916. Berg's notebook from this period (Figure 2.5) bears the usual military jargon of the k. und k. regime. We see that Berg was assigned to auxiliary service (office duty) on "17. II. 1916," that he still retains the title of *Einjähriger Freiwilliger Gefreiter* (the second lowest rank in the Austrian military), and that he is attending the Reinlgasse Volksschule in training for his new status.[15]

The following four pages of the notebook, in contrast, contain detailed diagrams of the scenic disposition for *Wozzeck*. Scholars have always considered Berg's pared down, *Pierrot*-like fifteen scenes of the opera a fait accompli. Here in contrast Berg lists 22 scenes from the Franzos/Landau version of the Büchner text arranged in a four- rather than three-act plan. The famous Tavern Garden Scene functions as the highest point of dramatic tension. (See Figures 2.6a–2.8a and the transcriptions, Figures 2.6b–2.8b). Berg also carefully tabulates the number of changes of scene, as well as the number of characters appearing in each scene. In this, the only existing sketch of an earlier, large-scale plan for the opera, Berg is seemingly so taken by Büchner's play that he is reluctant to discard even a single scene. (He most likely questions the scene of Wozzeck buying the knife from the Jewish merchant because of the offensive stereotyping of the latter.) Yet the Roman numerals in the margins reveal a later stage of planning; Berg superimposes Roman numerals that reflect the final selection of scenes totaling fifteen. On the last page of the sketch, Berg makes the surprising comparison between the projected *Wozzeck* and Debussy's *Pelléas et Mélisande*. In this diagram, it appears that *Pelléas et Mélisande* (which Berg greatly admired) suggested an ideal model for an opera with many

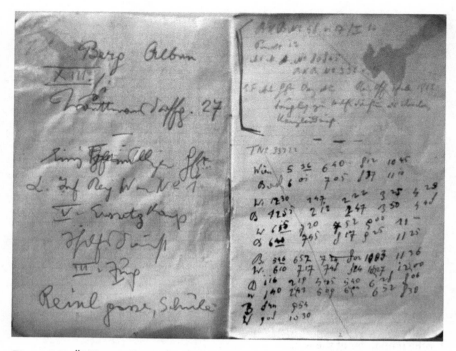

Figure 2.5: ÖNB Musiksammlung F 21 Berg 479/34 fols. 1ᵛ–2ʳ

short scenes (15) as well as transitional music between scenes.[16] Most importantly, though, Berg's sketch of the scenic disposition for *Wozzeck* suggests that although Berg had arrived for military service in 1915 armed with a newly purchased copy of Büchner's text, it was not until 1916 that he had his first chance to use it.[17]

This notebook from 1916 and its accompanying military ordinances allow us to substantially revise the chronology of the previously mentioned prewar sketch-book. The first half of this sketchbook does indeed contain sketches for the *Marsch* of the Three Pieces for Orchestra, which Berg composed in the summer of 1914. Berg has taken unusual care to organize the second half of the sketchbook; he has first hand-numbered the pages from 1 to 50, then stamped each page with a *numerator.* Initially the sketches skip from scene to scene in no particular order. (These could conceivably be the sketches that Berg's student Kassowitz reported seeing in 1914.)[18] By page 60, however, Berg is focusing on the "Street Scene," as he calls it, Act II, scene 2, including textual details that would have required Berg's Büchner text. We see one of these sketches in Figure 2.9a, transcribed in Figure 2.9b. It is a continuity draft of a fragment of Act II, scene 2. We can clearly see the word "*Schreck*" (horror) which appears in the early dialogue between the Captain and the Doctor, the only two characters appearing at this point in the scene. Of more interest, however, are the military ordinances and jargon covering the second half of the sketch. At the bottom of the sketch is the first ordinance on fol. 2 of the 1916 notebook: "B.K.B. No. 48 v.17. [II.] 1916 tauglich zu Hilfsdiensten geeignet"

(a)

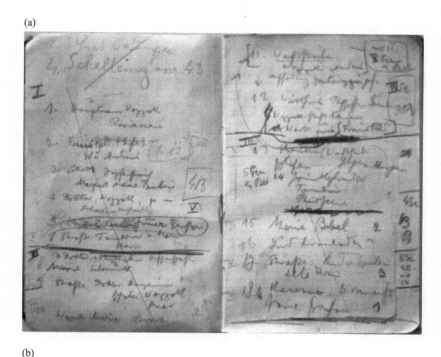

(b)

Fred Weidinger
4. Schelleingasse 43

I

   1. Hauptmann Wozzeck
          Rasierscene
   2. Freies Feld (hohe) - -
2.   W. u. Andres   [1.11)]
   3. Stadt Zapfenstreich
3   Margaret Marie Tambour | 4B
   4. Doktor, Wozzeck,   D - —— V
4   Erbsen, - unsterblich

   5. (eventuell Zimmer Fenster)

V 6   Straße Tambour u. Marie
          Kom[m]

II 7 Doktor u. Studenten Wissenschaft
VI 8 Marie Schmuck
VII 9 Straße Doktor Hauptmann
         später Wozzeck
               Haar   2
VIII 10 Wozzeck Marie Streit

[11. Wachtstube   mit 1.
                       V Scene
       Wozzeck Andres 4 Bilder
IX aufforderung zu tanzen gehn | IV Sc
   12. Wirtshaus Besoffene. Scene | 3B
   Wozzeck sieht tanzen
     Worte aus [Freies Feld]
III
  13 Kasern[e] (Wachtstub[e])
X   gegen Morgen
5 Scene Schlafen
4 Bild 14 heimkehrender [?]   7
        Tambour
        Streitscene   4.
XI 15   Marie Bibel   2   3
   16 Jud Kramladen   ?   B
XII 17 Straße: Kinder spielen 5 Sc
       Alte Frau   3 4B
XIII 18 Kaserne Er vermacht 16
       Seine Sachen   7

Figure 2.6: ÖNB Musiksammlung F 21 Berg 479/34 fols. 2ᵛ–3ʳ (catalog #: 296 & 297)

(a)

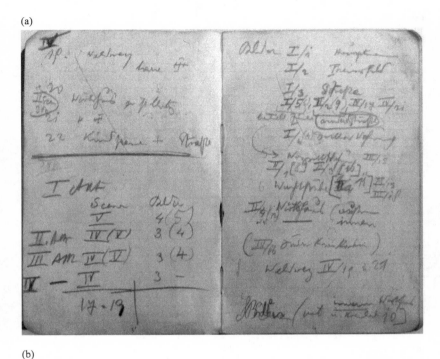

(b)

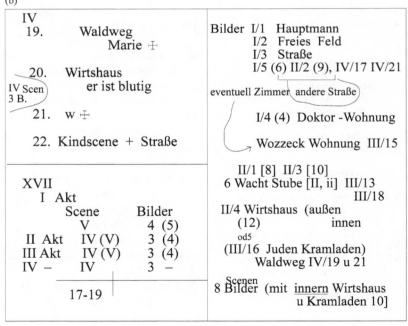

IV			Bilder I/1 Hauptmann

```
IV
  19.        Waldweg                    Bilder  I/1  Hauptmann
                     Marie ⊹                    I/2  Freies Feld
                                                I/3  Straße
   20.       Wirtshaus                          I/5 (6) II/2 (9), IV/17 IV/21
IV Scen⟩          er ist blutig
3 B.                                    eventuell Zimmer andere Straße
   21.     w ⊹
                                                I/4 (4) Doktor -Wohnung
   22. Kindscene + Straße
                                                Wozzeck Wohnung III/15

                                                II/1 [8]  II/3 [10]
XVII                                     6 Wacht Stube [II, ii]  III/13
    I Akt                                                        III/18
         Scene      Bilder              II/4 Wirtshaus (außen
             V       4 (5)                  (12)              innen
    II Akt  IV (V)   3 (4)                   od5
    III Akt IV (V)   3 (4)               (III/16 Juden Kramladen)
    IV –    IV       3 –                     Waldweg IV/19 u 21
                                                Scenen
           17-19                        8 Bilder (mit innern Wirtshaus
                                                 u Kramladen 10]
```

Figure 2.7: ÖNB Musiksammlung F 21 Berg 479/34 fols. 3ᵛ–4ʳ (catalog #: 298 & 299)

(a)

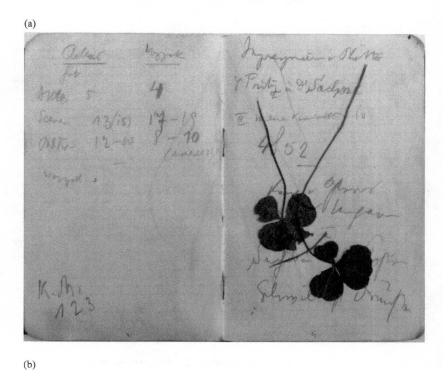

(b)

Pelleas hat	Wozzeck	
Akte 5	4	
Scenen 13 (i5)	17 - 19	
Bilder 12 - 10	8 - 10	
Wozzeck –	(eventuell 11, 12)	

Figure 2.8: ÖNB Musiksammlung F 21 Berg 479/34 fols. 4ᵛ–5ʳ (catalog #: 300)

(a)

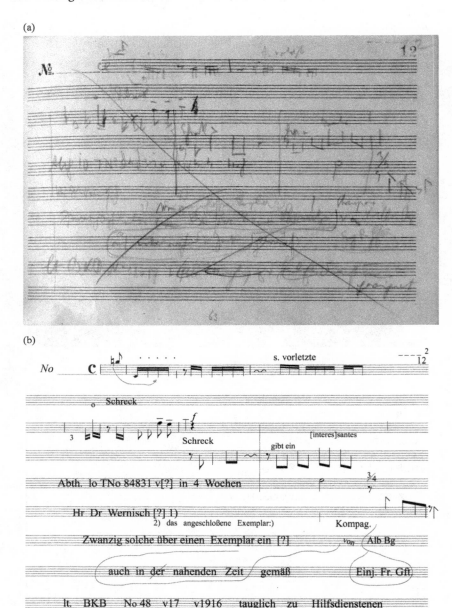

(b)

Figure 2.9: ÖNB Musiksammlung F 21 Berg 13/II p. 63 (catalog #: 056)

(qualified for auxiliary duties). On the left-hand side of the sketch (staff five) we see the Department of the War Ministry (*Abteilung* 10) to which Berg was assigned from May 1916 until the end of the war, and on staff six, a possible reference to one of his superiors, Dr. Wernisch.[19] Berg described his service in Abteilung 10 as

"2 1/2 *years*, *daily* service from 8 in the morning until 6–7 evenings [. . .] under a frightful superior (an idiotic drunk!) Humiliated during these years of suffering as a low-ranking officer, not composing a note."[20] (Ironically, his superior also had the rank of Captain, or *Hauptmann*.)

George Perle writes that the Doctor in *Wozzeck* (the second character appearing in this sketch) was modeled after "an inhuman military doctor."[21] Berg described one of these encounters to his wife: "The sick parade went like this, darling. M.O. [Medical Officer]: 'What's the matter with you?' I describe my condition (completely naked). M.O. squeezes my shoulder slightly. I say: 'A bit lower down.' His interest is not very great."[22]

On the right hand side of the sketch (staff 8) Berg lists his current military rank: *Einjähriger Freiwilliger Gefreiter* (Einj. Fr. Gft.) It became Berg's obsession in 1916 to achieve the rank of E. F. *Korporal*, which finally occurred in September. This places the draft sometime between May and September 1916.[23] In an August 22 letter to Helene, Berg writes, "For months I haven't done any work on *Wozzeck*. Everything suffocated, buried!"[24] This would further date the draft to May 1916. The sketch, using the same type of writing implement and blended almost inseparably into the letter draft, undoubtedly dates from the same time as well. It is tempting to imagine Berg suddenly motivated by "a frightful superior" and "an inhuman doctor" to create this scene. Whether or not it is true, it is clear that Berg did compose passages of the opera, however brief, later than 1914 and before the commonly-held date of inception, 1917.

1917–1918

I've been here for 10 days now, my dear Schoenberg. During the first week I was still suffering terribly from the effects of years of confinement: asthma attacks of such severity that on one occasion I really thought I would not survive the night. But now it's much better and, as happens every summer I spend here, the desire to work is—at last—beginning to stir again: and I'm working on the composition of the drama *Wozzeck* by Büchner, which I've been planning for more than three years. Of course, there is no chance for drafting out a larger section: In another week I lose my freedom again and the servitude in Vienna resumes, to last perhaps for years.[25]

   —Alban Berg to Arnold Schoenberg, August 13, 1917

Berg's student Willi Reich reports that Berg was working on Act II, scene 2 during this short reprieve from the War Ministry.[26] In a letter to Webern, Berg notes that he didn't begin composing seriously again until his next leave of absence from the War Ministry the following summer, when he actually managed to "finish something" and even hoped to complete another scene.[27] This is supported by the sketchbook, which shows abrupt changes in writing implements and content. For instance, Berg begins using a carnation pink pencil in notebooks from fall 1918. Sketches made with this same pencil appear beginning on page 72 of the sketchbook, suggesting that the remaining pages, that is, pages 72–99, may date from 1918. The few sketches for Act I, scene 2 at the end of the sketchbook identify the scene Berg hoped to (and did) complete in 1918.

It is also very apparent that Berg worked simultaneously with this sketchbook and his copy of the Büchner text. Figure 2.10a, for instance (transcribed in Figure 2.10b), shows one of Berg's initial sketches of dramatic action for Act I, scene 2. He compares the first strophe of Andres's hunting song "in unison," to "the sailors' choir in *Tristan*, Act I, that

(a)

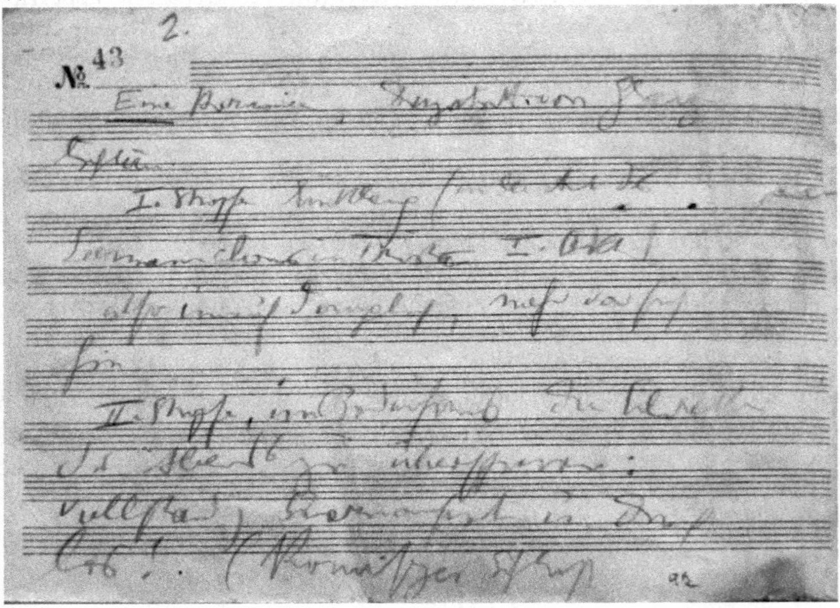

(b)

No _____

Eine Harmonie   Dazutritt von Glanz -

lichtern.

I. Strophe Einklang (in der Art des

Seemannchores in Tristan   I.   Akt)

also unauf dringlich, mehr vor sich

hin

II. Strophe, im Bedürfnis die Schrecken

des Abends zu   überschreien:

vollständig harmonisiert u. drauf

los!   (Komischer Schluß)

Figure 2.10: ÖNB Musiksammlung F 21 Berg 13/II p. 92 (catalog #: 085)

is, unobtrusive, more to oneself." Berg describes the emotionally heightened second strophe "completely harmonized," as "the need to scream above the horror of the evening." As we see from both this sketch and its corresponding passage in Berg's Büchner text (Figure 2.11), the three strophes of Andres's song become a structural element that generates the form of this scene, along with the three chords of the opening, which

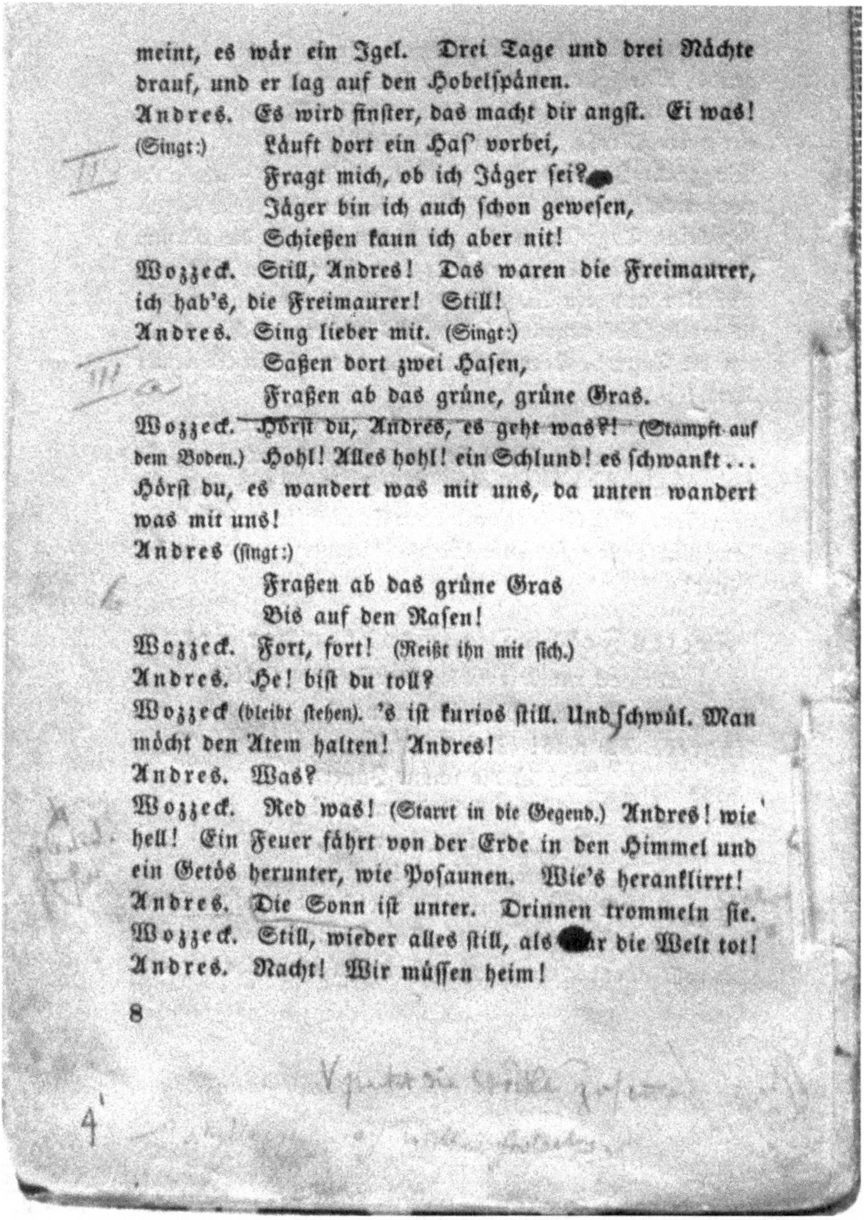

meint, es wär ein Igel. Drei Tage und drei Nächte drauf, und er lag auf den Hobelspänen.

Andres. Es wird finster, das macht dir angst. Ei was!

(Singt:) Läuft dort ein Has' vorbei,
Fragt mich, ob ich Jäger sei?
Jäger bin ich auch schon gewesen,
Schießen kann ich aber nit!

Wozzeck. Still, Andres! Das waren die Freimaurer, ich hab's, die Freimaurer! Still!

Andres. Sing lieber mit. (Singt:)
Saßen dort zwei Hasen,
Fraßen ab das grüne, grüne Gras.

Wozzeck. Hörst du, Andres, es geht was?! (Stampft auf dem Boden.) Hohl! Alles hohl! ein Schlund! es schwankt... Hörst du, es wandert was mit uns, da unten wandert was mit uns!

Andres (singt:)
Fraßen ab das grüne Gras
Bis auf den Rasen!

Wozzeck. Fort, fort! (Reißt ihn mit sich.)

Andres. He! bist du toll?

Wozzeck (bleibt stehen). 's ist kurios still. Und schwül. Man möcht den Atem halten! Andres!

Andres. Was?

Wozzeck. Red was! (Starrt in die Gegend.) Andres! wie hell! Ein Feuer fährt von der Erde in den Himmel und ein Getös herunter, wie Posaunen. Wie's heranklirrt!

Andres. Die Sonn ist unter. Drinnen trommeln sie.

Wozzeck. Still, wieder alles still, als wär die Welt tot!

Andres. Nacht! Wir müssen heim!

8

Figure 2.11: ÖNB Musiksammlung F 21 Berg 128, fol. 4ᵛ (catalog #: 262)

Figure 2.12: Examples of Austrian military calls from 1914

generate most of the musical material. Wozzeck cries out, "Three days and three nights afterward, and he was laid on the wood shavings." Berg selects triple meter to differentiate Wozzeck's music from the triplet compound duple meter for Andres, until, with Wozzeck's words, "Still, alles still, als wäre die Welt todt," Berg begins a "funeral march" which transitions into the military march of the opening of the next scene.[28] Given the apocalyptic images of this scene, which Glenn Watkins describes as "as vivid a projection of impending world doom as any to come out of the Great War [. . .]," Berg's fixation on the number three seems entirely appropriate.[29] Berg also makes two barely visible notations in the same text passage that are partially hidden by a peeled flap of the paper: "Gebet," ("prayer") and "Abgeblassen nach unten fortsetzen" (continue "dismissed" underneath). These are Austrian military signals, normally played on a bugle, appearing here in the military handbook for 1914, "Exerzierreglement für die k. u. k. Feldartillerie" (Drills for the k. and k. Field Artillery) (Figure 2.12). We can see in the corresponding location in the music how Berg has inserted these military signals, exactly as he specifies in his note, in a slightly atonal form, but certainly still recognizable to Austrians of that period (Example 2.1). Rather than a prewar projection of an

Example 2.1: Act I, scene II, mm. 315–318: Excerpted from trumpet and clarinet parts

opera, this sketchbook is a detailed visual record of a frustrating period of creative stagnation (tellingly supported by Berg's correspondence) until 1918, when Berg finally finished scenes I/2 and II/2. The end of the war would follow in November.

These two scenes completed in 1918 form an oddity in the autograph *Particell*. They are written in pencil on earlier paper types, apparently scavenged from previous works (Figure 2.13). The highly distressed, raglike texture of this paper suggests that Berg erased repeatedly, using the autograph *Particell* as a compositional medium.[30] In the following summer, he would finish the third through fifth scenes of Act I, taking up scene 1 (Wozzeck and the Captain), last.[31]

In the above letter to Schoenberg Berg also mentions the death of one of his students. The details, elaborated in an unpublished letter from

Figure 2.13: ÖNB Musiksammlung F 21 Berg 14 fol. 13ᵛ (catalog #: 326)

Gottfried Kassowitz, express the overall disenchantment with the war that had, by this time, overtaken nearly everyone:

I also have a very sad message to convey: Lieutenant Sluszanski died yesterday afternoon at 4:15. He is said by the nurse to have peacefully passed away. The whole thing affects me deeply, although actually I knew him less well. But I remember well the beautiful, long since passed time, when I always met him when I came to you in the afternoon for a lesson. What times! It's as if all that will never return so wonderfully, since one thing after another changes and becomes so different, that it, as in this case, can never be as it once was.[32]

The documents discussed thus far suggest the following revised chronology for *Wozzeck*:

- May 5 and 6, 1914: Berg attends two performances of *Wozzeck* and immediately decides to make it into an opera, initial sketches as reported by Kassowitz
- August 1915: Berg enlists in military, bringing newly purchased copy of *Wozzeck*, initial sketches in military notebook of scenic disposition
- May 1916: sketches in sketchbook 13/II of Act II, scene 2
- August 1917: more work on scenic disposition
- Summer 1918: Berg completes Act I, scene 2 and Act II, scene 2
- Summer 1919: Berg completes the remaining scenes for Act I, composing Act I, scene 1 last.

Berg had only completed two scenes of his opera in four grueling years and would progress no further until July of the following summer. The extant sketches for this period are limited but, nonetheless, more complete than for other years.

Table 2.1: Extant sketches for the years 1914 to 1918

F 21 Berg 479/34 fols. 1^v–5 (1916)
F 21 Berg 13/II pp. 50–71 (mostly 1916), pp. 72–99 (1918)
F 21 Berg 13/III (1918)
F 21 Berg 70/III fols. 9–10^v (1918) with later annotations as well
F 21 Berg 70/III fols. 1^v and 12–12^v. (1918)

CHAPTER Three

"Wir arme Leut:" 1919–1922

Dear Herr Berg,

Many thanks for letting me know that *Wozzeck* is finished. Unfortunately I am at present not in a position to bind myself in any way, as we are rather snowed under with commitments. Nor do I know how in the present state of our finances I can take on the responsibility of producing such demanding modern works, which requires an enormous amount of rehearsing.[1]

—Dr. Ernst Lert, General Manager of the Frankfurt Opera,
to Alban Berg, May 1922

Of course, the inflation alluded to in this letter affected not only Berg but the entire world. During the period 1917 to 1922 the Austrian Crown plummeted from 12 to 7,600 per U.S. dollar. In 1923, the U.S. dollar was the equivalent of 70,800 Crowns.[2] Berg's calendar from 1921 (Figure 3.1), still residing in a closet in his apartment in Hietzing, becomes a flurry of nervous expenditure lists. In calendars from the worst years of inflation, Berg actually superimposes dates from one calendar onto another, presumably to forestall buying a new calendar. Fortunately, these financial disasters also leave physical traces in the sketches. These clues, along with Berg's frequent "progress reports" to Kassowitz, Webern, and his wife make dating the remaining sketches fairly straightforward.

Finally liberated from the "slavery" of the War Ministry, Berg spent June 1st through September 10th at the Berghof.[3] Berg chose to compose scenes 3–5 of Act I first, and scene 1 of Act I later that summer. He writes to Kassowitz on the 22nd of July, "Now I've picked up the first scene of *Wozzeck* and will write to you about it soon."[4] The few surviving sketches for Act I confirm this order of composition: None of the sketches for scenes 2–5 contain consecutive measure numbers. (They are added in the finished *Particell*.)[5] And finally, Berg uses a new paper type in the *Particell* for the latter part of Act I, scene 4. He continues using this paper type in scene 5 and scene 1.

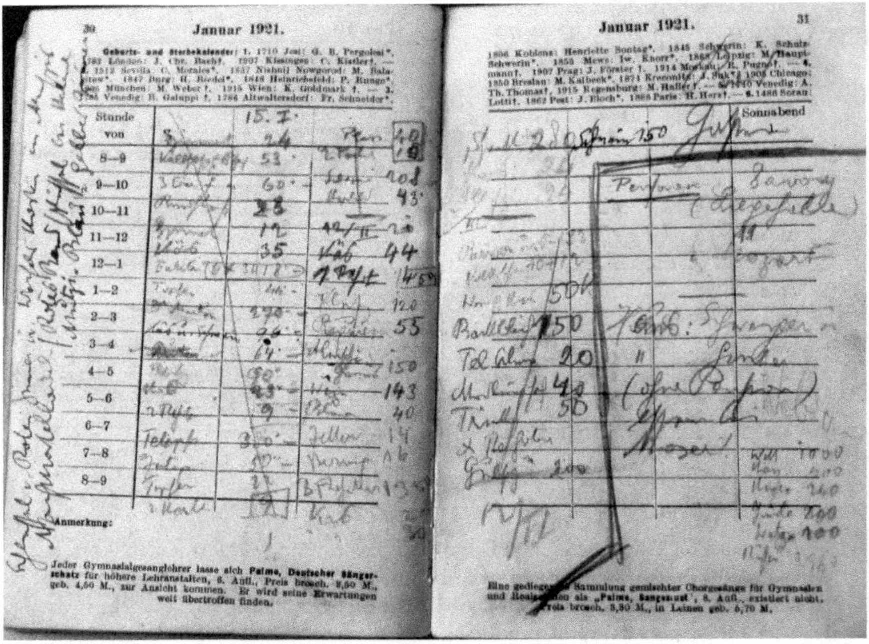

Figure 3.1: Berg's calendar for 1921 (uncatalogued) at Berg's apartment

Two days later, Berg's informs Kassowitz that he has completed a total of six scenes:

> With [the first scene] the first Act is completed. Five scenes: the above with the Captain, Wozzeck in the field above the city, Marie, Doctor, Marie and the Drum Major. From the second act only the street scene is finished: Captain, Doctor and Wozzeck.[6]

A second theme in Berg's letter to Kassowitz, boding ill toward Berg's progress on the opera, is Berg's frustration with Kassowitz's slow progress writing out the orchestral parts for Opus 6.

> The thought, that now in the last 4, 5, weeks, where I am in the middle of composition and leave the place, that I hoped to finish the second act—that I must interrupt all that, in order to write parts—that thought is horrible!!![7]

The composer Erwin Schulhoff, then working in Dresden as a "free artist," had approached Berg about a premiere of his Three Orchestral Pieces, Opus 6 in Dresden, to take place in December 1919. This premiere was part of a cycle of "Progress Concerts" that Schulhoff planned under the auspices of the Saxony Fund for Artists.[8] In Schulhoff's advertisements for the cycle, music is portrayed as a spiritual revolution, parallel to the political revolutions taking place in Europe at that time:

> Absolute art is revolution, it requires additional facets for development, leads to overthrow (coups) in order to open new paths (arises from the strongest psychic experience) and is the most powerful in music. [...] The idea of a revolution in art has evolved for decades, under whatever sun the creators live, in that for them art is a commonality of man. This is particularly true in music, because this art form is the liveliest, and as a result reflects the revolution most strongly and deeply—the complete escape from imperialistic tonality and rhythm, the climb to an ecstatic change for the better.[9]

Schulhoff, like Berg, had served in the Austrian army during World War I. But while Berg was relatively soon transferred to clerical work in the War Ministry, Schulhoff served on the Russian front, where he was wounded, and finished the war in an Italian prisoner of war camp. (This information elicits Berg's unfortunate comment that although he was not wounded and had not in been in battle, he had suffered during the war as much as Schulhoff.)

It is also not surprising that their correspondence includes analyses of their attitudes concerning World War I. In the same extended letter written November 27, 1919, Berg defensively responds:

> But one thing I have to say, however—that you are mistaken when you allude that I am an Imperialist or even a militarist. I wasn't one even once at the beginning of the war, and have it black on white, that I asked myself on August 14th whether a people who treat their greatest the way the Germans did and do, don't deserve to be conquered.[10]

In the end, Berg's Piano Sonata, Opus 1, and the Opus 2 songs, rather than the Three Orchestral Pieces, were performed in Schulhoff's series. Berg's String Quartet Opus 3, for which he also spent part of August writing out parts, is returned by Schulhoff's publisher Jatho.[11]

Of the four scenes composed during the summer of 1919, the extant sketches consist of only a single sketchbook and a few loose leaves, as shown in the summary of sketches for 1919 in Table 3.1.

Table 3.1: Summary of sketches for 1919

F 21 Berg 13/V fols. 3ᵛ–4ʳ (later annotations on 3ʳ)
F 21 Berg 13/VI fols. 3ʳ–3ᵛ (later annotations on 3ʳ)
F 21 Berg 13/X fol. 2ʳ
F 21 Berg 70/II fols. 1ʳ–10ᵛ
F 21 Berg 70/III fols. 1ʳ–11ʳ

1920–1921

Another enlightening letter to Kassowitz confirms that Berg was working on Act II, scene 1 at the beginning of this relatively long summer period of composition (the 2nd of July to the 6th of October).[12]

> Dear Friend,
>
> A week here. First sick, . . . then much business correspondence, finally again—the first attempts at composition: a sonata in the middle of *Wozzeck*, that is, the second act is overall a (5) movement symphony.
>
> In this regard I need something to smoke. Do you have something: cigarettes or tobacco. Please send! Here, against all expectation one gets <u>nothing</u>.[13]

Berg, like Freud, relied on tobacco to augment his creativity.

Berg writes to Schoenberg the same month, reporting his discovery of interval cycles, which he characteristically dismisses as "a theoretical trifle."[14] A musical statement of this discovery, as Perle points out, appears very prominently in Act II, scene 3,[15] and there is a sketch of the chart Berg sent to Schoenberg, F 21 Berg 70/III fol. 11^v, written on the back of sketches for Act I, scene 1 (Figure 3.2). (It was very common, because of general paper shortages during this period, for Berg to use every free scrap of paper available.) I will return to this sketch in Chapter 7 to explain—despite Berg's humble designation for his offering—its true significance.

Earlier that year, Berg had experienced the trauma and near rupture of relations with his siblings over the division of family finances.[16] As their discussions quickly degrade into insinuations, Berg is forced to defend his occupation as a composer while attempting to manage and sell the family house, the Berghof. Writing to his mother of his decision to leave Vienna in early January to travel to the Berghof, Berg expresses his frustration:

> This certainly does not mean that I am going because at the moment I have 'no proper occupation' in Vienna and can't get an allowance. Quite the reverse. I wish to emphasize, that
>
> (1) I have "a proper occupation" in Vienna. To wit my position in the Association, three pupils, your affairs, which, as it is, cost me two or three half-days a week and sometimes more.
>
> (2) I earn 850 Crowns a month therefrom, even without allowances.
>
> (3) For various reasons Helene is not going to the Berghof . . .
>
> I repeat: it's not because I "planned" to take over from Charly or have ever wanted to; or because I think my being there is a wonderful piece of luck for my family and a salvation for me in my indigent state; or because I "haven't anything really to do in Vienna"; or because I am a loafer who is not getting anything more from his mother and so lets himself be supported at the Berghof.[17]

Figure 3.2: ÖNB Musiksammlung F 21 Berg 70/III fol. 11ᵛ (catalog #: 253)

The "Association" that Berg refers to is the *Verein für musikalische Privataufführungen*, or Society for Private Musical Performances, which Schoenberg founded in November 1918. Active until 1922, this society furthered the performance of contemporary music and featured premiere performances by Eduard Steuermann, Rudolf Kolisch, and other distinguished artists. Performances were strictly for members of the *Vereign* only; music critics were banned from the audience. While a steady source of income, the duties associated with the *Verein* could also be incapacitating for Berg; already, by November 30, 1918, Berg is begging Schoenberg to be relieved of his position. In the end, he acts as performance director for the *Verein* until its dissolution in 1922.

How far did Berg get in this extended summer of composition? According to Berg's correspondence with his wife, he worked on Act II, scene 4 in both the summers of 1920 and 1921.[18] During this period, post WWI inflation becomes a deciding factor with its effect on paper production by 1921. If one compares the sketchbook for *Wozzeck* discussed earlier with the one originally dated 1914 by Ernst Hilmar (F 21 Berg 13/I) both use *Protokoll Schutzmarke* no. 70 ten-line sketchbook paper; however the color and size of the two papers is noticeably different. Paper types from this period are of like vintage: identical paper types, for instance, *Protokoll Schutzmarke* no. 70 ten-line paper, can exhibit drastic changes in quality and appearance from year to year. The ratio of rag to wood, the position of the brand stamp, and even the design of the "Nᵒ" that appears at the top of the page might vary. For the printing firm Josef Eberle, 1921 was a very bad year; the paper Berg used is highly brittle and has discolored to a deep walnut brown over time. This occurs in other papers produced by Josef Eberle in 1921 as well, making them extremely easy to recognize.

One source exhibiting these telltale characteristics, the sketchbook 13/I—and its removed interior pages, 13/VII—also includes a draft of a letter that nearly obliterates the musical sketches (Figure 3.3). Without too much effort one can

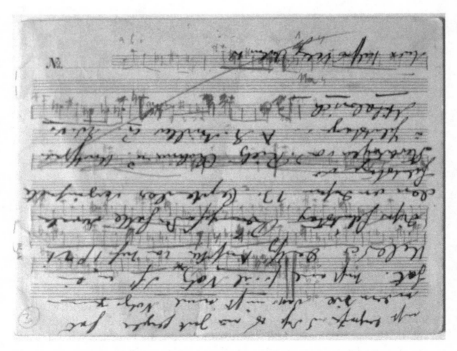

Figure 3.3: ÖNB Musiksammlung F 21 Berg 13/VII fol. 3ʳ (catalog #: 147)

make out the dates 13 September and 1921. The letter's painfully fulsome tone immediately suggests that it was addressed to Schoenberg:

> But as it is, I can tell you in writing what a festive day your birthday is for me and how clear it is to me that one day it will be a festive day for the whole world: a day for the world—taking time out from the routine of everyday life—to reflect upon its higher, its very highest qualities. And to find it incomprehensible that there was a time when it <u>didn't even take notice</u> of it.[19]

This sketchbook, then, including drafts of passages for the latter section of II/4 (beginning measures 589), Act II, scene 5, and Act III, scenes 2–5, is a fairly reliable source for the scenes Berg completed in this last summer of composition—according to his *Tagebuch* for 1921, July 25th through October 7th.[20] On page 30 of the sketchbook appears the annotation "9/23 Epilog," referring to the summary of themes at the end of Act III, scene 4. Shortly after this date, on September 28th, Berg writes to Webern: "Tomorrow I begin the last scene of *Wozzeck*. And then to Vienna."[21]

The conspicuous absence of sketches for Act III, scene 1 in this sketchbook, and the correspondence of paper type between Act II, scene 1 and Act III, scene 1 in the *Particell*, suggests that Berg completed the latter scene during the summer of 1920. He returned to Act II, scene 4 ("the most difficult of all") the following summer, finishing Act II and completing the remaining relatively short scenes of Act III.[22] A corresponding shift in paper type occurs in the autograph *Particell*, between this latter part of Act II, scene 4 and the following scene, the *Wachtstube*, Act II, scene 5. The autograph *Particell* is in fact so layered with different paper types from four years of composition that it reminds one of a tree with telltale growth rings designating each year of its existence.

Sketches from 1920 also frequently feature annotations in navy blue pencil. One would normally be loath to rely on a writing implement for chronology, but there are such large gaps between Berg's periods of composition that one does in fact see distinct changes in colored pencils from summer to summer. For instance, green pencil begins to appear in Berg's dated annotations in his notebooks in late December 1921, and the short score for *Wozzeck* is covered with corrections using this pencil. With all this evidence, we can now summarize the list of sketches for 1920–1921, as shown in Table 3.2.

Most of the annotations of orchestration, and many refinements of the short score, were completed after this point. Thus, the autograph *Particell* is an equally important element of Berg's compositional process on *Wozzeck*. In Figure 3.4, a *Particell* leaf of Act I, scene 2, measures 213–227, one is struck not only by the fragile condition of the paper and revisions of measure numbers in ink, but by the many annotations of orchestration in the score, as well as in the right-hand margin. Berg uses his own shorthand to list the instrumentation for the section in the corresponding right-hand margin, in the order that it would appear in the full score. The first line of the *Particell*, for instance will be orchestrated with one flute, two clarinets, one French horn, first and second violins, violas and 'cellos.

Table 3.2: Summary of sketches for 1920–1921

1920:

F 21 Berg 13/IV fols. 1ʳ, 2ᵛ, 3ʳ⁻ᵛ, 7ᵛ, 10ʳ–11ᵛ
F 21 Berg 13/VI fols. 1ʳ–2ʳ
F 21 Berg 13/VIII fols. 1–2ʳ
F 21 Berg 13/IX, 1ʳ–1ᵛ, 3–4ʳ
F 21 Berg 13/X (except for 2ʳ)
F 21 Berg 13/XI 1–3ᵛ
F 21 Berg 13/XII
F 21 Berg 13/XIII
F 21 Berg 13/XIV with later annotations
F 21 Berg 70/II fols. 11ʳ–11ᵛ
F 21 Berg 28/XXXVII fol. 14ᵛ

1921:

F 21 Berg 13/I
F 21 Berg13/IV fols. 4ʳ, 5ᵛ–6ᵛ, 8ʳ–8ᵛ, 11ʳ, 12ʳ–12ᵛ
F 21 Berg 13/VI fols. 2ᵛ, 4ʳ–5ᵛ
F 21 Berg 13/VII
F 21 Berg 13/VIII fol. 2ᵛ
F 21 Berg 13/IX fol. 2ʳ
F 21 Berg 13/X fols. 4ʳ⁻ᵛ

The writing out of the short score was entrusted to Berg's student, Fritz Heinrich Klein, and fascinating correspondence exists between Berg and Klein that mimics the master/student tone of Berg's letters to Schoenberg. In a letter dated May 1, 1922, Klein laments:

My dear Master,

I can't fulfill the request, to be already finished by Thursday. This hurts me all the more, in that it is my ambition, to always comply in everything; but my nerves have suddenly held a two-day strike.

—so that I slowly begin to work again, and on the 6th will be at the point of the second act.

—Outside of the 8–10 Wozzeck hours of my day, I must unfortunately cook fuel for the work machine . . .[23]

On May 19th, a further progress report:

Today, Friday, I'm at page 54. You can now, dear, honored master, definitely count on, that I (by 6–8 pages daily) in a week, that is, on the evening of the 26th, will be done with the third act, since this won't have more than 100 pages. I'm figuring that you'll send me the rest Tuesday evening the 23rd, which I shall certainly finish by our next Zusammenkunft (on the 27th, Saturday).[24]

Figure 3.4: ÖNB Musiksammlung F 21 Berg 14 fol. 14ʳ, Act I, scene 2, mm. 213– 227 (catalog #: 327)

Rather than having the work engraved simply for his own satisfaction, Berg shrewdly planned on using the piano-vocal score to send out to directors of opera houses.

For the funding of this expensive investment, Berg had to rely on wealthy friends. In Berg's letter to Schoenberg from July 17, 1922, he outlines his plan:

> *Wozzeck.* I have notified several music periodicals of the completion of the opera and have already received a promise from some that the notice will be "placed."

Table 3.3. Summary of chronology of composition from 1918 to 1921

1918	1919	1920	1921
II/2	I/3	II/1	II/4
I/2	I/4	III/1	II/5
	I/5	II/3	III/2
	I/1	II/4 (unfinished)	III/3
			III/4
			III/5
mm. 314	~600	513	479

> In addition, my sister's friend, May Keller, has agreed to have the piano score *engraved*. Her idea (and mine too) is as follows: a limited edition of the score available in the fall would enable me to distribute it to all eligible opera houses.[25]

The date, "16. VII. 22" at the end of the *Particell* marks the end of these revisions and Berg's completion of his opera, a little more than eight years from the time he saw Büchner's play.

Table 3.3 summarizes the evidence presented in this chapter—from correspondence, calendars, notebooks, and the sketches—for the chronology of the opera's composition.

At first glance, it would seem that Berg steadily increased his pace in each consecutive summer of composition. However, if one tabulates the measure numbers for the above scenes, his progress (except for 1914–18) is fairly uniform.

We began the second half of this study of chronology with an extended letter describing the inflation of the postwar period. A draft of a letter from 1921, from Berg to his brother Hermann and sister-in-law Alice, living in America, fills in unimaginable specifics about how these hardships affected Berg as he finished his opera.

In the initial draft of the letter, Berg reveals how inflation has impinged on his life as an artist and intellectual:

> I haven't attended the State Opera (former Court Opera) where I have no connections, for years. I as a musician! The very worst gallery seat costs 100–200K. Where are the good times when one bought books? One volume 2, 3500K!!!
>
> It's a crazy world we live in. What a contrast to the serene life in America, as you, dear Alice, describe it.[26]

In Berg's substantial revision of this letter, he focuses on daily necessities:

> Through Helene's phenomenal frugality and organization, we've gotten though this winter without buying ridiculously expensive vegetables and meat that is beyond our means. That is, to live simply on Quaker Oats, noodles, dumplings, polenta, rice, potatoes, coffee, cocoa, and in this way, have some variety. To keep me capable of working and to protect me from illness, I alone eat a tiny piece of meat every day.[27]

It seems that Berg identified with his protagonist not only in his fulfillment of military duties, but in abject poverty as well.

CHAPTER Four

The Critical Years: 1923–1925

I remain unshaken in my firm belief in this fate, I could write a book on this subject; but even more interesting is the fact that it always involves a fateful number. The number is 23![1]

—Berg to Schoenberg, June 10, 1915

True to his belief, in 1923 Berg experienced events in his professional career that established him for the first time as a leading twentieth-century composer. As a result of sending his engraved score of *Wozzeck* to music periodicals, articles evaluating the opera began appearing almost immediately in print. A short article by Erwin Stein in *Anbruch*, in January 1923, describing the forms in Berg's opera *Wozzeck*, was followed in April 1923 by a lengthier article by Ernst Viebig in *Die Musik*.[2] The opening of Viebig's article could not be more telling in its description of Berg's struggle, both in composing the opera and in making the opera known to the musical public:

One feels almost ashamed when faced with the courage of this composer, who dares to put his ideas so rigorously into action at the obvious risk of being ridiculed by his contemporaries. Here really is someone for whom there are no compromises.[3]

In April of 1923, Berg also began having discussions with Emil Hertzka, the director of Universal Edition, who expressed an interest in publishing *Wozzeck*. Universal Edition was the publisher of not only Schoenberg's works, but those of such famous twentieth-century composers as Béla Bartók, Frederick Delius, and Ernst Krenek. Berg's almost daily letters to his wife from this period reveal his lengthy negotiations with Hertzka about royalties.[4] Luckily, Alma Mahler not only interceded on Berg's behalf, but also raised the enormous sum necessary to pay off his debt for the original engraved score. As Berg describes in a letter to his wife from April 7, "Almschi says in her categorical way, in front of Werfel: 'I promise you with the help of Frau Bloch-Bauer I'll raise the money.'"[5]

In her autobiographical *And the Bridge is Love*, Alma Mahler specifies the financial difficulties Berg faced:

> Now the opera was finished. Alban and Helene Berg came to me, showed me the score, and asked me to accept the dedication of the work. They were in trouble: a friend who had lent them money to have the score printed was pressing for repayment. The matter weighed heavily on the Bergs, and having taken up collections in the past for Schönberg and others, I went on another begging tour and raised the missing sum in short order.[6]

In an undated letter (Figure 4.1) enclosed in an envelope labeled "Attention Check!" Alma Mahler writes in her larger-than-life spiraling handwriting:

> Dear Alban,
>
> Enclosed 7.000.000 and a number of things!!!___ I am beside myself that this chess move was successful.[7]

Equally important as this financial backing, Berg's compositions were beginning to be heard in important musical venues. The Three Pieces for Orchestra, Opus 6 (composed in 1914) for which Berg had interrupted his work on *Wozzeck* in the summer of 1919 in the desperate hope of a premiere, would finally be performed on June 5th (Präludium and Reigen movements) with Webern conducting. An even earlier work, Berg's Opus 3 String Quartet (1911), was finally premiered at the International Society for Contemporary Music in Salzburg. In Berg's effusive letter to his wife dated August 3, 1923, he describes the premiere as "artistically, the most wonderful evening of my life [. . .]"

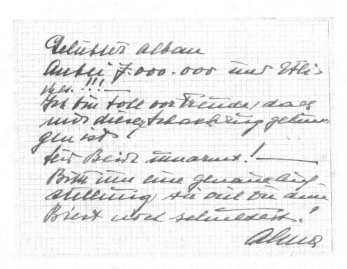

Figure 4.1: F 21 Berg 1058/137

At the end there was almost frantic applause. The quartet themselves came back twice, and kept looking for me in the audience. The third time I was called for, stepped on to the platform quite by myself, and was received with terrific enthusiasm by the whole audience—not one sound of booing. The applause continued, once more the five of us went up to the platform. Quite an important success for Salzburg and for such a small work of chamber music. The rest of the programme, surprisingly, rather fell off in comparison.[8]

With these highly successful performances came contact with influential musicians who could assure Berg performances of *Wozzeck*. The conductor Hermann Scherchen, whom Berg met at the Opus 3 premiere, suggested that Berg create a selection of excerpts of the opera—a Bruchstücke—to introduce it to the public in a more accessible form, a stratagem that Berg would use again for his second opera, *Lulu*.[9] These excerpts of some of the most attractive and accessible moments of the opera feature only the singer Marie, as well as her showpiece, the Lullaby of Act I, scene 3. (The Lullaby was also printed in Viebig's article from *Die Musik*.)

In a draft of a letter to Scherchen, Berg's uncertainty and anxiety over the non-premiere of Opus 6 in 1919 revisit him:

I enquire about that so precisely, because I need certainty before I occupy myself more intensively with the whole business. I've already taken on too much unnecessary work. Think of the orchestral pieces, for whose premiere I occupied myself in vain for four years.[10]

In this same draft (annotated by Scherchen) there are also discussions of the actual content of the Bruchstücke, specifically, the length and the singers involved. (At this point in time, April 1924, both Berg and Scherchen are considering a children's choir.) In later letters, they discuss the featured singer (who would eventually be replaced) and the number of rehearsals required.[11] The opening of a letter written by Berg in list format and quickly annotated by Scherchen reads:

Thanks, dear Herr Scherchen, for your letter from 7.3. Since I have a great deal of questions on the matter, I'll write in the form of a questionnaire, which you can send back to me filled out. Is the acceptance of my Wozzeck pieces for the Music Festival of the General German Music Society definite[?] ANSWER Definite![12]

The premiere of the Bruchstücke would occur in Frankfurt in June 1924, an event Willi Reich describes as "the sensation of the Festival."[13]

During the summer of 1923 Berg began composing his next work, the Chamber Concerto for piano, violin and 13 wind instruments. From Berg's open letter to Schoenberg of February 9, 1925 (Berg's fortieth birthday) we know that the dedication to Schoenberg is even more explicit than in *Wozzeck*.[14] In a sketchbook for the Chamber Concerto, F 21 Berg 74/V, one can clearly see Schoenberg's musical letters extracted from his theme: A-d S-c-h-b-e-g. The themes appearing below,

Figure 4.2: F 21 Berg 74/V fol. 2ᵛ

although not annotated, are for Anton Webern (A E B E) and Alban Berg (A B A E G) (Figure 4.2).[15]

The evolution of Berg's compositional style that begins to appear in sketches for *Wozzeck* from 1920 is now explicit, not only in this more obvious form of dedication, but in the musical language as well. For instance, the operations of retrograde, inversion, and retrograde inversion that modified the basic rhythm of Act III, scene 3 of *Wozzeck* are now applied to entire themes. On folio 20ᵛ (Figure 4.3), Berg assigns the second through fourth variations of the first movement the operations K (retrograde), U (inversion) and KU (retrograde inversion). Similarly, while Berg constructed large sections in *Wozzeck* that are formally symmetrical (for instance, the Inn Scene of Act II, scene 4), the Adagio movement of the Chamber Concerto is palindromic. Thus, the second half of the second movement is essentially a mirror image of the first half (Example 4.1).

As if in culmination of this glorious year of success, 1923, the meeting between Berg and Erich Kleiber took place on November 17, 1923 (bei Hertzka). Since Berg was not a skilled pianist, he arranged for Ernst Bachrich to play the score.[16] According to Reich, after hearing the second scene Kleiber exclaimed, "It's settled! I'm going to do the opera in Berlin, even if it costs me my job!"[17] That it was "Kleiber's decision" would be brought up repeatedly in reviews of the premiere. Rather than costing Kleiber his job, however, he would be unanimously heralded for his brilliant conducting of such a difficult contemporary work.

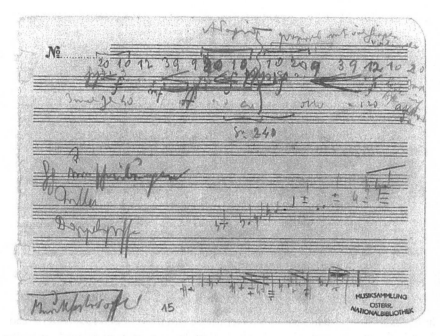

Figure 4.3: F 21 Berg 74/V fol. 15ʳ

Example 4.1: Chamber Concerto. Length of first half is same as second half.

20	10	12	39	9	20	10	10	20	9	39	12	10	20

$pp \!\! <\! f$ $\xrightarrow{}$ $\textit{ff}$ $<\! f$ p p f $\xrightarrow{\hspace{1cm}} f$

mf

240

Much of Berg's remaining musical activity in 1924 was devoted to Schoenberg, whether composing the Chamber Concerto, or editing a special issue of *Anbruch* in honor of Schoenberg's fiftiethth birthday. Appearing as the August/September issue, the new music periodical contains contributions from thirty authors, including an introductory note of thanks from Schoenberg himself.[18] Many of these contributions are anecdotal or congratulatory in nature (for instance, Erika Wagner describes the rehearsals for the premiere of *Pierrot Lunaire*). Others, like Berg's article at the end of the volume, are lengthy essays. Berg's essay foreshadows two ideas that will become critical in the remaining chapters of this book: Berg's innate talent for analysis—whether of his own works or those of his teacher—and the crisis of comprehension that was occurring in listeners attempting to understand modern works. Defending the complexity of Schoenberg's first string quartet (Opus 7), Berg writes:

Think of Bach's polyphony; of the structure of the themes—often quite free contrapuntally and rhythmically, of the classical and pre-classical composers, and of their highly skilled treatment of the principle of variation; of the Romantics, with their bold juxtapositions (which are still bold even today) of distantly related keys; of the new chordal formations in Wagner arrived at by chromatic alteration and enharmonic change, and their natural embodiment in tonality; and finally think of Brahms' art of thematic and motivic work, often penetrating into the smallest details.

It is clear that a music that unites in itself all these possibilities that the masters of the past have left behind would not only be *different* from a contemporary music where such a combination is not to be found (as I will show); it also—despite those properties that we recognized as the merits of good music, and despite its excessive richness in all the fields of music, or rather, just *because* of this—it also manages to be difficult to understand, which indeed Schoenberg's music is.[19]

1925

In Berg's correspondence with Fritz Heinrich Klein from March 1925, they already discuss the premiere of *Wozzeck*, which, Berg learns, has been delayed. In Klein's dutiful response to Berg's letter he complains:

> Dear cherished friend! I'm answering your letter immediately, and all the more because I can't express my anger quickly enough, that your *Wozzeck* is to be postponed again. Hopefully that's only nonsense, which I would sooner think, in that you've not received an official agreement. But are there logistic reasons for the postponement? No more time for examination–enough rehearsal? Then, however, the postponement is better than a half-prepared performance, which could really damage *Wozzeck*; that must be a consolation to you, even desirable.[20]

Two months later, in May 1925, Berg attends the ISCM Festival in Prague where the *Wozzeck* Bruchstücke will be performed for a second time. He is invited to stay at the villa of the Prague industrialist Herbert Fuchs-Robettin and his wife, Hanna Fuchs-Robettin. In a formal letter to the couple, significantly dated May 23rd, Berg writes:

> My very dear Mr. Fuchs-Robettin, honored Madam:
>
> I have the greatest need to express once more, in writing, my heartfelt thanks to you both for the unforgettable days in Prague. The manner in which you knew how to transform my reception into your magnificent home into a hospitality beyond compare—a hospitality in which one forgot that one was a guest—has made such a deep and lovely impression on me that I (can) not put it into words.[21]

In July, Berg writes his first "private" letter to Hanna Fuchs-Robettin, declaring his love and his plans to write a string quartet dedicated to her:

> Will I be granted the tranquility necessary to express in tones what I have expe-
> rienced since those days in Prague-Bubenec? I could not do it now: the incurable
> wound, which I fear I will carry around with me for the rest of my life, bleeds so
> incessantly that as yet I cannot touch one key or write down a single line of notes.
> I would most like to write songs. But how could I? The words of the texts would
> betray me. So it will have to be songs without words, which only the initiate, only
> you, will be able to read! Perhaps a string quartet.[22]

The effusive, desperate tone of Berg's letter is almost disturbing. But this same tone appears regularly in letters to other women in his life, including the mother of his child, his paramours, and even—in times of separation—his wife. One begins to suspect that Berg had an emotional addiction to long-distance relationships—a "ferne Geliebte" syndrome, if you will.
To Marie Scheuchl, probably in 1901:

> But for what purpose do I write all this!!! - You certainly know everything - - !!
> I wanted to at least attempt to show – how high you stand - - how heavenly high!
> - - - like your first namesake - - - - the holy Maria - - - you remain unblemished and
> pure - - for the one sin of humankind is scattered through the great, great, pain—
> washed pure - - as with Maria. - - - - - - - - - - that is my most inner conviction!!!! –
> From the depths of my soul!!! It is 1:00 in the morning![23]

Or, almost thirty years later, to Edith Edwards:

> What a splendid letter, what a wonderful writer! But I can't bring myself to say "Sie," as lit-
> tle possible not to call you "beloved." I called you that already in that moment when I first
> saw your dining room illuminated by the sun, that is, illuminated by you, the "du" that,
> tactlessly suddenly came from my lips, was born weeks earlier in my deepest being.[24]

George Perle revealed the explicit connection between Hanna Fuchs and Alban Berg in his 1978 article, "The Secret Program of the Lyric Suite."[25] But many of the sketches for the *Lyric Suite* are far less obvious in their dedication, or even identity. Fanning asks whether the sketch, F 21 Berg 70/I fols. 6^r–6^v, appearing in the midst of *Wozzeck* sketches might be a plan for the opening of Act III, scene 1.[26] In the bottom margin of the sketch (Figure 4.4) we see Berg's annotation, "herab die 7 und 5 Ton themen hinunter rutschen" (from here the 7 and 5 tone themes glide below), and the opening of Act III, scene 1, does in fact feature a seven-tone theme. However, on an intuitive level, something about the sketch seems wrong—whether it is the odd format of the paper, a now pristinely white PS No. 70 with rounded edges, the peculiar intensely pink tint of colored pencil, or the handwriting itself. On closer inspection, one can decipher the phrase between staves 8 and 9: "zurückgehn zur Urform des 4/8 Ton themen auf den 7ton Rhythmus" (return to the original form of the 4/8 tone theme from the 7-tone rhythm) which refers specifically to row operations performed in

Figure 4.4: F 21 Berg 70/I fol. 6ᵛ

the third movement of the *Lyric Suite*. In fact, the uneven left edge of the sketch fits with the trace of the stub in the sketchbook it comes from, F 21 Berg 76 (before fol. 13), and the pencil mark in the left-hand margin of the sketch continues onto the previous stub. This sketch, for the third movement of the *Lyric Suite*, describes in outline form the various configurations of the row that will be used throughout that movement. The date 29/9.25 appears on page 9ᵛ of the sketchbook.

The sketchbook also contains preliminary sketches for Berg's song "Schließe mir die Augen beide," completed that same summer. In the sketch of the twelve-tone rows for the song, which Berg composed (at least officially) in honor of Emil Hertzka and the 25th anniversary of Universal Edition, Berg's serial writing is already unexpectedly complex (Figure 4.5). Using an "all-interval series" discovered by Fritz Heinrich Klein that appears in the *Lyric Suite* as well, it features a secondary row derived by the exchange of intervals from the first row into corresponding positions in the second row.[27] Thus, in hexachord 1, the semitone, F-E-natural (dyad 1) becomes the semitone E-flat-D (dyad 5 of the derived row). The perfect fourth, G-D (dyad 5) of the source row becomes F-C (dyad 1 of the derived row). It is an example of what George Perle terms internal rearrangement of hexachord content, that is, the center interval forms a barrier between the two hexachords; intervals, however, may be rearranged within these hexachords.[28]

In the compositional sketch (appearing on the back side of the leaf), Berg uses Row I in a continually cycling form as the melodic line, allowing ever new intervals to begin lines of the text (Figure 4.6). For instance, in the line, "Und wie leise sich der Schmerz," the tritone B-F sets the words "der Schmerz" with the F sustained as a half note.

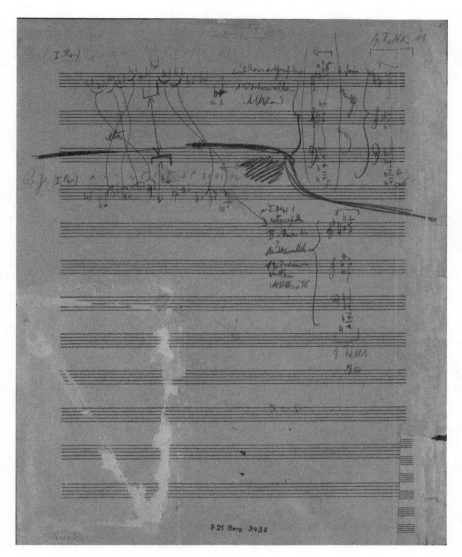

Figure 4.5: F 21 Berg 3438 fol. 1ʳ

Berg uses fragments of Row I in the left hand of the accompaniment. Meanwhile, the melodic line appearing above it in the right hand is labeled with both order numbers from Rows I and II. Like many similar passages in *Lulu*, the sketch suggests that despite the many musical effects that necessitated freedom with the twelve-tone method, Berg still felt the need to justify their derivation. These examples by no means represent a complete analysis of the song, but rather, an indication of how far Berg's compositional technique had evolved by the time of the premiere of *Wozzeck*.

Figure 4.6: F 21 Berg 3438 fol. 1ᵛ

Anatomy of a Premiere

Between Berg's correspondence with students and trusted friends, his twice-daily letters to his wife, a notebook devoted entirely to details of the premiere, and Berg's binder containing approximately 266 reviews, one could write a book on the premiere alone.[29]

Berg had received news about rehearsals of *Wozzeck* as early as September 29, 1925. Acting as an informant of sorts, Hanns Eisler writes with news received from Josef Schmidt about critical developments during rehearsals: the projected day of the premiere, which singers are assigned to the various roles, and the general attitude of the performers toward the opera. For instance, in a postcard from September 29, Eisler informs Berg of a change in the principal role:

> I learned something important about the progress of the Wozzeck rehearsals. They're working very hard on it. Now something seems (as Schrenk told me yesterday) not to be in order: various men (including Hörth, who is conducting) are not in agreement about Schwarz, who is to sing Wozzeck, and it is possible that this role will be replaced. That is not yet certain. In any case, Kleiber is decidedly working with the goal of very definitely premiering the work during your deadline of November.[30]

Soon after, Eisler sends a letter correcting important details of his earlier postcard:

> My news about Wozzeck appears false in retrospect. Schwarz *will* sing the title role after all. Schmid, who is actually here, with whom I was together twice and who is better informed about it than I, will write to you about it.
> ... Kemp won't sing [the part of] Marie.
> The premiere won't be until December.
> It's difficult to extract something factual from the backstage-gossip of the half-informed. (Unfortunately I don't know Kleiber.)
> As soon as I hear something again about Wozzeck, I'll write to you.[31]

And finally, on October 29th:

> Dear Herr Berg: Finally something authentic about Wozzeck.
> Casting: Wozzeck-------Schützendorf
>   Marie-----Strozzi
>   Tambourmajor------Loot
>   Performance-------14 December
> The ensemble rehearsals begin around the 12th through 14th November. At the moment everyone is moaning (with the exception of Kleiber) about the difficulty.[32]

Eventually Berg would witness rehearsals firsthand, as he traveled to Berlin in mid-November and again at the beginning of December. For this latter momentous occasion, Berg set aside an entire notebook devoted to details of the *Wozzeck* premiere.[33] As one looks through the pages of this small (10.5 × 15.5 cm) brown leather notebook, laden with every detail of Berg's minute planning for the single most important artistic moment of his life, one finally experiences the guilt of the voyeur. The notebook begins with Berg's preparations: clothes and other items he plans to pack. A day-by-day countdown of activities follows, beginning Wednesday the 25th (students with whom he will meet) through Sunday the 29th, when he will pack and bathe. On page 7ᵛ of the notebook is the first of several lists of friends, students, and acquaintances whom Berg expects to attend the premiere on the 14th (see Figure 4.7). On the following page it would appear that Berg is giving out free tickets to his students in order to "paper the house" and thus create his own cheering section. Other items in the notebook include Christmas lists, addresses of people in Berlin, addresses of Berlin hotels,

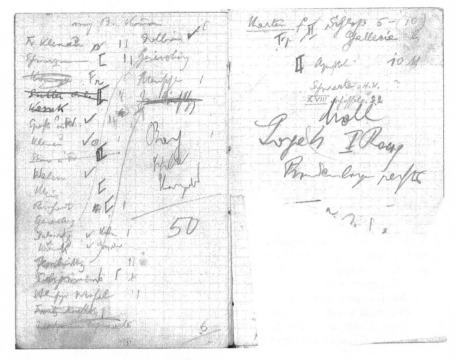

Figure 4.7: F 21 Berg 479/36 fols. 7ᵛ–8ʳ

and lists of expenses incurred while in Berlin. The only item of musical significance in the latter half of the notebook is a draft of a letter to Gerhardt Hauptmann on page 23(!) of the notebook, in which Berg expresses his interest in setting Hauptmann's play "Und Pippa Tanzt" as his next opera (Figure 4.8).

> Honored Master, You will have already been made aware by your publisher, that I have made the decision, I would like to create an opera out of your magnificent work, U. P. T. Your publisher has encouraged me to approach you directly, as to whether you would give me permission.[34]

In the latter half of this draft, Berg actually invites Hauptmann to the premiere of *Wozzeck*. It is unclear, however, if this draft materialized into a letter; two years later Berg is still writing to Alma Mahler, asking whether she will broach the subject to Hauptmann.[35]

It is a measure of Berg's rapport with his wife that he writes her twice daily during this period, reporting on the progress of rehearsals. In Chapter 5 we will examine a number of sketches for the Inn Scene (Act II, scene 4). In addition to the complexity of the form, reflected by Berg's many sketches, the coordination of the stage band and the orchestra, as well as the large numbers of characters that appear, made it an extremely difficult scene to realize in performance. There are daily references to rehearsals of this problematic scene in the letters he writes to

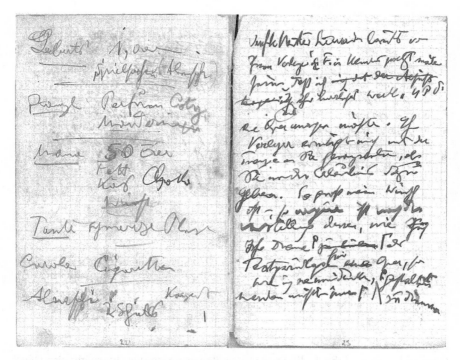

Figure 4.8: F 21 Berg 479/36 fols. 22ᵛ–23ʳ

her from December 1–7. (Helene Berg would arrive in Berlin on December 9.) Among them:

December night 1st–2nd, "Half past midnight."
Tomorrow, Wednesday, I'm having stage rehearsals with Hörth, also Thursday and Friday, when I hope to get the singers absolutely perfect. Especially the music in the Inn Scene, which is quite impossible so far and gives me real head-aches. Please don't talk about my doubts too much, and also be careful on the telephone when you're reporting to Stein. Say that it's a tough nut to crack but that we'll manage it.[36]

December 2, "afternoon."
This afternoon there's a very important rehearsal with guitar and accordion players, and clarinetists, so I hope the stage band will be good too.[37]

December 3, "at night."
The last Inn Scene also very good, but the big Inn Scene isn't quite satisfactory yet, although the staging is all right and full of brilliant touches. But I am afraid the musical side gets a bit lost because of all the problems and acting details. Besides which, the stage band is still bad, my biggest problem child, despite all the extra rehearsal. "What is going to happen?" says Wozzeck.[38]

Friday night 4–5th, December, 1 a.m.
. . . Today I'm more optimistic again about Wozzeck. A magnificent accordion player, an American virtuoso. So the biggest danger is eliminated.[39]

Saturday night 5th–6th December 1925, 1:30 a.m.
Today there was a rehearsal for the Inn Scene band, which went quite well; but the orchestral rehearsal with the complete stage "effects" was really chaotic, I really don't know how everything's going to work in a week's time. My only comfort is that Kleiber himself is a perfectionist. Particularly in this case, where he stands or falls by the success of the first night, and knows he must have his perfection *in time*. The sets are very beautiful.[40]

Monday, 7th December 1925, at night
Today we had the whole of Act 2. The Inn Scene is still a bit of a problem—getting a thing like that really satisfactory.
 . . . p.s. I am quite fit, despite working 16 hours a day, despite having irregular (but adequate) meals, walking through deep snow for two hours, and insufficient sleep. Today, for instance, I left before nine, was already working on the score in the underground; 10 to 11 stage music, 11 to 2 second Act, 2 to 3 production meeting, 3 to 5 lunch and talk "shop" with Schmid, 5 to 8 with Kleiber, discussing all the tempi. Accompanied him to the Kroll Opera, where we listened to a guest singer, 9:30 to 12:30 with Kleiber and Arravantinos (designer of the sets—a real artist too!), at the restaurant. Then home by the underground and through the snow with 10 lbs. of score under my arm.[41]

Another point of concern was the recent resignation of Max von Schillings, the General Director of the Berlin State Opera; Berg worried that this might also affect Kleiber's standing, to the point that he, too would have to resign. This is explained repeatedly in the pre-concert articles on *Wozzeck*, many of which describe the so-called "scandal" of the open rehearsal on December 12th. For example, in the *Nachtausgabe Berlin/Sonnabend die illustrierte Abendzeitung*:

Scenes of scandal in the State Opera

Tumult during the general rehearsal

Heated fight about the Wozzeck rehearsal

At the general rehearsal for Alban Berg's *Wozzeck* in the State Opera Unter den Linden that took place this afternoon before a densely filled house, it came to scenes of scandal, as was unaccustomed in the State Opera House. It became apparent how quickly the spirit of a house can suffer when from one day to the next the leader of a distinguished theater is removed, when one decides, to "dismiss" the Director "without notice," even before the right replacement for him has been found.[42]

There at least 51 articles reporting on the "scandal," and many, like this one, use it as an opportunity to question the decision to force Schillings to resign.

 For the details of the premiere itself, we can turn to Berg's binder of reviews, apparently collected by a clipping service and glued by Berg onto pages in his binder. Berg further sorts the reviews into categories. Besides the 51 "scandal" articles, and 15 pre-concert articles (interviews with Alban Berg, etc.), Berg makes the following distinctions for the premiere itself:

1. From leading critics (printed in brochure)

2. Positive

3. Serious, but rejecting

4. Less good or completely bad

5. Scandal 4th performance

6. Foreign speaking critics about the premiere

The two reviews of *Wozzeck* that Reich cites in his biography of the composer present the opera as an extreme dichotomy: either a masterwork or an auditory offense.[43] This impression is furthered by the reviews printed in the 1926 issue *Pult und Taktstock*, a musical periodical for conductors, in which a particularly offensive review (the same one cited by Reich) is categorized as "sewer odor" (*Kanalgeruch*).[44]

But if one analyzes the entire group of approximately 200 reviews in Berg's six categories, most of the critics appear to be sincerely grappling with the complexities of an atonal opera, whose dissonance and incomprehensibility surpasses anything thus far produced in this conservative genre. Indeed, many of their queries on the ability to hear a modern work will seem as relevant today as in 1925. In the following discussion, I will analyze the major points repeatedly discussed by these critics, citing sections from their reviews.

Who Is Alban Berg?

It is very clear that for most of the reviewers, Berg is an unknown quantity, and even more an enigma in that he is suddenly having an opera premiered by one of the most prestigious opera companies in the world. Even reviewers who are familiar with Alban Berg feel the need to fill in details of his life for their readers. He is invariably described as "a student of Schoenberg," but some reviews further stress what they perceive as his inexperience:

Nachtausgabe, L.R.
We are familiar with string quartets, orchestral songs, orchestra pieces and numerous chamber works from the Schoenberg student Alban Berg, who, in any case, had decided on this, his first dramatic work, and would have certainly completed it, if the war hadn't intervened, in which Berg served in the Austrian army until the end. While on leave Berg had already sketched individual scenes. In 1920 the opera was finished, and about a year ago accepted by the Berlin State Opera.[45]

Vossische Zeitung Berlin, Erwin Stein
Alban Berg was born in Vienna on February 9, 1885. His composition teacher was Arnold Schoenberg, with whom he still has a close friendship. Berg is considered one of the most radical representatives of modern music. He lives in Vienna.

His works are not numerous: a one-movement piano sonata, a book of songs, a string quartet in two movements (probably the most well known work of the composer) five orchestral songs, four pieces for clarinet and piano, three orchestral pieces, the opera *Wozzeck*, a recently written concerto for piano and violin with accompaniment of thirteen winds. Berg began composing *Wozzeck* in 1914. His conscription into the military, however, delayed the completion until after the war.[46]

Schlesische Zeitung, Breslau, Dr. Fr. Br.
Until now, we knew as good as nothing about Alban Berg. His *Wozzeck* is Opus 7.
　　Born of German parents in Vienna in 1885, he attended secondary school, became a civil servant in the Viennese city government, to then throw himself completely into music, which he came to know more closely through Arnold Schoenberg.
　　Before the outbreak of war he became acquainted with Georg Büchner's play through a Viennese performance.[47]

Schwäbischer Merkur, Stuttgart, Dr. Friedrich Schwabe
Berg, a now forty-year-old man, who up to this point has distinguished himself with chamber music, is a student of Arnold Schoenberg (who recently was appointed as director of the master class for composition in Berlin), has carried out the lessons of his master to their last consequences and stripped musical language of any euphony.[48]

While Alban Berg is an unknown, Büchner's "Woyzeck" is revered as a classic. According to Peter Gay, Büchner was experiencing a renewal in Weimar Germany:

Once again the Republic completed what the late Empire had begun. Carl Zuckmayer recalls that with the outbreak of the revolution, when the youth, filled with talent, excitement, and great need, looked for figures it could truly admire, Büchner became "the patron saint of the youth; a magnificent youth, rebellious, vital, and penetrated by the awareness of its public responsibility."[49]

Many of the reviewers even question Berg's decision to set the play to music. They repeatedly use the expression "vergewaltigt" (rapes), or, in this context, "overpowers" or "assaults," to describe the music's effect on the libretto:

Sozialistische Monatshefte, Max Butting
Can Büchner's work *be* set to music? In my opinion, Berg's music has assaulted it.
　　And despite this, Büchner's work shines through all of the complications of the music, usually stronger than the music, so that one never has the sense of a true unity between music and text. When the text, with its great differing individual weight has no skeleton, what holds this music together? It is certainly not to be seen in Berg's formal schemes of traditional musical forms.
　　While listening, I searched and found really nothing.[50]

Schwäbischer Merkur, Stuttgart
The way that Büchner decorated this forceful story with philosophical tinsel would be reason enough for a musician to keeps his hands off it; the unfolding events require no music. Secondly, however, Alban Berg wrote music for it, which according to our ideas to date is no music, but rather a horrible accumulation of wrong-sounding noises that attempt to paint the spiritual life of Wozzeck.[51]

It is to be expected that many reviewers discuss the performance difficulties in realizing atonality and *Sprechstimme*.

Deutsche Tonkünstler-Zeitung, Joachim Beck
Contrary to the spirit of the music, and despite the atonality, one might say. Atonality is the great, almost insolvable problem; before one can prove or dispute it down to its physical foundation, subjective, indecisive impressions speak for or against it. Even its most aggressive champions probably don't hear it as beautiful, but it may be genuine. And Alban Berg may also want to be genuine, not beautiful. He thus places himself in opposition to Western tonality.

   If one perceives historical tonality as primeval, as I do, then one would have to say that Berg is working against the spirit of music. In certain respects, that is not only hypothesis, but proof and confession: whoever rejects the singing, time honored voice, rejects a primary element of music.[52]

Nachrichten Stadt und Land, Oldenburg
Who knows whether his *Wozzeck* would have ever even been performed if the young, ambitious General Music Director from Vienna, Erich Kleiber, had not advocated for it? For the work teems with such difficulties that real courage and extraordinary conducting ability are necessary in order to bring it off. Only really big stages even have the possibility of mustering the necessary giant orchestra and auxiliary orchestras, and to find the time for the necessary rehearsals, which would take a year. If up to now I had thought that Strauss's *Elektra* or Schreker's *Die Gezeichneten* would have presented the greatest conceivable difficulties, a look in *Wozzeck's* piano reduction would very soon have convinced me that in comparison to it the other two works are easy, especially with regard to rhythm. With respect to range and hitting intervals, Berg demands the downright impossible from the singers, for whom he specifies Sprechgesang to a large extent, but not of the kind Wagner introduced, and also direct speaking. Of course it does not matter whether the notes always occur as notated in the score, for in the whole of *Wozzeck* there is no tonality to speak of. It is probably the most dissonant opera that has ever been created up to now.[53]

Surprisingly, what the reviewers object to even more frequently than the atonality and *Sprechstimme* is their inability to hear Berg's operatic forms (gigue, fugue, sonata) which were explained in pre-premiere articles:

Kölnische Zeitung, Dr. Heinz Pringsheim
The danger of fluttering away that was evident with such a loose structure of scenes is supposed to be eliminated by emphasizing the form-building elements of the music. The individual scenes, composed in closed, absolute musical forms, joined through transitions, are intended to mutually determine one another, and to fuse into a higher unity in an act [of the opera]: a new type of solution to the problem of a dramatic symphony. (The piano score appeared in the Viennese Universal Edition.) So says the composer himself, at least, and his fans, who must know it. Of course the attentive listener doesn't notice much of it.

   He hears neither the paper sarabandes, gavottes, gigues, passacaglias as such, nor would it be useful to him, if he could identify them with the help of a program analysis. Even then he would wonder no less how much this music strays in its ability to characterize. Except for details, it unfolds peripherally as a superfluous foreign body in relation to the plot.[54]

Oper und Ballet, *Berliner Volkszeitung*, Frank Warschauer
The contrasting of the individual works is indicated two-fold: once in the scene, then however, an independent meaning is insinuated for them.

And in this connection Berg speaks of a suite, a passacaglia, fantasy and fugue, inventions, and so on.

But these forms have no direct evidence of any kind; it is impossible to experience them. They appear as such on paper; just as with Schönberg the artistry and thinking of his constructions must be demonstrated for us beforehand: they are not audible, while there is no Bach fugue whose construction is not immediately comprehensible.[55]

Köln. *Volkszeitung*, Fritz Ohrmann
The first act is a succession of five character pieces with a passacaglia with 21 variations. The second is supposed to represent a symphony, while the third act is supposed to be built of six inventions (among them, one on a [single] tone!). I must be a somewhat backward musician, in that I heard nothing, absolutely nothing of all of these beautiful things. It was a real comfort to me, however, that several composers of rank sitting next to me also heard nothing.[56]

Germania, Berlin, Edmund Kühn
It is a pity that these "new directions" into which he moves by incorporating common concert forms in his dramatic/stage-realm—among others, the score supposedly includes a suite, twenty-one variations, a five-movement symphony (!)—are not recognizable as such! At least, one can puzzle out from this amalgamation what modern noise-makers of Alban Berg's type understand under "composing an opera." If their attacks on the good health of music and the good taste of the audiences were not so impertinent and unrelenting, one would have to laugh about them. But there is only one thing to say: When it comes to Schönberg and Schönberg-breeds: war into eternity unto those poisoners of the well of German music![57]

The barely concealed anti-Semitism in this last review would run rampant during the Third Reich, severely curtailing Berg's career as a composer. It is even more explicit in a number of other articles, but this one foreshadows the fixation with the term "healthy" in the 1930s. Geert Mak writes, "It is almost impossible to find a cultural essay from the 1930s in which terms such as "pure" and "healthy" do not appear. It was the leitmotif of the modern age.[58]

Trierische Landeszeitung, Trier
Atonality is slowly beginning to be a danger to our German cultural music, and it is high time that those still healthy progressive thinking musicians in Germany give everything to energetically confront this sinister movement. If jazz bands and nigger tunes invade our German cultural music, atonal hubbub on the other, both working off of texts without foundation, then the situation is indeed serious.[59]

Völkischer Kurier, München (L.M.)
On the other hand, however, party members of the atonalists see in Berg's "Wozzeck" something like a Gospel of the new music style coming down the path which forfeits everything, and would have to virtually finish off what our entire musical culture has represented up to now.

The essential aspect of this premiere is that the Berlin State Opera—where Kleiber now has absolute power—ever since the displacement of director Schillings, has become disloyal to the whole tradition that it was so proud of through the premiere of this work. The effects of Schillings' "dismissal without notice" are already beginning to manifest themselves. The atonal composers, meaning the Jews, are encroaching more and more onto the State Opera by evoking artificial successes through all means, by feigning great successes to the press, and then to appeal to them. Over the long or short run the Berlin State Opera will thus become an experimental stage on which lobbyists will luxuriantly flower. The paying public is the only hope, whose healthy instinct will hopefully keep them from stepping on the road, which Herr Kleiber is showing.[60]

These reviews allow us to re-experience a critical musical moment from the point of view of the cultivated, but not necessarily sympathetic, listener. This moment was far removed from the circumstances of the opera's genesis; the reviewers mention World War I only in the context of Berg's service, and no one seems to identify with the helplessness and penury of the opera's main character. Indeed, in 1925, Berlin was at the peak of the Weimar era, the equivalent of our "Roaring Twenties," when the humiliation of the previous decade must have seemed like past history, or was even intentionally pushed out of consciousness. Nonetheless, this brief period of experimentation and relative financial security allowed the premiere of a very difficult and controversial opera that required many more rehearsals than standard opera repertoire.

What is most striking, however, is the crisis of perception that the reviewers, and certainly the audience, experienced with this modern work. Beyond the novelty of the *Sprechstimme* and the amount of dissonance, they seemed unable to make sense of the music—as if atonality impinged on traditional forms to such a degree that they were no longer perceptible.

We now begin a detailed study of the sketches for the opera, beginning with a chapter that addresses this issue: Berg's genesis of traditional forms from Büchner's text.

CHAPTER Five

Berg's Büchner Text and the Genesis of Form

I lose my bearings studying Philosophy. I discover the poverty of the human mind from yet another perspective. For my sake! If only one could imagine the holes in our pants as palace windows, one could live like a king! But in reality we are freezing pitifully.[1]

—Georg Büchner

Büchner's expression of despair, underlined in one of Berg's editions of *Woyzeck*, beautifully encapsulates the overall theme of Berg's opera: the helplessness and relentless oppression of the poor. This is the same theme Berg highlights at the end of "A Word About *Wozzeck*": "the vast social implications of the work that by far transcend the personal destiny of Wozzeck."[2]

But one is equally struck by what Berg's many annotations reveal about the opera's form—the element, that in the same lecture he hoped "no one, from the moment the curtain parts until it closes for the last time, pays any attention to."[3] We see, of course, the expected deletions and editing of text by which Berg shaped his libretto. Berg's primary working copy of the play also contains many annotations and diagrams that literally chisel out the form for each scene of the opera, showing text as the genesis for his ideas on form, rather than form as an abstract idea that he superimposed on the text.

In this essay, we examine two scenes in proximity in the opera, but at extreme ends of the chronological spectrum: Act II, scene 2 and Act II, scene 4. The sketches for these scenes, completed in 1918 and 1921, appear in very different arrangements; the first, neatly self-contained in a sketchbook, the second, spread over the entire collection using every paper type imaginable. Both, however, reveal the genesis of Berg's ideas on form in an atonal idiom as well as how these ideas are fulfilled in his later compositional sketches.

Act II, scene 2 is one of the pivotal scenes of the opera, for Wozzeck is first alerted through the cruel taunting of the Captain and the Doctor of Marie's affair with the Drum Major. It portrays the initial stages of what Perle describes as "the disintegration of the one human relationship upon which his manhood and sanity depends."[4] Possibly because it was the first scene Berg composed, his sketches reveal an intensely detailed working out of the relation between text and form. In Berg's working copy of *Wozzeck*, he divides the text for the latter part of the scene featuring the Captain, the Doctor, and Wozzeck into twelve smaller sections, A–L, (originally, Roman numerals I–XII) based on the interjections of conversation among the three characters (Figure 5.1). Like the stanzas of Andres's song in Act I, scene 2, this section relies on a unifying idea: Marie's infidelity with the Drum Major. But it is also dynamic in character, building tension through the mounting distasteful evidence served up by the Doctor and Captain, ("What is it, Wozzeck? Didn't he find a hair from a beard in his spoon?"), climaxing in Wozzeck's frantic exit and cry, "God in heaven! A man might want to hang himself! Then he would know where he stood!"

In his revisions of the Büchner text, Berg removes extraneous words and intensifies the dialogue, taking Büchner's expressionistic style a step further. For instance, the Captain's comment, "Aber Er hat ein braves Weib, he?" is reduced to, "Aber Er hat doch ein braves Weib?!" Wozzeck's reply, "Jawohl! Was wollen Sie damit sagen, Herr Hauptmann?!" is changed to, "Was wollen Sie damit sagen, Herr Doktor, und Sie, Herr Hauptmann?!" Other than curtailing the Captain's egotistical rantings at the end of the scene by three sentences, and thus fixing the action on Wozzeck rather than the Captain, these are minor changes to the dialogue.

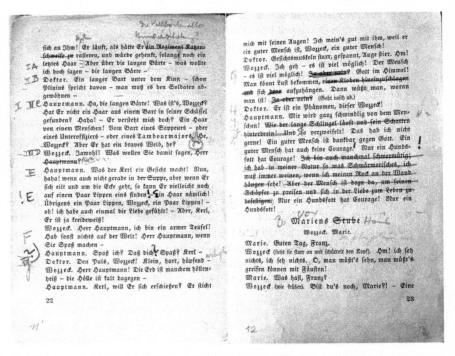

Figure 5.1: F 21 Berg 128 fols. 11ᵛ–12ʳ (catalog #: 276 & 277)

When Berg shaped the text for the "Street Scene," as he called it, he used the dramatic opportunity of the successive texts of these three characters and his earlier outline in the text to plan a three-subject fugue (Figures 5.2a and 5.3a and their transcriptions 5.2b and 5.3b). In general, Berg uses successive entrances of

(a)

(b)

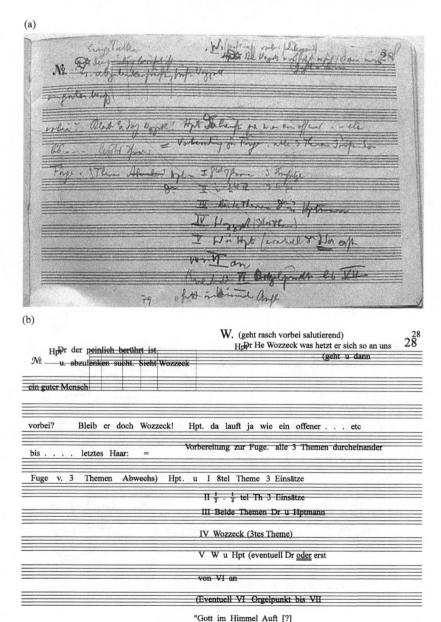

Figure 5.2: F 21 Berg 13/II p. 79 (catalog #: 072)

(a)

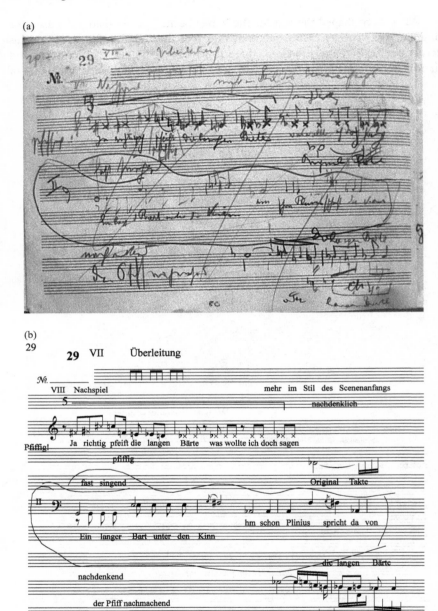

(b)

Figure 5.3: F 21 Berg 13/II p. 80 (catalog #: 073)

voices, whether in a fugue or canon, as an intensifying device. In addition to this fugue, one thinks of the canonic entrances in Act III, scene 3, exposing Wozzeck's crime, the staggered "B" of the interlude after Marie's murder, or the multiple statements of the twelve-tone melody during the murder itself.

Berg's outline indicates that the fugue will consist of a preparatory section (Vorbereitung zur Fuge) utilizing all three themes; seven sections of the fugue proper featuring expositions of the three themes (I, II, IV) and three developments (III, V, and VI); transition music for Wozzeck's exit (VII); and finally a Nachspiel (VIII) that returns to the style of the beginning of the scene. Given the number of annotations of "eventuell" (possibly), Berg's outline is remarkably consistent with his final result. As was his habit, Berg preceded this sketch with a psychological analysis of the Captain (Figure 5.4) whom he characterizes in surely his most seething vitriol against the military as:

> A nobody. With a very limited capacity to seem better than he is. A pretentious braggart. (Ein guter Mensch) He is totally taken by himself. A kind of remnant from military discipline, that straightaway vanishes behind the sickly smugness of military command.[5]

The chronology of the sketches shows that this sketch, like the one bearing a notation of Berg's orders for transfer to the War Ministry, undoubtedly dates from 1916, when Berg served under a "Hauptmann" he characterized as "an idiot drunk."

In Berg's next stage of sketching (Figure 5.3a staves 2–10), we see the first two subjects for the fugue, the themes for the Captain and the Doctor. Here, Berg must not only supply an acceptable subject for a fugue, but one that reflects the personality and changing psychological state of each character in that moment of the drama. The music functions like an actor whose tone, pacing, and dynamics personalize the text. For instance, Berg's added direction, "nachmachend" (imitating) appears immediately in context with the Doctor. The barbed falsetto melody that Berg gives him as he mimics the motions of the Drum Major with his cane quickly change the tone of this scene from the cruel to the painfully grotesque, climaxing in the Captain's long drawn-out "or that of a Tambourmajor's" (Example 5.1).

These sketches of themes and dramatic action allow Berg to construct a continuity draft of the opening of the fugue, featuring his characteristic rhythmic shorthand (Figures 5.5 and 5.6). Its shape, location in the fugue, and annotations of text leave no doubt, however, that Berg has sketched the first entrance of the Captain (measure 286) and the Doctor (measure 293). As Berg returns to section III of his outline (Figure 5.6 staves 7–10 and Figure 5.7) he characterizes Wozzeck during the development of the Doctor and Captain's themes as "becoming more uncertain" (unsicher werdend) (Figure 5.7 staff 3) until his exit in meaure 345 when the music "breaks up completely" (Figure 5.8), reflecting a state of agitation that Wozzeck can no longer bear. Berg's sketches of the dramatic subtleties of these three characters are now so covered with text and staging directions that they resemble a film script, which, as shown by the violent scratching out

(a)

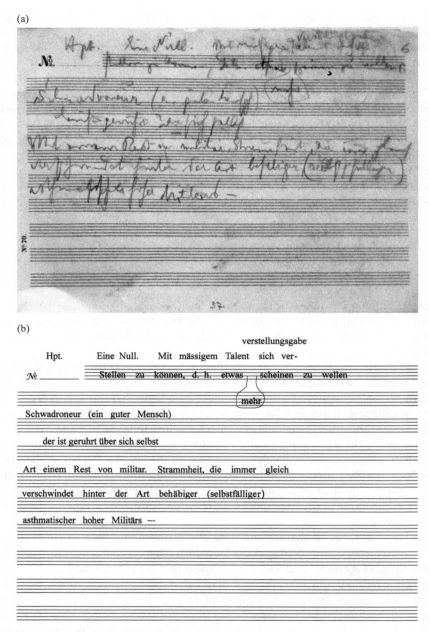

(b)

verstellungsgabe

Hpt. Eine Null. Mit mässigem Talent sich ver-

№. _____ ~~Stellen zu können, d. h. etwas~~ ~~scheinen zu wellen~~

mehr

Schwadroneur (ein guter Mensch)

der ist geruhrt über sich selbst

Art einem Rest von militar. Strammheit, die immer gleich

verschwindet hinter der Art behäbiger (selbstfälliger)

asthmatischer hoher Militärs —

Figure 5.4: F 21 Berg 13/II p. 57 (catalog #: 057)

Example 5.1: Act II, scene 2, mm. 298–308

in the sketch in Figure 5.9 (Section VI, development of Captain's, Doctor's and Wozzeck's themes), can apparently also "break up completely."

Wozzeck's theme (Subject III) does not appear until the very end of the sketches (Figure 5.8 staves 7–10); however, it has not yet attained its characteristic downward shape that so identifies it with our defeated (uncertain) protagonist. Both Perle and Petersen have suggested that this is the theme Berg writes to his wife about in 1918:

> I myself walked uphill very slowly, frequently resting, "according to regulations," and finally, as I proceeded with heavy steps, there actually occurred to me—though I wasn't planning to work—a long-sought idea for an entrance of Wozzeck's.[6]

Thus far, the sketches appearing in Berg's Büchner text and his sketchbook suggest the following compositional process:

1. Annotations of form in Büchner text
2. Psychoanalysis of one or more characters

(a)

(b)

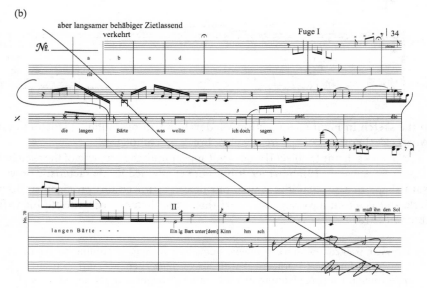

Figure 5.5: F 21 Berg 13/II p. 85 (catalog #: 078)

(a)

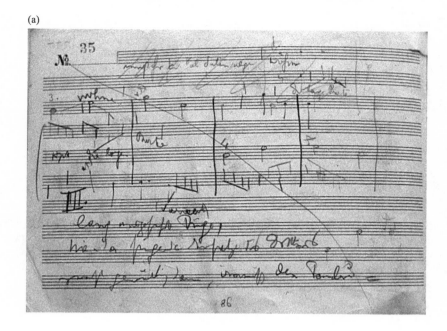

(b)

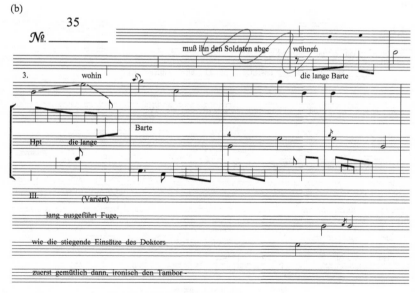

Figure 5.6: F 21 Berg 13/II p. 86 (catalog #: 079)

(a)

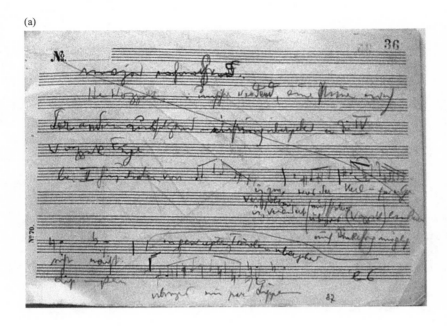

(b)

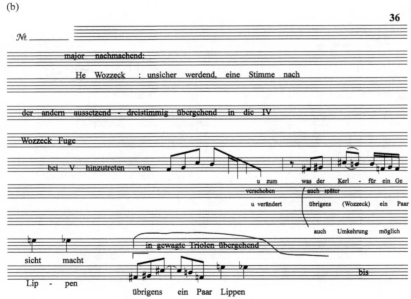

Figure 5.7: F 21 Berg 13/II p. 87 (catalog #: 080)

(a)

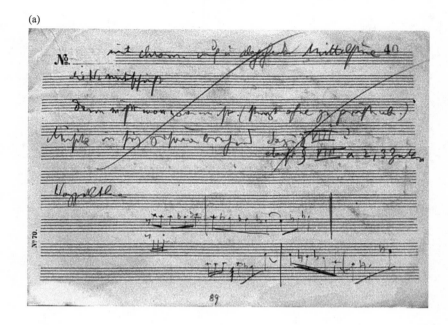

(b)

Figure 5.8:　F 21 Berg 13/II p. 89 (catalog #: 082)

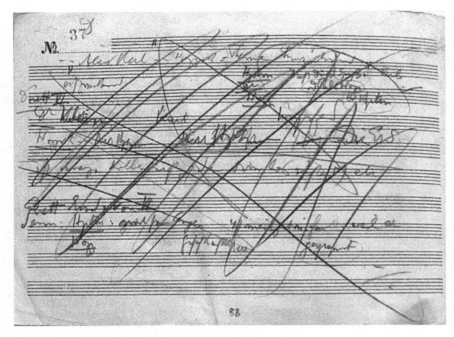

Figure 5.9: F 21 Berg 13/II p. 88 (catalog #: 081)

3. Outline showing function of formal sections
4. More detailed summary of dramatic effect and themes of each section
5. Continuity draft
6. Detailed draft in short score form

Berg's compositional process is already quite complex, but as Klaus Lippe has shown, Berg further revised sections of Act II, scene 2 at a later date, eliminating most of the *Sprechstimme* and even changing the transposition level of important themes.[7] (Note, for instance, that the Captain's theme in Figure 5.3 is sketched entirely in *Sprechstimme*, and the Doctor's theme in both the same sketch and the continuity draft in Figure 5.4 begin on G, not C, as in the published score.) Berg expresses his concerns about the viability of *Sprechstimme* for opera in a letter to Webern from 1918:

> And here is a point that causes me great concern: whether these kinds of melodramas are practical on stage. Whether human *Sprechstimme* is adequate for an opera house—despite the most careful instrumentation.[8]

With his designation "melodramas," Berg is referring to the Schoenbergian fore-runner *Pierrot Lunaire*, which he mentions earlier in the letter. In that this work is for chamber ensemble, however, it is clear why Berg would eventually depart from his model.

Berg's *La Valse*

Berg was faced with a very different challenge in constructing the form of the Tavern Scene, Act II, scene 4, which includes multiple ensembles and simultaneous action between large groups of characters. And like the previously discussed Street Scene, it is pivotal in the drama because Wozzeck now sees Marie and the Drum Major together for the first time. It thus forms a duality with the previously discussed scene, both in its symmetrical relation—flanking the central scene of the opera—and its content: while in Act II, scene 2, Wozzeck hears about the evidence for the first time, in Act II, scene 4 he actually witnesses it.

Berg complained in a letter to his wife of the difficulties he was having composing this scene, and it is the only scene, other than the previously discussed Act II, scene 2, that traversed two summers of composition.[9] Some of these difficulties no doubt had to do with the new compositional techniques Berg was innovating, but, as we shall see, they were also related to the scene's complex form.

As with Act II, scene 2, there are copious markings in Berg's Büchner text, but here they are more specific in their function. For instance, Berg notes that the scene will begin with a Ländler (A) and then move to the Trio I with the song of the Apprentice, interrupted by the Waltz, (section II) in which Wozzeck sees Marie and the Drum Major dancing (Figure 5.10). Rather than the trimming of dialogue

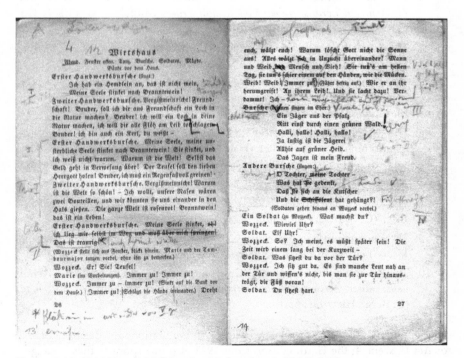

Figure 5.10: F 21 Berg 128 fols. 13ᵛ–14ʳ (catalog #: 280 & 281)

we saw in the previous scene, this scene requires heavy pruning; the entire speech of the second Apprentice in the opening of the scene is cut. And needless to say, Berg sanitizes his text of the highly anti-Semitic and mildly obscene line that ends the Apprentices' choral, "Let's piss on a cross so that a Jew dies."

Peter Petersen has discussed the text revisions of this scene based on the changes in the Witkowski edition, now *Woyzeck*, which appeared in 1920.[10] These minor changes include, for instance, the substitution of "liebe" for "meine," "du" for "sie," "Fuhrknecht" for Schiffsleut," etc. They are written with an indelible pencil in Berg's Büchner text, with a different character than the penciled in markings that make up the rest of the changes, and therefore may have been completed at a different time. Fanning notes that the revisions to Andres's song in the Witkowski edition appear in the sketches as well, suggesting that Berg acquired a copy and made these changes in 1921.[11]

If one tabulates all of Berg's editions of Büchner's *Wozzeck* (or *Woyzeck*) in his personal library at Hietzing and in various archives, they include the following:

1. The Franzos edition from 1879: *Georg Büchner, Sammtliche Werke und handschriftlicher Nachlaß;. Erste kritische Gesammt-Ausgabe.* Frankfurt am Main, J.D. Sauerländer. (In Berg's Hietzing apartment)

2. The Landau edition from 1909: *Georg Büchner, Gesammelte Schriften, in zwei Bänden.* Paul Cassirer. (In Berg's Hietzing apartment)

3. The Franz edition from 1912: *Georg Büchner, Dramatische Werke. Mit Erklärungen herausgegeben von Rudolf Franz.* München, G. Birk & Co. m.b.H. (In Berg's Hietzing apartment)

4. The Insel-Bücherei Nr. 92 from 1913: *Wozzeck/Lenz/Zwei Fragmente.* Leipzig, Roßberg'schen. (ÖNB Müsiksammlung F 21 Berg 128)

5. The Hausenstein edition from 1916: *Georg Büchner, Gesammelte Werke.* Leipzig, Insel. (Only typed introduction from this source, in ÖNB Musiksammlung F 21 Berg 127)

6. The Orplid-Büchlein from 1919: *Wozzeck/Ein Fragment.* Berlin-Charlottenburg, Axel Junker. (Harvard and Berg's Hietzing apartment)

7. The Witkowski edition from 1920: *Woyzeck.* Leipzig, Insel. (In Berg's Hietzing apartment)

8. The Insel-Bücherei from 1921: *Woyzeck/Eine Tragödie.* Hardt. Leipzig, Insel. (ÖNB Musiksammlung F 21 Berg 127)

9. The Bergemann edition from 1922: *Georg Büchner, Sämtliche Werke und Briefe.* Leipzig, Insel. (In Berg's Hietzing apartment)

10. The Zweig edition from 1923: *Georg Büchner, Sämtliche poetische Werke, nebst einer Auswahl seiner Briefe.* München und Leipzig, Rösl&Cie. (In Berg's Hietzing apartment)

The Witkowski edition of 1920 includes Berg's annotations and deletions of text for Act II, scene 4; the Hardt edition from 1921 also incorporates these changes. In any case, Berg's heavily annotated copy of Insel-Bücherei Nr. 92 alone makes it very clear, as George Perle posited long ago, that Berg used the Franzos edition in the Landau ordering, making very minor changes based on Witkowski.[12]

To accommodate the simultaneous events of Act II, scene 4, while still maintaining the chronological progression, Berg resorted to a master flow-chart format similar to that he created for the sonata form of *Lulu* in Act II, scene 1 (Figure 5.11).

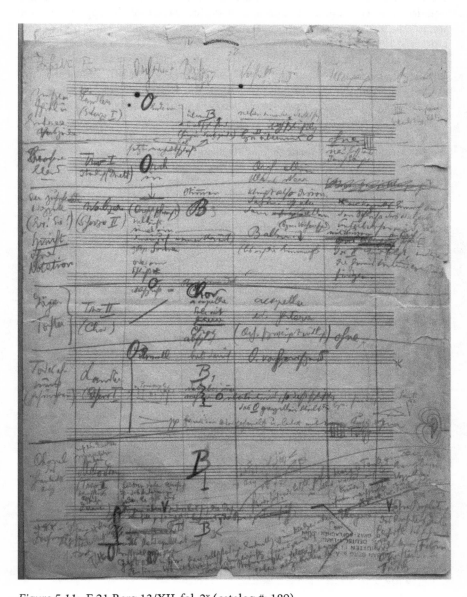

Figure 5.11: F 21 Berg 13/XII, fol. 2ᵛ (catalog #: 189)

One of the most fascinating and complex sketches for the opera, it shows Berg developing a seven-part form highlighting the dramatic occurrences of each section and summarizing the interaction between the stage music and the orchestra. The seven headings for the columns read from left to right: "content, form, orchestra, stage music, relation to each other, transition, and remarks." The seven chronological sections of the scene, appearing in the far left-hand column, read: "transition and entrance, drunken squalor, the watching Wozzeck (him! her!) <u>speaks</u> without notation, hunter daughter, foreboding of death, chorale of the apprentices, and songs." The forms for each of these sections (column 2) replicate some of the annotations in Berg's Büchner text. The first three sections (Scherzo I, Trio I, Scherzo II) are replicated in the second half of the scene after the central Trio II. Smaller symmetries occur as well: measures 447–455 from the first half appear in retrograde motion in the second half (641–649); the scalar patterns in the choir of Apprentices and Soldiers (measures 560–575) appear in retrograde motion in A1 (measures 581–589).

One has the sense that this outline, preserved in even the most fleeting sketches, served as a kind of lifeline through the difficulties of realizing this scene. For instance, in the critical section "the watching Wozzeck," Berg specifies that in contrast to the Duet of the previous Trio I Wozzeck "speaks without notation." Berg is concerned with the orchestration of the voice, which can move in a continuum from speaking, to Sprechstimme, to singing, as well as refinements of each of these three categories. For Wozzeck to speak without notation allows the greatest contrast between his voice and the already scaled-down tavern ensemble on stage. Berg further specifies that the orchestra should be silent during this section (Orchester schweigt) or perhaps an interjection during Wozzeck's text, "Sonne" (Why doesn't God put the sun out?), or at the end, where Wozzeck's interjections break off the end of the Waltz (column 7). And true to Berg's sketches, other than the abrupt gesture of the orchestra announcing Wozzeck's arrival (Example 5.2), a foreign element in

Example 5.2: Act II, scene 4, mm. 495–496

the midst of Marie and the Drum Major's carefree proceedings, these are the only sections of the waltz in which the orchestra participates.

In Berg's musical drafts of the Waltz (Scherzo II) he labels each subsection with Roman numerals I through VII (Figure 5.12). On a smaller scale, this division into seven is reflected in the 7/4 meter of the Song of the Apprentices and Soldiers (Trio II, measure 560) as well as the seven-note melody they sing. (Clearly, Berg is practicing a musical variant of fractal analysis, that is, the same organizational unit is replicated on different structural levels.) Initially Berg's drafts are so detailed

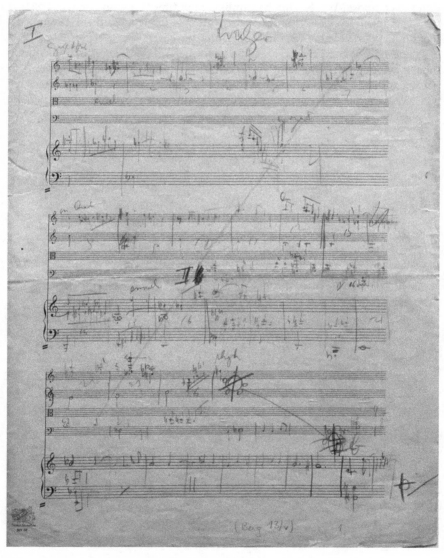

Figure 5.12: F 21 Berg 13/V fol. 1ʳ (catalog #: 123)

that they include tonalities here and there, for instance, the E-minor tonality that begins and ends the first section (measures 481–495) and the E-flat minor tonality that appears in section 2. But the sketches begin to quickly break down. We have scraps of manuscript paper, unidentified phrases (Figure 5.13), drafts, indicating almost nothing but staging directions (Figure 5.14); at the end of the summer, Berg sketched a fragment of a scene that he would have to complete the following year. The different writing implements and overlays in some of these drafts suggest that Berg completed them the following summer. Was Berg so unnerved by illness and the financial debilitation of the previous months that he no longer had the peace of mind to compose? Was he simply running out of time? Or conversely, did he find the quasi-tonal expressions of the Waltz so simple to compose that he completed them in the *Particell*? We can only conjecture.

Berg did not compose the repetition of Scherzo II (measures 670–736) until the following summer. But here it is accompanied by an increasingly complex ostinato pattern (Figure 5.15). Derived from a motivic figure in the waltz associated with the Tambourmajor, the ostinato begins to subsume the music of the interlude

Figure 5.13: F 21 Berg 13/V fol. 5ʳ (catalog #: 131)

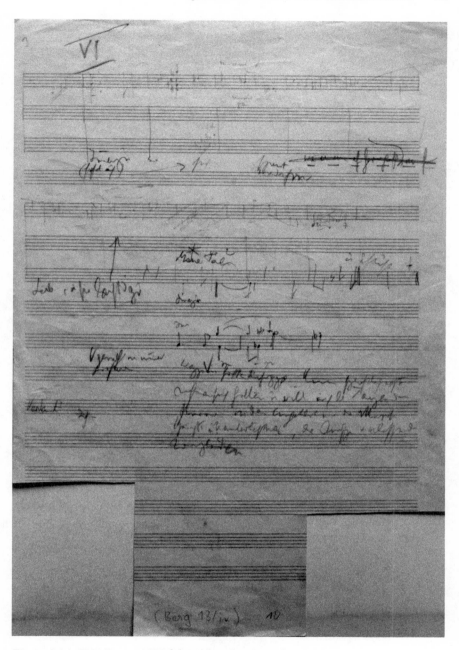

Figure 5.14: F 21 Berg 13/IV fol. 10ʳ (catalog #: 117)

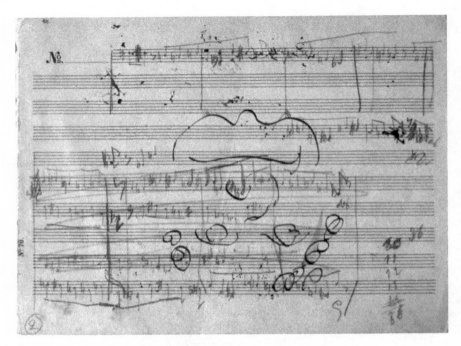

Figure 5.15: F 21Berg 13/VII fol. 2ʳ (catalog #: 145)

with its successive patterns of 3, 5, 7, 9, and 10 notes reflecting Wozzeck's painful obsession. The nightmarish quality of the interlude prepares Wozzeck's first line in the barracks of the next scene, in which he complains: "Andres! Andres! I can't sleep. When I close my eyes I see her, and hear the violins immer zu, immer zu."

   If the music for Act I, scene 2 is "as vivid a projection of world doom to come out of the Great War," then Berg's Waltz, with its decaying tonality and patterned ostinati, is the unraveling of the nineteenth century reconstituted into a tautly strung pattern from the twentieth.[13]

CHAPTER Six

Master of the Smallest Link:
The Sketches for Large-Scale Form

> It is not only the fate of this poor man, exploited and tormented by *all the world*,
> that touches me so closely, but also the unheard-of intensity of mood of the
> individual scenes. The combining of 4–5 scenes into *one* act through orchestral
> interludes tempts me also, of course. (Do you find anything similar in the *Pelléas* of
> Maeterlinck-Debussy!)[1]
>
> —Berg to Webern, August 19, 1918

The challenge of creating large-scale form had occupied Berg from the beginning—
even before he wrote this letter to Webern in 1918. In the sketches Berg completed
during officer training for the military in 1916, discussed in Chapter 2, he was able,
using Debussy's *Pelléas et Mélisande* as a model, to create a streamlined structure
of fifteen scenes that would move relentlessly to the tragedies of Act III. These fifteen scenes, like the ensemble of fifteen instruments in Act II, scene 3, reflect the
instrumentation of Schoenberg's Opus 9 Chamber Symphony. In his "Lecture on
Wozzeck" Berg comments:

> Apart from the obvious thematic relationships which make this Largo a self-
> contained movement it has one peculiarity: the instrumentation is that of chamber
> music and indeed corresponds exactly to the instrumentation of the Chamber
> Symphony of Arnold Schoenberg. I wanted here at this central point of the opera
> to pay homage to my teacher and master.[2]

In the above letter to Webern, Berg is concerned with the transitions between
scenes, that is, how individual scenes cohere into the larger form of an act. Adorno
pays homage in title (*Alban Berg: Master of the Smallest Link*) and text to Berg's
mastery of transitions:

> Its style is that of seamless correspondence. And it, too, carries the art of transition
> much further than Wagner ever conceived possible, carries it to the point of pervasive
> mediation. It does not shrink from extremes; Büchner's tragedy completely absorbs the
> profound melancholy of the music's German/Austrian tone, but with such coherence

and immanence of form as to give scenic embodiment to expression and pain, serving thereby, purely out of itself, as something like a posthumous court of appeals. The joined and interlaced quality of this music, its seamlessness, is decisive.[3]

The "seamlessness" that Adorno refers to can even refer to silence. The sketch in Figure 6.1a (transcribed in Figure 6.1b) shows Berg's initial solutions for the transitions between scenes of Act II, as well as a draft for the opening of Act III, scene 1,

(a)

Figure 6.1: F 21 Berg 13/XIII fol. 1v (catalog #: 191)   *(continued)*

(b)

Figure 6.1: cont.

which also acts as a transition—between the last scene of Act II and the first scene of Act III. In staves 3–6 Berg has sketched three successive versions of the opening of Act III. In the first version the curtain opens, followed by a pause and Marie's spoken words as she reads from the Bible. In the second version, Berg sets the strings one beat before Marie begins to read. Finally, in the third version, which

Berg annotates "besser!" (better!), he combines both ideas from the two previous sketches: Marie's words are preceded by four to five measures of sustained strings. This version conforms to the final score (Example 6.1) and forms a symmetrical relation with the silence at the end of Act II, as well as a quiet moment that would emphasize Marie's isolation and vulnerability. In Berg's "Lecture on *Wozzeck*," he comments on this symmetry:

> When the music of this act has finished, the last stage picture is held for a moment and then the curtain falls. Similarly (again in an attempt to establish a connection) the curtain to Act III rises before the music begins. The music first starts after a (silent) pause.[4]

Example 6.1: transition between Act II and Act III

The reverse side of the leaf (Figure 6.2a, transcribed in Figure 6.2b) shows a complete outline of the five scenes for Act III, in which Berg takes into account not only the setting of each scene and predominant activity (for instance, for scene 1, Marie in her room, reading the Bible), but also the time of day and subsequent lighting. The predominant musical form, the type of vocal delivery, and the nature of the transition from one scene to the next also figure prominently. One could consider this sketch an architectural overview, both musically and dramatically, of the entire act, which clarifies its structure by omitting foreground details. Each scene, for instance, features a different type of light depending on the setting and time of day: Marie reads her Bible "spät Nachts" (late at night); the murder in scene 2 takes place in the evening; the inn room of scene 3 is "schlecht beleuchtet" (badly lit); Wozzeck's suicide is "ganz finster"

(completely dark); followed finally by the contrast of scene 5, in which the children sing as a choir à la Debussy in "helle Morgensonne!" (bright morning sun!). Initially, the lighting, musical content, and characters of this scene function as a dramatic cleansing of the horrible darkness and sordidness of the previous scenes. Büchner (and Berg), however, quickly returns to a more painful and incongruous reality in the children's unselfconscious excitement about Marie's corpse and their blunt communication of the news to Marie's child: "You. Your mother is dead." Even worse, the boy registers no reaction, but continues to ride his hobbyhorse. Apparently, it is already too late to save this child; it only remains for him to experience a fate similar to his parents', that is, to begin the events of the opera yet again. Berg comments about the analogous musical effect:

> The closing scene of Act III, and thus of the whole opera, is based on constant quavers, a sort of *perpetuum mobile* movement, which depicts the games and the play of the poor working-class children amongst whom is the completely unsuspecting child of Marie and Wozzeck, now orphaned twice over. And yet, although it again clearly moves to cadence on to the closing chord, it almost appears as if it carries on. And it does carry on! In fact, the opening bar of the opera could link up with the final bar and in so doing close the whole circle.[5]

The music that precedes the final scene is a "großes Zwischenspiel mit Abschluß," (large interludium with conclusion). To emphasize the interludium's length and self-contained nature Berg encloses it in a box in his sketch. The sketch specifies that the hexachord, the unifying element of scene 4 (Waldweg am Teich) will dissolve into the D minor chord that begins (and ends) the interlude (column 2, staves 9–10). D minor brings an element of compassion, through which Berg expressed "a confession of the author who now steps outside the dramatic action on the stage. Indeed, as it were, an appeal to humanity through its representative, the audience." It would at first appear to be a reference to Schoenberg's D minor quartet.[6] In two letters to his wife, however, Berg makes explicit the association with his wife. On July 11, 1914, at the beginning stages of *Wozzeck*, Berg writes:

> I'd love to finish the little piano piece for you and get it down on paper, but it just won't take shape at present. Those few bars are really only a beginning, a sort of continuation and end, and of course I could join them up, but it would be just a school exercise, and even you wouldn't like that. I couldn't give my best in it, as I want to do. Perhaps the theme itself is not quite original, somehow derivative in mood and tone, although I can't think of any possible model for it.[7]

Berg's manuscript for this piano piece, F 21 Berg 48 (Figure 6.3), consists of three pages carefully copied in ink, and thus is at a later stage than what he reports to his wife in the above letter. The opening eight measures of the piece, and emphatic cadences in D minor beginning in the climax (measure 365), act as a tonal frame to the entire interlude, which quickly departs into atonality. Berg devotes six pages of sketches in his final sketchbook (dated 23. 9) to a kind of laundry list of themes that he intends to include in this final summation of the major *leitmotivic* ideas of the opera. In actual practice Berg creates a hierarchy in which some of these themes are barely audible, while "Wir arme Leut," the raison d'être of the opera, acts as its dramatic climax (Figures 6.4 and 6.5). On May 27, 1922, at the end of composition, Berg again writes to his wife:

> Pferschi, who do I owe *Wozzeck* to but you? Without you, and the peace you've given me through five years—peace for my soul and my body—I couldn't have

(a)

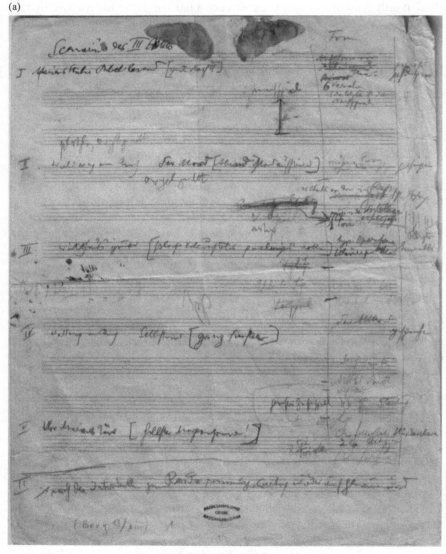

Figure 6.2: F 21 Berg 13/XIII fol. 1r (catalog #: 190)   *(continued)*

(b)

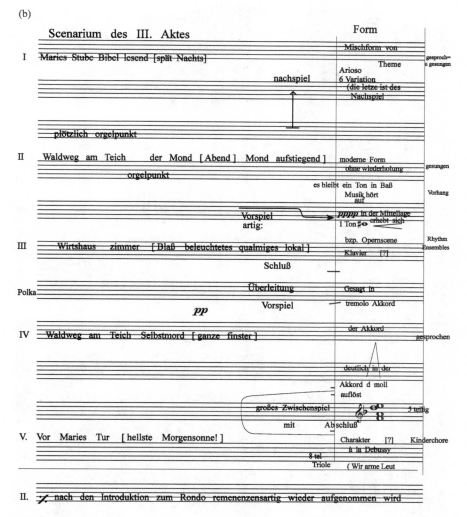

Figure 6.2: cont.

composed a single bar. The peace no one in the world except you could give me or have taken away from me. I mean to write this to Jeanette, too, and tell her that besides the Almighty I owe *Wozzeck* to three people: to her, for making it possible for me to work on it this last year and a half without financial worries; to Schoenberg as teacher (even though he wanted to take away my joy in it); and to my golden one for the reasons given above. The Interlude at the end I owe to you and you alone. You really composed it, I just wrote it down. That's a fact![8]

It is an indication of the span and flexibility of Berg's compositional style that the Interlude, begun in 1914 and concluded in 1921, is one of the most memorable moments of the opera.

Figure 6.3: F 21 Berg 48, fol. 1r

The *Gesamtkunstwerk* nature of *Wozzeck* is also reflected in the timing of the stage curtain, which is played like an instrument throughout the opera. Berg even focuses on this aspect in an early sketch in his Büchner text showing the transition music at the end of Act III, scene 2, and Act III, scene 3 (Figure 6.6a, transcribed in Figure 6.6b). In Berg's initial solution to the dramatic postlude after Marie's murder, the B, which appears first in the middle voices of the orchestra and spreads out symmetrically to the higher and lower instruments, is sustained for ten measures rather than two blocks of five measures. It leads immediately to the rhythmic

Figure 6.4: F 21 Berg 13/I p. 31 (catalog #: 032)

Figure 6.5: F 21 Berg 13/I p. 35 (catalog #: 036)

motive of Act III, scene 3, played by the bass drum, which foreshadows the same rhythm played on the inn piano at the beginning of scene 3. Berg specifies in his diagram that the stage curtain will open on the first note of scene 3 (as it does in the final score) (Example 6.2). Berg further notes that the postlude to scene 3 (Inn

(a)

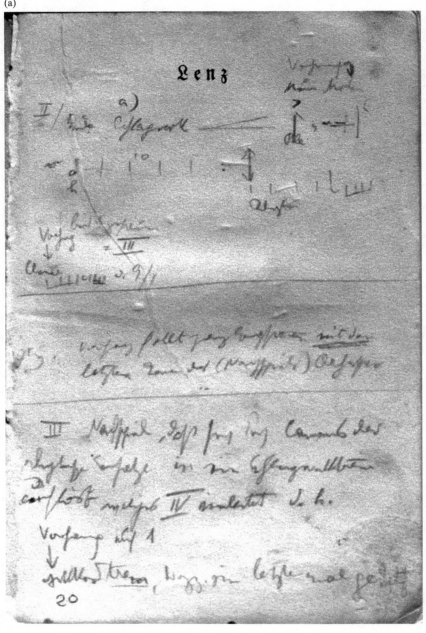

Figure 6.6: F 21 Berg 128 fol. 20ʳ (catalog #: 293)   *(continued)*

(b)

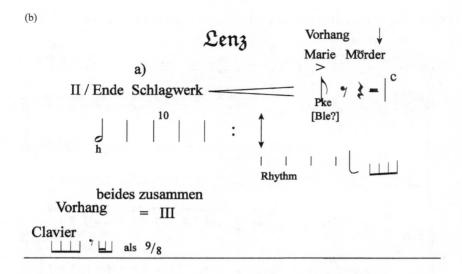

Vorhang sollt ganz engsten mit den
letzen Töne des (Nachspiels) Orchester

III. Nachspiel, das sich durch Canons der
rhythmische Einsätze in ein Schlagwerktrem
auflöst welches IV einleitet d. h.

Vorhang auf 1

Akkord trem, Wozz. zum letzten mal gehetzt

Figure 6.6: cont.

Scene), whose rhythmic canons dissolve into a drum roll, will use this element to
transition to the repeated hexachord at the beginning of the scene onto which the
curtain opens on beat 1. Berg writes, "Wozzeck zum letztenmal gehetzt" (Wozzeck
is hounded for the last time). In both of these instances, Berg uses a "pivot element,"
whether a rhythm, a pitch collection, or an articulation, to transition from the
scene itself, to the transition, and again to the next scene.

Example 6.2: Transition between Act III, scene 3 and Act III, scene 4

In a final fascinating sketch of large-scale form, Berg placed *Wozzeck* in the context of the remaining works he hoped to complete in his lifetime (Figure 6.7a, transcribed in Figure 6.7b). Labeled with opus numbers (which Berg discarded from *Wozzeck* on), this chart lists future compositions, including two more operas, through Opus 12. The three operas form a trilogy, "Die Drei W's": *Wozzeck, Vincent, and Wolfgang*, representing Knecht, Freund, and Herr (servant, friend, and gentleman). In true Bergian fashion, the second half of the central opera, *Vincent*, is the retrograde of its first half. Moreover, it features an orchestral interlude at its center, suggesting an idea that Berg would pursue in his second opera, *Lulu*. The subsidiary works that flank the central opera are both *a cappella* compositions, the first using a text by Berg's idol, Karl Kraus, and the second an *a cappella* choir, in retrograde. The final (subsidiary) work, Berg ominously labels "letztes Werk" (last work.) This gives a total of twelve opus numbers to Berg's life work, a number that by this time (1922) had attained significance far beyond the year in which Schoenberg composed *Pierrot Lunaire.* The total number of scenes for the three operas is a multiple of twelve (24). Finally, if we assign opus numbers to the major works Berg did complete, this number equals twelve as well.

(a)

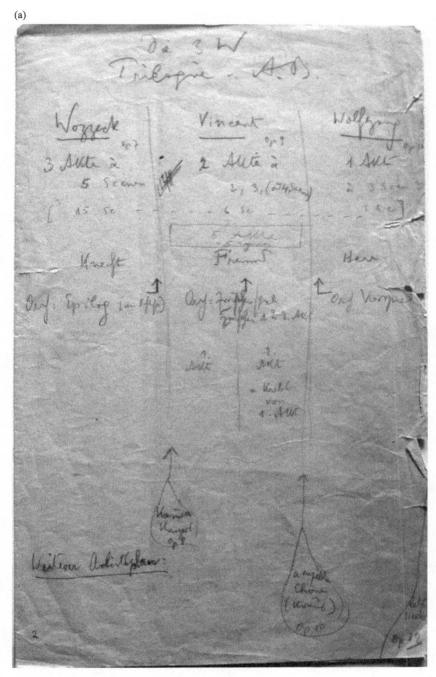

Figure 6.7: F 21 Berg 70/I fol. 2ʳ (catalog #: 200)   *(continued)*

(b)

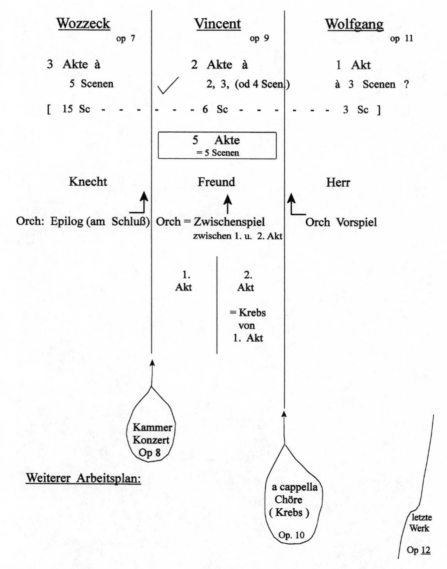

Die 3 W
Trilogué v. A. B.

<u>Wozzeck</u>   <u>Vincent</u>   <u>Wolfgang</u>

op 7   op 9   op 11

3 Akte à   2 Akte à   1 Akt

5 Scenen   2, 3, (od 4 Scen)   à 3 Scenen ?

[15 Sc - - - - - - 6 Sc - - - - - - 3 Sc]

5 Akte
= 5 Scenen

Knecht   Freund   Herr

Orch: Epilog (am Schluß)   Orch = Zwischenspiel   Orch Vorspiel
zwischen 1. u. 2. Akt

1.   2.
Akt   Akt

= Krebs
von
1. Akt

Kammer
Konzert
Op 8

<u>Weiterer Arbeitsplan:</u>

a cappella
Chöre
(Krebs)

Op. 10

letzte
Werk

Op 12

Figure 6.7: cont.

With this apparent episode of numerology we end this chapter and begin our final chapter, which deals in contrast, with the smallest level of organization, the various pitch structures indicated and analyzed in Berg's sketches for *Wozzeck*.

CHAPTER Seven

"Berg war Analysen freundlich gesinnt:"
Analyses of Pitch Structure in the Sketches for Wozzeck

Berg was well disposed toward analysis. His characteristically painstaking analyses of Schoenberg's works, of *Gurrelieder, Pelleas und Melisande*, and the First Chamber Symphony, were completed as a young man. Though published, they are not nearly as well known as they deserve to be; in particular, the analysis of the Chamber Symphony, a work that remains difficult even today, can be considered exemplary; a collected edition would be worthwhile.[1]

—Theodor Adorno

In the introduction to his chapter "Analysis and Berg," Adorno urges us to become acquainted with Berg's other persona: the music analyst. And although Adorno cites as evidence Berg's published analyses, Berg's jottings in his scores of Schoenberg's atonal works are equally insightful, particularly in the compositional techniques he had adopted in *Wozzeck*. Berg's heavily annotated score for *Pierrot Lunaire* (frequently cited by Berg as a model for *Wozzeck*) elucidates not only its forms and canonic devices, but also the more subtle techniques by which Schoenberg created motivic variation (Figure 7.1). Here, Berg's analysis of the final measures of "Nacht" shows how the network of transpositions of the initial three-note motive (E-G-E-flat) express a subsidiary chromatic motive that is used throughout the movement (Example 7.1). Similarly, in measures 8–9 he shows how the same three-note motive is defined by the contours of the vocal line (D-F-D-flat) (Example 7.2). In measure 12, Berg identifies how the successive transpositions of the motive (on E, G, and E-flat) express it on a higher structural plane (Example 7.3).

In Berg's score of Schoenberg's *Erwartung*, in contrast, he focuses on how the orchestra reflects subtle nuances of the Pappenheim text. Berg divides these depictions into two categories at the beginning of his analysis: "Impress[ionistic] Klänge" (impressionistic sounds), written in red colored pencil, and "Expression[istic] Themen" (expressionistic themes), written in blue colored pencil.[2] He then appropriately color-codes his annotations of the score so that red annotations are musical references to physical objects or events, while blue annotations reflect emotional

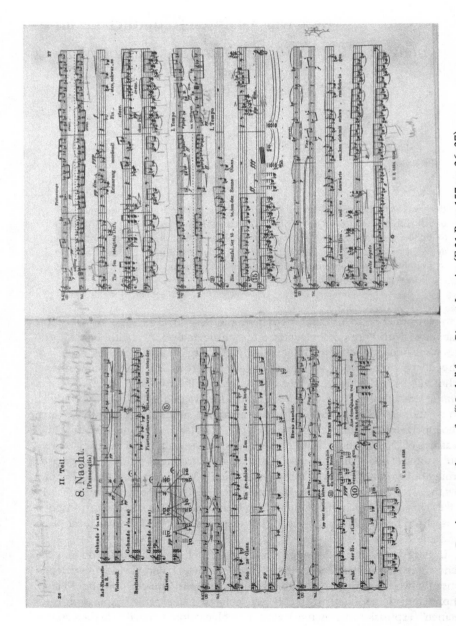

Figure 7.1: Berg's annotated score for "Nacht" from *Pierrot Lunaire* (F 21 Berg 157 pp. 26–27)

Example 7.1: Berg's network of transpositions of the three-note motive from "Nacht."

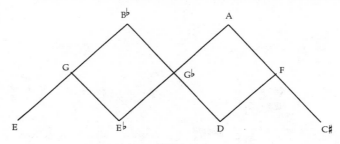

Example 7.2: Berg's analysis of measures 8–9 of "Nacht."

Example 7.3: Berg's analysis of the large-scale expression of the motive E-G-E-flat of measure 12 of "Nacht"

states. For instance, in the heavily annotated page of the score leading to the third scene (Figure 7.2), "Stamm" (trunk), "Licht" (light), "Schatten" (shadow), "Mond" (moon), and "tanzt etwas" (something dances) are annotated with red pencil. (Berg even differentiates the sonorities; for instance, Licht is D-F-C-E-G-B, Schatten is D-F-B-A-G-sharp, and Mond is D-E-C-E-flat.) The emotional states, annotated in blue, are "Andeutung des weitergehens des innern Geschehens" (indication of the continuation of the inner state), "ängstlich" (anxiously), and, on the following page, "sofort beherrscht" (immediately in command of [her emotions]).

Figure 7.2: Berg's annotated copy of *Erwartung*, measures 86–94 (F 21 Berg 156 p. 12)

Berg makes further indications of instrumentation in measure 88, notes on the emergence of light (measures 87–89) from the annotation in measure 87, "irgend etwas" (something or other) to "kommt Licht" (light comes) and "Erklärung" (explanation) measure 89. In general, the micro-timing of natural phenomena in this example, as well as the anxiety provoked by imagined events, recalls Act II, scene 2 of *Wozzeck* (Waldweg am Teich) or even Act I, scene 2 (freies Feld).

Finally, Berg bared his analytical persona about his own compositions to concert audiences in his pre-concert talks on *Wozzeck*, suggesting that, for him, even composition was an analytical experience.[3] We have already seen many examples of Berg's analyses of formal devices in *Wozzeck* that produce coherence, the primary topic of his presentations. But Berg also completed many analyses of pitch structure in his sketches that would have been too complex for a concert audience. Berg's palette of pitch structures in *Wozzeck* extends from debilitated tonality, to atonality, to serial writing, which, like orchestral color, he could select depending on the needs of the dramatic moment. Tonality and serial writing, the two extremes of Berg's palette, are more closed compositional systems than atonality: the resolution of a V7 chord, or the continuation of a serial ostinato requires more finite choices than atonality. The relative strictness of these mediums also required pre-compositional planning in the form of analytical sketches. In this chapter we shall study these sketches, following the evolution of Berg's compositional style established in Chapters 2–3.

Berg's initial analyses in the sketches show his experiments with tonality—not only in the folk idioms that he infuses with a kind of fractured tonality, allowing us to perceive a Ländler, a lullaby, or a march, but often in passages that analysts have treated as atonal. In Berg's first sketchbook for *Wozzeck*, a section dating from 1918 shows him working on the opening of Act I, scene 2 (Wozzeck and Andres in the field) (Figure 7.3a and its transcription, Figure 7.3b). In the center of the sketch, Berg experiments with a wedge formation that converges on E-flat in the bass. He makes the annotation, "Es (moll)" and then "Es dur und moll mit unaufgelösten d" (E-flat major and minor with unresolved D.") The sketch and Berg's annotation reveal two ideas about Berg's concept of atonality in this passage of the opera. First, he is working with a defined collection of notes—E-flat major combined with E-flat minor. Second, he consciously experiments with unresolved tendency tones within this collection—here, scale degree seven. These tendency tones act as a tonal foil for the collection, giving rise to the unsettling, unresolved quality we associate with atonal music.

Even though modal mixture of major and minor is a common tonal technique, it implies a large collection of notes: ten to be exact. How, then, did Berg establish E-flat as a tonal center? In the sketch, E-flat appears as a sustained bass note—a tonic, that is approached by a skeleton of a V7 chord in the lower two voices (B-flat, A-flat). This suggests one final and very crucial idea about Berg's concept of atonality: that it relies on hierarchy. Berg emphasized primary notes of a key, such as scale degrees one and five, while leaving tendency tones unresolved.

One sees this same technique so frequently in *Wozzeck* that it becomes almost a formula by which Berg balanced the emotional malaise of atonality with the expressiveness of tonality. For instance, in a sketch for Act III, scene 1, where Marie, overcome with remorse, reads passages from the Bible describing Christ's forgiveness of Mary Magdalene, Berg emphasizes the pitch B-natural, even though he labels the passage F minor in his sketches and gives it the corresponding key signature in the score (Figure 7.4). This B-natural acts as a tonal foil, similar to the unresolved leading tone in the previous sketch, and also reflects Marie's state of psychological anguish. (Later in the opera it will become the symbol of her murder.) This sympathy extends to Berg's psychoanalysis of her as well: Berg spares her the

(a)

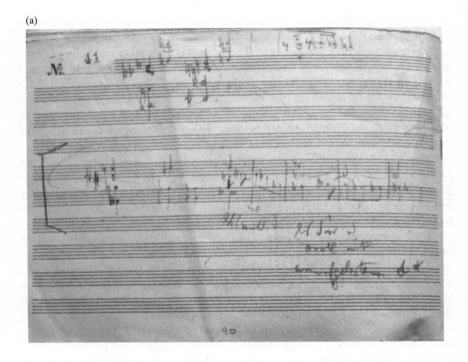

(b)

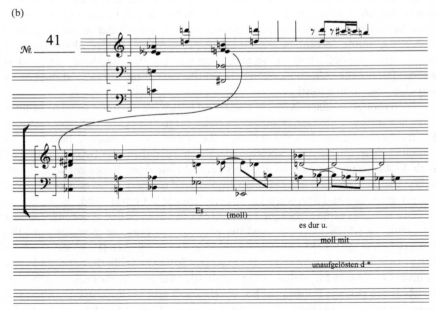

Figure 7.3: F 21 Berg 13/II p. 90 (catalog #: 083)

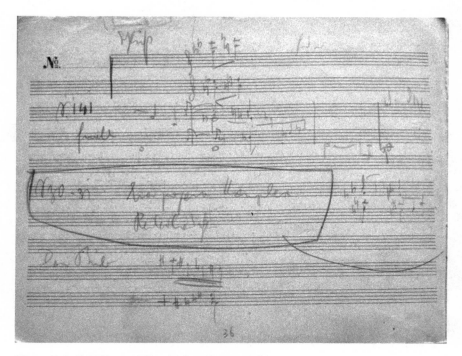

Figure 7.4: F 21 Berg 13/I p. 36 (catalog #: 037)

Example 7.4: Act II, scene 4, measures 589–90

scathing descriptions given to the Captain, the Doctor, and the Drum Major, noting only her sensuality and passivity.[4]

In the E-flat minor passage of the Tavern Scene of Act II, scene 4, Berg applies both techniques: the leading tone, D, becomes the goal of the passage rather than the tonic, and Berg again raises scale degree four as a tonal foil. The repeating E-flat minor triads, however, assure that the key is established so that it can then be deflected (Example 7.4).

Figure 7.5: F 21 Berg 70/I fol. 9ʳ (catalog #: 205)

In the following sketch, also likely completed in 1918, Berg experiments with a voice leading that is reminiscent of many passages from Hugo Wolf's songs. Berg comments, "in einigen Takten Auflösung dieser Quint g-c nach oben!" (within a number of measures the resolution of this fifth g-c above!). Berg's G-C pedal appearing in the bass clef, which foils the A-flat major tonality appearing above it, resolves over the course of three measures to a G-major triad in a different register. However, by the time C has resolved via C-sharp to the root, G, the other voices have moved to a different harmony (Figure 7.5). We could compare this gradual resolution to Wolf's "Mir ward gesagt"; Deborah Stein has described its "staggered resolution technique," in which "the overall effect . . . is a discontinuity between treble and bass, in which the clearest harmonic progression is undermined by melodic dissonance and the melodic motion is often disconnected from its expected harmonic support. As a result, the vocal line often sounds unstable and unfocused, and this aptly mirrors the anxiety and confusion in the text."[5]

By the following summer (1919), Berg was implementing serial ordering, but in a more comprehensive fashion than it appeared in the *Altenberg Lieder*. The row used in the Doctor's scene, Act I, scene 4, shows a peculiar genesis; written note by note (with some revision) in Berg's copy of his Büchner text (Figure 7.6). It would seem that Berg had established E-flat (alias S for Schoenberg) as the reference tone of his opera by 1918. Further, the genesis of Berg's twelve-tone theme may have been similarly related to significant numerology

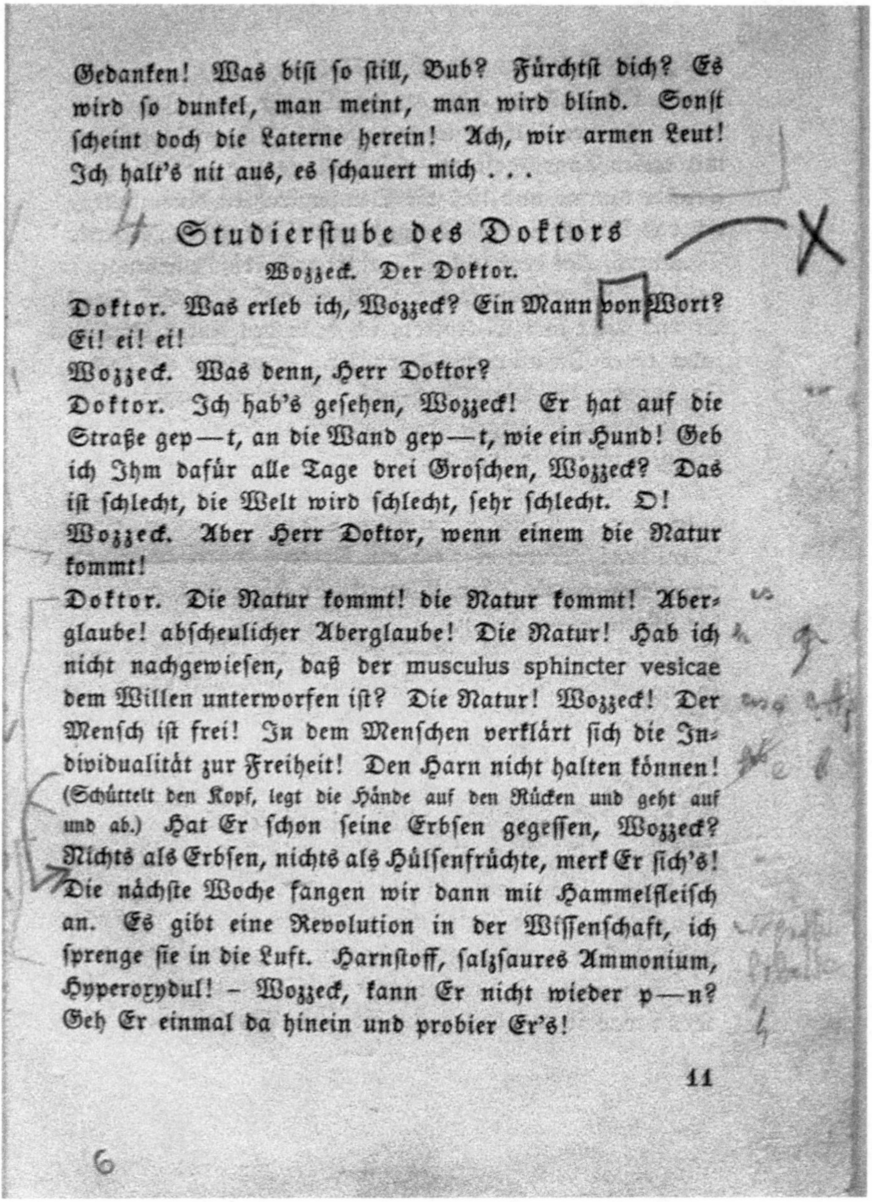

Gedanken! Was bist so still, Bub? Fürchtst dich? Es wird so dunkel, man meint, man wird blind. Sonst scheint doch die Laterne herein! Ach, wir armen Leut! Ich halt's nit aus, es schauert mich . . .

Studierstube des Doktors
Wozzeck. Der Doktor.

Doktor. Was erleb ich, Wozzeck? Ein Mann von Wort? Ei! ei! ei!

Wozzeck. Was denn, Herr Doktor?

Doktor. Ich hab's gesehen, Wozzeck! Er hat auf die Straße gep—t, an die Wand gep—t, wie ein Hund! Geb ich Ihm dafür alle Tage drei Groschen, Wozzeck? Das ist schlecht, die Welt wird schlecht, sehr schlecht. O!

Wozzeck. Aber Herr Doktor, wenn einem die Natur kommt!

Doktor. Die Natur kommt! die Natur kommt! Aberglaube! abscheulicher Aberglaube! Die Natur! Hab ich nicht nachgewiesen, daß der musculus sphincter vesicae dem Willen unterworfen ist? Die Natur! Wozzeck! Der Mensch ist frei! In dem Menschen verklärt sich die Individualität zur Freiheit! Den Harn nicht halten können! (Schüttelt den Kopf, legt die Hände auf den Rücken und geht auf und ab.) Hat Er schon seine Erbsen gegessen, Wozzeck? Nichts als Erbsen, nichts als Hülsenfrüchte, merk Er sich's! Die nächste Woche fangen wir dann mit Hammelfleisch an. Es gibt eine Revolution in der Wissenschaft, ich sprenge sie in die Luft. Harnstoff, salzsaures Ammonium, Hyperoxydul! – Wozzeck, kann Er nicht wieder p—n? Geh Er einmal da hinein und probier Er's!

11

Figure 7.6: F 21 Berg 128 fol. 6ʳ (catalog #: 265)

(the twelve of *Pierrot*'s date, 1912) rather than a twelve-tone row, per se. In his sketches in planning for the Doctor's scene, Berg is using the number twelve on multiple structural levels, just as he employed the number three in the second scene he composed, Act I, scene 2 (Freies Feld). Berg has divided his text into

dunkel is und nur noch ein roter Schein im Westen, wie von einer Esse, an was soll man sich da halten? (Schreitet im Zimmer auf und ab.)

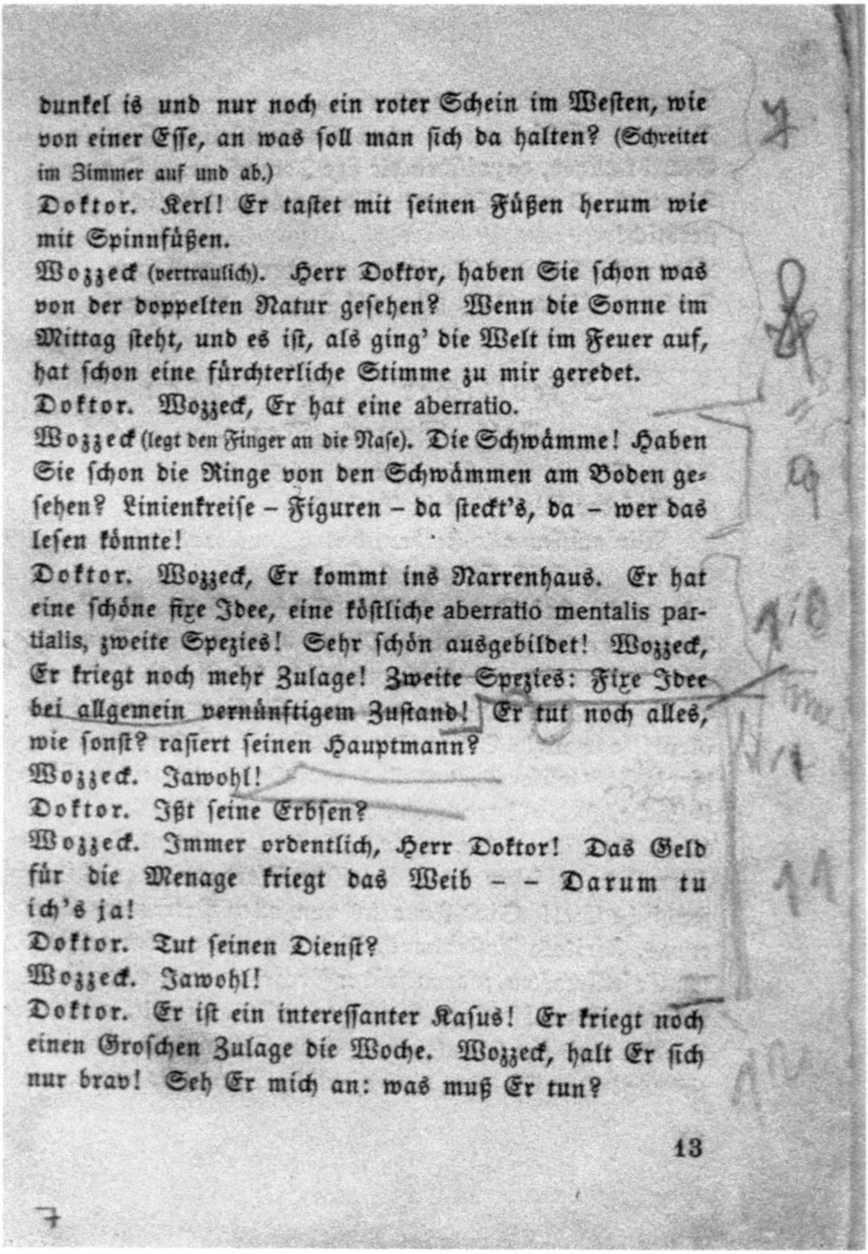

Doktor. Kerl! Er tastet mit seinen Füßen herum wie mit Spinnfüßen.

Wozzeck (vertraulich). Herr Doktor, haben Sie schon was von der doppelten Natur gesehen? Wenn die Sonne im Mittag steht, und es ist, als ging' die Welt im Feuer auf, hat schon eine fürchterliche Stimme zu mir geredet.

Doktor. Wozzeck, Er hat eine aberratio.

Wozzeck (legt den Finger an die Nase). Die Schwämme! Haben Sie schon die Ringe von den Schwämmen am Boden gesehen? Linienkreise – Figuren – da steckt's, da – wer das lesen könnte!

Doktor. Wozzeck, Er kommt ins Narrenhaus. Er hat eine schöne fixe Idee, eine köstliche aberratio mentalis partialis, zweite Spezies! Sehr schön ausgebildet! Wozzeck, Er kriegt noch mehr Zulage! Zweite Spezies: Fixe Idee bei allgemein vernünftigem Zustand! Er tut noch alles, wie sonst? rasiert seinen Hauptmann?

Wozzeck. Jawohl!

Doktor. Ißt seine Erbsen?

Wozzeck. Immer ordentlich, Herr Doktor! Das Geld für die Menage kriegt das Weib – – Darum tu ich's ja!

Doktor. Tut seinen Dienst?

Wozzeck. Jawohl!

Doktor. Er ist ein interessanter Kasus! Er kriegt noch einen Groschen Zulage die Woche. Wozzeck, halt Er sich nur brav! Seh Er mich an: was muß Er tun?

13

Figure 7.7: F 21 Berg 128 fol. 7ʳ (catalog #: 267)

twelve, rather than twenty-one variations, based on the minute shifts in topic during the Doctor's obsessive tirade (Figure 7.7). It is unfortunate that as of yet there are no compositional sketches of this scene that might illuminate its correspondingly complex rhythmic durations.[6]

Berg's penchant for numerology, and specifically that reflecting *Pierrot Lunaire*, is so encompassing in *Wozzeck* that it even reflects the total pitch content of later themes. We might cast a suspicious eye at passages utilizing three, or even twelve pitches. But twenty-one, the number of movements in *Pierrot*, and seven, the

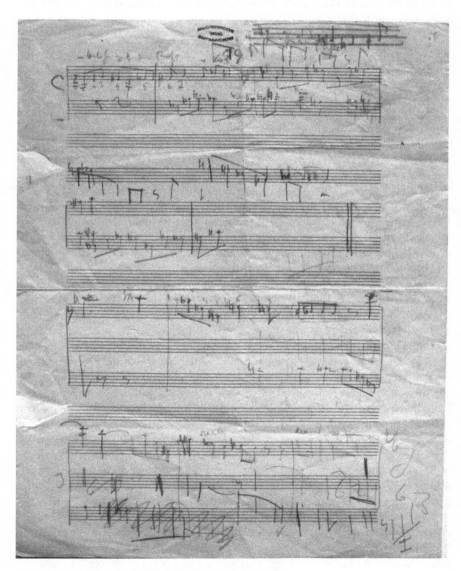

Figure 7.8: F 21 Berg 13/XIV fol. 2ᵛ (catalog #: 195)

number of movements in each act, is so improbable, that like Berg's Es symbolism, there can be little doubt. A glance at the score for Act II, scene 4, and Act III, scene 1, both composed in 1920, clearly show Berg's expression of the number seven in his meters, the number of variations, and total pitch content of themes. In Berg's sketch of the fugue for Act III, scene 1, he numbers each different pitch of the subject, totaling, of course, seven. The contrasting theme, "Heiland, ich möchte Dir die Füße salben," is also numbered 1–7 (Figure 7.8). These same themes appear in the opening of the scene, discussed in the previous chapter, as well as a twelve-note theme in the 'cellos and contrabasses that matches the appoggiatura-like character of the seven-note theme it accompanies.

Example 7.5: Petersen's "scheme #2"

I/1 T. 147, Solo Vl.	C	E	G	B	D	F	Gis	H	Dis	Fis	A	Cis
2. Zwölftonterzakkord	4	3	3	4	3	3	3	4	3	3	4	

Petersen has analyzed passages from Act I, scene 1, the final scene Berg completed in the summer of 1919, that reveal a twelve-tone content.[7] But rather than through a "horizontal" twelve-tone theme, as in Act I, scene 4, this is accomplished through various chord series, for example, Petersen's "Schema Nr. 2" featured in the solo 'cello of measure 147, in which the total content of the chords equals twelve pitches (Example 7.5). In one instance in the sketches for Act I, scene 1 (measures 151–153 beat 2) "Ich glaub' wenn wir in den Himmel kämen, so müßten wir donnern helfen!" (I believe if we went to Heaven, we'd have to help make thunder!), in which the accented triads portray the thunder, Berg appears to be taking stock of the total pitch content of the chord series, which he analyzes by quality (major, minor, diminished, augmented) as well (Figure 7.9).

Early in Berg's compositional summer of 1920, he presents Schoenberg with a chart, carefully completed in ink, of arrays of interval cycles generated by one through eleven semitones (Figure 7.10). This chart, first discovered by George Perle, consists of rows of successively larger melodic intervals which Berg has labeled in the left-hand margin: minor second, major second, minor third, major third, etc. The columns of the chart form the same interval series and are labeled by Berg at the bottom of a chart, in a diagram which also shows (with arrows) the equal division of the octave into minor thirds (top of diagram) and the inversional relationship of the intervals (the minor second is connected to the major seventh, the major second to the minor seventh, etc.) This same diagram is duplicated in the right-hand margin of the chart, under which Berg specifies, "Every single voice gives in the vertical the same chord" emphasizing the dual property of interval cycles: each horizontal is paired with a vertical column that expresses the same interval (Example 7.6).

Discovered "by chance" while composing his opera, Berg tactfully dismisses his discovery as "a theoretical trifle."[8] Perle cites only one instance of Berg's discovery: the two-beat passage in Act II, scene 3 in which Wozzeck describes Marie's infidelity as "a sin so thick and wide, it must stink enough to smoke the angels out of Heaven."[9] Composed that same summer, the passage features the simultaneous statements of interval cycles of one through four semitones played by a solo 'cello, viola, clarinet, and oboe (Example 7.6). Citing the passage as an example of word painting, Perle explains:

> But a closer inspection of the passage will reveal a more subtle analogy between music and words than the conventional one that associates the idea of ascension with rising musical patterns. Ignoring for the moment the solo violin part, we note that each of the remaining instruments fills the span between

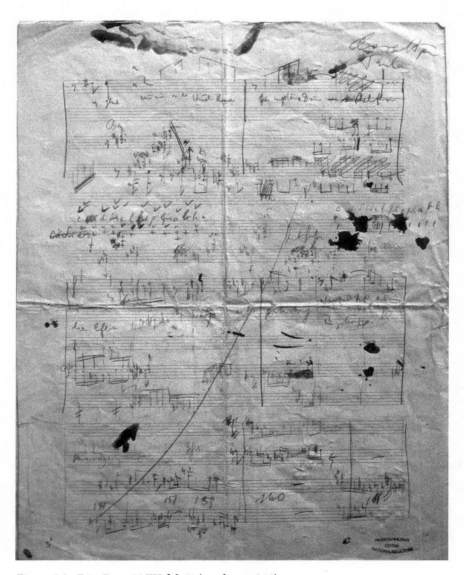

Figure 7.9: F 21 Berg 70/III fol. 5ᵛ (catalog #: 241)

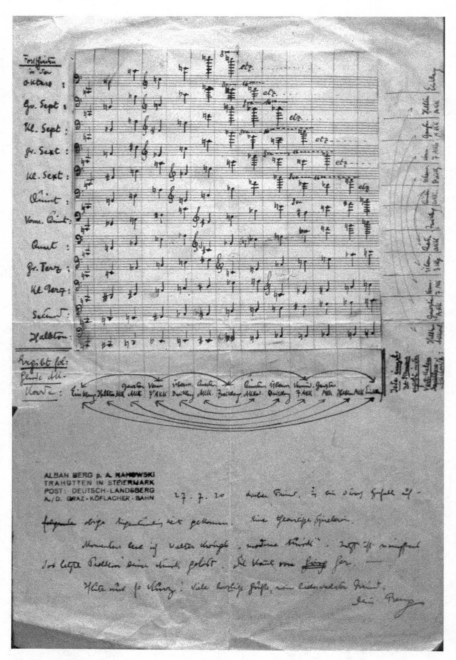

Figure 7.10: LOC1 (catalog #: 532)

Example 7.6: George Perle, Interval cycles in Act II, scene 3

the first and last notes of the figure assigned to it with successions of a single interval—of 1, 2, 3, and 4 semitones, respectively. The simultaneities are likewise uni-intervallic structures, successively generated by intervals of 0, 1, 2, 3, 4, 5, 6, and 7 semitones. Thus, commencing from the unison, each instrument progresses in a straight and "perfect" line to the final simultaneity, a four-note segment of the circle of perfect fifths. The solo violin part, representing Marie's sin rising to heaven, spoils the otherwise "perfect" design in its weaving and irregular ascent and in its interpolation of the "wrong" note into each of the simultaneities after the initial unison."[10]

If this short passage were the only example of interval cycles in *Wozzeck*, we might agree with Berg's modest assessment. The sketches, however, tell a very different story. A sketch of interval cycles, in preparation for the one in ink he sent in his letter of July 27 to Schoenberg, gives us additional insights into their properties (Figure 7.11). At the top of the sketch, (staves 1–3) Berg has connected intervals that divide the octave into symmetries—either an interval and its inversion, the minor third, or the minor thirds flanking a tritone. In his third diagram, most resembling the one in ink he sent to Schoenberg, Berg writes out the beginnings

Figure 7.11: F 21 Berg 70/III fol. 11ᵛ (catalog #: 253)

of each interval cycle, pairing the minor and major second, the minor and major third, etc., to save space. Note how even in a sketch, Berg meticulously retains the vertical alignments between interval series, demonstrating that successive pitch cycles replicate their pitch content both horizontally and vertically. Both dimensions, the horizontal and vertical, are critical to Berg's concept of interval cycles.

Unless Berg grafted passages utilizing his new discovery onto previously composed sections of *Wozzeck*, we would expect these passages, based on our study of the chronology of the opera, to be concentrated in Act II, scene 3

Figure 7.12: F 21 Berg 28/XXXVII fol. 14ᵛ (catalog #: 196)

through the remainder of the opera. Moreover, after expressing an interval cycle in its simplest form, we would expect Berg to progressively refine these statements, perhaps incorporating other parameters like rhythm and dynamics. In fact, in another sketch from the same summer, Berg has written a matrix of cyclic permutations of the number four in the left-hand margin (Figure 7.12):

Example 7.7: Summary of pitch content for measures 465–467

465	466	467
A A A G	G G $F^\#$ $F^\#$	$F^\#$ F F F
E E F F	F E^b E^b E^b	E^b E^b E^b E^b
D D^b D^b D^b	D^b D^b D^b D^b	D D D B^b
$F^\#$ $F^\#$ $F^\#$ $F^\#$	C C C G	G G A A
(4123)	*(3412)*	*(2341)*

12341

2341

3412

4123

Note that the successive rows as well as columns state the next cyclic per-mutation of the series: 1 2 3 4, 2 3 4 1, 3 4 1 2, and, finally, 4 1 2 3. The musical relevance becomes clear in Berg's sketch (on the same leaf) of mea-sures 465–467 of Act II, scene 4, the tavern scene. The pitch content of mea-sures 465–467 is summarized in Example 7.7. Counting the number of beats per measure before each voice arrives on a new pitch (in the order, bass to soprano) we see the following durations: In measure 465, 4 1 2 3; in measure 466, 3 4 1 2; and in measure 467, 2 3 4 1. (In the score Berg emphasizes musi-cally the arrival of each of these new pitches with a crescendo and *fp* accent.) These durations, of course, duplicate the fourth, third, and second row of the chart, while simultaneously maintaining the vertical order of the columns. The durations guarantee that only one voice will shift to a new pitch within a single beat. Thus, they are both in theory and their musical employment, the equivalent of Berg's interval cycles. We can contrast this almost mathematical control of the harmonic parameter with the sketch discussed above from Act I, scene 2 from 1918 in which the voice leading is entirely dependent on tonal parameters.

This passage in Act 2, scene 4 is preceded by two ostinati passages, (Examples 7.8 and 7.9). As described by Perle, these ostinati, with total dura-tions of eight eighth-notes and nine eighth-notes each, shift systematically to the next eighth-note, either forward or backward in the measure, until they return to the original metric position.[11] Thus, they also conform to Berg's numerical matrix, which is expandable to include more than four elements and can progress from top to bottom, or bottom to top, depending on whether the ostinati move systematically one beat forward or one beat backward in the measure. The following matrix, for example, illustrates Berg's ostinato with the duration of nine eighth-notes (Example 7.9, measures 456–467) moving progressively one eighth-note forward in a 4/4 meter until it reaches its original position. In the matrix, the boxes represent each ostinato statement and the numbers the metric placement of each eighth-note within the consecutive

Example 7.8: Ostinato, Act II, scene 4, measures 447–451

Example 7.9: Ostinato, Act II, scene 4, measures 456–457

4/4 measures. The first ostinato statement begins on the first eighth-note of the measure, the second ostinato statement on the second eighth-note of the measure, etc.

123456781

234567812

345678123

456781234

567812345

678123456

781234567

812345678

Our discussion of the ostinati has thus far been based on their rhythmic structure and behavior within the surrounding meter. Their pitch content is also regulated, however, and can either coincide with the rhythmic statements or partially intersect. In Berg's only detailed sketch of the chord series that

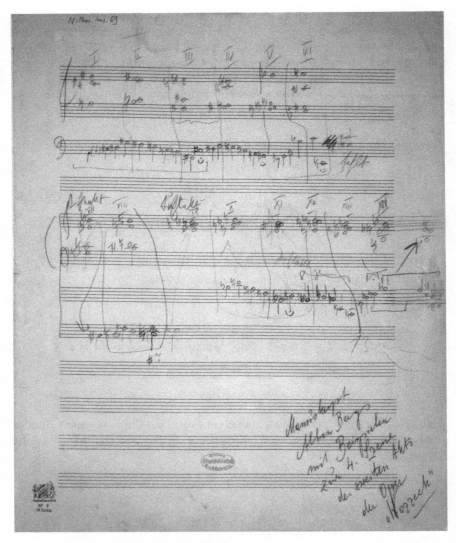

Figure 7.13: N Mus MS 69 fol. 1ʳ (catalog #: 517)

inhabits the ostinati of measures 456–464 (Figure 7.13) he does not reveal how the pitches themselves were generated, but rather how the fifteen-chord series (another reference to Schoenberg's Chamber Symphony) is utilized as a melody beginning in measure 608 (Example 7.10). Clearly, as Perle has described, Berg was using a chorale-like texture to mimic the Apprentice's grotesque drunken sermon. In Berg's sketches he describes him as "psalmadierend" (psalmadizing).[12]

Example 7.10: Act II, scene 4, measures 602–608

*) Die (durchwegs vom Bombardon gespielte) Choralmelodie ist durch besonders dicke Noten gekennzeichnet.

U. E. 7382

In the first ostinato discussed above (measures 447–453) the chords conform to the ostinati, neatly expressing two chords of four notes each in the space of a single ostinato (Example 7.8). In the second passage, however, Berg develops the relationship between rhythm and pitch by creating other patterns for the chord segments that intersect those of the ostinato. In this sketch for the passage (Figure 7.14), Berg not only indicates the beginning and end of each ostinato

Figure 7.14: F 21 Berg 13/V fol. 2ʳ (catalog #: 125)

statement with brackets, but he also numbers the members of the chord series from one to fifteen, allowing him to see the interaction of the two parameters. If we graph out the arrival of each of the fifteen chords within the ten rhythmic elements, or attacks of the ostinato (Example 7.11), we see the following interaction: After two initial statements in which the two parameters correspond exactly, Berg displaces the next two chordal statement by three elements (8–8),

Example 7.11: Interaction of pitch and rhythm, Act II, scene 2, measures 456–467

♪ ♪ ♪ ♪ ♪. ♪ ♪ ♪ ♪ ♪ ♩

①2 3 4 5 6 7 8 9 10
①2 3 4 5 6 7⑧9 10
1 2 3 4 5 6 7⑧9 10
1 2 3 4 5 6 7 8 9 ⑩
①2 3 4 5 6 7 8⑨10
①2 3 4 5 6 7⑧9 10
①2 3 4 5 6⑦8 9 10
①2 3 4 5⑥7⑧9 10
①

then begins a pattern alternating between a successively earlier arrival and a corresponding arrival (10–1–9–1–8–1–7–1–6) at which point he returns to the earlier statements displaced by three elements (8–8).

Berg extends these pitch/rhythm experiments in his last summer of composition, 1921, richly documented in his final sketchbook for the opera. The ostinati that end the scene are formulaic in nature: the number of measures that completes each ostinato determines the number of notes in the next pattern. (They are clearly examples of the "ostinati machines" coined by Derrick Puffett.)[13] Moreover, the ostinati have become so complex that Berg uses variables to represent their pitch content. For instance, the nine-note ostinato beginning measure 713 (F-sharp, G-sharp, B-flat, G, E, B, D, C-sharp, D-sharp, F-sharp) is notated with the variables, a b c d e f g h i a, with the "a" at the end indicating a repetition of the first melodic element (Figure 7.15). Placed in one of Berg's grids, we can more clearly see the interaction of pitch and meter. Example 7.12 shows the five-note ostinato of measures 697–703 (E, B-flat, A-flat, F-sharp, G,), in which the first note of each new statement replicates the original pitches of the ostinato, and each variable retains its original metric position in successive statements. Note that these successive statements produce a mirror image centered on the pitch A, the original element of the ositinato. Not only, as both Perle and Jarman have discussed, does Berg emphasize the symmetry of the entire scene by repeating entire ostinati in retrograde in the second half, but in this case, the ostinato itself is symmetrical, reflecting once more Berg's penchant for organic offshoots, or the replication of motivic shapes on different structural levels.[14]

The raucous choir of Soldiers and Apprentices is constructed similarly. In 7/4, using a seven-note theme, each vocal line adds another pitch until the total verticality equals the complete melodic statement (Example 7.13). In Berg's draft

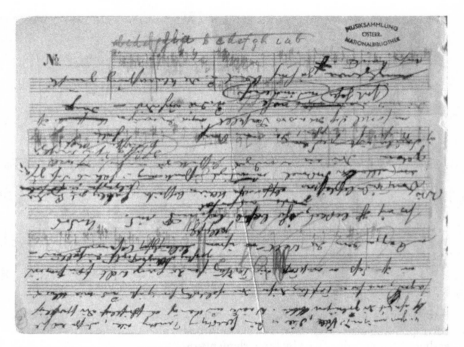

Figure 7.15: F 21 Berg 13/VII fol. 2ᵛ (catalog #: 146)

Example 7.12: Ostinato, Act II, scene 4, measures 697–703 expressed in variable notation

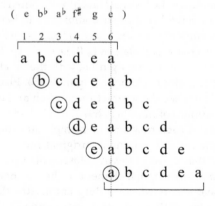

of this passage, which contain text changes based on the Witkowski edition of *Woyzeck*, Berg meticulously notates this accumulation of voices, along with measure numbers that are only one measure off compared to the final score (Figure 7.16). In the second half of his draft, Berg reverses the direction of the melodic pattern (down instead of up) and the function of the voices: they

Example 7.13: Act II, scene 4, measures 560–565

accumulate pitches from the top voice down, rather than from the bottom voice up (Example 7.14).

In his sketches of Act III, scene 4, Berg extends the concept of cyclic permutation to include simultaneous sonorities. In the sketch shown in Figure 7.17, Berg has written out twelve transpositions of the hexachord that is the basis of this scene, "Invention on a chord." Berg extracts chords by cyclically permuting the series of transpositions, a technique that would foreshadow the cyclically permuted rows for his opera *Lulu.* Berg makes the annotation in the center of the sketch, "Ganze Welt. Die 12 Akkorde in allen möglichen unregelmäßigen Einsätzen" (Whole world. The 12 chords in all possible unordered entrances). This refers to the text of Act III, scene 4, in which Wozzeck, searching for the knife with which he killed Marie, cries, "Will die ganze Welt es ausplaudern?" (Will the whole world tell everything?) (Example 7.15). In a similar moment in Act III, scene 2, at Marie's death, Berg used five canonic entrances of a twelve-note row using progressively smaller durations of entrance (five, four, three, and two quarter notes) to reflect the immediacy of Marie's murder (Example 7.16). This also results in a progressively larger vertical accumulation of the sonorities of the row.

In a draft of the end of Act III, scene 4, as the Captain and Doctor walk by the pond, the Captain says, "It's the water in the pond. The water is calling. No one has drowned for a long time." Berg notates cycling of the hexachord in interval cycles, first of perfect fourths, major thirds, minor thirds, etc. reflecting not only the gradual change of cycle, but also the interacting change in tempo

Figure 7.16: F 21 Berg 13/VI fol. 1ᵛ (catalog #: 134)

(Figure 7.18). One could view this section as a chromatic cycle regulated by a gradual de-acceleration.

In the final measures of Act III, scene 4, featuring the descending celeste figures, Berg again takes up the idea of the hexachord, but as an ordering of six elements, which he rotates using transpositions that allow the note "C" to arrive in different order positions. In the sketch (Figure 7.19) these are marked "6, 4, 2, and in retrograde form, 2, 1." In the passage itself, Berg uses rotations beginning on 1, 4, and in retrograde, 4, 2 (Example 7.17).

Example 7.14: Act II, scene 4, measures 581–586

Act III, scene 3, the Tavern Scene, is based almost entirely on imitative entrances of a rhythmic motive, expressed, yet again, as a seven-note theme. Berg's sketches for the scene are remarkable in their complexity, the result of specific operations, including multiple displacements (*verschiebungen*), and what Berg defines as inversion, applied to the initial rhythmic figure. If we rearrange the leaves based on the original ordering of this gathering, we see the genesis and evolution of some of the more complex operations. For instance, in the sketch shown in Figure 7.19 (transcribed in Figure 7.19b), Berg takes the initial canonic statement, "Blut, Blut, freilich, Blut" displaced by consecutive divisions

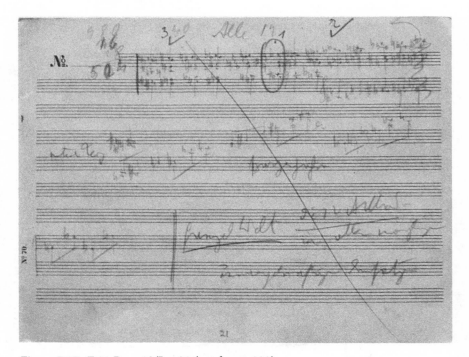

Figure 7.17: F 21 Berg 13/I p. 21 (catalog #: 022)

of the original two-beat entrance: one beat, one half beat, one fourth beat, etc. In a second sketch (Figure 7.20), which Berg labels inversion (on a horizontal axis?), Berg expresses the rhythm in retrograde. It is probably a similar operation that produces the durations of the haunting open fifths that conclude the opera, a word-painting device since Hugo Wolf for emptiness and isolation, and another reminder of not only the cyclic nature of the opera, but also the unending cycle of oppression, now replicated in a younger generation.

∞

In his introduction to the Bruckner Festival of September 2005, speaking of "how the new comes into the world," the physicist Anton Zeilinger claimed it is "not through deduction. Planck's, Einstein's and Schrödinger's discoveries in no way follow from what one knew before."[15] Berg's compositional discoveries in 1920 at first seem so mechanized and formulaic that they appear to have arisen spontaneously rather than from pre-existing compositional methods. Certainly Berg experimented with ostinati and twelve-tone collections as early as the *Altenberg Lieder*, a work we studied in Chapter 1 as a precursor

Example 7.15: Act II, scene 4, measures 268–272

to *Wozzeck*. The idea of horizontal space equaling that of a vertical one—the end result of interval cycles—is also a tenet expressed by Schoenberg in his *Harmonielehre* of 1911. It is the overwhelming frequency of these devices and finite relation to their precursor in *Wozzeck* that makes them different from earlier compositional methods. Yet, only the "informed" listener would hear a shift in compositional method. In this sense, Berg's "link" between the two compositional systems is as finessed as his transitions between scenes, discussed in Chapter 4.

Example 7.16: Act III, scene 2, measures 97–98

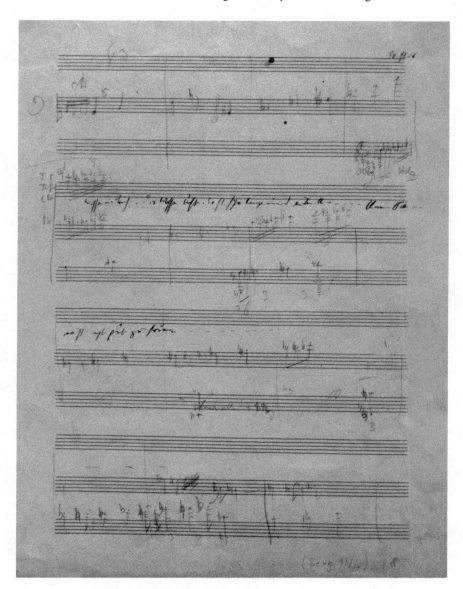

Figure 7.18:   F 21 Berg 13/IV fol. 8ʳ (catalog #: 113)

What is perhaps most impressive about Berg's compositional innovations in the later part of *Wozzeck* is that, as programmed as they are, they in no way distract from the drama, in fact, they perfectly complement the dramatic events that are portrayed. This dramatic priority is also expressed in Berg's sketches; as we observed in the previous chapter, Berg's first compositional act was to identify the

Example 7.17: Rotation of hexachord elements in Act III, scene 4, measures 306–307

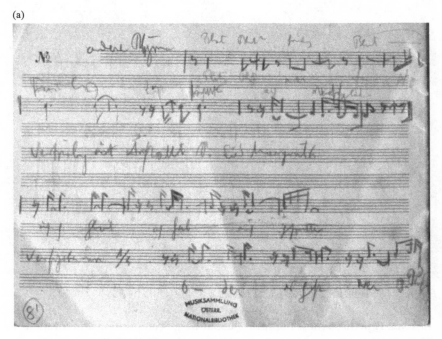

(a)

Figure 7.19: F 21 Berg 13/VII fol. 8ᵛ (catalog #: 158)   (*continued*)

(b)

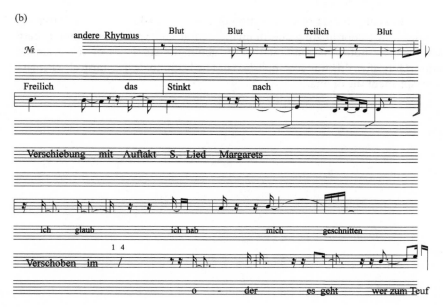

Figure 7.19: cont.

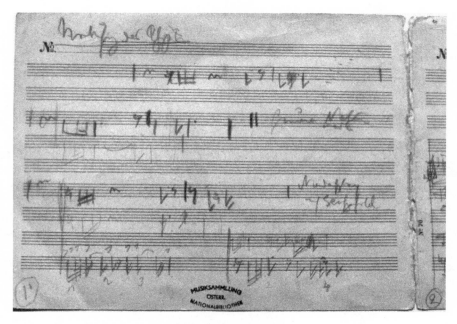

Figure 7.20: F 21 Berg 13/VII fol. 1ᵛ (catalog #: 144)

critical dramatic content of each section of a scene. In addition to the extremely complex chart coordinating the dramatic action and various ensembles, Berg made endless notes on additional leaves about the subtleties of the dramatic action. Only after this was accomplished did he begin to devise musical schemata to complement the drama.

Conclusion

> Tomorrow nothing and again nothing—I have to put up with all this because of this
> filthy war. I again put my hand to my brow (the gesture of saluting is just nonsense!)
> and ask myself why I do it, indeed why everyone around me doesn't salute and ask
> themselves the same thing. Three years stolen from the best period of my life, from
> age 18 to 48, then, let's say a tenth of this time completely lost.[1]
> —Alban Berg to Helene Berg, June 29, 1918

This paragraph of bitter frustration, written to his wife as he awaited a leave of seven precious weeks to work on his opera *Wozzeck*, is symptomatic of Berg's compositional career as a whole: in creating a total of twelve works, the last unfinished, he had only the summer months to devote to composition, and he would die prematurely at the age of 50, only ten years after the premiere of *Wozzeck*. It is doubtful if Berg could have imagined, after the financial success of *Wozzeck*, which allowed him to buy a car and a summer home, that he would be pitched back into financial instability even worse than that he had experienced during the hyper-inflation following World War I. The modernism of *Wozzeck*, so relevant to the daring experimentation of the twenties, would now work against him during the enforced conservatism of the Third Reich. Moreover, as a student of Schoenberg, Berg was perceived as tainted with the same "Jewish intellectualism" and performances of *Wozzeck* were banned.

A memorial article by Alfred Rosenzweig, printed one year after Berg's death, bears as its title Berg's initial military rank, "Einjährig-Freiwillige Titular-Gefreite Alban Berg: Toward the First Return of the Day of his Death on 24th December" and shows a thirty-year old Berg in his Austrian army uniform (Figure 8.1).[2] The article painfully documents with letters to Berg's wife and to his student Gottfried Kassowitz the physical sacrifices he endured serving in the Austrian army, yet, as Rosenzweig explains, it was his military experience that allowed Berg to identify with the humiliated protagonist of his most celebrated work:

> Berg faithfully performed this ten-hour service until the end of the war. Then he put
> away the uniform forever, and only a few people knew, as the famous composer at

the magnificent *Wozzeck* premiere in the Vienna State Opera in an elegant tailcoat—
the image of Oscar Wilde—approached the steps of the stage in order to address the
rapturous storm of applause, that the creator of this grandiose score had himself
experienced the suffering of this creature in uniform. That behind the hunted
Wozzeck stands as an invisible shadow the one-year volunteer, titular Corporal
Alban Berg.[3]

This book has entered into this intimate biographical realm of Berg's life, in citing
details from both his notebooks and his personal correspondence, but it is in deciphering the sketches themselves that one finds perhaps the clearest evidence of
Berg's admirable persistence, despite war, chronic illness, economic depression,
and the apathy of others, to create an atonal opera.

Many sketches by atonal composers—even Schoenberg and Webern—are dis-
appointing in the lack of insight they give into compositional process—Kramer's
"window of the artist's soul."[4] This is partially due to the very nature of atonality,
which, as a more open musical system, often does not require the complex pre-
compositional procedures of a difficult twelve-tone passage. Thus, one is frequently
confronted with a draft in the composer's hand, either very similar to the finished
passage, or with differences that one cannot qualify due to the extreme openness
of atonality.

Figure 8.1: Berg in uniform

In Berg's atonal sketches for *Wozzeck*, in contrast, even the act of assembling Büchner's aphoristic text into a traditional musical form was so difficult that we already see copious analyses in Berg's copies of Büchner's *Woyzeck*. These are often followed by five to six distinct compositional stages before Berg had achieved something resembling the finished passage.

While we might argue that Berg's lectures, as well as previous published analyses, have revealed the complex forms of the scenes and acts, the object of the most vehement criticism by Berg's reviewers, the sketches do also reveal details about the subtle textual and musical justifications for these forms, as well as the number symbolism—one of many of his acts of homage to Schoenberg—that allow the forms to cohere simultaneously on a fractal level. The sketches also make insightful comments on the transitions within and between these forms, which, based on the detail of his sketches,Berg valued as much as the forms themselves. In the case of Berg's *Marsch* from the Three Orchestral Pieces, which we studied in Chapter 1, the form is so complex that it is still an open question. Here Berg's sketches reveal a through-composed, modern form, which in retrospect seems as highly logical as those in *Wozzeck*.

Combining this biographical and sketch evidence has also allowed us to finally reveal the precise chronology of the opera's eight-year gestation, as well as the influences on Berg's life during each of these years. For instance, rather than a prewar premonition, Act I, scene 2 and Act II, scene 4, composed during Berg's initial service in the Austrian army, should be considered a painful exposé of the dehumanization of military life. Given Berg's feelings about his military superiors and doctors, it is not surprising that he chose to complete Act II, scene 2 first, nor that it was followed, in 1918, by Act I, scene 2, with its military signals, funeral march, and flight into insanity.

Like his opera *Lulu*, *Wozzeck* was composed over such a long and creatively volatile period that we can see a distinct evolution in his approach to atonality, always tempered, of course, with the dramatic needs of the moment. I have begun to view the atonality of the Second Viennese School as a transition of approximately twelve years from late tonality to the twelve-tone method these composers would utilize for the rest of their lives. It is astonishing how Berg clings initially to tonality, even in his analyses of the most non-tonal passages of *Pierre Lunaire*, and in his own initial sketches for *Wozzeck*, for instance, the opening of Act I, scene 2, where tonality—for most theorists—would be the analytical method of last choice. Berg returns to these "great tonal moments" in the most moving and contemplative passages of *Wozzeck*—the Interlude between Act III, scenes 4 and 5, or the opening of Act III. By 1921, the year of the discovery of the twelve-tone method, Berg's sketches show evidence that he is beginning to superimpose numeric configurations and apply operations that lead to a specificity of pitch, duration, and register that would prefigure Boulez, and certainly supersede those of Webern, championed for decades as the forerunner of modern music. In Chapter 1 I made a comparison between Kandinsky's expressionist paintings of 1908 and Berg's *Marsch* from Opus 6. Tellingly, by 1921, Kandinsky is expressing his own version of a more ordered universe: his paintings are still abstract, but the various blobs and wavy lines have transformed into perfect circles and arcs.

Perhaps the most important contribution of Berg's sketches is that they allow us to identify distinct stages in this broad spectrum of atonality, which in the opera *Wozzeck* is often treated as a uniform whole. I offer these various species of atonality, from consciously negated tonality to interval cycles, as analytical strategies to deal with a compositional system that is anything but uniform.

Thirty years ago, in his article, "Ideas of Order in Motivic Music," William Benjamin poetically described the challenges of analyzing atonal music:

> It seems as if we've finally begun to figure out how to get into those mysterious houses built just after the turn of the century by Schoenberg and Webern. To say that we've found the key does not, however, represent an apt way of narrowing the metaphor, since, for better or for worse, they built these houses without doors. At best they may seem to have painted door-like signs on their exteriors, or, in some cases, to have graced their façades with doors grouped in threes and fours, leading not to the inside but instead to one another and out. [...] Precision equipment for penetrating façades is not designed to be hurled like a demolition ball at the objects it is meant to transform. One is better off, on the whole, with crude tools employed with subtlety than with a refined technology for which one lacks the appropriate strategies.[5]

What, other than the composer's own sketches, will give us insights into these strategies?

Catalogue of the Sketches for *Wozzeck*

Introduction

www.oup.com/us/bergswozzeck

This catalogue and its accompanying scans place the extant sketches for *Wozzeck* together for the first time, allowing the researcher to view the entire collection and to make comparisons between sketches in different archives. The sketches are housed in seven archives: the Österreichische Nationalbibliothek in Vienna (ÖNB), Houghton Library at Harvard University (HL), the Alban Berg Stiftung in Vienna (ABS), the Beinecke Rare Book and Manuscript Library at Yale University (BRBL), the Staatsbibliothek Preussicher Kulturbesitz in Berlin (SBPK), the Library of Congress in Washington, D.C. (LOC), and the Bayerische Staatsbibliothek in Munich (BSB).

Format of the Catalogue

The sketches are listed using their archival call numbers, with the largest collection, that of the Österreichische Nationalbibliothek, listed first. Each section begins with a description of the materials contained in a specific archival folder. This is followed by a description of each individual leaf in that folder, indicating dimensions, writing implements, paper type, sketch content, physical condition, chronology, and any other pertinent information. This information allows searches based on the writing implement, date of completion, location in the opera, etc. I have retained the pagination/foliation from each archive, but explain errors (e.g. pages out of order) when they occur. While the *Particell* is not a sketch, per se, I have photographs of the entire source to show the process by which instrumentation was added.

Photographic Method

I photographed all the sketches in the companion website except those in the Staatsbibliothek Preussicher Kulturbesitz in Berlin, the Bayerische Staatsbibliothek in Munich, and the Alban Berg Stiftung in Vienna, for which scans were provided. As a researcher, I have found all too often that archival photographs, taken from documents flattened under Plexiglas and filmed using artificial light, appear very different from the original document. Since I have also had to rely a great deal on external evidence in my own research, I have photographed the sketches in such a way that their physical properties are maximized. One can see the various folds and flaws in the paper, as well as how the paper naturally lies. Since color will vary from computer to computer, I have provided a color index from *Dumont's Farbenatlas* to indicate the sketch's true color. The images have been scanned, when possible, at a high resolution. This allows magnification of important details without making the files too large for a website of this size. Blank pages and sketches other than those for *Wozzeck* are indicated in the catalogue, but not reproduced. Since I was asked to photograph these sketches as quickly as possible, usually in the midst of a busy reading room with varying degrees of natural light, I have edited the scans so that the color is uniform for a particular book or paper type, and often sharpened the image.

Chronology of the Sketches

The chronology of the *Wozzeck* sketches is extremely complicated and requires a meticulous assessment of all the evidence available. It is often clear that the sketches in an individual folder are a random assortment, dating from various years of composition, and are thus meaningless as chronological evidence. Instead, one turns to Berg's correspondence and the internal and external evidence presented by the sketches themselves.

Without Berg's frequent progress reports to Schoenberg, his students, and his wife, we would be hard pressed to date the sketches. Fortunately, he was a frequent correspondent, eager to comment on the work at hand. With this general outline, we can begin to examine the internal evidence of the sketches (content and presence of accurate measure numbers) to see which sketches are datable. Finally one looks at the external evidence: trends in paper types, writing implements, address stamps, etc. Paper types are occasionally helpful, but they can be equally misleading; Berg borrowed paper from previous works when he was short—a frequent event during the inflation years. Writing implements—especially shades of colored pencils—are stronger indicators of a specific year. Among the difficulties with colored pencils though, is that they change shade as the paper deteriorates, and that Berg also went back and annotated older sketches. When I was allowed to look at the collection of colored pencils retained in Berg's desk in his Hietzing apartment, the complexity of the issue of writing implements became especially apparent; there were at least ten colored pencils, with four shades of blue, some of which had red pencil at their other end. In general, I've tried to establish a balance between all the evidence available, including letters, calendars, and the sketches themselves. Based on this evidence, most of the sketches fall between 1918 and 1921.

Berg's Creative Process

As chaotic as Berg's sketches initially seem, they tend to fall into specific categories, depending on the stage of sketching and the goal to be accomplished. Particularly in sketchbooks, one can see a progression from form sketches based on the logic of the text, to motivic sketches inspired by fragments of text, to thematic sketches, to continuity drafts using rhythmic shorthand and indicating contours of melodies, and finally (occasionally) to fairly complete continuity drafts. Early continuity drafts are the most common type of sketch featured in this collection. It seems that Berg wanted to at least achieve a stage that would allow him to progress readily to the *Particell*. However, even the *Particell*, as I will discuss later, shows significant revision. This is also the source in which Berg made definitive choices for orchestration.

A Caveat

While this companion website will be far more useful than a microfilm, it will never take the place of viewing the original sketches in an archive. Rather, it is a study tool that allows one to easily become familiar with an entire collection while conserving the original sources. Anyone undertaking a serious study of Berg's sketches, and certainly anyone anticipating publication, must eventually view the original sources. No reproduction or simulation will ever replace the experience of touching, smelling, and looking directly at a piece of paper handled by the composer. I hope, nonetheless, that this will be a useful archival tool and a model for other collections—especially those that are so dispersed that studying the original is initially impractical.

I.   Sketches from the Music Division of the Österrichische Nationalbibliothek (ÖNB)

ÖNB Musiksammlung F 21 Berg 13/I

General Description

This sketchbook dates from Berg's last summer of composition. Although, as in 13/II, Berg used J.E. & Co. No. 70 sketchbook paper, it differs in color (Y40, M10) and dimensions (12.9 × 16.7). It is typical of the paper Berg used in 1921, which is poor in quality and slightly brittle, and it has darkened significantly over time. This sketchbook has been paginated, rather than foliated by the ÖNB.

As Petersen and Fanning have noted, this sketchbook of originally 50 pages is missing one of its gatherings, which is catalogued as 13/VII and should be placed between pages 14 and 15 in order to see the correct content and evolution of the sketchbook.[1] All gatherings in this sketchbook consist of four, nested bifolia (eight leaves). Like 13/II it is a significant source, which, including its missing gathering, contains sketches for II/4, II/5, and III/2–5.

Description of Individual Pages

001 – 13/I, front cover: Brown cardboard cover with "Wozzeck" written in Berg's hand. White label with "Wozzeck" written in Helene Berg's hand. 1921.

002 – 13/I, p. 1: (J.E. & Co. /No. 70 /10-stave /12.9 × 16.7 cm /M10 C00 Y40 S00) Blank. 1921.

003 – 13/I, p. 2: (J.E. & Co. /No. 70 /10-stave/12.9 × 16.7 cm /M10 C00 Y40 S00) Continuity draft of II/4, mm. 589–594. (Pencil.) 1921.

004 – 13/I, p. 3: (J.E. & Co. /No. 70 /10-stave /12.9 × 16.7 cm /M10 C00 Y40 S00) Continuity draft of II/4, mm. 595–597. (Pencil.) 1921.

005 – 13/I, p. 4: (J.E. & Co. /No. 70 /10-stave /12.9 × 16.7 cm /M10 C00 Y40 S00) Continuity draft of II/4, mm. 598–600, with some revisions. Melodic sketch of II/4 mm. 592–593 (Ländler melody) staff 1. Berg's annotation of accurate measure numbers (600) indicates that the previous sections of the opera were already composed. (Pencil.) 1921.

006 – 13/I, p. 5: (J.E. & Co. /No. 70 /10-stave /12.9 × 16.7 cm /M10 C00 Y40 S00) Continuity draft of II/4, mm. 603–604, 606–609. (Pencil.) 1921.

007 – 13/I, p. 6: (J.E. & Co. /No. 70 /10-stave /12.9 × 16.7 cm /M10 C00 Y40 S00) Notation of cantus firmus for II/4 mm. 604–610. Sketch of interval pattern for II/4 m. 643. (Pencil.) 1921.

008 – 13/I, p. 7: (J.E. & Co. /No. 70 /10-stave /12.9 × 16.7 cm /M10 C00 Y40 S00) Continuation of sketch from the previous page (staves 7–10) of II/4, mm. 611–614. Staves 1–6, Continuity draft of II/5 mm. 737–746. (Pencil.) 1921.

009 – 13/I, p. 8: (J.E. & Co. /No. 70 /10-stave /12.9 × 16.7 cm /M10 C00 Y40 S00) Staves 1–6: Sketch of chord series II/4 mm. 643–649. Measures 650–652 scratched out. Staves 7–10: II/4 mm. 615–617. (Pencil, black ink.) 1921.

010 – 13/I, p. 9: (J.E. & Co. /No. 70 /10-stave /12.9 × 16.7 cm /M10 C00 Y40 S00) Staves 1–6 preliminary sketch of music for II/4,

mm. 665–668. Sketch of II/4 mm. 618–620, (staves 7–10). Text does not line up with notes of cantus in same way as finished score. (Pencil, black ink.) 1921.

011 – 13/I, p. 10: (J.E. & Co. /No. 70 /10-stave /12.9 × 16.7 cm /M10 C00 Y40 S00) Staves 1–5, continuity draft of II/4 mm. 649–651. Staves 9–10, II/4 mm. 666–670. Staff 7, annotation of cantus firmus, according to Fanning, mm. 623–627.[2] (Pencil.) 1921.

012 – 13/I, p. 11: (J.E. & Co. /No. 70 /10-stave /12.9 × 16.7 cm /M10 C00 Y40 S00) Staves 1–5, continuity draft of II/4 mm. 653–657 and 660–661. Staff 7, remainder of cantus firmus. (Pencil.) 1921.

013 – 13/I, p. 12: (J.E. & Co. /No. 70 /10-stave /12.9 × 16.7 cm /M10 C00 Y40 S00) Continuity draft of II/4, mm. 685–693. Some notes of ostinato incorrectly notated. (Pencil.) 1921.

014 – 13/I, p. 13: (J.E. & Co. /No. 70 /10-stave /12.9 × 16.7 cm /M10 C00 Y40 S00) Continuation of sketch on previous page, II/4 mm. 694–695. Notes of ostinato are written incorrectly. (Pencil.) 1921.

015 – 13/I, p. 14: (J.E. & Co. /No. 70 /10-stave /12.9 × 16.7 cm /M10 C00 Y40 S00) Continuity draft of five-note ostinato, II/4, mm. 697–704. Covered by a draft (in ink) of a letter to Schoenberg from September 1921. (Pencil, black ink.) 1921.

016 – 13/I, p. 15: (J.E. & Co. /No. 70 /10-stave /12.9 × 16.7 cm /M10 C00 Y40 S00) Draft of III/3 mm. 161–165. Berg's accurate labeling of m. 165 again tells us that he had completed the opera up to this point. (Pencil, with black ink annotations from Berg's letter draft.) 1921.

017 – 13/I, p. 16: (J.E. & Co. /No. 70 /10-stave /12.9 × 16.7 cm /M10 C00 Y40 S00) Staves 3–6, III/3 mm. 166–168. (Pencil, covered with draft of Berg's letter in black ink.) 1921.

018 – 13/I, p. 17: (J.E. & Co. /No. 70 /10-stave /12.9 × 16.7 cm /M10 C00 Y40 S00) Orchestration sketch of II/4 mm. 614–617. Staves 6 and 8: sketch of rhythm, end of III/3? (Pencil.) 1921.

019 – 13/I, p. 18: (J.E. & Co. /No. 70 /10-stave /12.9 × 16.7 cm /M10 C00 Y40 S00) Motivic ideas for III/4, attached to various bits of text: "Messer—auch Chrom" (bottom of sketch), "da regt sich was" (staves 6–7), etc. Manipulations of hexachord for this scene. (Pencil.) 1921.

020 – 13/I, p. 19: (J.E. & Co. /No. 70 /10-stave /12.9 × 16.7 cm /M10 C00 Y40 S00) More motivic ideas for III/4, some attached to fragments of text: "Halsband" (staff 8). More manipulations of hexachord. (Pencil.) 1921.

021 – 13/I, p. 20:   (J.E. & Co. /No. 70 /10-stave /12.9 × 16.7 cm /M10 C00 Y40 S00) Melodic ideas (not used in this form) for II/4 vocal line m. 240 and ff. (Pencil.) 1921.

022 – 13/I, p. 21:   (J.E. & Co. /No. 70 /10-stave /12.9 × 16.7 cm /M10 C00 Y40 S00) Berg is experimenting with transpositions of the hexachord for III/4 as well as rotations and the resulting transposition. In the center of the sketch he arranges the hexachord to highlight various intervals "untere Terz," etc. In the bottom part of the sketch, he writes "ganze Welt die 12 Akkorden in allen möglichen unregelmässigen Einsätzen," referring to m. 268 and following. The hexachord entrances occur at irregular intervals. (Pencil.) 1921.

023 – 13/I, p. 22:   (J.E. & Co. /No. 70 /10-stave /12.9 × 16.7 cm /M10 C00 Y40 S00) More sketches of various expressions of the hexachord for III/4. (Pencil.) 1921.

024 – 13/I, p. 23:   (J.E. & Co. /No. 70 /10-stave /12.9 × 16.7 cm /M10 C00 Y40 S00) Sketches showing the interaction of simple triple meter with compound triple. (Pencil.) 1921.

025 – 13/I, p. 24:   (J.E. & Co. /No. 70 /10-stave /12.9 × 16.7 cm /M10 C00 Y40 S00) Early drafts of passages from III/4 along with bits of text: "rote Schnur um den Hals" (staves 7–10). Mm. 238–244. (Pencil.) 1921.

026 – 13/I, p. 25:   (J.E. & Co. /No. 70 /10-stave /12.9 × 16.7 cm /M10 C00 Y40 S00) Early draft of III/4 mm. 244–257. (Pencil.) 1921.

027 – 13/I, p. 26:   (J.E. & Co. /No. 70 /10-stave /12.9 × 16.7 cm /M10 C00 Y40 S00) Early draft of III/4 mm. 258–269. (Pencil.) 1921.

028 – 13/I, p.27:   (J.E. & Co. /No. 70 /10-stave /12.9 × 16.7 cm /M10 C00 Y40 S00) Rhythmic shorthand of early setting of III/4 mm. 270–271, 277, 281–284 (measures in sketch do not correspond exactly with final version.) (Pencil.) 1921.

029 – 13/I, p. 28:   (J.E. & Co. /No. 70 /10-stave /12.9 × 16.7 cm /M10 C00 Y40 S00) Continuity draft of III/4, mm. 316–320 (staves 8–10). In staves 1–6 Berg is experimenting with cyclic rotations of the hexachord upon which this scene is based. (Pencil, black ink.) 1921.

030 – 13/I, p. 29:   (J.E. & Co. /No. 70 /10-stave /12.9 × 16.7 cm /M10 C00 Y40 S00) Shorthand notation of various interval cycles appearing in III/4 (?). (Pencil.) 1921.

031 – 13/I, p. 30:   (J.E. & Co. /No. 70 /10-stave /12.9 × 16.7 cm /M10 C00 Y40 S00) List of leitmotifs for the Epilog to be harvested from various locations from the opera. At top margin appears "Epilog 23/9" referring to September 23, 1921. The annotated page numbers (S 52) refer to

their location in Berg's autograph *Particell.* On this page, "Captain (staff 3), Nature (staves 5–6), Friend (Andres) staff 10, Marie, staves 9–10. (Pencil.) 1921 .

032 – 13/I, p. 31: (J.E. & Co. /No. 70 /10-stave /12.9 × 16.7 cm /M10 C00 Y40 S00) Leitmotifs for Epilog, continued: "Wir arme Leut" (staff 1), Terzen (thirds) (staves 2–3). Continuation of "Natur" (staves 4–7), Doctor (staves 8–10), continuation of Marie theme, staves 8–10, right-hand corner of sketch. (Pencil, black ink.) 1921.

033 – 13/I, p. 32: (J.E. & Co. /No. 70 /10-stave /12.9 × 16.7 cm /M10 C00 Y40 S00) Leitmotifs for Epilog: Marie (Bible) staves 1–2, Drum major staves 4–6) (Lippen), Kind, Staff 9 (Was der Bub immer schläft), and Staves 9–10: Wozzeck, Alles Arbeit unter der Sonne S 65- Wir Arme Leut. (Pencil.) 1921.

034 – 13/I, p. 33: (J.E. & Co. /No. 70 /10-stave /12.9 × 16.7 cm /M10 C00 Y40 S00) Leitmotifs for Epilog: Doctor (staff 2), W[ozzeck,] Der Gehetzte, staves 4–5, etc. (Pencil.) 1921.

035 – 13/I, p. 34: (J.E. & Co. /No. 70 /10-stave /12.9 × 16.7 cm /M10 C00 Y40 S00) Leitmotifs for Epilog: Volk staves 1–2, W[ozzeck,] Es moll imponierte staff 4, staves 7–10 III/4 mm. 336–345, mainly rhythmic shorthand. (Pencil.) 1921.

036 – 13/I, p. 35: (J.E. & Co. /No. 70 /10-stave /12.9 × 16.7 cm /M10 C00 Y40 S00) Staves 7–10, draft of III/4 mm. 364–366. Staves 7–10 III/4 mm. 346–352. Mainly rhythmic shorthand. (Pencil.) 1921.

037 – 13/I, p. 36: (J.E. & Co. /No. 70 /10-stave /12.9 × 16.7 cm /M10 C00 Y40 S00) More leitmotifs for Epilog: F minor idea, staves 3–4, "Dein Bub," stave 9–10, etc. Chords for end of III/5 "Schluss" notated on staves 1–2. Annotated "G dur." (Pencil.) 1921.

038 – 13/I, p. 37: (J.E. & Co. /No. 70 /10-stave /12.9 × 16.7 cm /M10 C00 Y40 S00) Remaining leitmotifs for Epilog. (Pencil.) 1921.

039 – 13/I, p. 38: (J.E. & Co. /No. 70 /10-stave /12.9 × 16.7 cm /M10 C00 Y40 S00) Continuity draft of III/5 mm. 377–381. (Pencil.) 1921.

040 – 13/I, p. 39: (J.E. & Co. /No. 70 /10-stave /12.9 × 16.7 cm /M10 C00 Y40 S00) Continuity draft of III/5 mm. 387–389. (Pencil.) 1921.

041 – 13/I, p. 40: (J.E. & Co. /No. 70 /10-stave /12.9 × 16.7 cm /M10 C00 Y40 S00) Instrumentation sketch of II/1 mm. 139–140. (Pencil, black ink.) 1921.

042 – 13/I, back cover: Something written in Berg's hand with exclamation point that is illegible. (Pencil.) 1921.

ÖNB *Musiksammlung F 21 Berg 13/II*

General Description

A bound sketchbook of (originally) 50 leaves. The gatherings consist of four nested bifolia, or eight leaves. The paper type is J.E. & Co. No. 70 10-stave paper. This paper has red edges. The dimensions are 12.1×16.9. While this type of paper appears in other sources for the opera, it is from a different year, and varies in its color, layout of the staves, and dimensions. Color: Y10. This sketchbook has been paginated rather than foliated by the ÖNB. Berg has numbered the pages of the second half, then stamped them with a numerator. It contains sketches for Opus 6/III in the first half, and for *Wozzeck* II/2 and I/2 in the second half. This is the earliest document containing compositional sketches for the opera, and as such it offers valuable insights about the opera's inception. While many authors have assumed that the *Wozzeck* sketches in this sketchbook date from 1914 because of their proximity to the sketches for Opus 6/III, it is more likely that they were completed from 1916 to 1918, during the few respites that Berg had from military service. The sketchbook format allows us to see the development of a scene better than loose leaves. Berg bracketed many themes from this sketchbook and copied them onto leaves from 13/III and 70/I, presumably to use at a later date.

Description of Individual Leaves

043 – 13/II, p. 50:   (J.E. & Co. /No. 70 /10-stave /12.1 × 16.9 cm /M00 C00 Y10 S00) (Berg p. 1.) Various chords exhibiting symmetrical interval relations. Pencil. Berg appears to be "warming up," that is, freely experimenting with ideas, none of which appear in the opera. Most of these unused sketches feature triple meter. (Pencil.)

044 – 13/II, p. 51:   (J.E. & Co. /No. 70 /10-stave /12.1 × 16.9 cm /M00 C00 Y10 S00) (Berg p. 2.) Unused thematic ideas in triple meter. (Pencil.)

045 – 13/II, p. 52:   (J.E. & Co. /No. 70 /10-stave /12.1 × 16.9 cm /M00 C00 Y10 S00) (Berg p. 3.) Unused thematic ideas. (Indelible pencil.)

046 – 13/II, p. 53:   (J.E. & Co. /No. 70 /10-stave /12.1 × 16.9 cm /M00 C00 Y10 S00) (Not numbered by Berg. He has inserted this page by gluing it into the sketchbook at a later date.) Unused melodic ideas. (Pencil.)

047 – 13/II, p. 54:   (J.E. & Co. /No. 70 /10-stave /12.1 × 16.9 cm /M00 C00 Y10 S00) (Not numbered by Berg.) More unused ideas in triple meter. Annotations of "schnell." (Pencil.)

048 – 13/II, p. 55:   (J.E. & Co. /No. 70 /10-stave /12.1 × 16.9 cm /M00 C00 Y10 S00) (Berg p. 4.) More experimentation with symmetrical interval patters, staves 1–3 (thirds versus whole-tones). Annotation in ink staves 7–9, "Wirtshausscene" and "Polka." Berg notated themes for Act II, scene 4 long before he actually began to compose that scene. (Pencil, black ink.)

049 – 13/II, p. 56: (J.E. & Co. /No. 70 /10-stave /12.1 × 16.9 cm /M00 C00 Y10 S00) (Berg p. 5.) List of characters and vocal ranges. Includes characters eventually eliminated, for instance "Alte Frau" and "Jude." (Pencil.)

050 – 13/II, p. 57: (J.E. & Co. /No. 70 /10-stave /12.1 × 16.9 cm /M00 C00 Y10 S00) (Berg p. 6.) Psychological analysis of Captain: "Eine Null," (a nothing), etc. (Pencil.)

051 – 13/II, p. 58: (J.E. & Co. /No. 70 /10-stave /12.1 × 16.9 cm /M00 C00 Y10 S00) (Berg p. 7.) Unused thematic ideas in 4/4 meter. Indelible pencil, except for Berg's annotation of "7" in pencil in the top margin. (Indelible pencil, pencil.)

052 – 13/II, p. 59: (J.E. & Co. /No. 70 /10-stave /12.1 × 16.9 cm /M00 C00 Y10 S00) (Berg p. 8.) Fragment of the opening of II/2 (Captain's theme). (Pencil, smears of indelible pencil from the previous page.)

053 – 13/II, p. 60: (J.E. & Co. /No. 70 /10-stave /12.1 × 16.9 cm /M00 C00 Y10 S00) (Berg p. 9.) Sketches for "Zwischenspiel" (Interludium) in 4/4, which Berg characterizes as "Trauermarschartig" and "Langsam." These sketches are not used in the opera. (Pencil.)

054 – 13/II, p. 61: (J.E. & Co. /No. 70 /10-stave /12.1 × 16.9 cm /M00 C00 Y10 S00) (Berg p. 10.) Motivic ideas for II/2, Captain and Doctor. Fragments of text appear, "Und Sie selbst," etc. with rhythmic or pitch notation. (Pencil.)

055 – 13/II, p. 62: (J.E. & Co. /No. 70 /10-stave /12.1 × 16.9 cm /M00 C00 Y10 S00) (Berg p. 11.) Draft of II/2 mm. 193–197, predominantly a setting of the vocal lines using rhythmic notation. (Pencil.)

056 – 13/II, p. 63: (J.E. & Co. /No. 70 /10-stave /12.1 × 16.9 cm /M00 C00 Y10 S00) (Berg p. 12.) Draft of II/2 m.196 (last eighth-note in clarinet) through m. 201 (3/4 measure). Primarily rhythmic in which one can also see the general contours of the melodic lines. Staves 5–10 are covered with a draft of an unknown letter and a military ordinance (BKB No. 48017 from 1916) stating that Berg has been assigned to clerical duty. (Pencil.)

057 – 13/II, p. 64: (J.E. & Co. /No. 70 /10-stave /12.1 × 16.9 cm /M00 C00 Y10 S00) (Berg p. 13.) In this page and the following Berg begins experimenting with ideas for other scenes. The annotation "letzte Scene" appears at the top of the page; however, it isn't clear from the sketch's content whether he means the last scene of the opera, or perhaps the last scene of Act I. In any case, these sketches were discarded. The brackets around the sketches on this page and the next tell us that Berg copied them in another source (13/III) to be used later. (Pencil.)

058 – 13/II, p. 65: (J.E. & Co. /No. 70 /10-stave /12.1 × 16.9 cm /M00 C00 Y10 S00) (Berg p. 14.) Bracketed unused ideas to be copied into another source. Sketch of ideas for Wirtshausscene (II/4) with annotations "langsamer Walzertempo" (slow waltz tempo) and "Ländler." (Pencil.)

059 – 13/II, p. 66: (J.E. & Co. /No. 70 /10-stave /12.1 × 16.9 cm /M00 C00 Y10 S00) (Berg p. 15.) Return to draft of II/2, mm. 191–197. Berg indicates bits of accompaniment (not just the vocal line) in this draft. (Pencil.)

060 – 13/II, p. 67: (J.E. & Co. /No. 70 /10-stave /12.1 × 16.9 cm /M00 C00 Y10 S00) (Berg p. 16.) Draft of II/2 mm. 198–204. (Pencil.)

061 – 13/II, p. 68: (J.E. & Co. /No. 70 /10-stave /12.1 × 16.9 cm /M00 C00 Y10 S00) (Berg p. 17.) Staves 6–10 draft of orchestra II/2 mm. 192–196. Annotation between staves four and five: s(iehe) 15/16 referring to sketches on those pages of 13/II. (Pencil.)

062 – 13/II, p. 69: (J.E. & Co. /No. 70 /10-stave /12.1 × 16.9 cm /M00 C00 Y10 S00) (Berg p. 18.) Bracketed (unused) themes. (Pencil.)

063 – 13/II, p. 70: (J.E. & Co. /No. 70 /10-stave /12.1 × 16.9 cm /M00 C00 Y10 S00) (Berg p. 19.) Bracketed (unused) themes. (Pencil.)

064 – 13/II, p. 71: (J.E. & Co. /No. 70 /10-stave /12.1 × 16.9 cm /M00 C00 Y10 S00) (Berg p. 20.) Remainder of sketch from previous page. Annotation, "4taktartig" (in four beats), "in Akkorden" (in chords), and "pizz." (Pencil.)

065 – 13/II, p. 72: (J.E. & Co. /No. 70 /10-stave /12.1 × 16.9 cm /M00 C00 Y10 S00) (Berg p. 21.) Annotation at top of page "Fortsetzung v. 16" (continuation from p. 16). Sketch of rhythm of vocal line and occasional indications of accompaniment (in pink pencil). II/2, mm. 204–213. This is the same shade of pencil used in a letter from 1918 and thus may date from the same time. (Pencil, pink pencil.)

066 – 13/II, p. 73: (J.E. & Co. /No. 70 /10-stave /12.1 × 16.9 cm /M00 C00 Y10 S00) (Berg p. 22.) Sketch of rhythm of vocal line and occasional annotations of accompaniment in pink pencil. II/2, mm. 214–225. Annotation staff 6 "Verschobung" referring to the shift of one beat of the vocal line between the version shown on staff 6 and staff 7. (Pencil, pink pencil.)

067 – 13/II, p. 74: (J.E. & Co. /No. 70 /10-stave /12.1 × 16.9 cm /M00 C00 Y10 S00) (Berg p. 23.) Sketch of rhythm of vocal line. II/2 mm. 226–231. Annotation staff 6, "Fortsetzung Krebsgang. Walzer" etc. (Pencil, pink pencil.)

068 – 13/II, p. 75: (J.E. & Co. /No. 70 /10-stave /12.1 × 16.9 cm /M00 C00 Y10 S00) (Berg p. 24.) Sketch of II/2 mm. 232–243. Pitch notation of vocal line mm. 232–237. Although the contour is generally the same, the notes differ in the final score. Indications of accompaniment in those measures as well. (Pencil.)

069 – 13/II, p. 76: (J.E. & Co. /No. 70 /10-stave /12.1 × 16.9 cm /M00 C00 Y10 S00) (Berg p. 25.) Continuity draft of II/2 mm. 244–254, showing rhythm of vocal line and some indications of accompaniment. (Pencil.)

070 – 13/II, p. 77: (J.E. & Co. /No. 70 /10-stave /12.1 × 16.9 cm /M00 C00 Y10 S00) (Berg p. 26.) Continuity draft of II/2 mm. 255–258, 262–271,

253–258 (staff 5). Berg indicates the rhythm of the vocal line and very little accompaniment. (Pencil.)

071 – 13/II, p. 78: (J.E. & Co. /No. 70 /10-stave /12.1 × 16.9 cm /M00 C00 Y10 S00) (Berg p. 27.) Bracketed (unused) theme. (Pencil.)

072 – 13/II, p. 79: (J.E. & Co. /No. 70 /10-stave /12.1 × 16.9 cm /M00 C00 Y10 S00) (Berg p. 28.) Verbal annotations of the plan for II/2 (mm. 270–344), indicating sections of the Fugue with Roman numerals for the various sections. (Pencil.)

073 – 13/II, p. 80: (J.E. & Co. /No. 70 /10-stave /12.1 × 16.9 cm /M00 C00 Y10 S00) (Berg p. 29.) Verbal plan for the remainder of II/2 (approximately mm. 345–365). Remaining sections indicated with Roman numerals. Beginning on staff 2, Berg begins composing themes for the fugue, for instance, the Captain's theme, m. 286, and the Doctor's theme, m. 293. (Indelible pencil, pencil.)

074 – 13/II, p. 81: (J.E. & Co. /No. 70 /10-stave /12.1 × 16.9 cm /M00 C00 Y10 S00) (Berg p. 30.) Idea for the march music in II/2 (mm. 300 and following) as the Captain and Doctor taunt Wozzeck about the Drum Major. Notations of "Grosse Tr[ommel], Beck, etc. (Indelible pencil with some offset of indelible pencil from the previous page.)

075 – 13/II, p. 82: (J.E. & Co. /No. 70 /10-stave /12.1 × 16.9 cm /M00 C00 Y10 S00) (Berg p. 31.) Thematic sketch of II/2 mm. 286–288. (Pencil, with occasional offsets of indelible pencil from the next page.)

076 – 13/II, p. 83: (J.E. & Co. /No. 70 /10-stave /12.1 × 16.9 cm /M00 C00 Y10 S00) (Berg p. 32.) Headed "Vorbereitung zur Fuge" (preparation for fugue). Mostly thematic sketches for II/2 mm. 272–283. (Indelible pencil, pencil.)

077 – 13/II, p. 84: (J.E. & Co. /No. 70 /10-stave /12.1 × 16.9 cm /M00 C00 Y10 S00) (Berg p. 33.) Thematic sketches for II/2 mm. 278–285. Annotations of text for these measures, as well as "Umkehrung," staves 6–7. (Pencil, indelible pencil.)

078 – 13/II, p. 85: (J.E. & Co. /No. 70 /10-stave /12.1 × 16.9 cm /M00 C00 Y10 S00) (Berg p. 34.) Sketch of fugue, II/2 mm. 286–296. Berg uses a rhythmic shorthand to indicate the entrance of themes. (Pencil, indelible pencil.)

079 – 13/II, p. 86: (J.E. & Co. /No. 70 /10-stave /12.1 × 16.9 cm /M00 C00 Y10 S00) (Berg p. 35.) Sketch of II/2 mm. 295–298, showing entrances of Doctor's theme. Verbal annotations for section III of the fugue on staves 7–10. (Pencil, indelible pencil.)

080 – 13/II, p. 87: (J.E. & Co. /No. 70 /10-stave /12.1 × 16.9 cm /M00 C00 Y10 S00) (Berg p. 36.) More verbal annotations about sections III–V of the fugue. (Pencil, indelible pencil.)

081 – 13/II, p. 88: (J.E. & Co. /No. 70 /10-stave /12.1 × 16.9 cm /M00 C00 Y10 S00) (Berg p. 37.) Annotations of text for II/2 (section VI of the fugue) that have been violently scratched out with indelible pencil. (Pencil, indelible pencil.)

(Berg 38 and 39 are missing. Fragments of a stub can be seen in the margins. See ABS p. 14.)

082 – 13/II, p. 89:   (J.E. & Co. /No. 70 /10-stave /12.1 × 16.9 cm /M00 C00 Y10 S00) (Berg p. 40.) Verbal annotations describing the end of II/2 (m. 344 onward). Berg experiments with ideas for a "Wozzeck theme" on staves 7–10. (Indelible pencil, pencil.)

083 – 13/II, p. 90:   (J.E. & Co. /No. 70 /10-stave /12.1 × 16.9 cm /M00 C00 Y10 S00) (Berg p. 41.) Sketch of opening of I/2 mm. 201–202. Bracketed theme, staves 4–9, to be copied into another source. In Berg's annotations (staves 7–9) he indicated that this bracketed theme is a collection of pitches from E-flat major and E-flat minor, with an unresolved D (leading tone). (Pencil.)

084 – 13/II, p. 91:   (J.E. & Co. /No. 70 /10-stave /12.1 × 16.9 cm /M00 C00 Y10 S00) (Berg p. 42.) Thematic sketch of Andres's theme, II/2 mm. 212–222. The theme is similar in rhythm, but very different in pitch than the final version. (Pencil, indelible pencil.)

085 – 13/II, p. 92:   (J.E. & Co. /No. 70 /10-stave /12.1 × 16.9 cm /M00 C00 Y10 S00) (Berg p. 43.) Verbal annotations of overall plan for I/2 arranged around the strophes of Andres's song. Page contains rip between staves 3 and 4, is dirty and more yellowed than the previous leaves. (Indelible pencil, pencil.)

086 – 13/II, p. 93:   (J.E. & Co. /No. 70 /10-stave /12.1 × 16.9 cm /M00 C00 Y10 S00) (Berg p. 44.) Continuation of previous page. Verbal annotations describing the plan of I/2 from m. 257 "Still" to the end of the scene. Page is stained with an unknown brown material, has numerous folds, and the pencil annotations have become smeared. (Indelible pencil, pencil.)

087 – 13/II, p. 94:   (J.E. & Co. /No. 70 /10-stave /12.1 × 16.9 cm /M00 C00 Y10 S00) (Berg p. 45.) Annotation of chords, A, B, and C. A is identical to the first chord in I/2, and B is very similar to the chord appearing on beat 1 of m. 4. Motivic idea for "fort, fort" m. 278. The page is stained with an unknown brown material, has multiple folds, and the pencil is smeared. (Pencil.)

088 – 13/II, p. 95:   (J.E. & Co. /No. 70 /10-stave /12.1 × 16.9 cm /M00 C00 Y10 S00) (Berg p. 46.) Berg experiments with motivic ideas for I/2. Annotations of "lichterstreif," "es wird finster," etc. (Pencil.)

089 – 13/II, p. 96:   (J.E. & Co. /No. 70 /10-stave /12.1 × 16.9 cm /M00 C00 Y10 S00) (Berg p. 47.) Unidentified melody in 4/4. (Pencil, indelible pencil.)

090 – 13/II, p. 97:   (J.E. & Co. /No. 70 /10-stave /12.1 × 16.9 cm /M00 C00 Y10 S00) (Berg p. 48.) Blank, except for light "X." (Indelible pencil.)

091 – 13/II, p. 98:   (J.E. & Co. /No. 70 /10-stave /12.1 × 16.9 cm /M00 C00 Y10 S00) (Berg p. 49.) Blank.

ÖNB Musiksammlung F 21 Berg 13/III

General Description

One single leaf and two bifolia of J.E. & Co. Protokoll Schutzmarke No. 29, consisting of themes Berg copied, mostly from 13/II, for later use in *Wozzeck*. Most of these sketches probably date from 1914 and were recopied in 1918; however, there are also later additions in colored pencil. This type of paper, consisting of an oblong format and three beamed staves, appears very rarely in the *Wozzeck* sketches. The only other example is 70/I fols. 9ᵛ–10ᵛ, which also contains recopied themes from 13/II and clearly dates from the same time. Dimensions: 34.3 × 26.5. Color: Y10. This source has been foliated by the ÖNB.

Note: Fol. 1ᵛ (according to the paper structure) is catalogued as fol. 1ʳ.

Description of Individual Leaves

092 – 13/III, fol. 1ʳ: (J.E. & Co. /Protokoll Schutzmarke No. 29 /12-stave /34.3 × 26.5 cm /M00 C00 Y10 S00) Berg lists ideas for various themes, including a Walzer, and Ländler. The first theme (staves 1–2) appears on page 55 of 13/II (staves 4–7). The theme appearing on staves 5–6 is copied from staves 8–9 of the same page of 13/II. The Walzer (staves 8–9) appears in 13/II on staves 4–6 (p. 65). The final theme, the Ländler, appears on staves 6–10 of the same page of 13/II. (Pencil.)

093 – 13/III, fol. 1ᵛ: (J.E. & Co. /Protokoll Schutzmarke No. 29 /12-stave /34.3 × 26.5 cm /M00 C00 Y10 S00) Heading, "Walzer (für Strasse [illeg].) u. Wirthausscene." The annotation "S. 52" (above staff four) refers to p. 52 of the *Particell*; thus, there are certainly additions to this leaf from a later time. The blue pencil on this leaf appears frequently in sketches for 1920. The theme appearing on staves 11–12 is recopied from p. 53 of 13/II. The theme "schnell" staves 8–9, the theme beginning on E-natural to its right, and the theme beginning on G-sharp to its far right are copied from 13/II p. 54. The theme and chordal idea (middle and right, staves 11–12) are also copied from p. 54 of 13/II. The themes on staves 2–3 are copied from p. 51 of 13/II. All the remaining ideas on this leaf (in dark pencil and blue pencil) were probably composed in 1920. (Pencil, blue pencil.)

094 – 13/III, fol. 2ʳ: (J.E. & Co. /Protokoll Schutzmarke No. 29 /12-stave /34.3 × 26.5 cm /M00 C00 Y10 S00) Heading, "Themen." The paper is stained with dirt. This theme has been copied from 13/II p. 70. (Pencil.)

095 – 13/III, fol. 2ᵛ: (J.E. & Co. /Protokoll Schutzmarke No. 29 /12-stave /34.3 × 26.5 cm /M00 C00 Y10 S00) Heading, "Akkord

Verbindungen" (Chord connections). Berg duplicated the chords appearing in 13/II p. 50, staves 1–4. The third set is copied from 13/II p. 51, staff 8. (Pencil.)

096 – 13/III, fol. 3ʳ: (J.E. & Co. /Protokoll Schutzmarke No. 29 /12-stave /34.3 × 26.5 cm /M00 C00 Y10 S00) Blank. (Some pencil offset from 2ᵛ.)

097 – 13/III, fol. 3ᵛ: (J.E. & Co. /Protokoll Schutzmarke No. 29 /12-stave /34.3 × 26.5 cm /M00 C00 Y10 S00) Heading, "Themen" and "W. Fugentheme Strasse" ("Themes" and "W[ozzeck] fugue theme street"). Berg often referred to II/2 as the street scene. The theme appearing on staff 8 and 11–12 is recopied from 13/II p. 58. The theme and its variation appearing on staves 2–3 (right side) are copied from 13/II p. 89, staves 7–10. The rhythmic sketch (staff four) and the *gracioso* theme (middle, staff four) appear on p. 50 of 13/II. The theme on staves 5–6, far right, may have been written at a later time. Stains of unknown origin. (Pencil.)

098 – 13/III fol. 4ʳ: (J.E. & Co. /Protokoll Schutzmarke No. 29 /12-stave /34.3 × 26.5 cm /M00 C00 Y10 S00) Themes for "Strasse Zapfenstreich" and Polka. The *Zapfenstreich* is copied from p. 81 of 13/II. (Pencil, blue pencil.)

099 – 13/III, fols. 4ᵛ–5ᵛ: (J.E. & Co. /Protokoll Schutzmarke No. 29 /12-stave /34.3 × 26.5 cm /M00 C00 Y10 S00) Blank.

ÖNB Musiksammlung F 21 Berg 13/IV

General Description

Twelve leaves of sketches from various locations in *Wozzeck*. Many are fragments and appear to have been scavenged from other sources. All are individual leaves except for 1ʳ–2ᵛ and 5ʳ–6ᵛ, which are bifolia. Most of these sketches are for the early part of II/4 and were completed in 1920.

Description of Individual Leaves:

100 – 13/IV, fol. 1ʳ: (J.E. & Co. /DEPOSÉ No. 2 /12-stave /originally: 26.5 × 34.5 cm, now fragment: 26.5 × 26.6 cm /M00 C00 Y10 S00) Continuity draft of II/4 mm. 447–459. Measure numbers correspond to finished score. (Pencil.)

101 – 13/IV, fol. 1ᵛ–2ʳ: (J.E. & Co. /DEPOSÉ No. 2 /12-stave /originally: 26.5 × 34.5 cm, now fragment: 26.5 × 26.6 cm /M00 C00 Y10 S00) Arrangement of fragment of Schoenberg's Op. 9 Chamber Symphony (see Fanning).[3] (Indelible pencil.)

102 – 13/IV, fol. 2ᵛ: (J.E. & Co. /DEPOSÉ No. 2 /12-stave /originally: 26.5 × 34.5 cm, now fragment: 26.5 × 26.6 cm /M00 C00 Y10

	S00) Continuity draft of II/4 mm. 460–480. (Pencil, blue pencil, black ink.)
103 – 13/IV, fol. 3ʳ:	(J.E. & Co. /Protokoll Schutzmarke No. 4 /16-stave /34.7 × 26.3 cm /M00 C00 Y10 S00) Continuity draft of II/4 mm. 514–529. (Berg's Section IV of the Waltz). (Pencil, black ink.)
104 – 13/IV, fol. 3ᵛ:	(J.E. & Co. /Protokoll Schutzmarke No. 4 /16-stave /34.7 × 26.3 cm /M00 C00 Y10 S00) (Pencil, black ink.)
105 – 13/IV, fol. 4ʳ:	(J.E. & Co. /Protokoll Schutzmarke No. 3 /14-stave /34.4 × 26.4 cm /M00 C00 Y10 S00) Continuity draft of III/5 mm. 371–373. (Pencil, black ink.)
106 – 13/IV, fol. 4ᵛ:	(J.E. & Co. /Protokoll Schutzmarke No. 3 /14-stave /34.4 × 26.4 cm /M00 C00 Y10 S00) Blank.
107 – 13/IV, fol. 5ʳ:	(no brand /16-stave /26.6 × 34.8 cm /M00 C00 Y10 S00) Blank.
108 – 13/IV, fol. 5ᵛ:	(no brand /16-stave /26.6 × 34.8 cm /M00 C00 Y10 S00) Concept sketch. (Pencil.)
109 – 13/IV, fol. 6ʳ:	(no brand /16-stave /26.6 × 34.8 cm /M00 C00 Y10 S00) Continuity draft of III/1 mm. 61–67. (Pencil.)
110 – 13/IV, fol. 6ᵛ:	(no brand /16-stave /26.6 × 34.8 cm /M00 C00 Y10 S00) Continuity draft of III/2 mm. 81–91. (Pencil.)
111 – 13/IV, fol. 7ʳ:	(J.E. & Co. /Protokoll Schutzmarke No. 3 /14-stave /26.5 × 34.5 cm /M00 C00 Y10 S00) Continuity draft of II/1 mm. 109–130, 139–140, 164–166. Has been folded into eighths. (Pencil.)
112 – 13/IV, fol. 7ᵛ:	(J.E. & Co. /Protokoll Schutzmarke No. 3 /14-stave /26.5 × 34.5 cm /M00 C00 Y10 S00) Draft of II/1 mm. 139–40. Draft of letter from Helene Berg (erased) and draft of letter in Berg's handwriting: "Auch wäre es mir sehr angenehm wenn Sie mir einen Prospektus über das Bad, die Kurmittel u dgl erhalten könnte [crossed out]– eventuell per Nachnahme-übersenden wurden." 1920. Paper has been folded into fourths. (Pinkish-red pencil.)
113 – 13/IV, fol. 8ʳ:	(no brand /12-stave /25.4 × 33 cm /M00 C00 Y10 S00) Continuity draft of III/4 mm. 284–296.[4] (Pencil, black ink.)
114 – 13/IV, fol. 8ᵛ:	(no brand /12-stave /25.4 × 33 cm /M00 C00 Y10 S00) Continuity draft of III/4 mm. 297–315. (Pencil, black ink.)
115 – 13/IV, fol. 9ʳ:	(J.E. & Co. /Protokoll Schutzmarke No. 31 /30-stave /26.5 × 34.3 cm /M00 C00 Y10 S00) Paper has been folded into thirds. List of forms representing various characters in *Wozzeck*. "Suite Hauptmann," etc. Not clear if this is simply an outline for a talk. The instrumentation list on the same leaf is for the Chamber Concerto. Unidentifiable rhythmic pattern. (Pencil, indelible pencil.)

116 – 13/IV, fol. 9ᵛ: (J.E. & Co. /Protokoll Schutzmarke No. 31 /30-stave /variable width × 34.3 cm /M00 C00 Y10 S00) Unidentifiable rhythmic sketch. (Pencil.)

117 – 13/IV, fol. 10ʳ: (J.E. & Co. /Protokoll Schutzmarke No. 4 /16-stave /originally: 26.3 × 34.7 cm, now fragment: 24.8 × 34.5 cm /M00 C00 Y10 S00) Early draft of Section VI–VII of the Waltz (mm. 538–559) II/4. Primarily verbal annotations for Section VI (mm. 546–559). (Pencil.) 1920.

118 – 13/IV, fol. 10ᵛ: (J.E. & Co. /Protokoll Schutzmarke No. 4 /16-stave /originally: 26.3 × 34.7 cm, now fragment: 24.8 × 34.5 cm /M00 C00 Y10 S00) Continuity draft (with measure numbers) of section VII and VIII of the Waltz. (II/4 mm. 546–559). Berg's measure numbers are one more than in the printed score. (Pencil.) 1920.

119 – 13/IV, fol. 11ʳ: (J.E. & Co. /Protokoll Schutzmarke No. 4 /16-stave /originally 26.3 × 34.8 cm, now fragment: 25.4 (top) – 25.2 (bottom) × 34.8 cm /M00 C00 Y10 S00) Continuity draft for II/5 mm. 741–748. (Pencil.) 1921.

120 – 13/IV, fol. 11ᵛ: (J.E. & Co. /Protokoll Schutzmarke No. 4 /16-stave /originally 26.3 × 34.8 cm, now fragment: 25.4 (top) – 25.2 (bottom) × 34.8 cm /M00 C00 Y10 S00) Continuity draft of II/4 mm. 480–508. Sections I–II of Waltz. (Pencil with smudges of blue pencil in bottom margin.) 1920.

121 – 13/IV, fol. 12ʳ: (no brand /4.3 × 25.9 cm /M10 C00 Y40 S10) Strip of music paper showing vertical marks at regular intervals. Discoloration makes it appear like 1921 paper. (Pencil, black ink.)

122 – 13/IV, fol. 12ᵛ: (no brand /4.3 × 25.9 cm /M10 C00 Y40 S10) Instrumentation list with "Marie" "Woz." More vertical marks showing equal divisions. (Pencil, black ink.) 1921.

ÖNB Musiksammlung F 21 Berg 13/V

General Description

Five leaves of various types of music paper. Many are fragments, again indicating that Berg has salvaged them from other sources. The content of this folder is II/4 and I/1–2. All are single leaves except for fols. 3–4, which is a bifolio.

Description of Individual Leaves

123 – 13/V, fol. 1ʳ: (J.E. & Co. /Protokoll Schutzmarke No. 61 /18-stave (arranged 6+6+6) /26.5 × 34.5 cm /M00 C00 Y10 S00) Continuity draft of II/4 mm. 480–505. (Pencil, blue pencil, orange pencil.) 1920.

124 – 13/V, fol. 1ᵛ: (J.E. & Co. /Protokoll Schutzmarke No. 61 /18-stave (arranged 6+6+6) /26.5 × 34.5 cm /M00 C00 Y10 S00) Continuity draft of II/4 mm. 416–442. (Pencil, indelible pencil, blue pencil.) 1920.

125 – 13/V, fol. 2ʳ: (no brand /12-stave /originally: 25.5 × 32 cm, now fragment: 23.8 (top) – 23.5 (bottom) × 32 cm /M00 C00 Y10 S00) Same type of paper as 13/XIII. Continuity draft of II/4 mm. 455–465. Address stamp: ALBAN BERG WIEN XIII/1 TRAUTTMANSDORFFGASSE 27. (Pencil, blue pencil.) 1920.

126 – 13/V, fol. 2ᵛ: (no brand /12-stave /originally: 25.5 × 32 cm, now fragment: 23.8 (top) – 23.5 (bottom) × 32 cm /M00 C00 Y10 S00) Continuity draft of II/4 mm. 421–429. (Pencil.) 1920.

127 – 13/V, fol. 3ʳ: (no brand /16-stave /26.7 × 34.8 cm /M00 C00 Y10 S00) Borrowed from the *Particell*. Continuity draft of II/4 mm. 403–415. Annotation in black ink staves 9–10: "Wozzecks Verzweiflung umgekehrt" (Wozzeck's despair inverted). (Pencil, black ink.) 1920.

128 – 13/V, fol. 3ᵛ: (no brand /16-stave /26.7 × 34.8 cm /M00 C00 Y10 S00) Continuity draft of I/1–2 mm. 172–176, 184–200. Measure numbers correspond to final score. (Pencil, black ink.) 1919.

129 – 13/V, fol. 4ʳ: (no brand /16-stave /26.7 × 34.8 cm /M00 C00 Y10 S00) Continuity draft of I/I mm. 172–191. II/3 m. 394. Numerous glue spots and bleed-through from ink on verso side. (Pencil, black ink.) 1919.

130 – 13/V, fol. 4ᵛ: (no brand /16-stave /26.7 × 34.8 cm /M00 C00 Y10 S00) I/I m. 153 in ink (from *Particell*), and I/1 mm. 162–172. Measure numbers correspond to those in the *Particell*. (Pencil, black ink.) 1919.

131 – 13/V, fol. 5ʳ (J.E. & Co. /Protokoll Schutzmarke No. 61 /18-stave (arranged 6+6+6) /originally: 26.5 × 34.5 cm, now fragment: 26.5 × 22.8 /M00 C00 Y10 S00) Continuity draft of II/4, discarded. (Indelible pencil, pencil.) 1920.

132 – 13/V, fol. 5ᵛ (J.E. & Co. /Protokoll Schutzmarke No. 61 /18-stave (arranged 6+6+6) /originally: 26.5 × 34.5 cm, now fragment: 26.5 × 22.8 /M00 C00 Y10 S00) Continuity draft of waltz leading up to Section III (II/4 mm. 504), which has been discarded. (Pencil, blue pencil, orange pencil.) 1920.

ÖNB Musiksammlung F 21 Berg 13/VI

General Description

Six leaves of sketches, predominantly for II/4. Single leaves of various types of paper, except for fols. 1–2, a bifolio. Many of these sketches use the same blue/orange colored pencil as 13/V and undoubtedly date from the same summer (1920).

Description of Individual Leaves

133 – 13/VI, fol. 1ʳ: (no brand /12-stave /25.6 × 33.2 cm /M00 C00 Y10 S00) Has been folded in thirds. Early draft of Section III of the Waltz (II/4 mm. 504–513) differing radically from final version. (Pencil, orange pencil, blue pencil.) 1920.

134 – 13/VI, fol. 1ᵛ: (no brand /12-stave /25.6 × 33.2 cm /M00 C00 Y10 S00) Continuity draft of II/4 mm. 560–589. (Indelible pencil, black ink, blue pencil.) 1920.

135 – 13/VI, fol. 2ʳ: (no brand /12-stave /25.6 × 33.2 cm /M00 C00 Y10 S00) Concept sketch of II/4 mm. 590 and ff. Headed with "Todesahnung + Ländler I." (Pencil, smudges of black ink.) 1920.

136 – 13/VI, fol. 2ᵛ: (no brand /12-stave /25.6 × 33.2 cm /M00 C00 Y10 S00) Sketch of pitch ranges for Bombardon. (Orange pencil, pencil.) 1920.

137 – 13/VI, fol. 3ʳ: (J.E. & Co. /Protokoll Schutzmarke No. 3 /14-stave /26.5 × 34.2 cm /M00 C00 Y10 S00) Motivic ideas for I/V with annotations of text, for instance, staves 4–5, "er umfasst sie wieder," and staff 4, "eindränglich." This sketch should be studied with the New Haven source of the same material. (Pencil, orange pencil, blue pencil.) 1919.

138 – 13/VI, fol. 3ᵛ: (J.E. & Co. /Protokoll Schutzmarke No. 3 /14-stave /26.5 × 34.2 cm /M00 C00 Y10 S00) *Particell* leaf, in ink and pencil. I/4 mm. 635–655. (Black ink, pencil, orange pencil.) 1919.

139 – 13/VI, fol. 4ʳ: (no brand /12-stave /originally: 25.6 × 33 cm, now fragment: 23.1 × 33 cm /M00 C00 Y10 S00) Very porous. Continuity draft of II/4 mm. 600–604. (Pencil, black ink.) 1921.

140 – 13/VI, fol. 4ᵛ: (no brand /12-stave /originally: 25.6 × 33 cm, now fragment: 23.1 × 33 cm /M00 C00 Y10 S00) Continuity draft of II/4 mm. 605–609. (Pencil.) 1921.

141 – 13/VI, fol. 5ʳ: (no brand /12-stave /originally: 25.6 × 33 cm, now fragment: 24.2 × 33 cm /M00 C00 Y10 S00) Continuity draft of II/4 mm. 610–624. (Pencil.) 1921.

142 – 13/VI, fol. 5ᵛ: (no brand /12-stave /originally: 25.6 × 33 cm, now fragment: 24.2 × 33 cm /M00 C00 Y10 S00) Continuity draft of II/4 mm. 625–642. (Pencil, black ink.) 1921.

ÖNB Musiksammlung F 21 Berg 13/VII

General Description

The missing gathering for 13/I, to be placed between pages 14 and 15. The correct succession of the pages should be: 2ʳ, 2ᵛ, 3ʳ,3ᵛ,4ʳ,4ᵛ,5ʳ,5ᵛ,6ʳ,6ᵛ,1ʳ,1ᵛ. Like 13/I, the entire gathering dates from 1921.

Description of Individual Leaves

143 – 13/VII, fol. 1ʳ: (J.E. & Co. /No. 70 /10-stave /12.9 × 16.7 cm /M10 C00 Y40 S00) Rhythmic sketches of the rhythm for III/3. (Pencil.) 1921.

144 – 13/VII, fol. 1ᵛ: (J.E. & Co. /No. 70 /10-stave /12.9 × 16.7 cm /M10 C00 Y40 S00) More operations on the rhythmic pattern for III/3, including "Umkehrung" (inversion). (Pencil.) 1921.

145 – 13/VII, fol. 2ʳ: (J.E. & Co. /No. 70 /10-stave /12.9 × 16.7 cm /M10 C00 Y40 S00) Sketch of seven-tone ostinato, II/4 mm. 705–712, with some revision. Doodle of someone's face—Schoenberg's? (Pencil, black ink.) 1921.

146 – 13/VII, fol. 2ᵛ: (J.E. & Co. /No. 70 /10-stave /12.9 × 16.7 cm /M10 C00 Y40 S00) Continuation of ostinato sketch from previous page. Sketch of nine-note ostinato, II/4 mm. 713–723. (Pencil, with continuation of letter to Schoenberg from September 1921 in black ink.) 1921.

147 – 13/VII, fol. 3ʳ: (J.E. & Co. /No. 70 /10-stave /12.9 × 16.7 cm /M10 C00 Y40 S00) Continuation of ostinato sketch from previous page. Sketch of eleven-note ostinato, II/4 mm. 724–737 with some revision. (Pencil, with black ink from Schoenberg letter draft.) 1921.

148 – 13/VII, fol. 3ᵛ: (J.E. & Co. /No. 70 /10-stave /12.9 × 16.7 cm /M10 C00 Y40 S00) Sketch of ostinato for II/4 mm. 713–716. Rhythmic shorthand of II/5 mm. 746–751. Measure numbers by Berg are ten less than finished score. (Pencil.) 1921.

149 – 13/VII, fol. 4ʳ: (J.E. & Co. /No. 70 /10-stave /12.9 × 16.7 cm /M10 C00 Y40 S00) Continuation of sketch from previous page, but in more detail. Continuity draft of II/5 mm. 751–760 (staves 1–9). Staff 10: II/5 m. 750, last beat-751. (Pencil.) 1921.

150 – 13/VII, fol. 4ᵛ: (J.E. & Co. /No. 70 /10-stave /12.9 × 16.7 cm /M10 C00 Y40 S00) Continuation of sketch from previous page. Continuity draft using primarily rhythmic shorthand of II/5 mm. 761–773. (Pencil.) 1921.

151 – 13/VII, fol. 5ʳ: (J.E. & Co. /No. 70 /10-stave /12.9 × 16.7 cm /M10 C00 Y40 S00) Ideas for II/5. (Pencil.) 1921.

152 – 13/VII, fol. 5ᵛ: (J.E. & Co. /No. 70 /10-stave /12.9 × 16.7 cm /M10 C00 Y40 S00) More ideas for II/5. Annotation on staff 7 "fanfare." (Pencil.) 1921.

153 – 13/VII, fol. 6ʳ: (J.E. & Co. /No. 70 /10-stave /12.9 × 16.7 cm /M10 C00 Y40 S00) Ideas of III/2 with corresponding measure numbers: Staves 6–8 "Angst 103," Staves 6–8 far right, "B Liebe 104," etc. (Pencil, very dark indelible pencil.) 1921.

154 – 13/VII, fol. 6ᵛ: (J.E. & Co. /No. 70 /10-stave /12.9 × 16.7 cm /M10 C00 Y40 S00) Staves 1–3, continuity draft of end of III/2 mm. 107–108. Staves 5–10 sketches of rhythm to be used in III/3. (Pencil.) 1921.

155 – 13/VII, fol. 7ʳ: (J.E. & Co. /No. 70 /10-stave /12.9 × 16.7 cm /M10 C00 Y40 S00) Initial sketches for Margret's song, III/3 mm. 168–179. (Pencil.) 1921.

156 – 13/VII, fol. 7ᵛ: (J.E. & Co. /No. 70 /10-stave /12.9 × 16.7 cm /M10 C00 Y40 S00) Rhythmic shorthand for Wozzeck's song: "Es Ritten drei Reiter" III/3 mm. 144–152. (Pencil.) 1921.

157 – 13/VII, fol. 8ʳ: (J.E. & Co. /No. 70 /10-stave /12.9 × 16.7 cm /M10 C00 Y40 S00) Rhythmic shorthand for III/3 mm. 122–141 and setting of lines "Ich glaub' ich hab' mich geschnitten" through end of scene. (Pencil.) 1921.

158 – 13/VII, fol. 8ᵛ: (J.E. & Co. /No. 70 /10-stave /12.9 × 16.7 cm /M10 C00 Y40 S00) More manipulations of rhythmic motive for III/5 "andere Rhytmus" "verschoben" etc. (Pencil.) 1921.

ÖNB Musiksammlung F21 Berg 13/VIII

General Description

A bifolio of 16-stave paper (26.5 × 34.5) that has been folded in fourths. Sketches for II/3 and III/2. Color: Y30C10M10

Description of Individual Leaves

159 – 13/VIII, fol. 1ʳ: (no brand /16-stave /26.5 × 34.5 cm /M10 C10 Y30 S00) Continuity draft of II/3 mm. 383–389. (Pencil.) 1920.

160 – 13/VIII, fol. 1ᵛ: (no brand /16-stave /26.5 × 34.5 cm /M10 C10 Y30 S00) Continuity draft of II/3 mm. 390–397. Glue spot staff 8. (Pencil.) 1920.

161 – 13/VIII, fol. 2ʳ: (no brand /16-stave /26.5 × 34.5 cm /M10 C10 Y30 S00) Continuity draft of II/3 mm. 397–402. (Pencil, black ink.) 1920.

162 – 13/VIII, fol. 2ᵛ: (no brand /16-stave /26.5 × 34.5 cm /M10 C10 Y30 S00) Continuity draft of III/2 mm. 73–80, 100, and 103. This color matches that of the sketches for III/2 in the 1921 sketchbook (13/VII). (Pencil, dark indelible pencil.) 1921.

ÖNB Musiksammlung F 21 Berg 13/IX

General Description

Four individual leaves of various types of paper. Most contain sketches for II/1.

Description of Individual Leaves

163 – 13/IX, fol. 1ʳ: (no brand /12-stave paper /24.8 × 31.8 cm /M00 C00 Y10 S00) Continuity draft with accurate measure numbers for II/1 mm. 29–53, with some revision. This leaf has been folded numerous times. Traces of glue on right-hand margin. (Pencil.) 1920.

164 – 13/IX, fol. 1ᵛ: (no brand /12-stave paper /24.8 × 31.8 cm /M00 C00 Y10 S00) Staves 1–9: Continuity draft of II/1 mm. 6–29. Staves 10–12: Early sketch of II/1 mm. 2–6. Blotches of glue on bottom margin. (Pencil.) 1920.

165 – 13/IX, fol. 2ʳ: (J.E. & Co. /Protokoll Schutzmarke No. 3 /14-stave /originally: 26.5 × 34.5, now fragment: 26.5 × 27.2 cm /M00 C00 Y10 S00) Continuity draft of III/5 mm. 371–382, with accurate measure numbers. (Pencil, black ink.) 1921.

166 – 13/IX, fol. 2ᵛ: (J.E. & Co. /Protokoll Schutzmarke No. 3 /14-stave /originally: 26.5 × 34.5, now fragment: 26.5 × 27.2 cm /M00 C00 Y10 S00) Blank.

167 – 13/IX, fol. 3ʳ: (J.E. & Co. /Protokoll Schutzmarke No. 3 /14-stave /originally: 26.5 × 34.5, now fragment: 25.7 (top) – 25.9 (bottom) × 34.5 cm /M00 C00 Y10 S00) Originally a *Particell* leaf that was later used for sketches. Staves 1–4 *Particell* copy for II/1 mm. 81–82. Staves 5–14: II/1 109–123, mostly rhythmic setting of vocal line. (Pencil, black ink.) 1920.

168 – 13/IX, fol. 3ᵛ: (J.E. & Co. /Protokoll Schutzmarke No. 3 /14-stave /originally: 26.5 × 34.5, now fragment: 25.7 (top) – 25.9 (bottom) × 34.5 cm /M00 C00 Y10 S00) Continuity draft of II/1 mm. 106–108. (Pencil.) 1920.

169 – 13/IX, fol. 4ʳ: (no brand /14-stave /25 × 33.3 cm /M00 C00 Y10 S00) Has been folded in fourths. Continuity draft of II/1 mm. 93–108. (Pencil, specks of black ink.) 1920.

ÖNB Musiksammlung F21 Berg 13/X

General Description

Fragments of 12-stave and 16-stave paper, containing mostly sketches for the sonata, II/1. The paper type of leaves 2–4 is used in other sketches for II/1, I/5 and probably dates from 1920. Color: Y10.

Description of Individual Leaves:

170 – 13/X fol. 1r: (no brand /12-stave /11.3 × 16.3 cm /M00 C00 Y10 S00) II/3 m. 400 with orchestration. (Pencil, red pencil.) 1920.

171 – 13/X fol. 1v: (no brand /12-stave /11.3 × 16.3 cm /M00 C00 Y10 S00) (Pencil.) 1920.

172 – 13/X fol. 2r: (no brand /16-stave /11.4 × 26.5 cm /M00 C00 Y10 S00) Sketch of I/1 "Courante" with text "Was ist heut' für ein Wetter? "Süd-nord," etc. with continuity draft of this section differing substantially from final score. (Pencil.) 1919.

173 – 13/X fol. 2v: (no brand /16-stave /11.4 × 26.5 cm /M00 C00 Y10 S00) "f moll" theme. Fanning suggests perhaps from III/1, mm. 33–35.5 (Pencil.) 1920.

174 – 13/X fol. 3r: (no brand /16-stave /11.1 × 26.6 cm /M00 C00 Y10 S00) Motivic ideas for "Kind" section of II/1. Partial leaf. (Pencil.) 1920.

175 – 13/X fol. 3v: (no brand /16-stave /11.1 × 26.6 cm /M00 C00 Y10 S00) Blank. 1920.

176 – 13/X fol. 4r: (no brand /16-stave /11.4 × 26.5 cm /M00 C00 Y10 S00) Form sketch for II/1. Partial leaf of 16-stave paper. (Pencil.) 1920.

177 – 13/X fol. 4v: (no brand /16-stave /11.4 × 26.5 cm /M00 C00 Y10 S00) Theme for a waltz, not used in final version. (Pencil.) 1920.

ÖNB Musiksammlung F 21 Berg 13/XI

General Description

Two single leaves and a bifolio (2–3) of sketches from II/1 and II/5. All Y10, except for leaf 4.

Description of Individual Leaves

178 – 13/XI, fol. 1r: (no brand /12-stave /24.6 × 31.8 cm /M00 C00 Y10 S00) Sketch of *Wozzeck* II/1 early rhythmic sketch. Headed "Symphonie, 5 Bildern 1. Sonatensatz" mm. 6–60. Paper has been folded multiple times. (Pencil.) 1920.

179 – 13/XI, fol. 1v: (no brand /12-stave /24.6 × 31.8 cm /M00 C00 Y10 S00) Early draft of II/1 mm. 49–60. (Pencil.) 1920.

180 – 13/XI, fol. 2r: (no brand /16-stave /26.7 × 34.8 cm /M00 C00 Y10 S00) Has been folded into fourths. Continuity draft of II/3 mm. 372–375, and 364–373. (Pencil.) 1920.

181 – 13/XI, fol. 2v: (no brand /16-stave /26.7 × 34.8 cm /M00 C00 Y10 S00) Continuity draft of II/1–II/2 mm. 162–172. Continuation of sketch on 3r. (Pencil, black ink.) 1920.

182 – 13/XI, fol. 3r: (no brand /16-stave /26.7 × 34.8 cm /M00 C00 Y10 S00) Continuity draft of II/1 mm.139, 141–161. Measure numbers in sketch are same as in final score. (Pencil, black ink.) 1920.

183 – 13/XI, fol. 3v: (no brand /16-stave /26.7 × 34.8 cm /M00 C00 Y10 S00) Continuity draft of II/3 mm. 374–382. Rhythmic sketch of

vocal line, staves 14–15, II/3 mm. 395–397. Glue spots on upper half of leaf. (Pencil.) 1920.

184 – 13/XI, fol. 4ʳ: (no brand /14-stave /originally: 33 × 45 cm, now fragment: 25 × 33 cm /M10 C00 Y40 S00) Continuity draft of II/5 mm. 797–805. Glue abrasion staff 6. Measure numbers in sketch are eleven less than in finished score. (Pencil, black ink.) 1921.

185 – 13/XI, fol. 4ᵛ: (no brand /14-stave /originally: 33 × 45 cm, now fragment: 25 × 33 cm /M10 C00 Y40 S00) Continuity draft of mm. 806–818. (Pencil.) 1921.

ÖNB Musiksammlung F 21 Berg 13/XII

General Description

Berg's master form chart of II/4 with many annotations about dramatic action. 1920.

Description of Individual Leaves

186 – 13/XII, fol. 1ʳ: (22 × 33.8 cm /M00 C00 Y20 S00) Rental form "Löbliche k. k. Steuer-Administration, etc. Form outline for movements of three acts. Rhythmic sketch for "Reiter am Rhein." More detailed annotations about section of II/4 (trio, etc.). Glued to leaf 2. (Pencil, smears of blue indelible pencil.) 1920.

187 – 13/XII, fol. 1ᵛ: (22 × 33.8 cm /M00 C00 Y20 S00) More notes about transitions between sections in II/4. (Pencil, dark indelible pencil.) 1920.

188 – 13/XII, fol. 2ʳ: (no brand /12-stave /25.6 × 33 cm /M20 C10 Y40 S00) Detailed outline of form for II/4. Paper has numerous rips on right-hand margin. Right-hand margin is heavily smeared. [Pencil, blue pencil (like 13/IV), indelible pencil.] 1920.

189 – 13/XII, fol. 2ᵛ: (no brand /12-stave /25.6 × 33 cm /M20 C10 Y40 S00) Blank, except for small, unidentified rhythmic sketch at bottom of page. (Pencil, black ink.) 1920.

ÖNB Musiksammlung F 21 Berg 13/XIII

General Description

A single leaf of twelve-stave paper which has been folded into fourths. Like 13/XI, fol. 1 it is a sketch of the form of Act II "Symphonie in 5 Sätzen." It also uses the same paper type and was most likely completed at the same time, in the summer of 1920. On the back of the leaf Berg outlines the Scenarium for Act III.

Description of Individual Leaves

190 – 13/XIII, fol. 1ʳ: (no brand /12-stave /24.6 × 31.8 cm /M00 C00 Y10 S00) (Same paper type as 13/XI fol. 1.) Outline of the Scenarium for Act III, including location of scene, type of light, transition between scenes, musical form, and vocal delivery. (Pencil, black ink.) 1920.

191 – 13/XIII, fol. 1ᵛ: (no brand /12-stave /24.6 × 31.8 cm /M00 C00 Y10 S00) Outline of form for Act II. Two drafts of opening of Act II/1followed by outlines of the form for each scene and how they transition between each other. (Pencil, black ink.) 1920.

ÖNB Musiksammlung F 21 Berg 13/XIV

General Description

Two leaves of 14-stave paper (no brand) containing sketches for III/1. Assuming that Berg jumped ahead and completed III/1 before finishing II/4, these sketches would date from 1920—at the very latest, 1921. The dark purple pencil included in these sketches appears in the 1921 sketchbook.

Description of Individual Leaves

192 – 13/XIV, fol. 1ʳ: (no brand /14-stave /25.7 × 33 cm /Y30 M10 C10) Has been folded into fourths width-wise. Rips in right-hand margin. Continuity draft of III/1 mm. 26–35. (Pencil, dark indelible pencil.)

193 – 13/XIV, fol. 1ᵛ: (no brand /14-stave /25.7 × 33 cm /Y30 M10 C10) Continuity draft of III/1 mm. 17–29. (Pencil, dark indelible pencil.)

194 – 13/XIV, fol. 2ʳ: (no brand /14-stave /25.7 × 33 cm /Y30 M10 C10) Has been folded into eighths. Continuity draft of III/1 mm. 33–40. Rips at left margin. (Pencil, dark indelible pencil.)

195 – 13/XIV, fol. 2ᵛ: (no brand /14-stave /25.7 × 33 cm /Y30 M10 C10) Continuity draft of III/1 mm. 52–63. With analysis of themes with seven notes. (Pencil, some bleed-through from dark indelible pencil on recto side.)

ÖNB Musiksammlung F 21 Berg 28/XXXVII

General Description

Sketches for Act II/4 that are found in Berg's sketches for Lulu.

Description of Individual Leaves

196 – 28/XXXVII, fol. 14ᵛ: (no brand /12-stave /25.5 (top) – 25.4 (bottom) × 32.8 (left) – 33 (right) cm /M00 C00 Y10 S00) Continuity draft of II/4 mm. 465–470. Numeric notation in left-hand margin refers to interval cycles used to designate the harmonic rhythm of the four voices, mm. 465–468. (Pencil, black ink.)

197 – 28/XXXVII, fol. 17ʳ: (no brand /12-stave /25.5 (top) – 25.4 (bottom) × 32.8 (left) – 33 (right) cm /M00 C00 Y10 S00) Continuity draft of II/4 mm. 471–481. (Pencil, black ink.)

ÖNB Musiksammlung F 21 Berg 48

General Description

Berg's pre-opus piano sonatas. The only leaf relating to *Wozzeck* is fol. 9ʳ, the opening measures of which Berg used for the Interlude in Act III between scenes 4 and 5.[6]

Description of Individual Leaves

198 – 48, fol. 9ʳ: (JE & Co. Protokoll Schutzmarke No. 10/12-stave /26.2 × 34.4 cm /M10 C00 Y40 S00) Pre-opus piano sonata No. 4, mm. 1–21. (Black ink.) 1908.

ÖNB Musiksammlung F 21 Berg 74/XV

General Description

According to Fanning, "lecture notes on rondo form, with examples from Beethoven Piano Sonatas op. 13 and op. 31 no. 1."[7] The only sketch relating to *Wozzeck* is fol. 1ʳ.

Description of Individual Leaves

199 – 74/XV, fol. 1ʳ: (no brand /12-stave /25.7 × 32.7 cm /M10 C00 Y40 S00) Instrumentation sketch of II/1 mm. 211–218. Annotated with "Mödling Donnerstag Kurs." (Pencil, black ink, blue pencil.)

ÖNB Musiksammlung F21 Berg 70/I

General Description

A potpourri of sketches, mainly for the Chamber Concerto. The only sketches relating to *Wozzeck* are fols. 2ʳ–3ᵛ, 8ᵛ, and 9ʳ–10ᵛ (both 2ʳ–3ᵛ and 9ʳ–10ᵛ are bifolia). 9^r–10^v are the same paper type as F 21 Berg 13/III (Protokoll Schutzmarke No. 29) and probably date from 1918. They also consist of thematic ideas Berg copied from 13/II. Color: Y10. Fols. 13^r–15^v functioned as a cover for the sketches of II/2. When the three fragments are fitted together (13^r with 14^v and 15^r), they form a single leaf of 20-stave paper, labeled "Originalmanuscript (bleistiftgeschrieben) den II Scene des II. Aktes /dort ersetzt durch Kopie (tintengeschrieben) /vollständig/" Y40M10. The source F 21 Berg 70/I has been foliated by the ÖNB.

Description of Individual Leaves

200 – 70/I, fol. 2^r: (21 × 34 cm /M20 C00 Y40 S00) A fascinating chart showing *Wozzeck* as part of a trilogy of three operas: *Wozzeck, Vincent,* and *Wolfgang*. Chart is headed, "Die Drei W Trilogy v. AB." The Chamber Concerto and a choral work using a text by Karl Kraus are interim works between the three operas. Small design on back (2^v and 3^r). (Pencil, black ink.) 1925?

201 – 70/I, fol. 2^v: (21 × 34 cm /M20 C00 Y40 S00) Blank (as far as sketch content). (Pencil.)

202 – 70/I, fol. 3^r: (21 × 34 cm /M20 C00 Y40 S00) Blank (as far as sketch content). (Pencil.)

203 – 70/I, fol. 3^v: (21 × 34 cm /M20 C00 Y40 S00) Blank (as far as sketch content). (Pencil.)

204 – 70/I, fol. 8^v: (no brand /24-stave /fragment: 26.5 × 28.2 cm /M00 C00 Y10 S00) Rhythmic sketch for I/5 mm. 677–680, staves 4–5. Originally bifolio of 24-stave paper folded in quarters. (Pencil, indelible pencil, red pencil, offset of blue pencil.) 1919.

205 – 70/I, fol. 9^r: (J.E. & Co. /Protokoll Schutzmarke No. 29 /12-stave /26.5 × 34.4 cm /M00 C00 Y10 S00) Thematic sketches recopied from 13/II, headed "Wozzeck skizzen, Diverses." The theme on staves 5–6 is copied from 13/II p. 90 (staves 5–10). The theme appearing on staves 7–9 is recopied from 13/II p. 78. Entire bifolio has been folded in half. (Pencil.) 1918.

206 – 70/I, fol. 9^v: (J.E. & Co. /Protokoll Schutzmarke No. 29 /12-stave /26.5 × 34.4 cm /M00 C00 Y10 S00) More thematic ideas. The theme appearing on staves 7–10 is recopied from 13/II p. 55 (staves 1–3). The theme on staves 11–12 is copied from 13/II p. 69 (staves 1–6). The theme and last idea on staves 1–3 are copied from 13/II p. 52. (Pencil.) 1918.

207 – 70/I, fol. 10^r: (J.E. & Co. /Protokoll Schutzmarke No. 29 /12-stave /26.5 × 34.4 cm /M00 C00 Y10 S00) The Zwischenspiel theme (staves 2–3) and its variation (staves 5–6) are copied from 13/II p. 60. The theme appearing on staves 8–9 is copied from page 69 of 13/II (staves 6–10). The idea to the far right on staff 8 (Terzen) and the following theme on staves 11–12 are copied from 13/II p. 70 (staves 1–6). (Pencil.) 1918.

208 – 70/I, fol. 10ᵛ: (J.E. & Co. /Protokoll Schutzmarke No. 29 /12-stave /26.5 ×
34.4 cm /M00 C00 Y10 S00) Discarded chord successions.
(Pencil.) 1918.

ÖNB *Musiksammlung F21 Berg 70/II*

General Description

The second sketchbook Berg completed for *Wozzeck*, containing primarily sketches
for I/3. Five nested bifolia of 6-stave paper, with one leaf of another paper type inserted
at the end of the sketchbook. 25.3 × 15.7. Color: Y40M10. All of the sketches (except
for the inserted leaf) date from 1919. This source has been foliated by the ÖNB.

Description of Individual Leaves

209 – 70/II, Cover: The cover of the sketchbook reads: "Notenheft für <u>Helene
Nahowski</u>," with her name written in her hand. (Black ink.)
1919.

210 – 70/II, fol. 1ʳ: (no brand /6-stave /25.5 × 15.7 cm /M10 C00 Y40 S00)
I/3 mm. Early draft 329–332 (staves 1–4). Staves 5–6, beats
3–4 m. 332–333, first beat. Remainder, staves 5–6: another
draft of 329–332. (Pencil.) 1919.

211 – 70/II, fol. 1ᵛ: (no brand /6-stave /25.5 × 15.7 cm /M10 C00 Y40 S00)
Draft of I/3 mm. 326–334, not yet corresponding exactly to
the final score. (Pencil.) 1919.

212 – 70/II, fol. 2ʳ: (no brand /6-stave /25.5 × 15.7 cm /M10 C00 Y40 S00)
Draft of I/3 mm. 335–341. (Pencil.) 1919.

213 – 70/II, fol. 2ᵛ: (no brand /6-stave /25.5 × 15.7 cm /M10 C00 Y40 S00)
Continuity draft of I/3 mm. 342–349. (Pencil.) 1919.

214 – 70/II, fol. 3ʳ: (no brand /6-stave /25.5 × 15.7 cm /M10 C00 Y40 S00)
Continuity draft of I/3 mm. 350–361. (Pencil.) 1919.

215 – 70/II, fol. 3ᵛ: (no brand /6-stave /25.5 × 15.7 cm /M10 C00 Y40 S00) Draft
of I/3 mm. 372–399. Berg has labeled sections of the lullaby
with letters so that he can use them as shorthand when the
song repeats. (Indelible pencil, pencil, black ink.) 1919.

216 – 70/II, fol. 4ʳ: (no brand /6-stave /25.5 × 15.7 cm /M10 C00 Y40 S00)
Draft labeled "Thema Scene I/4," which has the character,
particularly in the bass, of the theme appearing at m. 525
and ff. Staves 5–6: mm. 394–395. (Pencil, indelible pencil.)
1919.

217 – 70/II, fol. 4ᵛ: (no brand /6-stave /25.5 × 15.7 cm /M10 C00 Y40 S00)
Drafts of mm. I/3 mm. 396–403. (Pencil.) 1919.

218 – 70/II, fol. 5ʳ: (no brand /6-stave /25.5 × 15.7 cm /M10 C00 Y40 S00)
Continuity draft of I/3 mm. 404–416. Differs significantly
from final version. (Pencil.) 1919.

219 – 70/II, fol. 5ᵛ: (no brand /6-stave /25.5 × 15.7 cm /M10 C00 Y40 S00) Draft of I/3, mm. 363–370. (Pencil, indelible pencil, orange-red pencil.) 1919.

220 – 70/II, fol. 6ʳ: (no brand /6-stave /25.5 × 15.7 cm /M10 C00 Y40 S00) Draft of I/3 mm. 369–371. (Pencil.) 1919.

221 – 70/II, fol. 6ᵛ: (no brand /6-stave /25.5 × 15.7 cm /M10 C00 Y40 S00) Continuity draft of I/3 mm. 417–423 and 426–427. Differs significantly from final version. (Pencil.) 1919.

222 – 70/II, fol. 7ʳ: (no brand /6-stave /25.5 × 15.7 cm /M10 C00 Y40 S00) Continuity draft of I/3 mm. 428–433. (Pencil, black ink.) 1919.

223 – 70/II, fol. 7ᵛ: (no brand /6-stave /25.5 × 15.7 cm /M10 C00 Y40 S00) Continuity draft of I/3 mm. 434–439. (Pencil.) 1919.

224 – 70/II, fol. 8ʳ: (no brand /6-stave /25.5 × 15.7 cm /M10 C00 Y40 S00) Continuity draft of I/3 mm. 440–446. (Pencil.) 1919.

225 – 70/II, fol. 8ᵛ: (no brand /6-stave /25.5 × 15.7 cm /M10 C00 Y40 S00) Continuity draft of I/3 mm. 447–454. (Pencil.) 1919.

226 – 70/II, fol. 9ʳ: (no brand /6-stave /25.5 × 15.7 cm /M10 C00 Y40 S00) Continuity draft of I/3 mm. 453–458. Measure number 258 annotated by Berg at end of this draft indicates that he had not yet composed scene 1. (Pencil, teal blue pencil.) 1919.

227 – 70/II, fol. 9ᵛ: (no brand /6-stave /25.5 × 15.7 cm /M10 C00 Y40 S00) Continuity draft of I/3 mm.459–467. (Pencil.) 1919.

228 – 70/II, fol. 10ʳ: (no brand /6-stave /25.5 × 15.7 cm /M10 C00 Y40 S00) Continuity draft of I/3 mm. 468–473 and 477–479. (Pencil.) 1919.

229 – 70/II, fol. 10ᵛ: (no brand /6-stave /25.5 × 15.7 cm /M10 C00 Y40 S00) Continuity draft of I/3 mm. 480–481. (Pencil.) 1919.

230 – 70/II, fol. 11ʳ: (no brand /16-stave /25.9 × 11.6 cm /M00 C00 Y10 S00) Continuity draft of III/1 mm. 45–51. Fragment of 16-staff paper that has been folded in half. No brand, but like 70/III fol. 5. Top section of leaf. This sketch probably dates from 1920. (Pencil, black ink.) 1920.

231 – 70/II, fol. 11ᵛ: (no brand /16-stave /25.9 × 11.6 cm /M00 C00 Y10 S00) Early draft of III/1 mm. 45–51 using rhythmic shorthand. (Pencil, black ink.) 1920.

ÖNB Musiksammlung F 21 Berg 70/III

General Description

Twelve leaves of various types of music paper and an envelope, containing primarily sketches for I/1. All single leaves except for 4–5 and 8–9 which are bifolia. Leaves 1 and 3 have been separated and should follow each other based on content of the sketch and paper profile in the following order: 1ᵛ, 1ʳ, 3ʳ, 3ᵛ.

Description of Individual Leaves

232 – 70/III, fol. 1ʳ: (J.E. & Co. /Protokoll Schutzmarke No. 3 /14-stave /26.5 × 34.7 cm /M00 C00 Y10 S00) Continuity draft of I/I mm. 58–114. Paper has been folded into fourths horizontally. Attached to a fragment of fol. 3. Paper marked with pin pricks. (Pencil.) 1919.

233 – 70/III, fol. 1ᵛ: (J.E. & Co. /Protokoll Schutzmarke No. 3 /14-stave /26.5 × 34.7 cm /M00 C00 Y10 S00) Verbal annotations about Drum Major and musical accompaniment for I/5. Staves 6–14 continuity draft of I/2 mm. 286–295. (Pencil.) 1918 and 1919.

234 – 70/III, fol. 2ʳ: (J.E. & Co. /Protokoll Schutzmarke No. 3 /14-stave /26.5 × 34.7 cm /M00 C00 Y10 S00) Continuity draft of I/1 mm. 42–57. Paper has been folded in half. Has same pattern of pin pricks as fol. 1. (Pencil, black ink.) 1919.

235 – 70/III, fol. 2ᵛ: (J.E. & Co. /Protokoll Schutzmarke No. 3 /14-stave /26.5 × 34.7 cm /M00 C00 Y10 S00) Fairly complete draft of I/1 mm. 1–19. [Pencil, black ink smudge, teal blue pencil (like 13/ IV).] 1919.

236 – 70/III, fol. 3ʳ: (J.E. & Co. /Protokoll Schutzmarke No. 3 /14-stave /26.5 × 34.7 cm /M00 C00 Y10 S00) Continuity draft of I/1 mm. 78–109. Paper has been folded horizontally in fourths. Glue spots right and left center. (Pencil.) 1919.

237 – 70/III, fol. 3ᵛ: (J.E. & Co. /Protokoll Schutzmarke No. 3 /14-stave /26.5 × 34.7 cm /M00 C00 Y10 S00) Continuity draft of I/1 mm. 20–41. Large ink spill. (Pencil, black ink.) 1919.

238 – 70/III, fol. 4ʳ: (no brand /16-stave /26.6 × 34.8 cm /M00 C00 Y10 S00) Continuity draft of I/1 mm. 127–135. Glue spot in upper right margin. Paper has been folded into fourths. (Pencil, spot of black ink.) 1919.

239 – 70/III, fol. 4ᵛ: (no brand /16-stave /26.6 × 34.8 cm /M00 C00 Y10 S00) Continuity draft of I/1 mm. 136–143. (Pencil, black ink.) 1919.

240 – 70/III, fol. 5ʳ: (no brand /16-stave /26.6 × 34.8 cm /M00 C00 Y10 S00) Continuity draft of I/1 mm. 144–153. [Pencil, black ink, teal blue pencil (like 13/IV) as minor edits.] 1919.

241 – 70/III, fol. 5ᵛ: (no brand /16-stave /26.6 × 34.8 cm /M00 C00 Y10 S00) Continuity draft of I/1 mm. 151–161 with accurate measure numbers. Paper has many black ink spots and glue spots. (Pencil, black ink.) 1919.

242 – 70/III, fol. 6ʳ: (envelope /21.3 × 12.9 cm /M20 C00 Y60 S10) Envelope of telegram that has been used for a draft of a letter to Schoenberg. Draft asks about "Mitglieder Zahl, Trudel, general Veranstaltung 6 od. 7 Uhr," etc. No sketches. (Pencil.) 1919.

243 – 70/III, fol. 6ᵛ: (envelope / 21.3 × 12.9 cm / M20 C00 Y60 S10) Envelope postmarked "3. XII 18" Letter draft probably dates from following summer (1919). (Pencil.) 1919.

244 – 70/III, fol. 7ʳ: (J.E. & Co. /Protokoll Schutzmarke No. 2 /12-stave /26.5 × 34.5 cm /M00 C00 Y10 S00) Continuity draft of I/1 mm. 129–138, mainly rhythmic setting of text. Paper has been folded into fourths. Has same diagonal line of pin pricks as fols. 1 and 2. (Pencil, indelible pencil.) 1919.

245 – 70/III, fol. 7ᵛ: (J.E. & Co. /Protokoll Schutzmarke No. 2 /12-stave /26.5 × 34.5 cm /M00 C00 Y10 S00) Continuity draft of I/1 mm. 109–128. (Pencil, indelible pencil.) 1919.

246 – 70/III, fol. 8ʳ: (J.E. & Co. /Protokoll Schutzmarke No. 2 /12-stave /26.5 × 34.5 cm /M00 C00 Y10 S00) Continuity draft of I/5 mm. 691–699. Paper has been folded into half. (Pencil, orange-red pencil.) 1919.

247 – 70/III, fol. 8ᵛ: (J.E. & Co. /Protokoll Schutzmarke No. 2 /12-stave /26.5 × 34.5 cm /M00 C00 Y10 S00) Continuity draft of I/5 mm. 700–707 (Pencil, orange-red pencil.) 1919.

248 – 70/III, fol. 9ʳ: (J.E. & Co. /Protokoll Schutzmarke No. 2 /12-stave /26.5 × 34.5 cm /M00 C00 Y10 S00) Continuity draft of I/5 mm. 707–713. (Pencil, orange-red pencil, teal blue pencil.) 1919.

249 – 70/III, fol. 9ᵛ: (J.E. & Co. /Protokoll Schutzmarke No. 2 /12-stave /26.5 × 34.5 cm /M00 C00 Y10 S00) Continuity draft of I/5 mm. 714–717 (Pencil, red-orange pencil, indelible pencil.) 1919.

250 – 70/III, fol. 10ʳ: (J.E. & Co. /Protokoll Schutzmarke No. 3 /14-stave /26.5 × 34.5 cm /M00 C00 Y10 S00) Motivic sketches, mostly for I/5. Staff 4 shows Captain's theme. Spots of black ink. Paper has been folded in half and has same diagonal line of pin pricks as fols. 1 and 2. Glue spot staves 8–11. (Pencil, orange-red pencil, teal blue pencil, indelible pencil.) 1919.

251 – 70/III, fol. 10ᵛ: (J.E. & Co. /Protokoll Schutzmarke No. 3 /14-stave /26.5 × 34.5 cm /M00 C00 Y10 S00) Outline of French Suite, English Suite, Mazurka, etc. Showing rhythmic patterns and form of movements. (Pencil, black ink spots.) 1919.

252 – 70/III, fol. 11ʳ: (J.E. & Co. /Protokoll Schutzmarke No. 2 /12-stave /26.5 × 34.5 cm /M00 C00 Y10 S00) Fairly complete draft of I/1 mm. 115–127. Has been folded into fourths. Section of paper removed from staves 2–5, left-hand margin. Same diagonal line of pin pricks as fols. 1 and 2. (Pencil.) 1919.

253 – 70/III, fol. 11ᵛ: (J.E. & Co. /Protokoll Schutzmarke No. 2 /12-stave /26.5 × 34.5 cm /M00 C00 Y10 S00) Draft of chart of interval cycles that Berg sent to Schoenberg in a letter from 1920. Discolorations in paper. (Pencil and black ink.) 1920.

254 – 70/III, fol. 12ʳ: (J.E. & Co. /DEPOSÉ No. 2 /12-stave /26.5 × 34.7 cm /M00 C00 Y10 S00) Continuity draft of I/2 mm. 303–325. (Pencil.) 1918.

255 – 70/III, fol. 12ᵛ: (J.E. & Co. /DEPOSÉ No. 2 /12-stave /26.5 × 34.7 cm /M00 C00 Y10 S00) Drafts of I/2 mm. 211–212 and 303–305. Annotation between staves 9 and 10: "Trommel beginn des Zwischenspiels." (Pencil, small revisions in orange-red pencil.) 1918.

ÖNB Musiksammlung F 21 Berg 128

General Description

Georg Büchner/Wozzeck/Zwei Fragmente/Im Insel Verlag zu Leipzig – Lenz, Insel Bücherei Nr. 92. 11.7 × 18.4. This source has been foliated by the ÖNB.

Description of Individual Leaves

256 – 128, fol. 1ʳ: Title page.

257 – 128, fol. 2ʳ: Newspaper cutting of performance of "Wozzeck" that Berg attended in Vienna "Residenzbühne Rotenturmstrasse 20.-Fleischmarkt 1. Anfang 8 Uhr. Ende von 1/2 10 Uhr. Zum erstenmal: Wozzeck von Georg Büchner." List of roles and actors. Annotated by Berg in pencil "5./V./14". (Pencil.)

258 – 128, fol. 2ᵛ: Blank.

259 – 128, fol. 3ʳ: Small annotations: line number, etc. (Pencil.)

260 – 128, fol. 3ʳ: Small annotations: line number, Arie, etc. (Pencil.)

261 – 128, fol. 4ʳ: Small revisions of text, crossing out of text Berg will omit. (Pencil, indelible pencil.)

262 – 128, fol. 4ᵛ: Division of I/2 into sections I, II, and IIIa and b based on Andres's song. Notes on type of military signal Berg will add in right-hand margin and bottom margin. (Pencil, indelible pencil, drops of black ink.)

263 – 128, fol. 5ʳ: Addition of stage directions and song "Eioe popei," etc. for I/3. (Pencil.)

264 – 128, fol. 5ᵛ: Addition of stage directions, I/3. (Pencil, indelible pencil.)

265 – 128, fol. 6ʳ: Analysis of I/4 into 12 sections. Annotation of notes of Doctor's 12-tone theme in right-hand margin. (Pencil.)

266 – 128, fol. 6ᵛ: Division of I/4 into 12 sections. (Pencil and indelible pencil.)

267 – 128, fol. 7ʳ: Division of I/4 into 12 sections. (Pencil and indelible pencil.)

268 – 128, fol. 7ᵛ: Revisions of text for end of I/4. (Pencil, orange pencil.)

269 – 128, fol. 8ʳ: Striking out of eliminated scene. (Pencil.)

270 – 128, fol. 8ᵛ: Small annotations to text of I/5. At bottom of page "Komm!" (Pencil.)

271 – 128, fol. 9ʳ: Striking out of unused scene. (Pencil.)

272 – 128, fol. 9ᵛ: Striking out of unused scene, additions of stage directions to II/1. (Pencil.)

273 – 128, fol. 10ʳ: Revisions of text, addition of stage directions for II/1. (Pencil.)

274 – 128, fol. 10^v: Revisions of text, addition of stage directions for II/1. (Pencil.)

275 – 128, fol. 11^r: Revisions of text. Annotation of 3/4 in top margin. (Pencil, indelible pencil.)

276 – 128, fol. 11^v: Division of text into sections A–F based on sections of the fugue. Revisions of text. (Pencil, indelible pencil.)

277 – 128, fol. 12^r: Further division of text into G–L based on sections of fugue. Revisions (particularly deletions) of text. Stage directions for II/3. (Pencil.)

278 – 128, fol. 12^v: Revisions of text for II/3, addition of stage directions and line of text numbers. (Pencil.)

279 – 128, fol. 13^r: Striking out of unused scene. Annotations to text "Orig" in dark indelible pencil that may date from a later time (1921?). (Indelible pencil.)

280 – 128, fol. 13^v: Analysis of II/4 based on sectional forms (Trio I, etc.). Addition of stage directions. (Pencil.)

281 – 128, fol. 14^r: Analysis of II/4 based on sectional forms (Trio II, etc.). Annotations in indelible pencil are revisions of text based on later edition. May date from 1921. (Pencil, indelible pencil.)

282 – 128, fol. 14^v: More analysis of II/4 based on sectional forms. Addition of stage directions. (Pencil.)

283 – 128, fol. 15^r: Striking out of unused scene. Addition of stage directions to II/5. Notations of rhythm. Indelible pencil annotation "Walzer VI schliesst" may date from a later time (1921). (Pencil, indelible pencil.)

284 – 128, fol. 15^v: Striking out of scene. Division of III/1into A and B themes. Division of whole into VIII sections. (Pencil.)

285 – 128, fol. 16^r: More division of III/1 into 8 sections, A and B themes. (Pencil.)

286 – 128, fol. 16^v: Striking out of unused scene. (Pencil.)

287 – 128, fol. 17^r: Striking out of unused scenes. (Pencil.)

288 – 128, fol. 17^v: Striking out of unused scene. Revisions of text and stage directions for III/2. (Pencil.)

289 – 128, fol. 18^r: Revisions of text and addition of stage directions for III/2 and III/3. Notations of musical events in III/1. (Pencil.)

290 – 128, fol. 18^v: Revisions of text and additions of stage directions for III/3. (Pencil.)

291 – 128, fol. 19^r: Revisions of text, addition of stage directions and musical events for III/4. (Pencil.)

292 – 128, fol. 19^v: Revisions of text and addition of stage directions for III/4 and III/5. (Pencil.)

293 – 128, fol. 20^r: Analysis of transitions between acts. (Pencil.)

294 – 128, fol. 38^r: Berg's underlining in text in blue pencil. Der Torso "Wozzeck" hat erst ... Discussion of Landau ordering. (Blue pencil.)

295 – 128, fol. 38^v: Analysis of II/5 into sections, revisions of text, additions of stage directions. Additions of syllable numbers in margin of next page. (Pencil.)

ÖNB Musiksammlung F 21 Berg 479/34

General Description

A small black notebook (5 × 14.5 cm) containing 22 pages of paper in graph format. This notebook, although undated, has notes from Berg's army service as Hilfsdienst. The military ordinance listed on p. 2 dates from 17/II 16, that is February 17, 1916. This notebook has been foliated by the ÖNB. On pp. 2ᵛ–4ᵛ are sketches for the scenic disposition of *Wozzeck*.

Description of Individual Leaves

296 – 479/34 fol. 2ᵛ: (notebook paper, graph format /5 × 14.5 cm /M00 C00 Y10 S00) A tabulation of the scenes, number of stage settings, consisting of fours acts. (Pencil.) 1916.

297 – 479/34 fol. 3ʳ: (notebook paper, graph format /5 × 14.5 cm /M00 C00 Y10 S00) A continuation of the tabulation of scenes and stage setting, through Act III, which in this version ends with the barracks scene. (Pencil.) 1916.

298 – 479/34 fol. 3ᵛ: (notebook paper, graph format /5 × 14.5 cm /M00 C00 Y10 S00) Continuation of the compilation on 3ʳ, through the end of Act IV (Kindscene), and a tabulation of the number of scenes and stage settings. (Pencil.) 1916.

299 – 479/34 fol. 4ʳ: (notebook paper, graph format /5 × 14.5 cm /M00 C00 Y10 S00) Tabulation of stage settings for *Wozzeck*. (Pencil.) 1916.

300 – 479/34 fol. 4ᵛ: (notebook paper, graph format /5 × 14.5 cm /M00 C00 Y10 S00) A comparison of the number of scenes, acts, and stage settings of *Pélleas* and *Wozzeck*. (Pencil and indelible pencil.) 1916.

ÖNB Musiksammlung F 21 Berg 14

General Description

Berg's autograph *Particell* (short score) of *Wozzeck* consisting of 96 leaves and containing his annotations of orchestration from which the full score was produced. This manuscript dates from Berg's entire period of composition in that he accumulated pages as he composed the opera. Thus, when Berg writes that he has finished the first act in 1919, this means that he has completed the *Particell* pages through that material. The paper types of the *Particell* also reflect (more accurately than the sketches themselves) the various kinds of paper Berg used during the years 1914 to 1922. The date appearing at the end of the *Particell* indicates when he had finished orchestration. Leaves of various types of paper bound with string by Berg. Measure numbers in *Particell* correspond to score.

Description of Individual Leaves

301 – 14 fol. 1ʳ: (J.E. & Co. /Protokoll Schutzmarke No. 3 /14-stave /34.4 × 26.4 cm /M00 C00 Y10 S00) (Pencil.)

302 – 14 fol. 1ᵛ: (J.E. & Co. /Protokoll Schutzmarke No. 3 /14-stave /34.4 × 26.4 cm /M00 C00 Y10 S00) Blank.

303 – 14 fol. 2ʳ: (J.E. & Co. /Protokoll Schutzmarke No. 3 /14-stave /34.4 × 26.4 cm /M00 C00 Y10 S00) Title page. (Black ink, pencil.)

304 – 14 fol. 2ᵛ: (J.E. & Co./Protokoll Schutzmarke No. 3 /14-stave /34.4 × 26.4 cm /M00 C00 Y10 S00) Dedication page. (Black ink.)

305 – 14 fol. 3ʳ: (J.E. & Co. /Protokoll Schutzmarke No. 3 /14-stave /34.4 × 26.4 cm /M00 C00 Y10 S00) Personen, Orchester. (Black ink, pencil.)

306 – 14 fol. 3ᵛ: (J.E. & Co. /Protokoll Schutzmarke No. 3 /14-stave /34.4 cm /M00 C00 Y10 S00) Scenarium. (Black ink, pencil, green pencil.)

307 – 14 fol. 4ʳ: (J.E. & Co. /Protokoll Schutzmarke No. 3 /14-stave /34.4 × 26.4 cm /M00 C00 Y10 S00) I/1 mm. 1–12. Address stamp: ALBAN BERG WIEN XIII TRAUTTMANSDORFFGASSE 27. (Black ink, pencil, green pencil.)

308 – 14 fol. 4ᵛ: (J.E. & Co. /Protokoll Schutzmarke No. 3 /14-stave /34.4 × 26.4 cm /M00 C00 Y10 S00) I/1 mm. 13–21. (Black ink, pencil.)

309 – 14 fol. 5ʳ: (J.E. & Co. /Protokoll Schutzmarke No. 3 /14-stave /34.4 × 26.4 cm /M00 C00 Y10 S00) I/1 mm. 22–32. (Black ink, pencil, green pencil.)

310 – 14 fol. 5ᵛ: (J.E. & Co. /Protokoll Schutzmarke No. 3 /14-stave /34.4 × 26.4 cm /M00 C00 Y10 S00) I/1 mm. 33–43. (Black ink, pencil, green pencil.)

311 – 14 fol. 6ʳ: (J.E. & Co. /Protokoll Schutzmarke No. 3 /14-stave /34.4 × 26.4 cm /M00 C00 Y10 S00) I/1 mm. 44–53. (Black ink, pencil, green pencil.)

312 – 14 fol. 6ᵛ: (J.E. & Co. /Protokoll Schutzmarke No. 3 /14-stave /34.4 × 26.4 cm /M00 C00 Y10 S00) I/1 mm. 54–64. Paste-on covering bottom-right staff. (Black ink, pencil, green pencil.)

313 – 14 fol. 7ʳ: (J.E. & Co. /Protokoll Schutzmarke No. 3 /14-stave /34.4 × 26.4 cm /M00 C00 Y10 S00) I/1 mm. 65–76. (Black ink, pencil, green pencil.)

314 – 14 fol. 7ᵛ: (J.E. & Co. /Protokoll Schutzmarke No. 3 /14-stave /34.4 × 26.4 cm /M00 C00 Y10 S00) I/1 mm. 77–91. Patch on bottom-right lower staff. (Black ink, pencil, dark indelible pencil.)

315 – 14 fol. 8ʳ: (J.E. & Co. /Protokoll Schutzmarke No. 3 /14-stave /34.4 × 26.4 cm /M00 C00 Y10 S00) I/1 mm. 92–104. (Black ink, pencil, dark indelible pencil.)

316 – 14 fol. 8ᵛ: (J.E. & Co. /Protokoll Schutzmarke No. 3 /14-stave /34.4 × 26.4 cm /M00 C00 Y10 S00) I/1 mm. 105–121. (Black ink, pencil, green pencil, red pencil.)

317 – 14 fol. 9ʳ: (J.E. & Co. /Protokoll Schutzmarke No. 3 /14-stave /34.4 × 26.4 cm /M00 C00 Y10 S00) I/1 mm. 122–131. (Black ink, pencil, green pencil, red pencil.)

318 – 14 fol. 9ᵛ: (J.E. & Co. /Protokoll Schutzmarke No. 3 /14-stave /34.4 × 26.4 cm /M00 C00 Y10 S00) I/1 mm. 132–138. (Black ink, pencil, green pencil.)

319 – 14 fol. 10ʳ: (no brand /16-stave /26.5 × 34.5 cm /M00 C00 Y10 S00) I/1 mm. 139–146. (Black ink, pencil, green pencil.)

320 – 14 fol. 10ᵛ: (no brand /16-stave /26.5 × 34.5 cm /M00 C00 Y10 S00) I/1 mm. 147–152. (Black ink, pencil.)

321 – 14 fol. 11ʳ: (no brand /16-stave /26.5 × 34.5 cm /M00 C00 Y10 S00) I/1 mm. 153–161. (Black ink, pencil, green pencil.)

322 – 14 fol. 11ᵛ: (no brand /16-stave /26.5 × 34.5 cm /M00 C00 Y10 S00) I/1 mm. 162–171. (Black ink, pencil, green pencil.)

323 – 14 fol. 12ʳ: (no brand /16-stave /26.5 × 34.5 cm /M00 C00 Y10 S00) I/1 mm. 172–182. (Black ink, pencil, green pencil.)

324 – 14 fol. 12ᵛ: (no brand /16-stave /26.5 × 34.5 cm /M00 C00 Y10 S00) I/1 mm. 183–190. (Black ink, pencil, green pencil.)

325 – 14 fol. 13ʳ: (no brand /16-stave /26.5 × 34.5 cm /M00 C00 Y10 S00) I/1 mm. 192–200. (Black ink, pencil, green pencil.)

326 – 14 fol. 13ᵛ: (J.E. & Co. /DEPOSÉ No. 2 /12-stave /34.3 × 25.4 cm /M00 C00 Y10 S00) Glued to back of 13ʳ. Beginning of I/2, mm. 201–212. Paste-on glued to bottom, now removed. (Pencil, black ink, green pencil.)

327 – 14 fol. 14ʳ: (J.E. & Co. /DEPOSÉ No. 2 /12-stave /34.3 × 25.4 cm /M00 C00 Y10 S00) I/2 mm. 213–227. Paste-on over right half of staves 7–9. (Pencil, black ink, green pencil, red pencil.)

328 – 14 fol. 14ᵛ: (J.E. & Co. /DEPOSÉ No. 2 /12-stave /34.3 × 25.4 cm /M00 C00 Y10 S00) I/2 mm. 228–244. Paste-on over staves 4–10. (Pencil, black ink, green pencil, dark indelible pencil.)

329 – 14 fol. 15ʳ: (J.E. & Co. /Protokoll Schutzmarke No. 6 /20-stave /34.2 × 26.6 cm /M00 C00 Y10 S00) I/2 mm. 245–258. (Pencil, black ink, green pencil.)

330 – 14 fol. 15ᵛ: (J.E. & Co. /Protokoll Schutzmarke No. 6 /20-stave /34.2 × 26.6 cm /M00 C00 Y10 S00) I/2 mm. 259–270. (Pencil, black ink, blue pencil, green pencil, red pencil.)

331 – 14 fol. 16ʳ: (J.E. & Co. /Protokoll Schutzmarke No. 5 /18-stave /34.3 × 26.7 cm /M00 C00 Y10 S00) I/2 mm. 271–289. Paste-on of three staves of 14-stave paper over staves 14–18. Paper has been

folded in fourths. [Pencil, black ink, green pencil, red pencil, blue pencil (M10 C90).]

332 – 14 fol. 16ᵛ: (J.E. & Co. /Protokoll Schutzmarke No. 5 /18-stave /34.3 × 26.7 cm /M00 C00 Y10 S00) I/2 mm. 290–308. Paste-on of 14-line paper over staves 1–5. (Pencil, black ink, green pencil.)

333 – 14 fol. 17ʳ: (J.E. & Co. /Protokoll Schutzmarke No. 5 /18-stave /34.3 × 26.7 cm /M00 C00 Y10 S00) I/2 mm. 309–327. Paper has been folded into fourths. (Pencil, black ink, indelible pencil.)

334 – 14 fol. 17ᵛ: (J.E. & Co. /Protokoll Schutzmarke No. 5 /18-stave /34.3 × 26.7 cm /M00 C00 Y10 S00) I/3 mm. 328–343. (Pencil, black ink.)

335 – 14 fol. 18ʳ: (J.E. & Co. /DEPOSÉ No. 3 /14-stave /26.5 × 34.7 cm /M00 C00 Y10 S00) I/3 mm. 344–363. Paper repair in left-hand upper corner. Hole in paper between staves 11 and 12, right-hand side. (Pencil, black ink, red pencil.)

336 – 14 fol. 18ᵛ: (J.E. & Co. /DEPOSÉ No. 3 /14-stave /26.5 × 34.7 cm /M00 C00 Y10 S00) I/3 mm. 362–371. Paste-on in lower left-hand corner. (Black ink, pencil.)

337 – 14 fol. 19ʳ: (no brand /12-stave paper /32.8 × 24.7 cm /M00 C00 Y10 S00) I/3 mm. 372–388. Paper has been folded into fourths. (Black ink, pencil)

338 – 14 fol. 19ᵛ: (no brand /12-stave paper /32.8 × 24.7 cm /M00 C00 Y10 S00) I/3 mm. 389–406. Paste-on of same type of paper over staves 1–9. (Black ink, pencil.)

339 – 14 fol. 20ʳ: (J.E. & Co. /Protokoll Schutzmarke No. 6 /20-stave /34.2 × 26.6 cm /M00 C00 Y10 S00) I/3 mm. 407–429. (Black ink, pencil, green pencil.)

340 – 14 fol. 20ᵛ: (J.E. & Co. /Protokoll Schutzmarke No. 6 /20-stave /34.2 × 26.6 cm /M00 C00 Y10 S00) I/3 mm. 430–444. Paper has been folded into fourths. (Black ink, pencil.)

341 – 14 fol. 21ʳ: (J.E. & Co. /Protokoll Schutzmarke No. 6 /20-stave /34.2 × 26.6 cm /M00 C00 Y10 S00) I/3 mm. 445–453. Paper has been folded into fourths. (Black ink, pencil.)

342 – 14 fol. 21ᵛ: (J.E. & Co. /Protokoll Schutzmarke No. 6 /20-stave /34.2 × 26.6 cm /M00 C00 Y10 S00) I/3 mm. 454–465. Paste-on over bottom three staves, lower right-hand corner. (Black ink, pencil, green pencil, blue pencil.)

343 – 14 fol. 22ʳ: (J.E. & Co. /Protokoll Schutzmarke No. 6 /20-stave /34.2 × 26.6 cm /M00 C00 Y10 S00) I/3 mm. 467–475. (Black ink, pencil, green pencil.)

344 – 14 fol. 22ᵛ: (J.E. & Co. /Protokoll Schutzmarke No. 6 /20-stave /34.2 × 26.6 cm /M00 C00 Y10 S00) I/3 mm. 476–488. (Black ink, pencil, green pencil.)

345 – 14 fol. 23ʳ: (J.E. & Co. /Protokoll Schutzmarke No. 8a /26-stave /34.4 × 26.3 cm /M00 C00 Y10 S00) I/4 mm. 488–499. Paper has been folded in half. (Black ink, pencil.)

346 – 14 fol. 23^v: (J.E. & Co. /Protokoll Schutzmarke No. 8a /26-stave /34.4 × 26.3 cm /M00 C00 Y10 S00) I/4 mm. 500–502. Originally glued to next page. (Black ink, pencil, blue pencil.)

347 – 14 fol. 24^r: (J.E. & Co. /Protokoll Schutzmarke No 6 /20-stave /34.2 × 26.6 cm /M00 C00 Y10 S00) PSA. I/4 mm. 500–507. Originally glued to 23^v. (Black ink.)

348 – 14 fol. 24^v: (J.E. & Co. /Protokoll Schutzmarke No 6 /20-stave /34.2 × 26.6 cm /M00 C00 Y10 S00) I/4 mm. 500–501. (Black ink, pencil.)

349 – 14 fol. 25^r: (J.E. & Co. /Protokoll Schutzmarke No 6 /20-stave /34.2 × 26.6 cm /M00 C00 Y10 S00) I/4 mm. 508–518. Paper folded in half. Paste-on on top staff. (Black ink, pencil.)

350 – 14 fol. 25^v: (J.E. & Co. /Protokoll Schutzmarke No 6 /20-stave /34.2 × 26.6 cm /M00 C00 Y10 S00) I/4 mm. 519–527. Paste-on over staves 8–9, left-hand side. (Black ink, pencil.)

351 – 14 fol. 26^r: (J.E. & Co. /Protokoll Schutzmarke No 6 /20-stave /34.2 × 26.6 cm /M00 C00 Y10 S00) I/4 mm. 528–537. (Black ink, pencil.)

352 – 14 fol. 26^v: (J.E. & Co. /Protokoll Schutzmarke No 6 /20-stave /34.2 × 26.6 cm /M00 C00 Y10 S00) I/4 mm. 538–552. Bottom staff inked in. (Black ink, pencil.)

353 – 14 fol. 27^r: (J.E. & Co. /Protokoll Schutzmarke No 6 /20-stave /34.2 × 26.6 cm /M00 C00 Y10 S00) I/4 mm. 553–561. Paper has been folded in half. (Black ink, pencil, blue pencil.)

354 – 14 fol. 27^v: (J.E. & Co. /Protokoll Schutzmarke No 6 /20-stave /34.2 × 26.6 cm /M00 C00 Y10 S00) I/4 mm. 562–585. Paste-on over staves 12–15, left-hand side. (Black ink, pencil, blue pencil, red pencil.)

355 – 14 fol. 28^r: (J.E. & Co. /Protokoll Schutzmarke No. 3 /14-stave /34.4 × 26.2 cm /M00 C00 Y10 S00) I/4 mm. 586–600. (Black ink, pencil, red pencil, blue pencil.)

356 – 14 fol. 28^v: (J.E. & Co. /Protokoll Schutzmarke No. 3 /14-stave /34.4 × 26.2 cm /M00 C00 Y10 S00) I/4 mm. 601–612. (Black ink, pencil, blue pencil, indelible pencil, red pencil.)

357 – 14 fol. 29^r: (J.E. & Co. /Protokoll Schutzmarke No. 3 /14-stave /34.4 × 26.2 cm /M00 C00 Y10 S00) I/4 mm. 613–622. (Black ink, pencil, blue pencil.)

358 – 14 fol. 29^v: (J.E. & Co. /Protokoll Schutzmarke No. 3 /14-stave /34.4 × 26.2 cm /M00 C00 Y10 S00) I/4 mm. 623–634. (Black ink, pencil.)

359 – 14 fol. 30^r: (J.E. & Co. /Protokoll Schutzmarke No. 3 /14-stave /34.4 × 26.2 cm /M00 C00 Y10 S00) I/4 mm. 635–655. (Black ink, pencil, blue pencil.)

360 – 14 fol. 30^v: (J.E. & Co. /Protokoll Schutzmarke No. 3 /14-stave /34.4 × 26.2 cm /M00 C00 Y10 S00) I/4 mm. 656–666. (Black ink, pencil, blue pencil, red pencil.)

361 – 14 fol. 31ʳ: (J.E. & Co. /Protokoll Schutzmarke No. 3 /14-stave /34.4 × 26.2 cm /M00 C00 Y10 S00) I/5 mm. 667–675. (Black ink, pencil.)

362 – 14 fol. 31ᵛ: (J.E. & Co. /Protokoll Schutzmarke No. 3 /14-stave /34.4 × 26.2 cm /M00 C00 Y10 S00) I/5 mm. 676–684. Paper has been folded into fourths. (Black ink, pencil, red pencil.)

363 – 14 fol. 32ʳ: (J.E. & Co. /Protokoll Schutzmarke No. 3 /14-stave /34.4 × 26.2 cm /M00 C00 Y10 S00) I/5 mm. 685–692. (Black ink, pencil, red pencil.)

364 – 14 fol. 32ᵛ: (J.E. & Co. /Protokoll Schutzmarke No. 3 /14-stave /34.4 × 26.2 cm /M00 C00 Y10 S00) I/5 mm. 693–700. (Black ink, pencil, red pencil, blue pencil.)

365 – 14 fol. 33ʳ: (J.E. & Co. /Protokoll Schutzmarke No. 3 /14-stave /34.4 × 26.2 cm /M00 C00 Y10 S00) I/5 mm. 701–708. Paper has been folded into fourths. (Black ink, pencil, red pencil.)

366 – 14 fol. 33ᵛ: (J.E. & Co. /Protokoll Schutzmarke No. 3 /14-stave /34.4 × 26.2 cm /M00 C00 Y10 S00) I/5 mm. 709–717. Paste-on over staff 6, left-hand side. Address stamp: ALBAN BERG WIEN XIII TRAUTTMANSDORFFGASSE 27. (Black ink, pencil, red pencil.)

367 – 14 fol. 34ʳ: (J.E. & Co. /Protokoll Schutzmarke No. 3 /14-stave /34.4 × 26.2 cm /M00 C00 Y10 S00) II/1 mm. 1–16. Same address stamp as above. Paste-on over staves 5–6, middle. (Black ink, pencil, red pencil.)

368 – 14 fol. 34ᵛ: (J.E. & Co. /Protokoll Schutzmarke No. 3 /14-stave /34.4 × 26.2 cm /M00 C00 Y10 S00) II/1 mm. 17–31. (Black ink, pencil.)

369 – 14 fol. 35ʳ: (J.E. & Co. /Protokoll Schutzmarke No. 3 /14-stave /34.4 × 26.2 cm /M00 C00 Y10 S00) II/1 mm. 32–46. Paper has been folded into fourths. Paste-on on staves 1–4. (Black ink, pencil.)

370 – 14 fol. 35ᵛ: (J.E. & Co. /Protokoll Schutzmarke No. 3 /14-stave /34.4 × 26.2 cm /M00 C00 Y10 S00) II/1 mm. 47–55. (Black ink, pencil.)

371 – 14 fol. 36ʳ: (J.E. & Co. /Protokoll Schutzmarke No. 3 /14-stave /34.4 × 26.2 cm /M00 C00 Y10 S00) II/1 mm. 56–68. (Black ink, pencil.)

372 – 14 fol. 36ᵛ: (J.E. & Co. /Protokoll Schutzmarke No. 3 /14-stave /34.4 × 26.2 cm /M00 C00 Y10 S00) II/1 mm. 69–80. Paste-on over staves 11–14. (Black ink, pencil.)

373 – 14 fol. 37ʳ: (J.E. & Co. /Protokoll Schutzmarke No. 3 /14-stave /34.4 × 26.2 cm /M00 C00 Y10 S00) II/1 mm. 82–92. Paste-on over staves 11–14. (Black ink, pencil, green pencil.)

374 – 14 fol. 37ᵛ: (J.E. & Co. /Protokoll Schutzmarke No. 3 /14-stave /34.4 × 26.2 cm /M00 C00 Y10 S00) II/1 mm. 93–104. (Black ink, pencil.)

375 – 14 fol. 38^r: (J.E. & Co. /Protokoll Schutzmarke No. 3 /14-stave /34.4 × 26.2 cm /M00 C00 Y10 S00) II/1 mm. 105–113. (Black ink, pencil, green pencil.)

376 – 14 fol. 38^v: (J.E. & Co. /Protokoll Schutzmarke No. 3 /14-stave /34.4 × 26.2 cm /M00 C00 Y10 S00) II/1 mm. 114–128. (Black ink, pencil, green pencil.)

377 – 14 fol. 39^r: (J.E. & Co. /Protokoll Schutzmarke No. 6 /20-stave /34.2 × 26.6 cm /M00 C00 Y10 S00) II/1 mm. 129–144. Paper has been folded into fourths. (Black ink, pencil, red pencil.)

378 – 14 fol. 39^v: (J.E. & Co. /Protokoll Schutzmarke No. 6 /20-stave /34.2 × 26.6 cm /M00 C00 Y10 S00) II/1 mm. 145–170. (Black ink, pencil.)

379 – 14 fol. 40^r: (J.E. & Co. /Protokoll Schutzmarke No. 6 /20-stave /34.2 × 26.6 cm /M00 C00 Y10 S00) II/2 mm. 171–179. (Pencil, black ink.)

380 – 14 fol. 40^v: (J.E. & Co. /Protokoll Schutzmarke No. 6 /20-stave /34.2 × 26.6 cm /M00 C00 Y10 S00) II/2 mm. 180–188. (Pencil, black ink.)

381 – 14 fol. 41^r: (J.E. & Co. /Protokoll Schutzmarke No. 6 /20-stave /34.2 × 26.6 cm /M00 C00 Y10 S00) II/2 mm. 189–197. (Pencil, black ink.)

382 – 14 fol. 41^v: (J.E. & Co. /Protokoll Schutzmarke No. 6 /20-stave /34.2 × 26.6 cm /M00 C00 Y10 S00) II/2 mm. 198–217. (Pencil, black ink.)

383 – 14 fol. 42^r: (J.E. & Co. /DEPOSÉ No. 2 /12-stave /34.3 × 25.4 cm /M00 C00 Y10 S00) II/2 mm. 218–227. (Pencil, black ink.)

384 – 14 fol. 42^v: (J.E. & Co. /DEPOSÉ No. 2 /12-stave /34.3 × 25.4 cm /M00 C00 Y10 S00) II/2 mm. 228–238. (Pencil, black ink.)

385 – 14 fol. 43^r: (J.E. & Co. /DEPOSÉ No. 2 /12-stave /34.3 × 25.4 cm /M00 C00 Y10 S00) II/2 mm. 239–249. (Pencil, black ink.)

386 – 14 fol. 43^v: (J.E. & Co. /DEPOSÉ No. 2 /12-stave /34.3 × 25.4 cm /M00 C00 Y10 S00) II/2 mm. 250–258. (Pencil, black ink.)

387 – 14 fol. 44^r: (J.E. & Co. /Protokoll Schutzmarke No. 3 /14-stave /34.4 × 26.2 cm /M00 C00 Y10 S00) II/2 mm. 259–271. (Pencil, black ink.)

388 – 14 fol. 44^v: (J.E. & Co. /Protokoll Schutzmarke No. 3 /14-stave /34.4 × 26.2 cm /M00 C00 Y10 S00) Blank.

389 – 14 fol. 45^r: (J.E. & Co. /DEPOSÉ No. 3 /14-stave /26.5 × 34.7 cm /M00 C00 Y10 S00) Labeled "Strasse 2[.]Scene Hptm, Wozzeck u Dr." (Pencil.)

390 – 14 fol. 45^v: (J.E. & Co. /DEPOSÉ No. 3 /14-stave /26.5 × 34.7 cm /M00 C00 Y10 S00) II/2 mm. 271–279. (Pencil, black ink.)

391 – 14 fol. 46^r: (J.E. & Co. /DEPOSÉ No. 3 /14-stave /26.5 × 34.7 cm /M00 C00 Y10 S00) II/2 mm. 280–289. (Pencil, black ink.)

392 – 14 fol. 46^v: (J.E. & Co. /DEPOSÉ No. 3 /14-stave /26.5 × 34.7 cm /M00 C00 Y10 S00) II/2 mm. 290–299. (Pencil, black ink.)

393 – 14 fol. 47ʳ: (J.E. & Co. /DEPOSÉ No. 3 /14-stave /26.5 × 34.7 cm /M00 C00 Y10 S00) II/2 mm. 300–310. (Pencil, black ink.)

394 – 14 fol. 47ᵛ: (J.E. & Co. /DEPOSÉ No. 3 /14-stave /26.5 × 34.7 cm /M00 C00 Y10 S00) II/2 mm. 311–321. (Pencil, black ink.)

395 – 14 fol. 48ʳ: (J.E. & Co. /DEPOSÉ No. 3 /14-stave /26.5 × 34.7 cm /M00 C00 Y10 S00) II/2 mm. 322–331. (Pencil, black ink.)

396 – 14 fol. 48ᵛ: (J.E. & Co. /DEPOSÉ No. 3 /14-stave /26.5 × 34.7 cm /M00 C00 Y10 S00) II/2 mm. 332–338. (Pencil, black ink.)

397 – 14 fol. 49ʳ: (J.E. & Co. /DEPOSÉ No. 3 /14-stave /26.5 × 34.7 cm /M00 C00 Y10 S00) II/2 mm. 339–344. (Pencil, black ink.)

398 – 14 fol. 49ᵛ: (J.E. & Co. /DEPOSÉ No. 3 /14-stave /26.5 × 34.7 cm /M00 C00 Y10 S00) II/2 mm. 345–353. (Pencil, black ink.)

399 – 14 fol. 50ʳ: (J.E. & Co. /DEPOSÉ No. 3 /14-stave /26.5 × 34.7 cm /M00 C00 Y10 S00) II/2 mm. 354–363. (Pencil, black ink.)

400 – 14 fol. 50ᵛ: (J.E. & Co. /DEPOSÉ No. 3 /14-stave /26.5 × 34.7 cm /M00 C00 Y10 S00) II/2 mm. 369–376. Paper has been folded into fourths. (Pencil, black ink, red ink.)

401 – 14 fol. 51ʳ: (J.E. & Co. /Protokoll Schutzmarke No. 5 /18-stave /34.3 × 26.7 cm /M00 C00 Y10 S00) II/3 mm. 377–382. (Black ink, pencil.)

402 – 14 fol. 51ᵛ: (J.E. & Co. /Protokoll Schutzmarke No. 5 /18-stave /34.3 × 26.7 cm /M00 C00 Y10 S00) II/3 mm. 383–387. (Black ink, pencil.)

403 – 14 fol. 52ʳ: (J.E. & Co. /Protokoll Schutzmarke No. 5 /18-stave /34.3 × 26.7 cm /M00 C00 Y10 S00) II/3 mm. 388–395. Paste-on over staff 18, left-hand side. (Black ink, pencil.)

404 – 14 fol. 52ᵛ: (J.E. & Co. /Protokoll Schutzmarke No. 5 /18-stave /34.3 × 26.7 cm /M00 C00 Y10 S00) II/3 mm. 396–401. (Black ink, pencil.)

405 – 14 fol. 53ʳ: (J.E. & Co. /Protokoll Schutzmarke No. 5 /18-stave /34.3 × 26.7 cm /M00 C00 Y10 S00) II/3 mm. 401–411. Paste-on over staves 15–16, right-hand side. (Black ink, pencil.)

406 – 14 fol. 53ᵛ: (J.E. & Co. /Protokoll Schutzmarke No. 5 /18-stave /34.3 × 26.7 cm /M00 C00 Y10 S00) II/3 mm. 412–437. (Black ink, pencil.)

407 – 14 fol. 54ʳ: (J.E. & Co. /Protokoll Schutzmarke No. 5 /18-stave /34.3 × 26.7 cm /M00 C00 Y10 S00) II/4 mm. 437–448. Paste-on over staves 11–12, right-hand side. (Black ink, pencil.)

408 – 14 fol. 54ᵛ: (J.E. & Co. /Protokoll Schutzmarke No. 5 /18-stave /34.3 × 26.7 cm /M00 C00 Y10 S00) II/4 mm. 449–461. Paste-on over staves 3–7. (Black ink, pencil, red pencil.)

409 – 14 fol. 55ʳ: (J.E. & Co. /Protokoll Schutzmarke No. 5 /18-stave /34.3 × 26.7 cm /M00 C00 Y10 S00) II/4 mm. 462–467. (Black ink, pencil, red pencil, green pencil.)

410 – 14 fol. 55ᵛ: (J.E. & Co. /Protokoll Schutzmarke No. 5 /18-stave /34.3 × 26.7 cm /M00 C00 Y10 S00) II/4 mm. 468–472. (Black ink, pencil, green pencil.)

411 – 14 fol. 56ʳ: (J.E. & Co. /Protokoll Schutzmarke No. 5 /18-stave /34.3 × 26.7 cm /M00 C00 Y10 S00) II/4 mm. 473–480. Paste-on over staves 14–18. (Black ink, pencil.)

412 – 14 fol. 56ᵛ: (J.E. & Co. /Protokoll Schutzmarke No. 5 /18-stave /34.3 × 26.7 cm /M00 C00 Y10 S00) II/4 mm. 481–505. Paste-on over staves 11–12, right-hand side. (Black ink, pencil, red ink, green pencil.)

413 – 14 fol. 57ʳ: (J.E. & Co. /Protokoll Schutzmarke No. 5 /18-stave /34.3 × 26.7 cm /M00 C00 Y10 S00) II/4 mm. 506–522. Paste-on over staves 10–13 and staves 17–18. (Black ink, pencil, red ink.)

414 – 14 fol. 57ᵛ: (J.E. & Co. /Protokoll Schutzmarke No. 5 /18-stave /34.3 × 26.7 cm /M00 C00 Y10 S00) II/4 mm. 523–547. Paste-on over staves 3–4 and 8–9. (Black ink, pencil, red ink.)

415 – 14 fol. 58ʳ: (J.E. & Co. /Protokoll Schutzmarke No. 3 /14-stave /34.4 × 26.4 cm /M00 C00 Y10 S00) II/4 mm. 548–565. Paste-on over staves 3–4 and 7–8. (Black ink, pencil, red ink.)

416 – 14 fol. 58ᵛ: (J.E. & Co. /Protokoll Schutzmarke No. 3 /14-stave /34.4 × 26.4 cm /M00 C00 Y10 S00) II/4 mm. 566–577. Paste-on over staves 8–9. (Black ink, pencil.)

417 – 14 fol. 59ʳ: (J.E. & Co. /Protokoll Schutzmarke No. 3 /14-stave /34.4 × 26.4 cm /M00 C00 Y10 S00) II/4 mm. 578–586. Paste-on over staves 3–4. (Black ink, pencil, red pencil.)

418 – 14 fol. 59ᵛ: (J.E. & Co. /Protokoll Schutzmarke No. 3 /14-stave /34.4 × 26.4 cm /M00 C00 Y10 S00) II/4 mm. 587–593. Paste-on over staves 2 and 7. (Black ink, pencil.)

419 – 14 fol. 60ʳ: (J.E. & Co. /Protokoll Schutzmarke No. 3 /14-stave /34.4 × 26.4 cm /M00 C00 Y10 S00) II/4 mm. 594–599. (Black ink, pencil, red ink.)

420 – 14 fol. 60ᵛ: (J.E. & Co. /Protokoll Schutzmarke No. 3 /14-stave /34.4 × 26.4 cm /M00 C00 Y10 S00) II/4 mm. 600–605. (Black ink, pencil.)

421 – 14 fol. 61ʳ: (J.E. & Co. /Protokoll Schutzmarke No. 6 /20-stave /34.2 × 26.6 cm /M00 C00 Y10 S00) II/4 mm. 606–615. (Black ink, pencil, red ink.)

422 – 14 fol. 61ᵛ: (J.E. & Co. /Protokoll Schutzmarke No. 6 /20-stave /34.2 × 26.6 cm /M00 C00 Y10 S00) II/4 mm. 616–623. (Black ink, pencil, red ink.)

423 – 14 fol. 62ʳ: (J.E. & Co. /Protokoll Schutzmarke No. 6 /20-stave /34.2 × 26.6 cm /M00 C00 Y10 S00) II/4 mm. 624–632. (Black ink, pencil, red ink.)

424 – 14 fol. 62ᵛ: (J.E. & Co. /Protokoll Schutzmarke No. 6 /20-stave /34.2 × 26.6 cm /M00 C00 Y10 S00) Blank.

425 – 14 fol. 63ʳ: (J.E. & Co. /Protokoll Schutzmarke No. 3 /14-stave /34.4 × 26.4 cm /M00 C00 Y10 S00) II/4 mm. 624–632 (sketch). (Black ink, pencil.)

426 – 14 fol. 63ᵛ: (J.E. & Co. /Protokoll Schutzmarke No. 3 /14-stave /34.4 × 26.4 cm /M00 C00 Y10 S00) II/4 mm. 633–640. Paste-on over staves 2–4. (Black ink, pencil, red ink.)

427 – 14 fol. 64ʳ: (J.E. & Co. /Protokoll Schutzmarke No. 3 /14-stave /34.4 × 26.4 cm /M00 C00 Y10 S00) II/4 mm. 641–656. (Black ink, pencil, red ink.)

428 – 14 fol. 64ᵛ: (J.E. & Co. /Protokoll Schutzmarke No. 3 /14-stave /34.4 × 26.4 cm /M00 C00 Y10 S00) II/4 mm. 657–663. (Black ink, pencil, red ink.)

429 – 14 fol. 65ʳ: (J.E. & Co. /Protokoll Schutzmarke No. 4 /16-stave /34.7 × 26.3 cm /M10 C00 Y40 S00) II/4 mm. 677–688. Paper type changes here to dark brown paper, like 13/I. This is a clue about the last year of composition. Paste-on over staves 13–16. Smells different than other paper. (Black ink, pencil, red ink, green pencil.)

430 – 14 fol. 65ᵛ: (J.E. & Co. /Protokoll Schutzmarke No. 4 /16-stave /34.7 × 26.3 cm /M10 C00 Y40 S00) II/4 mm. 689–704. Paste-on over staff 2, left-hand side. (Black ink, pencil, green pencil.)

431 – 14 fol. 66ʳ: (J.E. & Co. /Protokoll Schutzmarke No. 4 /16-stave /34.7 × 26.3 cm /M10 C00 Y40 S00) II/4 mm. 705–720. Small paste-on m. 711. (Black ink, pencil, green pencil, red ink.)

432 – 14 fol. 66ᵛ: (J.E. & Co. /Protokoll Schutzmarke No. 4 /16-stave /34.7 × 26.3 cm /M10 C00 Y40 S00) II/4 mm. 721–730. (Black ink, pencil, green pencil.)

433 – 14 fol. 67ʳ: (J.E. & Co. /Protokoll Schutzmarke No. 4 /16-stave /34.7 × 26.3 cm /M10 C00 Y40 S00) II/4 mm. 731–740. (Black ink, pencil, green pencil.)

434 – 14 fol. 67ᵛ: (J.E. & Co. /Protokoll Schutzmarke No. 4 /16-stave /34.7 × 26.3 cm /M10 C00 Y40 S00) II/5 mm. 741–749. Paste-ons over staves 11–16 and staff 1 (middle). (Black ink, pencil.)

435 – 14 fol. 68ʳ: (J.E. & Co. /Protokoll Schutzmarke No. 4 /16-stave /34.7 × 26.3 cm /M10 C00 Y40 S00) II/5 mm. 750–757. Paste-on attached to top of page 69ʳ and ᵛ labeled Klavierauszug Takt 757. (Black ink, pencil, green pencil.)

436 – 14 fol. 68ᵛ: (J.E. & Co. /Protokoll Schutzmarke No. 4 /16-stave /34.7 × 26.3 cm /M10 C00 Y40 S00) II/5 mm. 758–776. (Black ink, pencil.)

437 – 14 fol. 69ʳ: (J.E. & Co. /Protokoll Schutzmarke No. 4 /16-stave /34.7 × 26.3 cm /M10 C00 Y40 S00) II/5 m. 757. (Black ink, pencil.)

438 – 14 fol. 69ᵛ: (J.E. & Co. /Protokoll Schutzmarke No. 4 /16-stave /34.7 × 26.3 cm /M10 C00 Y40 S00) Blank. (Pencil.)

439 – 14 fol. 70ʳ: (J.E. & Co. /Protokoll Schutzmarke No. 4 /16-stave /34.7 × 26.3 cm /M10 C00 Y40 S00) II/5 mm. 767–774. (Black ink, pencil.)

440 – 14 fol. 70ᵛ: (J.E. & Co. /Protokoll Schutzmarke No. 4 /16-stave /34.7 × 26.3 cm /M10 C00 Y40 S00) II/5 mm. 775–784. (Black ink, pencil, red pencil.)

441 – 14 fol. 71ʳ: (J.E. & Co. /Protokoll Schutzmarke No. 4 /16-stave /34.7 × 26.3 cm /M10 C00 Y40 S00) II/5 mm. 785–792. (Black ink, pencil.)

442 – 14 fol. 71ᵛ: (J.E. & Co. /Protokoll Schutzmarke No. 4 /16-stave /34.7 × 26.3 cm /M10 C00 Y40 S00) II/5 mm. 793–802. Paste-on over staff 12. (Black ink, pencil.)

443 – 14 fol. 72ʳ: (J.E. & Co. /Protokoll Schutzmarke No. 4 /16-stave /34.7 × 26.3 cm /M10 C00 Y40 S00) II/5 mm. 803–809. (Black ink, pencil.)

444 – 14 fol. 72ᵛ: (J.E. & Co. /Protokoll Schutzmarke No. 4 /16-stave /34.7 × 26.3 cm /M10 C00 Y40 S00) II/5 mm. 803–818. Address stamp at bottom right: ALBAN BERG WIEN XIII, etc. (Black ink, pencil.)

445 – 14 fol. 73ʳ: (J.E. & Co. /Protokoll Schutzmarke No. 4 /16-stave /34.7 × 26.3 cm /M10 C00 Y40 S00) Cover labeled III Akt Particell. Address stamp at bottom right. (Pencil.)

446 – 14 fol. 73ᵛ: (J.E. & Co. /Protokoll Schutzmarke No. 4 /16-stave /34.7 × 26.3 cm /M10 C00 Y40 S00) Beginnings of a sketch. (Pencil, black ink.)

447 – 14 fol. 74ʳ: (J.E. & Co. /Protokoll Schutzmarke No. 3 /14-stave /34.4 × 26.4 cm /M00 C00 Y10 S00) III/1 mm. 1–14. Not discolored like previous paper. Address stamp in lower right-hand corner. (Black ink, pencil, red pencil.)

448 – 14 fol. 74ᵛ: (J.E. & Co. /Protokoll Schutzmarke No. 3 /14-stave /34.4 × 26.4 cm /M00 C00 Y10 S00) III/1 mm. 15–25. Paste-on over staves 10–14 is 75ʳ⁻ᵛ. (Black ink, pencil, green pencil, red pencil.)

449 – 14 fol. 76ʳ: (J.E. & Co. /Protokoll Schutzmarke No. 3 /14-stave /34.4 × 26.4 cm /M00 C00 Y10 S00) III/1 mm. 25–36. Stain between staves 13 and 12. (Black ink, pencil, red pencil, green pencil.)

450 – 14 fol. 76ᵛ: (J.E. & Co. /Protokoll Schutzmarke No. 3 /14-stave /34.4 × 26.4 cm /M00 C00 Y10 S00) III/1 mm. 37–46. (Black ink, pencil, green pencil.)

451 – 14 fol. 77ʳ: (J.E. & Co. /Protokoll Schutzmarke No. 3 /14-stave /34.4 × 26.4 cm /M00 C00 Y10 S00) III/1 mm. 47–57. Paste-ons over staves 1–4 and 6–9. (Black ink, pencil.)

452 – 14 fol. 77ᵛ: (J.E. & Co. /Protokoll Schutzmarke No. 3 /14-stave /34.4 × 26.4 cm /M00 C00 Y10 S00) III/1 mm. 58–65. Paste-on over staff 12, right-hand side. (Black ink, pencil.)

453 – 14 fol. 78ʳ: (J.E. & Co. /Protokoll Schutzmarke No. 3 /14-stave /34.4 × 26.4 cm /M00 C00 Y10 S00) III/2 mm. 66–75. (Black ink, pencil.)

454 – 14 fol. 78ᵛ: (J.E. & Co. /Protokoll Schutzmarke No. 3 /14-stave /34.4 × 26.4 cm /M00 C00 Y10 S00) III/2 mm. 75–80. (Black ink, pencil.)

455 – 14 fol. 79ʳ: (J.E. & Co. /DEPOSÉ No. 4 /16-stave /34.2 × 26.1 cm /M00 C00 Y10 S00) III/2 mm. 80–85. (Black ink, pencil, red pencil, blue pencil.)

456 – 14 fol. 79ᵛ: (J.E. & Co. /DEPOSÉ No. 4 /16-stave /34.2 × 26.1 cm /M00 C00 Y10 S00) III/2 mm. 86–91. (Black ink, pencil.)

457 – 14 fol. 80ʳ: (J.E. & Co. /DEPOSÉ No. 4 /16-stave /34.2 × 26.1 cm /M00 C00 Y10 S00) III/2 mm. 92–98. (Black ink, pencil.)

458 – 14 fol. 80ᵛ: (J.E. & Co. /DEPOSÉ No. 4 /16-stave /34.2 × 26.1 cm /M00 C00 Y10 S00) III/2 mm. 99–102. (Black ink, pencil.)

459 – 14 fol. 81ʳ: (J.E. & Co. /DEPOSÉ No. 4 /16-stave /34.2 × 26.1 cm /M00 C00 Y10 S00) III/2 mm. 103–104. (Black ink, pencil.)

460 – 14 fol. 81ᵛ: (J.E. & Co. /DEPOSÉ No. 4 /16-stave /34.2 × 26.1 cm /M00 C00 Y10 S00) III/3 mm. 105–117. Paste-on staves 13–16, bottom middle. (Black ink, pencil, green pencil.)

461 – 14 fol. 82ʳ: (J.E. & Co. /DEPOSÉ No. 4 /16-stave /34.2 × 26.1 cm /M00 C00 Y10 S00) III/3 mm. 118–142. Paste-on staves 7–8. (Black ink, pencil, red ink.)

462 – 14 fol. 82ᵛ: (J.E. & Co. /DEPOSÉ No. 4 /16-stave /34.2 × 26.1 cm /M00 C00 Y10 S00) III/3 mm. 143–155. Paste-ons over staves 2–3, 10, and 13–14. (Black ink, pencil, red pencil, green pencil.)

463 – 14 fol. 83ʳ: (J.E. & Co. /DEPOSÉ No. 4 /16-stave /34.2 × 26.1 cm /M00 C00 Y10 S00) III/3 mm. 156–169. Paste-ons over top margin, left, staves 11–12 right. (Black ink, pencil, green pencil.)

464 – 14 fol. 83ᵛ: (J.E. & Co. /DEPOSÉ No. 4 /16-stave /34.2 × 26.1 cm /M00 C00 Y10 S00) III/3 mm. 170–181. Paste-ons over staves 2–3, 6–7, and 10–11. (Black ink, pencil, red ink.)

465 – 14 fol. 84ʳ: (J.E. & Co. /Protokoll Schutzmarke No. 4 /16-stave /34.7 × 26.3 cm /M10 C00 Y40 S00) III/3 mm. 182–190. (Black ink, pencil.)

466 – 14 fol. 84ᵛ: (J.E. & Co. /Protokoll Schutzmarke No. 4 /16-stave /34.7 × 26.3 cm /M10 C00 Y40 S00) III/3 mm. 191–203. (Black ink, pencil.)

467 – 14 fol. 85ʳ: (J.E. & Co. /Protokoll Schutzmarke No. 4 /16-stave /34.7 × 26.3 cm /M10 C00 Y40 S00) III/3 mm. 204–211. Paste-on over staff 11, right. (Black ink, pencil.)

468 – 14 fol. 85ᵛ: (J.E. & Co. /Protokoll Schutzmarke No. 4 /16-stave /34.7 × 26.3 cm /M10 C00 Y40 S00) III/3 mm. 212–217. (Black ink, pencil, green pencil.)

469 – 14 fol. 86ʳ: (J.E. & Co. /Protokoll Schutzmarke No. 4 /16-stave /34.7 × 26.3 cm /M10 C00 Y40 S00) III/3 mm. 218–219, III/4 mm. 220–225. (Black ink, pencil.)

470 – 14 fol. 86ᵛ: (J.E. & Co. /Protokoll Schutzmarke No. 4 /16-stave /34.7 × 26.3 cm /M10 C00 Y40 S00) III/4 mm. 226–237. (Black ink, pencil, red pencil, green pencil.)

471 – 14 fol. 87ʳ: (J.E. & Co. /Protokoll Schutzmarke No. 4 /16-stave /34.7 × 26.3 cm /M10 C00 Y40 S00) III/4 mm. 238–244. (Black ink, pencil.)

472 – 14 fol. 87ᵛ: (J.E. & Co. /Protokoll Schutzmarke No. 4 /16-stave /34.7 × 26.3 cm /M10 C00 Y40 S00) III/4 mm. 245–254. Paste-on over staves 7–11. (Black ink, pencil, red pencil.)

473 – 14 fol. 88^r: (J.E. & Co. /DEPOSÉ No. 4 /16-stave /34.2 × 26.1 cm /M00 C00 Y10 S00) III/4 mm. 255–260. (Black ink, pencil, red pencil, green pencil.)

474 – 14 fol. 88^v: (J.E. & Co. /DEPOSÉ No. 4 /16-stave /34.2 × 26.1 cm /M00 C00 Y10 S00) III/4 mm. 261–271. (Black ink, pencil.)

475 – 14 fol. 89^r: (J.E. & Co. /DEPOSÉ No. 4 /16-stave /34.2 × 26.1 cm /M00 C00 Y10 S00) III/4 mm. 272–280. Paste-on over staves 3–4, right. (Black ink, pencil, green pencil.)

476 – 14 fol. 89^v: (J.E. & Co. /DEPOSÉ No. 4 /16-stave /34.2 × 26.1 cm /M00 C00 Y10 S00) III/4 mm. 281–287. Paste-on over staves 8 (right) and staves 13–14 (left). (Black ink, pencil, green pencil, red pencil.)

477 – 14 fol. 90^r: (J.E. & Co. /DEPOSÉ No. 4 /16-stave /34.2 × 26.1 cm /M00 C00 Y10 S00) III/4 mm. 288–301. (Black ink, pencil.)

478 – 14 fol. 90^v: (J.E. & Co. /DEPOSÉ No. 4 /16-stave /34.2 × 26.1 cm /M00 C00 Y10 S00) III/4 mm. 302–314. Paste-on over staves 8–9, right. (Black ink, pencil.)

479 – 14 fol. 91^r: (J.E. & Co. /DEPOSÉ No. 4 /16-stave /34.2 × 26.1 cm /M00 C00 Y10 S00) III/4 mm. 315–331. (Black ink, pencil, red pencil.)

480 – 14 fol. 91^v: (J.E. & Co. /DEPOSÉ No. 4 /16-stave /34.2 × 26.1 cm /M00 C00 Y10 S00) III/4 mm. 332–346. (Black ink, pencil, red pencil.)

481 – 14 fol. 92^r: (J.E. & Co. /DEPOSÉ No. 4 /16-stave /34.2 × 26.1 cm /M00 C00 Y10 S00) III/4 mm. 347–358. (Black ink, pencil, red pencil.)

482 – 14 fol. 92^v: (J.E. & Co. /DEPOSÉ No. 4 /16-stave /34.2 × 26.1 cm /M00 C00 Y10 S00) III/4 mm. 359–371. (Black ink, pencil, red pencil.)

483 – 14 fol. 93^r: (J.E. & Co. /Protokoll Schutzmarke No. 3 /14-stave /34.4 × 26.2 cm /M10 C00 Y40 S10) III/5 mm. 372–375. (Black ink, pencil, red pencil.)

484 – 14 fol. 93^v: (J.E. & Co. /Protokoll Schutzmarke No. 3 /14-stave /34.4 × 26.2 cm /M10 C00 Y40 S10) III/5 mm. 376–379. (Black ink, pencil.)

485 – 14 fol. 94^r: (J.E. & Co. /Protokoll Schutzmarke No. 3 /14-stave /34.4 × 26.2 cm /M10 C00 Y40 S10) III/5 mm. 380–384. (Black ink, pencil.)

486 – 14 fol. 94^v: (J.E. & Co. /Protokoll Schutzmarke No. 3 /14-stave /34.4 × 26.2 cm /M10 C00 Y40 S10) III/5 mm. 385–388. (Black ink, pencil.)

487 – 14 fol. 95^r: (J.E. & Co. /Protokoll Schutzmarke No. 3 /14-stave /34.4 × 26.2 cm /M10 C00 Y40 S10) III/5 mm. 389–402. Dated in bottom right-hand corner: Sonntag 16.7.22. (Black ink, pencil.)

488 – 14 fol. 95^v: (J.E. & Co. /Protokoll Schutzmarke No. 3 /14-stave /34.4 × 26.2 cm /M10 C00 Y40 S10) Notes on "Spieldauer 3. Akt." (Pencil.)

489 – 14 fol. 96^r: (J.E. & Co. /Protokoll Schutzmarke No. 3 /14-stave /34.4 × 26.2 cm /M10 C00 Y40 S10) Blank.

490 – 14 fol. 96^v: (J.E. & Co. /Protokoll Schutzmarke No. 3 /14-stave /34.4 × 26.2 cm /M10 C00 Y40 S10) Computations in pencil. (Pencil.)

II. Sketches from the Alban Berg Stiftung (ABS)

General Description

Two bifolia and eight leaves containing *Particell*-like first version of the opening of II/2, a title page, "Wozzeck, Strasse, S. 20 bis 23," and further drafts and sketches for the same scene. These manuscripts were recently discovered in Berg's study during renovation.

Description of Individual Leaves

491 – title page[r]: (J.E. & Co. /DEPOSÉ No. 2 /12-stave /26.5 × 34.5 cm /M00 C00 Y10 S00) "Wozzeck, Strasse, S. 20 bis 23" and two measures of unidentified sketches. (Black ink.)

492 – title page[v]: (J.E. & Co. /DEPOSÉ No. 2 /12-stave /26.5 × 34.5 cm /M00 C00 Y10 S00) Blank.

493 – p. 1: (J.E. & Co. /DEPOSÉ No. 2 /12-stave /26.5 × 34.5 cm /M00 C00 Y10 S00) Bifolio. Draft of II/2 mm. 171–179. (Pencil.)

494 – p. 2: (J.E. & Co. /DEPOSÉ No. 2 /12-stave /26.5 × 34.5 cm /M00 C00 Y10 S00) Draft of II/2, mm.180–185. (Pencil, black ink.)

495 – p. 3: (J.E. & Co. /DEPOSÉ No. 2 /12-stave /26.5 × 34.5 cm /M00 C00 Y10 S00) Draft of II/2 mm. 186–191. (Pencil, black ink.)

496 – p. 4: (J.E. & Co. /DEPOSÉ No. 2 /12-stave /26.5 × 34.5 cm /M00 C00 Y10 S00) Draft of II/2 mm. 192–197. (Pencil, black ink.)

497 – p. 5: (J.E. & Co. /DEPOSÉ No. 2 /12-stave /26.5 × 34.5 cm /M00 C00 Y10 S00) Single leaf. Draft of II/2 mm. 198–205. (Pencil, black ink.)

498 – p. 6: (J.E. & Co. /DEPOSÉ No. 2 /12-stave /26.5 × 34.5 cm /M00 C00 Y10 S00) Draft of II/2, mm. 206–217. (Pencil.)

499 – p. 7: (J.E. & Co. /DEPOSÉ No. 2 /12-stave /26.5 × 34.5 cm /M00 C00 Y10 S00) Bifolio. Draft of II/2 mm. 259–271. (Pencil.)

500 – p. 8: (J.E. & Co. /DEPOSÉ No. 2 /12-stave /26.5 × 34.5 cm /M00 C00 Y10 S00) Draft of II/2 mm. 272–277. (Pencil.)

501 – p. 9: (J.E. & Co. /DEPOSÉ No. 2 /12-stave /26.5 × 34.5 cm /M00 C00 Y10 S00) Draft of II/2 mm. 278–287. (Pencil.)

502 – p. 10: (J.E. & Co. /DEPOSÉ No. 2 /12-stave /26.5 × 34.5 cm /M00 C00 Y10 S00) Draft of II/2 mm. 288–297. (Pencil.)

503 – p. 11: (J.E. & Co. /DEPOSÉ No. 2 /12-stave /26.5 × 34.5 cm /M00 C00 Y10 S00) Single leaf. Draft of II/2 mm. 289–300, 313–322. (Pencil.)

504 – p. 12: (J.E. & Co. /DEPOSÉ No. 2 /12-stave /26.5 × 34.5 cm /M00 C00 Y10 S00) Draft of II/2 mm. 313–318. (Pencil.)

505 – p. 13: (J.E. & Co. /DEPOSÉ No. 2 /12-stave /26.5 × 34.5 cm /M00 C00 Y10 S00) Single leaf. Draft of II/2, mm. 326–338. (Pencil, black ink spots.)

506 – p. 14:	(J.E. & Co. /DEPOSÉ No. 2 /12-stave /26.5 × 34.5 cm /M00 C00 Y10 S00) Draft of II/2, mm. 335–365 with affixed leaf of 13/II pp. 38–39. (Pencil, red pencil. Affixed leaf, pencil, indelible pencil.)
507 – p. 15:	(no brand /12-stave /25 × 33 cm /M00 C00 Y10 S00) Single leaf. Draft of II/2, mm. 298–307. (Pencil.)
508 – p. 16:	(no brand /12-stave /25 × 33 cm /M00 C00 Y10 S00) Draft of II/2, mm. 308–312. (Pencil.)
509 – p. 17:	(J.E. & Co. /Protokoll Schutzmarke No. 3 /14-stave /26.5 × 34.9 cm /M00 C00 Y10 S00) Draft of II/2 mm. 322–328. (Pencil.)
510 – p. 18:	(J.E. & Co. /Protokoll Schutzmarke No. 3 /14-stave /26.5 × 34.9 cm /M00 C00 Y10 S00) Draft of II/2 mm. 330–337. (Pencil, red pencil.)
511 – p. 19:	(no brand /12-stave /25.7 × 33 cm /M00 C00 Y10 S00) Single leaf. Draft of II/2 mm. 338–343. (Pencil.)
512 – p. 20:	(no brand /12-stave /25.7 × 33 cm /M00 C00 Y10 S00) Draft of II/2 mm. 351–363. (Pencil.)
513 – p. 21:	(J.E. & Co. /Protokoll Schutzmarke No. 6 /20-stave /26.3–26.5 × 34.3 cm /M00 C00 Y10 S00) Single leaf. Draft of II/2 mm. 248–266. (Pencil, blue pencil.)
514 – p. 22:	(J.E. & Co. /Protokoll Schutzmarke No. 6 /20-stave /26.3–26.5 × 34.3 cm /M00 C00 Y10 S00) Draft of II/2 mm. 253–258, 271–272. (Pencil.)

III. Sketches from the Staatsbibliothek Preussischer Kulturbesitz (SBPK)

General Description

One single leaf and one bifolio containing sketches for III/4 and II/4.

Description of Individual Leaves

515 – N. Mus. MS. 68, 1ʳ:	(no brand /12-stave /25 × 32.8 cm /M10 C00 Y20 S10) A single leaf of 12-stave paper in full score format for III/3 mm. 209–215. Contains many annotations about instrumentation. Measure numbers correspond to full score. (Pencil, black ink.) 1921.
516 – N. Mus. MS. 68, 1ᵛ:	(no brand /12-stave /25 × 32.8 cm /M10 C00 Y20 S10) A letter from Helene Berg to "Herr Professor Wildgans" indicating that she gave him this sketch in 1955. (Black ink.) 1921.

517 – N. Mus. MS. 69, 1ʳ: (J.E. & Co. /Protokoll Schutzmarke No. 2 /12-stave /26.5 × 34.5 cm /M00 C00 Y10 S00) Concept sketch for II/4, mm. 447–465. (Pencil, orange pencil.) 1920.

518 – N. Mus. MS. 69, 1ᵛ: (J.E. & Co. /Protokoll Schutzmarke No. 2 /12-stave /26.5 × 34.5 cm /M00 C00 Y10 S00) Blank. 1920.

519 – N. Mus. MS. 69, 2ʳ: (J.E. & Co. /Protokoll Schutzmarke No. 2 /12-stave /26.5 × 34.5 cm /M00 C00 Y10 S00) Blank. 1920.

520 – N. Mus. MS. 69, 2ᵛ: (J.E. & Co. /Protokoll Schutzmarke No. 2 /12-stave /26.5 × 34.5 cm /M00 C00 Y10 S00) Blank. 1920.

IV. Sketches from the Beinecke Rare Book and Manuscript Library, Yale University (BRBL)

Music Deposit 16

General Description

A single leaf of 18-stave paper containing sketches for I/5. J.E. & Co. Protokoll Schutzmarke No. 5, 18 linig. Originally the first leaf of a bifolio. Has been folded into fourths. This sketch was sold to the Beinecke Library by Erich Alban Berg, the composer's nephew.

Description of the individual leaves

521 – Music Deposit 16, 1ʳ: (J.E. & Co. /Protokoll Schutzmarke No. 5 /18-stave /34.3 × 26.7 cm /M00 C00 Y10 S00) Continuity draft of I/5 mm. 682–688. (Pencil, black ink.) 1919.

522 – Music Deposit 16, 1ᵛ: (J.E. & Co. /Protokoll Schutzmarke No. 5 /18-stave /34.3 × 26.7 cm /M00 C00 Y10 S00) Motivic sketches for the remainder of the scene, with occasional annotations "Abschluss Kampf A," staff 1, "Höhepunkt," left-hand margin, between staves 8 and 9, "Begleitfigur für Kampf," staff 7, etc. (Pencil, blue pencil.) 1919.

V. Sketches from Houghton Library, Harvard University (HL)

General Description

Georg Büchner, The Orplid-Büchlein from 1919: *Wozzeck /Ein Fragment*. Berlin-Charlottenburg, Axel Junker. Contains annotations and paste-ons in Berg's hand.

See Perle.[8] 13.7 × 8.6 cm. Good condition. Call number: GC8.B8604 W.1919. Listed below is a summary of the most important pages of this source.

Description of Individual Leaves

523 – GC8.B8604 W.1919, front cover [r]:	"Wozzeck"
524 – GC8.B8604 W.1919, flyleaf [r]:	Address stamp: ALBAN BERG WIEN/XIII/I TRAUTTMANSDORFFGASSE 27.
525 – GC8.B8604 W.1919, p. 1:	(13.7 × 8.6 cm /M10 C10 Y40 S20) No annotations, but bleed-through from black ink on previous page.
526 – GC8.B8604 W.1919, p. 2:	(13.7 × 8.6 cm /M10 C10 Y40 S20) List of characters. Berg's inserted paste-on. (Black ink.)
527 – GC8.B8604 W.1919, p. 3:	(13.7 × 8.6 cm /M10 C10 Y40 S20)List of characters. Recto side of paste-on, on which Berg has written "(in der Fassung von Karl Emil Franzos) Oper in drei Akten (15 Scenen) von Alban Berg Op. 7 (Textbuch)." "Wozzeck" has been corrected by Berg to "Woyzeck." (Black ink.)
528 – GC8.B8604 W.1919, pp. 4–5:	(13.7 × 8.6 cm /M10 C10 Y40 S20) Berg's handwritten Scenarium and annotations to opening of I/1. (Black ink, red pencil.)
529 – GC8.B8604 W.1919, pp. 62–63:	(13.7 × 8.6 cm /M10 C10 Y40 S20) Berg's annotations to the continuation of II/5. (Black ink.)

VI.   Sketches from the Bayerische Staatsbibliothek (BSB)

General Description

Mus. Ms. 12913: A single leaf of sketches for I/4. These are the only sketches extant for I/4 in any archive. 12-stave paper, 31.5 × 22.9 cm. Paper is very discolored. Small rips at edge of paper have been repaired. All sides except for left-hand edge have been trimmed.

Description of Individual Leaves

530 – Mus. Ms. 12913, 1[r]:	(no brand /12-stave /31.5 × 22.9 cm /M10 C00 Y40 S00) I/4 mm. 510–516 1/2 (Variation 3). Remaining measure shows chord progression of Variation 4 (mm. 417–421). (Pencil.) 1919.
531 – Mus. Ms. 12913, 1[v]:	(no brand /12-stave /31.5 × 22.9 cm /M10 C00 Y40 S00) Detailed draft for Variation 1: mm. 496–503. (Pencil.) 1919.

VII.   Sketches from the Library of Congress (LOC)

Arnold Schoenberg Correspondence

General Description

532 and 533: A single leaf containing a chart of Berg's master arrays of interval cycles, which he sent to Schoenberg in a letter of July 27, 1920.[9]

William Remsen Strickland Collection, Box 19, Folder 8

General Description

534 and 535: A single leaf of a sketch for Act II, scene 5.

Description of Individual Leaves

534 – Box 19, Folder 8, fol. 1^r
(no brand /14-stave /33 × 45 cm /M10 C00 Y40 S00) Continuity draft of II/5 mm. 779–788. This leaf was originally the left-hand leaf of a bifolio with ONB 13/XI, fol. 4. Glue abrasion staff 9. Measure numbers in sketch are eleven less than in finished score. (Pencil, black ink.) 1921.

535 – Box 19, folder 8, fol. 1^v:
(no brand /14-stave /33 × 45 cm /M10 C00 Y40 S00) Continuity draft of II/5 mm. 789–796. This leaf was originally the left-hand leaf of a bifolio with ONB 13/XI, fol. 4. Various erasure abrasions. Measure numbers in sketch are eleven less than in finished score. "Tambourmajor!" written at top of sketch in Helene Berg's handwriting. (Pencil.) 1921.

NOTES

Abbreviations

ABS   Alban Berg Stiftung, Vienna
BRBL   Beinecke Rare Book and Manuscript Library, Yale University, New Haven
BSB   Bayerische Staatsbibliothek, Munich
HL   Houghton Library, Harvard University, Cambridge
LOC   Library of Congress, Washington, D.C.
ÖNB   Österrichische Nationalbibliothek, Vienna
SBPK   Staatsbibliothek Preussicher Kulturbesitz, Berlin

Introduction

1. Douglas Jarman, *Alban Berg: Wozzeck* (Cambridge: Cambridge University Press, 1989), 117.

2. Georg Büchner, *Büchner's Woyzeck, Nach den Handschriften neu hergestellt und kommentiert von Henri Poschmann* (Frankfurt am Main and Leipzig: Insel Verlag, 1985), 2.

3. See Georg Büchner, *Woyzeck, Faksimile, Transcription, Emendation und Lesetext Buch und CD-Rom, 2. Ausgabe, Herausgegeben von Enrico De Angelis* (Munich: K. G. Saur, 2000).

4. Friedemann Sallis, "Coming to Terms with the Composer's Working Manuscripts," in *A Handbook to Twentieth-Century Musical Sketches*, ed. Patricia Hall and Friedemann Sallis (Cambridge: Cambridge University Press, 2004), 45.

5. David Fanning, "Berg's Sketches for *Wozzeck*: A Commentary and Inventory," *Journal of the Royal Music Association* 112.2 (1986–87): 280–322.

6. Klaus Lippe, "'*Wozzeck* | Strasse | S. 20 bis 23' Ein Beitrag zur Philologie des *Wozzeck*-Particells," in *Alban Berg Studien, VI*, ed. Regina Busch and Klaus Lippe (Vienna: Universal Edition, 2008), 80–95.

7. George Perle, *The Operas of Alban Berg*, vol. 1, *Wozzeck* (Berkeley and Los Angeles: University of California Press, 1980), 25.

8. Büchner, *Büchner's Woyzeck*, 125.

9. Juliane Brand, Christopher Hailey, and Donald Harris, eds., *The Berg–Schoenberg Correspondence: Selected Letters* (New York: W. W. Norton, 1987), 451.

10. Rosemary Hilmar, *Katalog der Musikhandschriften, Schriften und Studien Alban Berg im Fond Alban Berg und der weiteren handschriftlichen Quellen im Besitz der Österreichischen Nationalbibliothek, Alban Berg Studien, I* (Vienna: Universal Edition, 1980).

11. Peter Petersen, *Alban Berg Wozzeck, Eine semantische Analyse unter Einbeziehung der Skizzen und Dokumente aus dem Nachlaß Bergs* (Munich: Edition Text + Kritik GmbH, 1985).

12. Fanning, "Berg's Sketches for *Wozzeck*," 295.

13. Richard Kramer, "The Sketch Itself," in *Beethoven's Compositional Process*, ed. William Kinderman (Lincoln: University of Nebraska Press, 1991), 3.

Chapter 1

1. Juliane Brand, Christopher Hailey, and Donald Harris, eds., *The Berg–Schoenberg Correspondence: Selected Letters* (New York: W. W. Norton, 1987), 75–76.

2. George Perle, *The Operas of Alban Berg*, vol. 1, *Wozzeck* (Berkeley and Los Angeles: University of California Press, 1980), 7.

3. Douglas Jarman, *Alban Berg: Wozzeck* (Cambridge: Cambridge University Press, 1989), 154.

4. Theodor W. Adorno, *Alban Berg: Master of the Smallest Link*, trans. Juliane Brand and Christopher Hailey (Cambridge: Cambridge University Press, 1991), 66.

5. Adorno, *Alban Berg*, 63.

6. Willi Reich, *The Life and Work of Alban Berg*, trans. Cornelius Cardew (London: Thames and Hudson, 1965), 40–41.

7. See Kathryn Bailey, "Berg's Aphoristic Pieces," in *The Cambridge Companion to Berg*, ed. Anthony Pople (Cambridge: Cambridge University Press, 1997), 83; and Christoph Khittl, "The Other Altenberg Song Cycle: A Document of Viennese Fin-de-Siècle Aesthetics," in *Encrypted Messages in Alban Berg's Music*, ed. Siglind Bruhn (New York and London: Garland, 1998), 137.

8. Mark DeVoto, "Some Notes on the Unknown *Altenberg Lieder*," *Perspectives of New Music* 5.1 (Autumn/Winter, 1966), 37–74.

9. Perle, *Operas*, vol. 1, *Wozzeck*, 18.

10. Jarman, *The Music of Alban Berg*, 177. Mark DeVoto, "Alban Berg's 'Marche Macabre'," *Perspectives of New Music* 22.1/2 (Autumn 1983/ Summer 1984), 386–447.

12. Derrick Puffett, "Berg, Mahler and the Three Orchestral Pieces Op. 6," in *The Cambridge Companion to Berg*, ed. Anthony Pople (Cambridge: Cambridge University Press, 1997), 139.

13. Melchior von Borries, *Alban Bergs Drei Orchesterstücke Op. 6 als ein Meisterwerk atonaler Symphonik* (Weimar: Verlag und Datenbank für Geisteswissenschaften, 1996), and Donald McLean, "A Documentary and Analytical Study of Alban Berg's Three Pieces for Orchestra" (Ph.D. diss., University of Toronto, 1997).

14. Alban Berg, *Sämtliche Werke, III. Abteilung: Musikalische Schriften und Dichtungen, Band 1:Analysen musikalischer Werke von Arnold Schönberg*, ed. Rudolf Stephan and Regina Busch (Vienna: Universal Edition, 1994), xx.

15. McLean, "Alban Berg's Three Pieces for Orchestra," 349–50.

16. See, for instance, Kandinsky's "Blaue Reiter" paintings of the same era, including "Composition VII."

Chapter 2

1. "Ich habe den Wozzeck vor dem Krieg aufgeführt gesehn u. einen so ungeheuren Eindruck gehabt, daß ich <u>sofort</u> (auch nach einem 2ten Anhören) den Entschluß faßte, ihn in Musik zu setzen." Handschriftensammlung, Wiener Stadt- und Landesbibliothek, I. N. 185.592. Note that Berg uses the spelling that appeared in his Franzos/Landau edition: *Wozzeck*, not the later *Woyzeck* of the Bergemann edition (1920).2. See, for instance,

David Fanning, "Berg's Sketches for *Wozzeck*: A Commentary and Inventory," *Journal of the Royal Musical Association* 112.2 (1986–87): 280–322; Peter Petersen, *Alban Berg, Wozzeck, Eine semantische Analyse unter Einbeziehung der Skizzen und Dokumente aus dem Nachlaß Bergs* (Munich: Edition Text + Kritik GmbH, 1985), 79; and Ernst Hilmar, *Wozzeck von Alban Berg: Entstehung—erste Erfolge—Repression (1914–1935)* (Vienna: Universal Edition, 1975), 33. George Perle, who bases his chronology on the published letters, maintains, in contrast, that Berg completed very little work on *Wozzeck* until the summers of 1917 and 1918. George Perle, *The Operas of Alban Berg*, vol. 1, *Wozzeck* (Berkeley and Los Angeles: University of California Press, 1980), 188.

3. See Gottfried Kassowitz, "Lehrzeit bei Alban Berg," *Österreichische Musikzeitschrift* 23 (1968): 6–7, 325.

4. "Es fällt mir schwer, der Bitte, etwas über meine Oper 'Wozzeck' zu sagen, heute nachzukommen; heute, wo es zehn Jahre her sind, daß ich sie zu komponieren begann." ÖNB Musiksammlung, F 21 Berg 110/V, fol. 85ᵛ.

5. Handschriftensammlung, Wiener Stadt- und Landesbibliothek, I. N. 185.612.

6. The most frequently mentioned passage reflecting Berg's experience in the military is that of the snoring soldiers in the barracks of Act II, scene 5, which Berg described in real life as "polyphonic breathing, gasping and groaning." See Willi Reich, *Alban Berg* (New York: Vienna House, 1974), 43.

7. See Perle's discussion of these passages in *Operas*, vol. 1, *Wozzeck*, 19.

8. Alban Berg, *Letters to His Wife*, trans. Bernard Grun (New York: St. Martin's Press, 1971), 229.

9. ÖNB Musiksammlung, F 21 Berg 432/19. Berg was "called up" a year earlier but was rejected for health reasons. See Juliane Brand, Christopher Hailey, and Donald Harris, eds., *The Berg–Schoenberg Correspondence: Selected Letters* (New York: W. W. Norton, 1987), 220–21.

10. See, for instance, Berg's letters to Gottfried Kassowitz from this period in the Wiener Stadt- und Landesbibliothek. The most detailed source on this era is Rosemary Hilmar, "Kriegsjahren, 1914–1918," *Alban Berg* (Vienna: Verlag Hermann Böhlaus Nachf, 1978).

11. Berg, *Letters to His Wife*, 183.

12. Berg, *Letters to His Wife*, 187.

13. "Verzeih' wenn ich Dich auf etwas aufmerksam mache, was mir sehr wichtig zu sein scheint. Wissen Deine Vorgesetzten wie es mit Deiner Sehkraft bestellt ist? Bist Du Dir selbst darüber ganz klar, was Du deinen Augen zutrauen kannst u. was Du von ihnen erwarten kannst? . . . Sollst Du Deine Vorgesetzten nicht nochmals darauf aufmerksam machen, bevor Du an die Front gehst?" Handschriftensammlung, Wiener Stadt- und Landesbibliothek, I. N. 185.558.

14. See Berg's promotion list in his military records, F 21 Berg 467 fol. 5ʳ.

15. One-year volunteer, private first class.

16. See also Berg's letter to Webern of August 19, 1918 (Wiener Stadt- und Landesbibliothek, I. N. 185.592).

17. Berg, *Letters to His Wife*, 179. In his notebook, ÖNB Musiksammlung, F 21 Berg 479/37–8 fol. 17ᵛ, Berg lists "Büchner" as one of the items he will be taking with him to military training.

18. Gottfried Kassowitz, "Lehrzeit bei Alban Berg," 325. At a later point in time (probably 1918) Berg systematically brackets material from the sketchbook not destined for I/2 or II/2 and recopies these themes and motives on twelve-staff paper, ÖNB Musiksammlung, F 21 Berg 13/III and 70/I, fols. 9ʳ–10ᵛ.

19. See Berg's list of military promotions, F 21 Berg 467 fol. 5ʳ.

20. Perle, *Operas*, vol. 1, *Wozzeck*, 21.

21. Perle, *Operas*, vol. 1, *Wozzeck*, 56.

22. Berg, *Letters to His Wife*, 186.

23. See Berg's annotation of the ordinance, F 21 Berg 479/51 fol. 25ᵛ, as well as Hilmar, *Alban Berg*, 124–5.

24. Berg, *Letters to His Wife*, 197.

25. Brand, Hailey, and Harris, eds., *Berg–Schoenberg Correspondence*, 266.

26. Reich, *Alban Berg*, 45.

27. Handschriftensammlung, Wiener Stadt- und Landesbibliothek, I. N. 185.592.

28. I am tempted to cite Paul Fussell here, who in his brilliant study of symbolism in English literature from the time of the Great War cites the persistent appearance of threes, as well as sunsets (and sunrises) as times of heightened emotional states (this despite that Büchner wrote the play in the 1830s). The "three-ness," however, is almost entirely the work of Berg. Paul Fussell, *The Great War and Modern Memory* (Oxford: Oxford University Press, 1975).

29. Glenn Watkins, *Proof Through the Night: Music and the Great War* (Berkeley: University of California Press, 2003), 236.

30. The only other sketches for Act I, scene 2, are three pages of large-format paper which coordinate with the annotations in both Berg's Büchner text and the sketchbook, ÖNB Musiksammlung, F 21 Berg 70/III, fols. 1ᵛ and 12ʳ–12ᵛ.

31. See Berg's letters to Kassowitz, Handschriftensammlung, Wiener Stadt- und Landesbibliothek, I. N. 200.904 and I. N. 201.706. The new paper type used for scene 5 in the *Particell* matches that of scene 1.

32. "Eine sehr traurige Mitteilung habe ich Ihnen auch zu machen: Der Leutnant Sluszanski ist gestern um 1/4 5 Uhr nachmittags gestorben. Er soll, wie die Pflegerin erzählte, ganz ruhig eingeschlafen sein. Mir ging die ganze Sache sehr nahe, obwohl ich ihn ja eigentlich weniger gekannt habe; aber ich erinnerte mich so recht der schönen längst vergangenen Zeit, da ich ihn immer traf, wenn ich nachmittags zu Ihnen hinaus zur Stunde kam. Was für Zeiten! Mir ist, als könnte das alles nie mehr so schön wiederkommen, da so eins nach dem andern sich ändert und zwar so anders wird, dass es, wie in gegebenem Falle niemehr so werden kann wie einst." ÖNB Musiksammlung, F 21 Berg 920/11.

Chapter 3

1. Alban Berg, *Letters to His Wife*, trans. Bernard Grun (New York: St. Martin's Press, 1971), 302.

2. Berg, *Letters to His Wife*, 288.

3. See Berg's Musik-Kalender for 1919 (at his apartment in Vienna) with its annotation on p. 101, and Berg's letter to Schulhoff of September 4, 1919, announcing his return to Vienna on September 10th. Ivan Vojtêch, ed., "Arnold Schoenberg, Anton Webern, Alban Berg: Unbekannte Briefe an Erwin Schulhoff," in *Miscellanea Musicologica XVIII* (Prague: Nákladem University Karlovy, 1965), 31.4. "Jetzt habe ich die 1. Scene des Wozzeck nachgeholt und werde Ihnen gelegentlich darüber Schreiben." Handschriftensammlung, Wiener Stadt- und Landesbibliothek, I. N. 200.904.

5. See, for example, ÖNB Musiksammlung F 21 Berg 70/II, which contains drafts of Act I, scene 3. "Damit ist der I. Akt vollendet, 5 Scenen: die obige beim Hauptmann, Wozzeck am Feld vor der Stadt, bei Marie, beim Arzt, Marie u. Tambourmajor.—Vom II. Akt ist nur die Scene auf der Straße: Hptmann, Arzt u. Wozzeck fertig." Handschriftensammlung, Wiener Stadt- und Landesbibliothek, I. N. 201.706.

7. "Wie gern teilte ich diesen Optimismus aus; dann der Gedanke, das ich mich jetzt die letzten 4,5 Wochen, wo ich mitten in komponieren bin u., vom Fleck komme, ja gehofft hatte mit den 2. Akt fertig zu werden—das ich also, all das unterbrechen soll, um Stimmen

heraus zu schreiben—der Gedanke ist scheußlich!!!" Handschriftensammlung, Wiener Stadt- und Landesbibliothek, I. N. 185.612.

8. Vojtêch, "Unbekannte Briefe," 32.

9. Vojtêch, "Unbekannte Briefe," 32.

10. "Aber das Eine muss ich Ihnen doch sagen, dass Sie sich sehr irren, wenn Sie mich als Imperialisten oder gar militaristen wähnen. Ich war es nicht einmal zu Beginn des Krieges u. habe es schwarz auf weiss, dass ich mich in August 14 gefragt habe, ob ein Volk, dass seine Grössten so behandelt, wie es den Deutsche tat u. tut, es nicht verdient, besiegt zu werden." Vojtêch, "Unbekannte Briefe," 51.

11. See Berg's letter to Kassowitz, Handschriftensammlung, Wiener Stadt- und Landesbibliothek, I. N. 200.897.

12. See Berg's letter to Webern, Handschriftensammlung, Wiener Stadt- und Landesbibliothek, I. N. 185.604, written in a train on his way back to Vienna.

13. "Lieber Freund,

Eine Woche hier. Zuerst krank, . . . dann viele geschäftliche Korrespondenzen, schließlich wieder—die ersten Komponierversuche: einer Sonatensatz mitten im Wozzeck d.h. der 2te Akt ist überhaupt eine (bzw 5) sätzige Symphonie . . .

Dazu brauch ich was zu rauchen! Haben Sie schon etwas: Zigarette oder Tabak. Bitte schicken! Hier kriegt man entgegen meiner Erwartungen nichts." Handschriftensammlung, Wiener Stadt- und Landesbibliothek, I. N. 201.709.

14. Juliane Brand, Christopher Hailey and Donald Harris, eds., The Berg–Schoenberg Correspondence: Selected Letters (New York: W. W. Norton, 1987), 283.

15. George Perle, The Operas of Alban Berg, vol. 1, Wozzeck (Berkeley and Los Angeles: University of California Press, 1980), 125.

16. Berg, Letters to His Wife, 251–67.

17. Berg, Letters to His Wife, 250.

18. Berg, Letters to His Wife, 278 and 280.

19. Brand, Hailey, and Harris, eds., Berg–Schoenberg Correspondence, 312.

20. See Berg's diary for 1921 in his Vienna apartment with its annotations on the 25th of July, "Reise nach Trahütten," and 7th of October, "Retour nach Wien." David Fanning also concludes that Act III, scene 1 was composed in 1920 based on the internal evidence of the sketchbooks F 21 Berg 13/I and 13/VII.

21. "Morgen beginne ich mit den letzten Scene des Wozzeck. Und dann nach Wien." Wiener Stadt- und Landesbibliothek, I. N. 185.614.

22. See also Berg's letter to Webern of August 17, 1921 in which he reports that the second act is finished, the third only one fourth. Wiener Stadt- und Landesbibliothek, I. N. 185.610.

23. "Meinem lieben Meister,

Kann ich leider den Wunsch, schon Donnerstag fertig zu sein, nicht erfüllen. Dies schmerzt mich umsomehr, als es mein Ehrgeiz ist, immer in allem zu entsprechen; aber meine Nerven haben plötzlich einen zweitägigen Streik abgehalten.

—so dass ich wieder langsam beginne, zu arbeiten und am 6. mit dem II. Akt zur Stelle sein werde.

—Außer den 8–10 Wozzeckstunden meines Tages muß ich leider meistens noch Öl für die Arbeitmachine kochen . . ." ÖNB Musiksammlung F 21 Berg 935.

24. "Heute, Freitag halte ich bei Seite 54. Sie können nun, lieber, verehrter Meister, bestimmt damit rechnen, dass ich (bei 6–8 Seiten täglich) heut in einer Woche, also am 26. abends mit dem 3. Akt fertig werde falls dieser nicht viel mehr als 100 Seiten haben wird – Ich rechne damit, dass Sie mir spätestens Dienstag den 23. abends den Rest schicken werden, den ich dann bis zu unserer nächsten Zusammenkunft (am 27., Samstag) sicher fertig mache." ÖNB Musiksammlung F 21 Berg 935.

25. Brand, Hailey, and Harris, eds., *Berg–Schoenberg Correspondence*, 316.

26. "In der Staatsoper (ehemalige Hofoper) wo ich keine Beziehungen habe, komm ich daher seit Jahren nicht. Ich als Musiker! Der allerschlechteste Galleriesitz kostet 100–200 K . . . Wo ist die schöne Zeit, wo man sich Bücher kaufte? Ein Band 2, 3500 K!!!, der früher 5, 6, Mark kostete . . .

Es ist ein närrische Welt in die wir leben. Welch ein Kontrast zu dem abgeklärten Leben in Amerika, wie Du liebe Alice es schilderst." Herwig Knaus, *Alban Berg, Handschriftliche Briefe, Briefentwürfe und Notizen*, Quellenkataloge zur Musikgeschichte herausgegeben von Richard Schaal, vol. 29 (Wilhelmshaven: Florian Noetzel Verlag, 2004), 30.

27. "Bei der unerhörten Sparsamkeit und Einteilbarkeit Helenes haben wir es diesen Winter wirklich zuwege gebracht, ohne das wahnsinnig teure Gemüse und das untererschwingliche Fleisch zu kaufen, also von einfachen Mehlspeisen, Quäker Oats, Nudeln, Nockerln, Polenta, Reis, Erdäpfeln, Kaffee, Kakao zu leben und dabei sogar Abwechslung zu haben. Um mich speziell arbeitsfähig zu erhalten und vor Krankheit zu schützen, esse ich als einziger täglich ein kleines Stückerl Fleisch." Knaus, *Alban Berg*, 31.

Chapter 4

1. Juliane Brand, Christopher Hailey, and Donald Harris, eds., *The Berg–Schoenberg Correspondence: Selected Letters* (New York: W. W. Norton, 1987), 245.

2. Willi Reich, *The Life and Work of Alban Berg*, trans. Cornelius Cardew (London: Thames and Hudson, 1965), 56.

3. Douglas Jarman, *Alban Berg: Wozzeck* (Cambridge: Cambridge University Press, 1989), 139.

4. Alban Berg, *Letters to His Wife*, trans. Bernard Grun (New York: St. Martin's Press, 1971), 310–18.

5. Berg, *Letters to His Wife*, 314.

6. Alma Mahler-Werfel, *And the Bridge is Love* (New York: Harcourt, Brace, 1958), 168.

7. "Geliebter Alban, Anbei 7.000.000 und etliches!!!–Ich bin toll vor Freude, daß mir dieser Schachzug gelungen ist." ÖNB Musiksammlung, F 21 Berg 1058/137.

8. Berg, *Letters to His Wife*, 325–6.

9. See Margaret Notley's splendid article outlining the process by which Berg produced a "propaganda suite" that could be performed during the Third Reich. Margaret Notley, "Berg's *Propaganda* Pieces: The 'Platonic Idea' of *Lulu*," *The Journal of Musicology*, 28.2 (2008): 94–142.

10. "Ich frage das alles so genau. Weil ich bevor ich mich mit der ganzen Idee intensiver beschäftige[n] möchte, <u>Sicherheiten</u> brauche. Ich habe schon zu viel Unnötiges in meinen eigenen Angelegenheiten unternommen. Denken Sie an die Orchesterstücke, um deren Aufführung ich mich 4 Jahre lang vergeblich bemüht habe," Herwig Knaus, *Alban Berg, Handschriftliche Briefe, Briefentwürfe und Notizen*, Quellenkataloge zur Musikgeschichte Herausgegeben von Richard Schaal, vol. 29 (Wilhelmshaven: Florian Noetzel Verlag, 2004), 316.

11. Knaus, *Alban Berg*, 170.

12. "Dank, lieber Herr, Scherchen, für Ihren Brief vom. 7.3. Da ich zu der Angelegenheit selbst eine ganze Anzahl <u>Fragen</u> habe, schreibe ich Ihnen in Form eines Fragebogens, dessen Kopie Sie bitte beantwortet an mich zurückgehn lassen mögen. Ist die Annahme meiner Wozzeck=Bruchstücke für das Musikfest des Allg. D. Musikvereins definitive[?] ANTWORT Definitiv!" Knaus, *Alban Berg*, 169.

13. Reich, *Alban Berg*, 57.

14. Brand, Hailey, and Harris, eds., *Berg–Schoenberg Correspondence*, 334–7.

15. ÖNB Musiksammlung, F 21 Berg 74/V. See also Douglas Jarman's detailed study of the sketches, "Some Notes on the Composition of Berg's *Kammerkonzert*," in *Alban Berg Studien, VI*, ed. Regina Busch und Klaus Lippe (Vienna: Universal Edition, 2008), 12–33.

16. *Briefwechsel Arnold Schönberg – Alban Berg*, Bd. 3.2, Juliane Brand, Christopher Hailey und Andreas Meyer, eds. (Mainz: Schott, 2007), 212. See also Berg's letter draft to Eduard Steuermann, F 21 Berg 475/104, published in Herwig Knaus and Thomas Leibnitz, eds., *Alban Berg. Briefentwürfe, Aufzeichnungen, Familienbriefe, Das "Bergwerk."* Aus den Beständen der Musiksammlung der Österreichischen Nationalbibliothek; hg. und bearbeitet von Herwig Knaus und Thomas Leibnitz, (=Quellenkataloge zur Musikgeschichte 35, hg. von Richard Schaal), (Wilhelmshaven: Florian Noetzel, 2006), 111.

17. Reich, *Alban Berg*, 58.

18. *Arnold Schoenberg zum fünfzigsten Geburtstage, 13. September 1924*. Special issue of *Musikblätter des Anbruch* 6 (August-September, 1924).

19. Reich, *Alban Berg*, 201.

20. "Lieber, teurer Freund! Deinen Brief beantworte ich gleich, umsomehr als ich nicht genügend schnell der Empörung darüber Ausdruck geben kann, daß man Deinen Wozzeck abermals verschieben will. Hoffentlich ist es doch nur Tratsch, was ich eher glaube, eben weil Du keine offizielle Verständigung erhalten hast. Oder es sind sachliche Gründe der Verschiebung da? Keine Zeit mehr zum gebührend-genügend Studium? Dann ist aber die Verschiebung besser als seine halbfertige Aufführung, die dem 'Wozzeck' sehr schaden könnte; das muß Dir ein Trost sein, ja sogar erwünscht . . . Den Klavierauszug mache ich natürlich; wie ich denn stets bereit bin, Deiner Kunst zu dienen. Aber ein Honorar nehme ich von Dir nicht an. Oder hast Du gemeint, die U.E. wird mich honorieren? Dieser erlaube ich es." ÖNB Musiksammlung, F 21 Berg 935/66.

21. Constantin Floros, *Alban Berg and Hanna Fuchs: The Story of a Love in Letters*, trans. Ernest Bernhardt-Kabisch (Bloomington and Indianapolis: Indiana University Press, 2008), 14.

22. Floros, *Alban Berg and Hanna Fuchs*, 20–21.

23. "Doch wozu schreib' ich das alles!!! – Weißt du es doch alles selbst - - !! – Ich wollte nur versuchen zu zeigen – wie hoch du dastehst - - wie himmlisch hoch! - - - So wie deine 1te Namensträgerin - - - die heilige Maria - - so stehst du unbefleckt und rein da - - denn die eine menschliche Sünde ist durch den großen-großen Schmerz verteidigt – reingewaschen - - wie bei Maria. - - - - - - - - - das ist meine innerste Überzeugung!!!!- Aus meiner Seele heraus!!! Es ist 1 Uhr nachts!" ÖNB Musiksammlung, F 21 Berg 474.

24. ÖNB Musiksammlung, F 21 Berg 3274/1. Transcribed in Herwig Knaus and Wilhelm Sinkovicz, *Alban Berg. Zeitumstände – Lebenslinien* (St. Pölten/Salzburg: Residenz Verlag, 2008), 360: "Welch' herrlicher Brief, welch' wunderbare Schreiberin! Aber ihr 'Sie' zu sagen, bringe ich nicht zustande, und ebensowenig sie nicht 'Geliebte' zu nennen. So nannte ich sie schon in dem Augenblick, als ich sie zum erstenmal in den Sonnen durchleuchteten, also von ihr durchleuchteten Speisesaal sah u. das 'Du', das so 'taktlos': plötzlich auf meinen Lippen war, war wochenlang vorher in meinem tiefsten Inneren geboren."

25. George Perle, "The Secret Program of the Lyric Suite," *International Alban Berg Society Newsletter* 5 (June 1977), 4–12.

26. David Fanning, "Berg's Sketches for *Wozzeck*: A Commentary and Inventory," *Journal of the Royal Musical Association* 112.2 (1987), 299.

27. For a detailed study of the correspondence between Klein and Berg, as well as their discussion of the special properties of these rows, see Arved Ashby, "Of *Modell-Typen* and *Reihenformen*: Berg, Schoenberg, F. H. Klein, and the Concept of Row Derivation," *Journal of the American Musicological Society* 48.1 (1995), 67–105.

28. George Perle, *Serial Composition and Atonality* (Berkeley University of California Press, 1981), 72–3.

29. ÖNB Musiksammlung, F 21 Berg 479/36 and ÖNB Musiksammlung, F 21 Berg 3123.

30. "Sehr geehrter Herr Berg! Ich erfahre sehr zunötigst von dem Fortgang der Wozzeckproben. Es wird sehr fest daran gearbeitet. Nur etwas scheint (wie mir Schrenk gestern erzählte) nicht in Ordnung zu sein: mit Schwarz, der den Wozzeck singen soll sind verschiedene Herrn, (u.a. Hörth) der Regie führt) nicht einverstanden und es ist möglich, dass diese Rolle umbesetzt wird (mit einem hiesigen sehr gut rein werdenden Baritonisten) das ist noch nicht sicher. In jedem Fall arbeitet Kleiber fest mit der Absicht das Werk <u>ganz bestimmt</u> dein Termin (November) herauszubringen." ÖNB Musiksammlung, F 21 Berg 686/7.

31. Eisler letter of September 10, 1925. "Sehr verehrter Herr Berg! Meine Nachrichten über Wozzeck stellen sich nachträglich als falsch heraus. Schwarz singt doch die Titelrolle. Schmid, mit dem ich schon bevor doch hier ist, 2 mal beisammen war, ist darüber besser orientiert wie ich u. wird Ihnen darüber schreiben.

Die Kemp wird die Marie nicht singen.

Die Uraufführung wird erst im Dezember sein.

<u>Es ist schwer aus den Koulissentratsch der halb informierten etwas Tatsächliches herauszuholen.</u> (Kleiber kenne ich leider nicht.) . . .

Sobald ich wieder etwas über Wozzeck höre, schreibe ich." ÖNB Musiksammlung, F 21 Berg 686/8.

32. Sehr geehrter Herr Berg endlich etwas authentisches über Wozzeck:

Besetzung: Wozzeck - - - - - - Schützendorf (also doch nicht Schwarz!)

            Marie - - - - - - - - Strozzi

            Tambourmajor - - - - - Loot

            Aufführung - - - - - - - 14 Dezember

Die Ensembleproben beginnen ca 12–14 November. Vorläufig jammert alles (bis auf Kleiber) über die Schwierigkeit. In Eile sehr herzlichst Ihr Eisler" ÖNB Musiksammlung, F 21 Berg 686/14.

33. ÖNB Musiksammlung, F 21 Berg 479/36.

34. "Verehrter Meister, Sie werden bereits von Ihrem Verleger F. in Kenntnis gesetzt werden sein, daß ich mich mit der Abschluß trage, ich aus Ihr[em] herrlichen Werk 'U P ť' eine Oper machen möchte. Ihr Verleger ermutigt mich mit der Frage an Sie heranzutreten, ob ich Sie mir die Erlaubnis dazu geben." ÖNB Musiksammlung F 21 Berg 432/21 36ᵛ.

35. Herwig Knaus and Wilhelm Sinkovicz, *Alban Berg, Zeitumstände—Lebenslinien* (St. Pölten, Salzburg: Residenz Verlag, 2008), 297.

36. Berg, *Letters to His Wife*, 347.

37. Berg, *Letters to His Wife*, 349.

38. Berg, *Letters to His Wife*, 351.

39. Berg, *Letters to His Wife*, 352.

40. Berg, *Letters to His Wife*, 353.

41. Berg, *Letters to His Wife*, 353–4.

42. "Skandalszenen in der Staatsoper

Tumult bei der Generalprobe.

Erregter Kampf um die Wozzeck-Aufführung

Bei der Generalprobe zu Alban Berg Oper *Wozzeck* in der Staatsoper Unter den Linden, die heute nachmittag vor dichtgefülltem Hause stattfand, kam es zu Skandalszenen, wie man sie bisher im Staatlichen Opernhause nicht gewohnt war. Es zeigte sich, wie schnell der Geist eines Hauses leiden kann, wenn man einem vornehmen Theater von heute auf morgen seinen Führer nimmt, wenn man sich entschließt, den Intendanten "fristlos" zu "entlassen," noch ehe man gleichzeitig auch den geeigneten Ersatz für ihn gefunden hat." ÖNB Musiksammlung, F 21 Berg 3123/16.

43. Reich, *Alban Berg*, 61–62.

44. *Pult und Taktstock, Fachzeitschrift für Dirigenten* (Vienna: Universal Edition, 1926), 26.

45. "Streichquartette, Orchesterlieder, Orchesterstücke und gezählte Kammermusikwerke kennen wir von dem Schönberg-Schüler Alban Berg, der sich allerdings schon vor dem Kriege nun auch zu diesem, seinem ersten dramatischen Werk entschlossen hatte und es sicher beendet haben würde, wäre nicht der Krieg dazwischen gekommen, an dem Alban Berg bis zum Ende in der österreichischen Armee teilnahm. In Urlaubswochen hatte Alban Berg schon einzelne Szenen aufgezeichnet. Im Jahre 1920 ward dann die Oper vollendet, und vor etwa einem Jahr erwarb sie das Berliner Staatstheater." ÖNB Musiksammlung, F 21 Berg 3123/6.

46. "Alban Berg ist am 9. Februar 1885 in Wien geboren. Sein Kompositionslehrer war Arnold Schönberg, mit dem ihn auch heute noch herzliche Freundschaft verbindet. Berg gilt als einer der radikalsten Vertreter der musikalischen Moderne. Er lebt in Wien.

Seine Werke sind nicht zahlreich: eine einsätzige Klaviersonate, ein Heft Lieder, ein Streichquartett in zwei Sätzen (wohl das bekannteste Werk des Komponisten), fünf Orchesterlieder, vier Stücke für Klarinette und Klavier, drei Orchesterstücke, die Oper *Wozzeck* und ein kürzlich geschriebenes Konzert für Klavier und Geige mit Begleitung von dreizehn Bläsern. Berg hat die Komposition des *Wozzeck* im Jahre 1914 begonnen. Seine Einberufung zum Militärdienst gestattete ihm aber die Beendung erst nach dem Krieg." ÖNB Musiksammlung, F 21 Berg 3123.

47. "Von Alban Berg wußte man bis dahin so gut wie nichts. Sein Wozzeck ist Opus 7.

1885 in Wien von deutschen Eltern geboren, besuchte er die Realschule, ward nach der Reifeprüfung Beamter in der Wiener Stadthalterei, um sich ganz der Musik in die Arme zu werfen, der er durch Arnold Schönberg näher trat.

Vor Kriegsausbruch lernte er das Schauspiel Georg Büchners in einer Wiener Aufführung kennen." ÖNB Musiksammlung, F 21 Berg 3123/98.

48. "Berg, ein jetzt 40jähriger Mann, der bisher mit Kammermusik hervorgetreten ist, ist Schüler von Arnold Schönberg, der kürzlich als Leiter einer Meisterklasse für Komposition nach Berlin berufen wurde, hat die Lehren seines Meisters bis in die letzten Konsequenzen durchgeführt und die Sprache der Musik von jeglichem Wohlklang entkleidet." ÖNB Musiksammlung, F 21 Berg 3123/97.

49. Peter Gay, *Weimar Culture: The Outside as Insider* (New York: Harper and Row, 2001), 54.

50. "Kann Büchners Werk überhaupt komponiert werden? Bergs Musik hat es nach meiner Empfindung vergewaltigt.

Und trotzdem wirkt es stark durch all die Kompliziertheiten der Musik hindurch, wirkt meist stärker als die Musik, so daß man nie die Empfindung einer wahren Einheit von Musik und Dichtung hat. Wenn die Dichtung mit ihrer großen andersartigen Eigengewichtigkeit kein Skelett gibt, wo liegt das Zusammenhaltende für diese Musik? In den von Berg zugrunde gelegten formalen Schemen alter Kunst ist es bestimmt nicht zu sehen.

Während des Hörens suchte ich und fand eigentlich nichts." ÖNB Musiksammlung, F 21 Berg 3123/82.

51. "Wie Büchner diese abstoßende Geschichte mit philosophischen Flittern behängt hat, wäre schon Grund genug für einen Musiker gewesen, die Finger davon zu lassen; die Vorgänge verlangen eben nach keiner Musik. Zum zweiten aber hat Alban Berg eine Musik dazu geschrieben, die nach unseren bisherigen Begriffen keine Musik ist, sondern eine ungeheure Anhäufung von mißtönenden Geräuschen, die sich bemühen, das Seelenleben Wozzecks zu malen." ÖNB Musiksammlung, F 21 Berg 3123/96.

52. "Gegen den Geist der Musik und trotz der Atonalität, möchte man sagen. Die Atonalität ist das große, fast unlösbare Problem; bevor man sie nicht, herunter bis zu ihrer

physikalischen Grundlage, beweisen oder leugnen kann, werden subjektive, unmaßgebliche Eindrücke dafür oder dagegen sprechen. Als schön hört sie wohl auch nicht ihr heftigster Verfechter, aber wahr mag sie sein. Und wahr, nicht schön möchte auch Alban Berg sein. Er stellt sich damit in Gegensatz zur abendländischen Tonkunst, soweit sie war und wirkt, soweit sie sich von den übrigen, charakterologischen Künsten unterscheidet. Wenn man, wie ich, die geschichtliche Tonalität als urtümlich empfindet, wird man sagen müssen, daß Berg gegen den Musikgeist arbeitet. In gewisser Hinsicht ist das nicht nur Hypothese, sondern Beweis und Eingeständnis: wer auf die singende, in der Zeit ruhende Menschenstimme verzichtet, verzichtet auf ein musikalisches Hauptelement." ÖNB Musiksammlung F 21 Berg 3123/79.

53. "Wer weiß, ob sein Wozzeck überhaupt je aufgeführt worden wäre, wenn nicht der aus Wien stammende junge, ehrgeizige Generalmusikdirektor Erich Kleiber sich dafür eingesetzt hätte? Denn das Werk strotzt dermaßen von Schwierigkeiten, daß wirklich Mut und außerordentliche Dirigentenfähigkeiten dazu gehören, um es herauszubringen. Nur ganz große Bühnen haben überhaupt die Möglichkeit, daß erforderliche Riesenorchester mit Nebenorchestern zu besetzen und für die fast ein Jahr benötigenden Proben Zeit zu finden. Wenn ich bisher geglaubt hatte, das die *Elektra* von Strauß oder die *Gezeichneten* von Franz Schreker die denkbar größten Schwierigkeiten darböten, so überzeugte mich der Einblick in den Klavierauszug des *Wozzeck* sehr bald davon, daß im Vergleich zu diesem jene beiden Werke, namentlich auch in rhythmischer Hinsicht, leicht sind. Geradezu Unmögliches in Bezug auf Umfang und Treffen der Intervalle verlangt Berg von den Sängern, für die er zum guten Teil einen Sprechgesang, jedoch nicht wie den von Wagner eingeführten, und direktes Sprechen vorschreibt. Freilich kommt es nicht darauf an, ob die Töne auch immer ganz so gebracht werden, wie die Partitur sie verzeichnet, denn von Tonalität ist im ganzen *Wozzeck* keine Rede. Er ist wohl die dissonanzenreichste Oper, die bisher geschaffen worden ist." ÖNB Musiksammlung, F 21 Berg 3123/99.

54. "Die Gefahr des Zerflatterns, die bei einem so lockern Szenengefüge auf der Hand lag, sollte durch Betonung der formbildenen Elemente der Musik gebannt werden; die in geschlossenen, "absolut" musikalischen Formen komponierten einzelnen Szenenbilder, durch Überleitungen miteinander verbunden, sollten sich wie die Sätze einer Sinfonie gegenseitig bedingen und im Akt zu einer höheren Einheit verschmelzen: eine neuartige Lösung des Problems der dramatischen Sinfonie. (Der Klavierauszug ist in der Wiener Universal-Edition erschienen.) So wenigstens sagt der Komponist selbst und seine Exegeten, die es ja wissen müssen. Der aufmerksame Hörer merkt davon zunächst allerdings nicht viel.

Weder hört er die papierten Sarabanden, Gavotten, Giguen, und Passacaglien als solche heraus, noch würde es ihm viel nützen, wenn er sie etwa mit Hilfe einer Programmanalyse feststellen könnte. Er würde sich auch dann nicht weniger darüber wundern, wie sehr dieser Musik die Fähigkeit zu charakterisieren abgeht. Sie läuft, von Einzelheiten abgesehen, als überflüssiger Fremdkörper neben der Handlung her." ÖNB Musiksammlung, F 21 Berg 3123/101.

55. "Die Kontrastierung der einzelnen Stücke wird zweifach gedeutet; einmal szenisch, dann aber wird ihnen noch ein selbständiger Sinn insinuiert und in diesem Zusammenhang spricht Berg von einer Suite, einer Passacaglia, einer Sinfonie, Phantasie und Fuge, Inventionen usw.

Aber diese Formen haben keinerlei unmittelbare Evidenz; es ist unmöglich, sie zu erleben, sie stehen als solche auf dem Papier; ebenso wie einem bei Schönberg die Künstlichkeit und Durchdachtheit seiner Konstruktionen vordemonstriert werden muß; zu hören ist sie nicht, während es keine Bachsche Fuge gibt, deren Aufbau nicht unmittelbar zu erfassen ist." ÖNB Musiksammlung, F 21 Berg 3123/89.

56. "Der erste Akt ist eine Folge von fünf Charakterstücken mit einer Passacaglia von 21 Variationen, der zweite soll eine Symphonie vorstellen, während der dritte Akt sich auf sechs Inventionen (darunter einer über einen Ton!) aufbauen soll. Ich bin wohl ein etwas

zu rückständiger Musiker, daß ich von all diesen schönen Sachen nichts, aber auch gar nichts gehört habe. Es war mir aber ein rechter Trost, daß mehrere Komponisten von Rang, die neben mir saßen, auch nichts herausgehört hatten." ÖNB Musiksammlung, F 21 Berg 3123/102.

57. "Schade, daß 'neue Bahnen,' die er wandelt durch Einbeziehung konzertmäßiger Formen in das bühnendramatische Reich – die Partitur soll angeblich eine Suite, 21 Variationen, eine fünfsätzige Sinfonie u.a. enthalten (!) – so gar nicht zu erkennen sind! Immerhin lässt sich aus dieser Verquickung (?) herausbuchstabieren, was die modernen Geräuschfabrikanten vom Schlage Alban Bergs unter 'Oper komponieren' verstehen. Wären ihre Angriffe auf die gute Gesundheit der Musik und den guten Geschmack des Publikums nicht so unverschämt und hartnäckig, müßte man über ihr Gebaren lachen. So aber gibt's nur noch eins: was um Schönberg und Schönberg-Zucht ist, den Brunnenvergiftern der deutschen Musik Fehde für alle Zeiten!" ÖNB Musiksammlung, F 21 Berg 3123/100.

58. Geert Mak, *In Europe*, trans. Sam Garrett (New York: Pantheon, 2007), 390.

59. "Die Atonalität fängt allmählich an, für unsere deutsche Kulturmusik gefährlich zu werden, und es wäre an der Zeit, daß die noch gesund-fortschrittlich denkenden Musiker Deutschlands alles daran setzen würden, um dieser unheimlichen Bewegung etwas Energisches entgegenzustellen. Wenn auf der einen Seite Jazz-Band- und Niggerweisen, auf der anderen atonaler Wirrwarr, beide mit bodenlosen Texten arbeitend, auf unsere deutsche Kulturmusik einstürmen, dann ist die Lage wirklich Ernst zu nehmen." ÖNB Musiksammlung, F 21 Berg 3123/108.

60. "Auf der anderen Seite sehen jedoch die Parteigänger der Atonalen in Bergs "Wozzeck" so etwas wie ein Evangelium des neuen Musikstils, der da kommt, und der alles verwirkt und schlechterdings erledigen müßte, was unsere ganze bisherige Musikkultur ausgemacht hat.

Das Wesentliche an dieser Uraufführung ist jedenfalls dies, daß die Berliner Staatsoper, an der Kleiber nach der Verdrängung des Intendanten von Schillings nunmehr eine uneingeschränkte Macht ausübt, durch die Aufführung des Werkes ihrer gesamten Tradition untreu geworden ist, auf die sie bisher so stolz war. Die Auswirkung der "fristlosen Entlassung" von Schillings beginnen sich bereits zu zeigen: Die Atonalen, d.h. die Juden, bringen mehr und mehr in die Staatsoper ein, indem sie künstliche Erfolge mit allen Mitteln herbeiführen, in ihrer Presse große Erfolge vortäuschen und sich dann darauf berufen. Auf diese Weise muß die Berliner Staatsoper über kurz oder lang zu einer Experimentierbühne werden, an der die Kliquenwirtschaft üppige Blüten treiben wird." ÖNB Musiksammlung, F 21 Berg 3123/104.

Chapter 5

1. "Ich werde ganz dumm in dem Studium der Philosophie; ich lerne die Armseligkeit des menschlichen Geistes wieder von einer neuen Seite kennen. Meinetwegen! Wenn man sich nur einbilden könnte, die Löcher in unseren Hosen seien Palastfenster, so könnte man schon wie ein König leben! So aber friert man erbärmlich." Georg Büchner, *Gesammelte Schriften, in zwei Bänden*, vol. 1, ed. Paul Landau (Berlin: P. Cassirer, 1909), 202.

2. Douglas Jarman, *Alban Berg: Wozzeck* (Cambridge: Cambridge University Press, 1989), 153.

3. Jarman, *Alban Berg: Wozzeck*, 153.4. George Perle, *The Operas of Alban Berg*, vol. 1, *Wozzeck* (Berkeley and Los Angeles: University of California Press, 1980), 39.

5. "Eine Null. Mit massigem Talent (Verstellungsgabe) sich verstellen zu können, d.h. etwas mehr scheinen zu wollen Schwadroneur (ein guter Mensch) leicht gerührt über sich selbst. Art einem Rest von militär. Strammheit, die immer gleich verschwindet hinter der

Art behäbiger (selbstgefälliger) asthmatischer hoher Militärs" ÖNB Musiksammlung F 21 Berg 13/II 57.

6. Perle, *Operas*, vol. 1, *Wozzeck*, 189.

7. Klaus Lippe, "'*Wozzeck* | Strasse | S. 20 bis 23' Ein Beitrag zur Philologie des *Wozzeck*-Particells," in *Alban Berg Studien, VI*, ed. Regina Busch and Klaus Lippe (Vienna: Universal Edition, 2008), 80–95. I would like to thank Klaus Lippe for making me aware of the Witkowski edition of *Woyzeck* at Berg's apartment in Hietzing.

8. "... u. hier ist ein Punkt, der mich mit Besorgnis erfüllt: Ob nämlich auf der *Bühne* solche <u>Melodramen</u> praktikabel sind. Ob die menschliche <u>Sprech</u> stimme trotz zartester Instrumentation ein Bühnenhaus <u>ausreicht</u>." Wiener Stadt- und Landesbibliothek, I. N. 185.592.

9. Alban Berg, *Letters to His Wife*, trans. Bernard Grun (New York: St. Martin's Press, 1971), 278.

10. Peter Petersen, *Alban Berg, Wozzeck, Eine semantische Analyse unter Einbeziehung der Skizzen und Dokumente aus dem Nachlaß Bergs* (Munich: Edition Text + Kritik GmbH, 1985), 11–40.

11. David Fanning, "Berg's Sketches for *Wozzeck*: A Commentary and Inventory," *Journal of the Royal Musical Association* 112.2 (1987), 302.

12. George Perle, "Woyzeck and Wozzeck," *Musical Quarterly* 53.2 (April 1967), 206ff.

13. Glenn Watkins, *Proof Through the Night: Music and the Great War* (Berkeley: University of California Press, 2003), 236.

Chapter 6

1. "Es ist nicht nur des Schicksal dieses von <u>aller Welt</u> ausgenutzten u. gequälten armen Menschen, was mir so nahe geht, sondern auch die unerhörte Stimmungsgehalt der einzelnen Scenen. Die Verbindung von immer 4–5 Scenen zu einem Akt danach Orchesterzwischenspiele verlockte mich natürlich auch noch. (Was ähnliches findest du in Maeterlincks-Debussys Pelleas!)" Handschriftensammlung, Wiener Stadt- und Landesbibliothek IN 185.592.

2. Douglas Jarman, *Alban Berg: Wozzeck* (Cambridge: Cambridge University Press, 1989), 164.

3. Theodor W. Adorno, *Alban Berg: Master of the Smallest Link*, trans. Juliane Brand and Christopher Hailey (Cambridge: Cambridge University Press, 1991), 85.

4. Jarman, *Alban Berg: Wozzeck*, 157.

5. Jarman, *Alban Berg: Wozzeck*, 156.

6. Jarman, *Alban Berg: Wozzeck*, 169.

7. Alban Berg, *Letters to His Wife*, trans. Bernard Grun (New York: St. Martin's Press, 1971), 158–9.

8. Berg, *Letters to His Wife*, 300–1.

Chapter 7

1. Theodor W. Adorno, *Alban Berg, Master of the Smallest Link*, trans. Juliane Brand and Christopher Hailey (Cambridge: Cambridge University Press, 1991), 35.

2. The following authors have also studied Berg's annotations in his score of *Erwartung*: Siegfried Mauser, *Das expressionistische Musiktheater der Wiener Schule* (Regensburg: Gustav Bosse Verlag, 1982), 58–80; Werner Grünzweig, *Ahnung und Wissen, Geist und Form: Alban*

Berg als Musikschriftsteller und Analytiker der Musik Arnold Schönbergs. Alban Berg Studien V (Vienna: Universal Edition, 2000), 173–5; and Kathryn Whitney, "Schoenberg's 'Single Second of Maximum Spiritual Excitement': Compression and Expansion in *Erwartung*," *Journal of Music Theory* 47.1 (Spring 2003): 155–214.

3. Alban Berg, "A Lecture on *Wozzeck*" in *Alban Berg: "Wozzeck,"* ed. Douglas Jarman (Cambridge: Cambridge University Press, 1989), 154–70.

4. Peter Petersen, *Alban Berg*, Wozzeck: *Eine semantische Analyse unter Einbeziehung der Skizzen und Dokumente aus dem Nachlaß Bergs* (Munich: Edition Text + Kritik GmbH, 1985), 188.

5. Deborah J. Stein, *Wolf's Lieder and Extensions of Tonality* (Ann Arbor: UMI Research Press, 1985), 162.

6. A single leaf held at the Bayerische Staatsbibliothek contains the only existing sketches for I/4; however these sketches focus on pitch content.

7. Petersen, *Alban Berg*, 102–6.

8. Juliane Brand, Christopher Hailey, and Donald Harris, eds., *The Berg–Schoenberg Correspondence: Selected Letters* (New York: W. W. Norton, 1987), 283.

9. George Perle, *The Operas of Alban Berg*, vol. 1, "*Wozzeck*" (Berkeley and Los Angeles: University of California Press, 1980), 124–5.

10. Perle, *Operas*, vol. 1, "Wozzeck," 124.

11. Perle, *Operas*, vol. 1, "Wozzeck," 144.

12. Perle, *Operas*, vol. 1, "Wozzeck," 144.

13. Derrick Puffett, "Berg, Mahler and the Three Orchestral Pieces, Op. 6," in *The Cambridge Companion to Berg*, ed. Anthony Pople (Cambridge: Cambridge University Press, 1997), 136–7.

14. Perle, *Operas*, vol. 1, "*Wozzeck*," 144, and Douglas Jarman, *The Music of Alban Berg* (Berkeley and Los Angeles: University of California Press, 1979), 190–1.

15. "Linzer Brucknerfest: Back to the roots; Anton Bruckner's 9. Symphonie: ein würdiger Festival-Auftakt," *Die Presse*, September 13, 2005.

Conclusion

1. "All das muß ich mir, morgen nichts und wieder nichts – und wegen diesen Sau-Kriegs bieten lassen. Ich greif' mir noch mal an die Steiner (die Geste des Saluzierens ist ja was sühnloses !) u. frag mich wieso ich dazu komm, ja wieso meine Umwelt sich nicht an die Stirn greift u sich fragt, wieso ich dazu komme. Drei wird gestohlene Jahre: aus der besten Zeit meines Lebens: sagen wir vom 18. bis zum 48. Lebensjahr, also ein zehntel dieser Zeit aber auch ganz verloren." Alban Berg to Helene Berg, 29. VI. 1918. ÖNB Musiksammlung, F 21 Berg 1581/1918/26.

2. *Der Wiener Tag* 25. XII. 1936, memorial article by Alfred Rosenzweig.

3. "Bis Kriegsende versah Alban Berg getreulich diesen zehnstündigen Dienst. Dann legte er die Uniform für immer ab, und nur wenige Menschen wußten, als der berühmte Komponist bei der festlichen *Wozzeck* Premiere in der Wiener Staatsoper im eleganten Frack—ein Ehrenbild Oscar Wildes—an die Bühnenrampe trat, um für die begeisterten Beifallstürme zu danken, dass der Schöpfer dieser grandiosen Partitur das Leid der gehetzten Kreatur in Uniform an sich selbst erlebt hat, dass hinter dem Wozzeck als unsichtbarer Schatten der Einjährig-Freiwillige Titular-Gefreite Alban Berg steht." ÖNB Musiksammlung F 21 Berg 3271.

4. Richard Kramer, "The Sketch Itself," in *Beethoven's Compositional Process*, ed. William Kinderman (Lincoln and London: University of Nebraska Press, 1991), 3.

5. William E. Benjamin, "Ideas of Order in Motivic Music," *Music Theory Spectrum* 1 (1979), 23.

Catalogue

1. Peter Petersen, *Alban Berg*, Wozzeck: *Eine Semantische Analyse unter Einbeziehung der Skizzen und Dokumente aus dem Nachlaß Bergs* (München, 1985), 77–8. David Fanning, "Berg's Sketches for *Wozzeck*: A Commentary and Inventory," *Journal of the Royal Music Association* 112.2 (1986–7), 287–93.

2. Fanning, "Berg's Sketches for *Wozzeck*," 296.

3. Fanning, "Berg's Sketches for *Wozzeck*," 301.

4. See ABS 50–1.

5. Fanning, "Berg's Sketches for *Wozzeck*," 300.

6. Ulrich Krämer, *Alban Berg als Schüler Arnold Schönbergs: Quellenstudien und Analyses zum Frühwerk. Alban Berg Studien IV* (Vienna: Universal Edition, 1996), 164.

7. Fanning, "Berg's Sketches for *Wozzeck*," 302–3.

8. George Perle, *The Operas of Alban Berg*: Wozzeck (Berkeley, 1980), 28.

9. See *The Berg–Schoenberg Correspondence: Selected Letters*, ed. Juliane Brand, Christopher Hailey, and Donald Harris (New York and London, 1987), 283.

BIBLIOGRAPHY

Adorno, Theodor W. *Alban Berg: Master of the Smallest Link*. Trans. Juliane Brand and Christopher Hailey. Cambridge: Cambridge University Press, 1991.

Ashby, Arved. "Of *Modell-Typen* and *Reihenformen*: Berg, Schoenberg, F. H. Klein, and the Concept of Row Derivation." *Journal of the American Musicological Society* 48.1 (1995): 67–105.

Bailey, Kathryn. "Berg's Aphoristic Pieces." In *The Cambridge Companion to Berg*, ed. Anthony Pople, 83–110. Cambridge: Cambridge University Press, 1997.

Benjamin, William E. "Ideas of Order in Motivic Music." *Music Theory Spectrum* 1 (1979): 23–34.

Berg, Alban. "A Lecture on *Wozzeck*." In *Alban Berg: "Wozzeck,"* ed. Douglas Jarman, 154–70. Cambridge: Cambridge University Press, 1989.

———. *Letters to His Wife*. Trans. Bernard Grun. New York: St. Martin's Press, 1971.

Brand, Juliane, Christopher Hailey, and Donald Harris, eds. *The Berg–Schoenberg Correspondence, Selected Letters*. New York: W. W. Norton, 1987.

Büchner, Georg. *Büchner's Woyzeck, Nach den Handschriften neu hergestellt und kommentiert von Henri Poschmann*. Frankfurt am Main and Leipzig: Insel Verlag, 1985.

———. *Gesammelte Schriften, in zwei Bänden*. Vol. 1. Ed. Paul Landau. Berlin: P. Cassirer, 1909.

———. *Woyzeck, Faksimile, Transcription, Emendation und Lesetext Buch und CD-Rom, 2. Ausgabe*, Herausgegeben von Enrico De Angelis. Munich: K. G. Saur, 2000.

DeVoto, Mark. "Alban Berg's 'Marche Macabre.'" *Perspectives of New Music* 22.1/2 (Autumn 1983/ Summer 1984): 386–447.

———. "Some Notes on the Unknown Altenberg Lieder." *Perspectives of New Music* 5.1 (Autumn/ Winter 1966): 37–74.

Fanning, David. "Berg's Sketches for *Wozzeck*: A Commentary and Inventory." *Journal of the Royal Music Association* 112.2 (1986–87): 280–322.

Floros, Constantin. *Alban Berg and Hanna Fuchs: The Story of a Love in Letters*. Trans. Ernest Bernhardt-Kabisch. Bloomington: Indiana University Press, 2008.

Fussell, Paul. *The Great War and Modern Memory*. Oxford: Oxford University Press, 1975.

Gay, Peter. *Weimar Culture: The Outside as Insider*. New York: Harper and Row, 2001.

Grünzweig, Werner. *Ahnung und Wissen, Geist und Form: Alban Berg als Musikschriftsteller und Analytiker der Musik Arnold Schöenbergs*. Alban Berg Studien V. Vienna, Universal Edition, 2000.

Hilmar, Ernst. *Wozzeck von Alban Berg: Entstehung—erste Erfolge—Repression (1914–1935)*. Vienna: Universal Edition, 1975.

Hilmar, Rosemary. *Katalog der Musikhandschriften, Schriften und Studien Alban Berg im Fond Alban Berg und der Weiteren Handschriftlichen Quellen im Besitz der Österreichischen Nationalbibliothek*. Alban Berg Studien I. Vienna: Universal Edition, 1980.

———. "Kriegsjahren, 1914–1918." In *Alban Berg*. Vienna: Verlag Hermann Böhlaus Nachf, 1978.

Jarman, Douglas. *Alban Berg: Wozzeck*. Cambridge: Cambridge University Press, 1989.

———. *The Music of Alban Berg*. Berkeley and Los Angeles: University of California Press, 1979.

———. "Some Notes on the Composition of Berg's *Kammerkonzert*." In Alban Berg Studien VI, ed. Regina Busch and Klaus Lippe, 12–33. Vienna: Universal Edition, 2008.

Kassowitz, Gottfried. "Lehrzeit bei Alban Berg." *Österreichische Musikzeitschrift* 23 (1968): 323–30.

Khittl, Christoph. "The Other Altenberg Song Cycle: A Document of Viennese Fin-de-Siècle Aesthetics." In *Encrypted Messages in Alban Berg's Music*, ed. Siglind Bruhn, 137–56. New York and London: Garland, 1998.

Knaus, Herwig. "Alban Berg, Handschriftliche Briefe, Briefentwürfe und Notizen." In *Quellenkataloge zur Musikgeschichte Herausgegeben von Richard Schaal*, Vol. 29. Wilhelmshaven: Florian Noetzel Verlag, 2004.

Knaus, Herwig, and Wilhelm Sinkovicz. *Alban Berg, Zeitumstände—Lebenslinien*. St. Pölten, Salzburg: Residenz Verlag, 2008.

Kramer, Richard. "The Sketch Itself." In *Beethoven's Compositional Process*, ed. William Kinderman. Lincoln: University of Nebraska Press, 1991.

Krämer, Ulrich. *Alban Berg als Schüler Arnold Schönbergs: Quellenstudien und Analyses zum Frühwerk*. Alban Berg Studien IV. Vienna: Universal Edition, 1996.

Lippe, Klaus. " '*Wozzeck* | Strasse | S. 20 bis 23' Ein Beitrag zur Philologie des *Wozzeck*-Particells." In Alban Berg Studien VI, ed. Regina Busch and Klaus Lippe, 80–95. Vienna: Universal Edition, 2008.

Mak, Geert. *In Europe*. Trans. Sam Garrett. New York: Pantheon, 2007.

Mahler-Werfel, Alma. *And the Bridge is Love*. New York: Harcourt, Brace, 1958.

Mauser, Siegfried. *Das expressionistische Musiktheater der Wiener Schule*. Regensburg: Gustav Bosse Verlag, 1982.

McLean, Donald. "A Documentary and Analytical Study of Alban Berg's Three Pieces for Orchestra." Ph.D. diss., University of Toronto, 1997.

Notley, Margaret, "Berg's *Propaganda* Pieces: The 'Platonic Idea' of *Lulu*." *The Journal of Musicology* 28.2 (2008): 95–142.

Perle, George. *The Operas of Alban Berg*, vol. 1, *Wozzeck*. Berkeley and Los Angeles: University of California Press, 1980.

———. "The Secret Program of the Lyric Suite." *International Alban Berg Society Newsletter* 5 (June 1977): 4–12.

———. *Serial Composition and Atonality*. Berkeley: University of California Press, 1981.

———. "Woyzeck and Wozzeck." *Musical Quarterly* 53:2 (April 1967): 206–19.

Petersen, Peter. *Alban Berg: Wozzeck, Eine semantische Analyse unter Einbeziehung der Skizzen und Dokumente aus dem Nachlaß Bergs*. Munich: Edition Text + Kritik GmbH, 1985.

Pult und Taktstock, Fachzeitschrift für Dirigenten. Vienna: Universal Edition, 1926.

Puffett, Derrick. "Berg, Mahler and the Three Orchestral Pieces Op. 6." In *The Cambridge Companion to Berg*, ed. Anthony Pople, 111–44. Cambridge: Cambridge University Press, 1997.

Reich, Willi. *The Life and Work of Alban Berg*. Trans. Cornelius Cardew. London: Thames and Hudson, 1965.

———. *Alban Berg*. New York: Vienna House, 1974.

Sallis, Friedemann. "Coming to Terms with the Composer's Working Manuscripts." In *A Handbook to Twentieth-Century Musical Sketches*, ed. Patricia Hall and Friedemann Sallis. Cambridge: Cambridge University Press, 2004.

Stein, Deborah J. *Wolf's Lieder and Extensions of Tonality.* Ann Arbor: UMI Research Press, 1985.

von Borries, Melchior. *Alban Bergs Drei Orchesterstücke Op. 6 als ein Meisterwerk atonaler Symphonik.* Weimar: Verlag und Datenbank für Geisteswissenschaften, 1996.

Vojtêch, Ivan, ed. "Arnold Schoenberg, Anton Webern, Alban Berg: Unbekannte Briefe an Erwin Schulhoff." In *Miscellanea Musicologica XVIII*, 31–83. Prague: Nákladem University Karlovy, 1965.

Watkins, Glenn. *Proof through the Night: Music and the Great War.* Berkeley: University of California Press, 2003.

Whitney, Kathryn. "Schoenberg's 'Single Second of Maximum Spiritual Excitement': Compression and Expansion in *Erwartung*." *Journal of Music Theory* 47.1 (Spring 2003): 155–214.

INDEX